RIDE A PALE HORSE

Helen MacInnes

FAWCETT CREST • NEW YORK

A Fawcett Crest Book
Published by Ballantine Books
Copyright © 1984 by Helen MacInnes

Library of Congress Catalog Card Number: 84-9037

ISBN 0-449-20726-9

This edition published by arrangement with Harcourt Brace Jovanovich, Publishers

Printed in Canada

First Ballantine Books Edition: October 1985

In memory of Gilbert

And I looked, and behold a pale horse:
and his name that sat on him was Death,
and Hell followed with him.

—REVELATION VI, 8

1

THE ROOM WAS COMFORTABLE ENOUGH, ADEQUATE BUT dull, totally unimaginative, a cream-walled box with everything else colored brown. Someone in Prague had ordered the essentials—bed, dresser, table, chairs, desk, a small state-controlled radio—straight out of a catalogue. Or perhaps this was the regulation room, repeated one hundred and ten times in this country hotel, judged suitable for foreign guests and the minor Czechoslovak officials who floated around in the background with polite advice and constant guidance.

Karen Cornell stopped pacing over the nine-by-twelve brown carpet, halted at the window. Even its view, showing her a driveway that circled a garden of scarlet geraniums and white begonias before it swept down an avenue through thick woods, did not lift her depression. It only reminded her once more of six days of helpful supervision. For there, drawn close to the hotel entrance, was a neat line of black Fiats, the cars provided for the visiting journalists to see them safely into Prague and back again.

Their drivers were linguists, and escorts, too. Once in Prague, they stayed by your side. If you wanted a stroll through the streets, a look at shops and people, they went with you, friendly and obliging. After all, you couldn't speak Czech, could you? You could get lost so easily, be late for tight schedule of meetings, lunches, entertainments. But now the escorts, ever dutifully lined up with their cars, did not seem to have much business. This was the sixth day, when meetings had ended and the only luncheon had been an early farewell downstairs to the eight West Europeans and one American who represented the press of the free world. The Eastern-bloc journalists, forty-eight of them, were probably sleeping off the dumplings (good) and the beer (excellent); they weren't leaving until tomorrow or the next day. The West Europeans, like this American, were waiting for all the notes they had made to be returned from the censors, worrying while they waited and eyed their watches. Damn all censors, Karen Cornell was thinking as she left the window, didn't they know we all have planes to catch? It was now almost three o'clock: she was to move out of the hotel by four-thirty for her flight to Vienna. She'd pack her bag and stop looking at the desk, where she had expected her notes to be lying in their envelopes once she had escaped from the luncheon.

There was nothing, but nothing, in her notes that could possibly rile a censor. Her system of classifying them by envelopes, each with the subject of its contents clearly marked on its top left-hand corner, was simple, time-saving, and invaluable for ready reference. So what was delaying those blasted censors? There were only two or three pages in each envelope; nothing unexpected, nothing exciting had happened at the Prague Convocation for Peace, which she had been covering for four days. (The fifth day was a country jaunt, a visit to a thriving village of farms, planned and supervised by the state, that made a vivid contrast to the inefficiency of another village, where farmers were trying to cling to their pre-1968 ideas of possession.) Convocation for Peace...the usual faces, the usual speeches. All wanted peace, all condemned the United States. A thousand strong in agreement and fervor, except for two West German women who had managed to be included with the Greens and tried to suggest that *all* nuclear weapons should be discarded by *everyone*. Their protest had been drowned out in three minutes, and they were escorted efficiently out of the hall, two small pebbles disappearing into a deep pond with only a little plop to bear witness to their existence.

But, thought Karen, I didn't put that brief interlude into my notes. I'm carrying it out in my head. And that was the stupidity of censorship. It could black out your written lines, but what about your mind?

Convocation—an impressive word, serious, benevolent, religious almost. And there had been Christians around, mingling with the atheists, quite forgetting that they had been denounced as enemies when religion was declared the opium of the people. Short memories?

So the journalists had been convoked, too, to give their seal of approval. And they came, hoping they could talk with the representatives, but finding as usual that only a few were available for any real discussion. Specially selected, of course: a strong wall of unshakable opinion, fervent, dedicated, against which the Westerners' arguments made not one crack. But that wasn't her main assignment here. The special correspondent of the monthly *Washington Spectator*, published and owned by *the* Hubert Schleeman, had been invited for quite another reason. Schleeman had been given the firm impression that there was to be an interview for Karen Lee Cornell with—no less—the President of the Socialist Federated Republic himself.

Schleeman's contact, the press aide at the Czechoslovak Embassy in Washington, had impressed on him the need for absolute discretion; no talk, no rumors to be circulated about this exceptional opportunity, or other papers and periodicals would be pestering his office.

Silence had been kept, secrecy was intact, and Karen had arrived in Prague on an ego trip that floated as high as a helium balloon.

This wasn't the first of her political interviews: Mitterrand last year; Helmut Schmidt on his way out of office; Kohl on his way in. Before that giddy accumulation of names, there had been a seven-year apprenticeship in the art of interviewing. First, a monthly column in the *Spectator* dealing with Washington personalities, foreign as well as home-grown. Next, brief interviews with congressmen; a longer one with a governor; full-length with two congressional committee chairmen, a new justice of the Supreme Court, a top aide at the White House. She had earned her way.

Yes, she reminded herself in mounting bewilderment, dismay, frustration, anger, we kept our word, Schleeman and I. And Jimmy Black, my editor, the only other person to hear about this project, kept his lips tightly buttoned, too. Not one word or whisper from us. Yet the interview fell through. No excuse offered, either; not one word of regret. No interview was possible this week. Or next. Totally impossible at present. Schleeman must have misunderstood.

If so, this was a first for Schleeman. He had never yet misunderstood a quiet invitation from any embassy or even misinterpreted a suggestion. He will be flaming mad. As I am. And I have the additional fear that somehow, some way, the blame for the failure of this assignment will be dumped on me. A remark I made, an attitude I displayed, made them doubt I was a suitable interviewer. That could be the little sound wave traveling back to Schleeman's quick ear. He wouldn't believe it. Or would he?

But I've been so damned careful, so circumspect. Not like Tony Marcus, the *London Observer*'s man, whose quick tongue was irrepressible. "So," he had said when they first met, "you're the spectator and I'm the observer, but I rather think we'll be only two of the sheep shepherded around." And when she had smiled discreetly, said nothing, he had added, "Have you noticed the eminently respectable journalists gathered at the West European table? Was that why we have been invited? To legitimize all these bastards?" His amused glance swept around the clusters of Eastern-bloc newsmen. "Dutiful lot, aren't they? There was really no need to come here. They don't have to write anything. They just add a phrase or two to the handouts." She had smiled again, turned away, pretended to seek out Duvivier of *Le Monde*, whom she had met in Paris last year.

She snapped the locks of her bag. Packing complete. Ready to leave, except for her briefcase, open and waiting for her files to be jammed in when they came back from the censors. You're a coward, she told herself. Tony Marcus may write an objective column, but he has the courage to be frank when he speaks. You may as well admit it: you wouldn't be so full of small criticisms and anger today if you had been given that interview yesterday. Your ego is punctured, deflated completely, lying in shreds around your feet. And what about your career? What happens to all your plans if news of this slap-in-the-face gets around. It could, too. There would be plenty who would laugh, and some who would crow with delight. She hadn't reached this stage in her life without making enemies. Because she was thirty-seven and left them behind, because she was a woman who got the promotions? At first they had said her husband probably wrote her stuff, a successful novelist who knew how to put words together. But she had gone on writing her own material after he had died, more and more sure of her craft. So then success was blamed on her face and figure—she knew how to use them, didn't she? Did she? Hell, no, she thought: a face and figure added to difficulties. Some people immediately believed you were brainless.

Three o'clock. All was far from well. If she didn't get her envelopes back—then, perhaps, she had to reconstruct most of her notes, such as they were, from memory.

It was sharp enough, thank heaven. ("Ah yes," her dear critics said, "she's wired for sound. Must carry a recording machine wherever she goes.")

"Stop this!" she told her reflection in the dresser's mirror. "You're turning paranoid. Stop it!" This gargoyle face glaring back at her would really delight her competition. So she calmed down, combed her dark hair back into proper place, added powder and lipstick, studied the neckline of her blue silk shirt, tried to take comfort in the way its color emphasized her eyes. My notes, she thought again, if they aren't returned, does that mean a reprimand of some kind? She didn't even know how to reach the censors' office to try to prod them into action. Or perhaps that wouldn't be wise. Not wise at all. Censors might not like being prodded, even in the gentlest fashion.

Her telephone rang. It was perched on the extension of the headboard on her bed. She dropped lipstick and compact on top of her handbag and reached it on its second ring.

"Miss Cornell?"

"Yes."

"My name is Vasek. I'm in charge of press relations."

His English was good, his accent fair. Vasek? In charge of press relations? One of the really important guys who kept a low profile? (It was the unimportant men in this regime who were much on view.)

"Miss Cornell? Are you still there?"

"I am."

"Have you enjoyed your visit? If you have any comments, I'd be glad to hear them. I'm sure any small difficulties could be easily explained."

"Could they?"

"I think so. Why don't you join me downstairs? I am telephoning from the lobby. I am sure a little talk could put your mind to rest. I am sorry you have been disappointed."

Sorry . . . The first apology given. "Indeed I have been. You know about that?"

"Yes. Regrettable. But perhaps—" Vasek paused. "All is not lost yet, Miss Cornell."

A last chance to get that interview? A change of mind in high places? Quickly, she calculated the time of her appointment in Vienna tomorrow afternoon against a morning flight from here. She could manage it. "I could stay for this evening—" she began and was interrupted.

"Why don't we talk? Will you join me downstairs? I'll be waiting near the elevator."

"Give me three minutes."

Josef Vasek replaced the receiver and turned to his assistant. "She's coming."

"Do you think it will do any good? She scarcely spoke a word at the luncheon today. She's a tough customer."

And that is what I'm betting on, thought Vasek. She's my gamble. "Well, we can't send her away antagonized. It doesn't pay to make enemies of the foreign press, does it? I'll talk to her in the garden, calm her down."

"All you'll hear will be complaints."

"Perhaps I should hand this job over to you, Bor."

"No, thank you. I'll just string along and admire your technique."

"Fine. Or, better still, why don't we save time? You deal with Duvivier. He's in the bar, I think. He's worrying about his friend—that *Observer* reporter who left without saying good-bye to him. Reassure him, can you?"

"I'll manage that. Here she comes, all cream and peaches. But she's a tough lady. I warned you." Averting his eyes from the elevator door, Bor moved off and made his way through the crowded lobby toward the bar.

2

KAREN CORNELL STEPPED OUT OF THE ELEVATOR. NEAR its door there were several people grouped, and she could recognize them all. Not one was named Vasek. Then she saw a man—a stranger she had glimpsed only once or twice, usually in the distance. None of her colleagues had met him either or could give her his name. He was probably of some importance. He might be wearing an ill-fitted double-breaster, but that unctuous little squirt called Bor—always impeccably dressed—had just left him with a bow of deference which he barely acknowledged. Medium height, middle-aged, and carrying too much weight around his waistline. (A sedentary job or a bulky jacket?) He was pretending not to notice her. She halted, controlled a rising excitement. If this was Vasek, let him make the first move: he knew damned well who she was.

He began walking, but not toward her. He seemed to be heading for the side entrance to the lobby that led out onto the terrace and a flower garden. Then it appeared as if he had caught sight of her when he glanced at the group in front of the elevators. He halted, turned, came forward through the crowd of people.

"Miss Cornell. My name is Vasek. I don't believe we have met. I am glad to have this chance to wish you a good journey. You are leaving tonight?"

"This afternoon."

"So soon? I hope your visit was enjoyable."

"I'd have preferred a more central hotel."

"But why, Miss Cornell?" He was astonished. "There was always a car for your convenience." His tone was soothing, his face a mask of politeness. "Have you any other comments?" But there was a sudden gleam of humor in his light-gray eyes.

"I was under the impression I was to be granted—"

"Didn't you have your interview yesterday with the Minister of Agriculture?"

A five-minute lecture, she reminded herself, before we were given a tour of model farms. Her impatience grew. "Yes. But I expected—"

"A moment, please, Miss Cornell. Too much noise here. Shall we try the terrace? Then we won't need to raise our voices."

She had the feeling that these sentences were as much for Bor's benefit—the man had appeared almost magically beside Vasek—as for hers.

Vasek spoke with Bor in a quick interchange of Czech, and Bor left—rather grudgingly, it seemed to Karen—with his usual bows. "Nothing important," Vasek said to her. Just an excuse. Bor hadn't found the French journalist in the bar. "He was looking for someone. I told him to try the man's bedroom." Anywhere, Vasek thought angrily, anywhere except at my elbow. "This way, Miss Cornell." He led her toward the terrace.

"If Bor is looking for one of my colleagues, he'll find him trying to track down the censors." A neat way to introduce my own worry, she thought. "I should be doing that myself. I'm leaving here at four-thirty. I haven't yet received my notes, and I—"

"You'll have them before you leave. I'm afraid the terrace is a bit crowded, too." He looked around the array of occupied chairs and urged her toward the steps into the garden. He said clearly, "I know you've had certain problems. Why not tell me your complaints? I can explain anything that is puzzling you, and I am sure you will feel much better. Can't have you leaving with unanswered questions, can we?"

But once they had reached the flower beds and were strolling leisurely on a path that took them a little distance from the terrace, his voice dropped. "Don't show surprise or shock at anything I say. You will argue with me, and I shall appear to be explaining away your doubts. Yes, you should interrupt me naturally, but *no* comments on what I am telling you. No astonishment, please!" For she had turned her head to look at him with her eyes wide and her lips parted. "When we reach that patch of grass ahead of us, we'll stop for a little. My back will be to the terrace, so you will face it. Eyes will be watching us. And there is one highly skilled lip reader among them. That is why you must stay absolutely normal. What you say will be known." He fell silent, stopped to look at a rosebush.

She stopped, too, but kept her face averted from the terrace. "My turn to talk?" I'm on the verge of a story, she told herself, excitement once more stirring. I feel it, I sense it, I can smell it. All that playacting of his in the lobby, all that little pantomime on the terrace of attempting to pacify a complaining guest—yes, he is a man in trouble, bigger than any of those I thought I had.

"Briefly. We haven't much time—ten minutes at most."

"Then I'll go on asking about my notes." Her face turned to admire the yellow rosebush they had passed. She halted briefly. "Why the delay? My material didn't need to be censored. It's absolutely harmless," she ended with considerable indignation.

He looked back, too, at the cluster of flowers, long enough to let any watcher see his lips. "Harmless? We must be the judge of that. And I assure you, we only hope

to make everything easier for our guests when they pass
through the airport. Let me explain." They resumed their
leisurely stroll, their faces now unseen from the terrace.
"Good," he said. "You're very good, Miss Cornell. Now
let's get to that stretch of grass."

"Why not the sundial in the center of the rose bed?
When I seem pacified, you could appear to be explaining
its design to me."

He smiled; not just a gleam in his eyes, this time, but
a smile that freed the pale expressionless face from its
controlled mask. "A pretty picture. But the dial is bugged.
So are these garden benches."

"What?"

"No astonishment, Miss Cornell!"

Is this more playacting, but now for my benefit? The
sudden suspicion grew, kept her silent.

He seemed to read her thoughts. "I am being serious,
Miss Cornell. Believe me. This may be the most serious
decision I shall ever make. My life is in your hands."
They had reached the stretch of grass, their slow pace
dwindling to a halt. They stood there, quite naturally it
seemed, Karen facing him, his back to the terrace.

She recovered herself. *My* hands? "Thank you for
explaining. But I still have some doubts. Yesterday, for
instance—" Yesterday, what? "The agriculture people
didn't really answer my question about acid rain. I've
heard much of your forest land is being killed by it. Is
that true?"

The mask had been dropped; there was a tightening of
worry, almost a desperation, on his lips. His eyes searched
hers. He drew a deep breath. "I am planning to defect.
Will you help me?"

"I thought it was the other way around," she said, then
bit her lip. Nearly a mistake, she told herself, and managed to laugh. "Tell me more about this acid rain problem.
It's widespread. We have it also."

"Will you help?" His eyes, light gray, intense, were

pleading. "I am putting you in danger, I know. But you will be helping your country too."

She stared at him. Then she nodded.

His hand had slipped quietly into the inside pocket of his double-breasted jacket, pulled out the top of a Manila envelope. He held it for a moment, just long enough for her to see *Tuesday: Village Visits*. Her handwriting, partly smudged by the coffee she had upset over the envelope; a proper mess that had left the envelope stained enough to be discarded into her wastepaper basket last night. She had rescued the two pages of her notes and added them to the envelope filled with official handouts from the Ministry of Agriculture. The basket had been emptied of its trash while she had breakfast on the terrace this morning. In spite of herself, her eyes widened, her mouth fell open. Quickly, she recovered. "Really?" she asked. "How—how extraordinary!"

The envelope disappeared back into Vasek's pocket; his arms were folded as he went on talking in a low, strained voice. "You will find that envelope among the others on your desk when you return to your room. Do not open it. Just take it out—to America—among the rest of your notes. And deliver it to Peter Bristow. You know him. He will see it is given immediate attention."

"But I hardly know—" she broke out, and stopped in time. She shrugged. "I really *am* ignorant. You were saying that acid rain is spreading? Into Austria? Even Switzerland?" And it's true; I hardly know Peter Bristow— I've met him only once, and then briefly. Naturally enough. He's CIA or something hush-hush, and I'm the press. As soon as he heard my name, he made a diplomatic retreat.

"You can always reach Bristow through Schleeman. They are friends."

He is too well informed, knows everything he shouldn't know. Warily, she looked at the white face. "An immediate problem, you say? Even Sweden and Norway are concerned. Yes, it would be a good subject to write about. If only I could learn more," she said slowly, "make sure of the facts. Reporters should be accurate, check all references. I really do need to know more than I do." Can you catch my meaning? she asked him silently. She needed to be told what was in that envelope. Would he get it?

He did. One hand briefly touched his jacket, just where its inside pocket was hidden. "No drugs, no currency, no diamonds. The envelope holds three letters. They are my insurance that I will be accepted by your government. I wrote these letters, taking the names of your Secretaries of State and of Defense. Also, of your President. You have heard of disinformation? These three brief documents are excellent examples—if I may say so. Of course, much praise must go to the expert forgers who could supply the signatures. It was a difficult undertaking, but it was successful. So far, the letters haven't been given out to the press. Then I discovered that the delay is official policy: two events, only hinted at in the letters, are actually to take place. The letters will be made public, but skillfully, once the events have been attempted. They could start a major upheaval—riots, wild protests, an end to the Western alliance. Then, as I see it, war would ensue. A hideous war."

There was silence. At last, Karen said, "What would be the cause of—of so much damage?"

"Two political assassinations, almost simultaneous."

She felt her face go rigid and dropped her head as if she were studying the grass at her feet. "When?" she risked, lips scarcely moving.

"That is still being decided. They must be arranged carefully. All blame must fall on the Americans."

"That shouldn't be difficult," she said bitterly. Not the way things were going. Can I believe him? Is this really possible—is it true?

"How long will you stay in Vienna? A few hours, I hope. That envelope is urgent."

"I can see that." If true, if true . . . "I'm a very curious person, you know. I think I must study the material on acid rain before I—before I can write about it." I am out of my depth and sinking fast, she thought. "But I'll start some research when I reach home—that's on Friday. I'll be only a day in Vienna, but I think Schleeman will expect me to get back to Washington and start explaining to him why that interview did not take place. The trouble is, I don't know why it didn't. Couldn't you persuade someone at the top to let me do the interview this evening? Just one hour—that's all I ask. I'll stay here overnight and keep my engagement in Vienna tomorrow."

"Couldn't you cancel it? Every day counts."

"It's another interview, with someone who isn't yet elected to the top job in Austria. But I'm betting on him. He will expect me to be there. And I do keep my commitments."

"I'm glad of that," Vasek told her grimly. He became thoughtful. "Yes, you must appear to act normally. A rush to Washington might be—" He shrugged. "Remember, attract no attention; draw no suspicion. Someday we'll meet again, and you can have full rights to this story. When? I don't know. Soon, I hope. And don't misunderstand me: I am still a Communist, but not one who believes he will advance our cause by forcing a world war. Tell Peter Bristow that. He may not yet know my present name, but he has quite a file on my past history." There was a fleeting smile. "I hear that Bristow has labeled it 'Farrago.' Don't forget: Farrago." He paused, and it seemed as if that reminded him of something else, for he spoke urgently. "Talk only to Peter Bristow. He, alone, receives the envelope. No one else."

"Really?" she asked, and pretended boredom. Fully twelve minutes had passed since they had entered the rose garden, and that worried her.

"No one." The words were snapped out. "There is a man in Bristow's unit—" he hesitated—"but I'll name him, among others, when I reach safety. My second insurance," he explained, and smiled broadly. "Now it's time to return. After we say good-bye in the lobby, delay for twenty minutes before you reach your room. Your envelopes, all of them, will be waiting for you. You are ready to leave?"

She nodded. She felt numb, so many conflicting emotions surging through her that rational thought had become a jumble. They walked back to the terrace, past two of the bugged benches. He was asking if her stay at the hotel had been comfortable, and she seized that topic like a life line. He had sensed she needed one, perhaps. Very pleasant place, she said, but she still wished she could have been somewhere in Prague itself, could have wandered through the city, attended a theater, visited a café, just watched the world stroll by. (Yes, there *was* a woman, center front row of the terrace, binoculars quickly lowered as Karen glanced in her direction. And a man at a side table, with a telescopic-lens camera, seemingly entranced with the rose bed.)

"Next visit," Vasek promised her as they passed through the terrace, "I'll see that you have a room in the most central hotel." They reached the lobby, some people standing and talking, fat armchairs stuffed with other guests who had become exhausted with conversation. He halted near one of the smoothly polished red-granite pillars, pressed her hand in a tight grip. "Thank you," he said almost inaudibly. She left him quickly; Bor was approaching. Now for a natural-looking delay. The bar seemed the logical place, where she'd find Tony Marcus and let him do the talking for the next twenty minutes.

3

THE BAR WAS SMALL, WITH TABLES CLOSELY PACKED, BUT at this time of day only half filled. As always, its heavy draperies on the windows were closed and the electric lights brilliant. Not a secretive place where people could be lost in the shadows or feel like making romantic assignations. She found Duvivier and Engel facing each other at a corner table. "Where's Tony Marcus?" she asked. "I hoped he'd give me a quip or two to cheer me on my way." The two men, pulling out a chair for her, looked as if they could use some cheering up, too.

"He's detained," Engel said.

"What?" She looked at Duvivier.

"For questioning," he said.

"When?" she asked, and waved aside the offer of a drink.

Engel said, "I saw him leaving with a plainclothesman on either side. Around eleven last night."

Duvivier was more pessimistic than usual. "Idiot! They searched his room while we were at dinner and found some papers—some material, anyway—that he hadn't turned in to the censors."

"What kind of material?" Karen asked. Oh, Lord, she thought, what have I got myself into?

"Could have been a case of forgetfulness," Engel suggested.

"Could have been something no censor would let him take out of the country." Duvivier shook his head. "Let us hope not."

"When I reach Hamburg, I had better notify the British Consulate," Engel said.

"I'll contact their embassy in Paris," Duvivier agreed. "Officials here have attacks of forgetfulness, too."

"Perhaps," said Karen uncertainly, "perhaps Tony will walk into the lobby before we leave."

The two men looked at her and then exchanged glances. Out of kindness to this sweet innocent, they made no comment. "Have that drink," Duvivier said, and began to talk about the Convocation for Peace as he signed to a waiter. Engel joined in the conversation. Karen kept silent.

Suddenly, she interrupted. "What makes me really mad is that none of us needs holier-than-thou talk about peace. We all want it—except the crazies. I *want* a Convocation for Peace, a real one, with every government that has nuclear weapons making an honest agreement to scrap every rocket and missile they possess."

"Every government?" Duvivier smiled at Engel. "White wine for the lady," he told the waiter.

"Yes. Yours, too, Yves. And England, India, Israel, Pakistan, South Africa, China—even the ones just at the planning stage, like Argentina—every single one of them, along with Russia and the United States."

"And supervision?" Engel asked.

"Of course. Just stop the power plays, the fears, the stupidity."

"A wonderful world," Duvivier said.

"Why not? Let the United Nations put some muscle

into their fat. It would give them more to do than listen to speeches and debates. What's the use of all their projects if the world goes up in flames?"

"True, true," murmured Duvivier, and wished he still held such a hopeful view of mankind's reasonable attitudes. Again he changed the subject. "What do you think of friend Bor? I see him hovering at the door."

Bor had watched Karen Cornell depart in the direction of the bar. To Vasek, who seemed about to leave the lobby, too, he said, "Thirsty lot, these journalists. But you seemed to have unruffled her feathers. How did you manage it?"

"Not difficult." Vasek looked at his watch. "I'm expecting a call—"

"What did you talk about?"

"Acid rain. And a room with a view of Wenceslaus Square. Censors, too—she objects to them as a matter of principle."

"Acid rain?" Bor stared at Vasek. The other two complaints had been expected.

"Yesterday she asked questions at the Agriculture Ministry and got few answers."

"So you supplied them?" Bor's grin was wide.

"I did my best. Now, I do have to get to my office before four o'clock—there's a call coming in. I think you'd better deal with that Hamburg fellow."

"Engel?"

"He's leaving around five, I believe. So send him away in a good mood."

"What about Rome?"

"I'll see Aliotto if I have time."

"He could be useful if you are still making that visit to Italy next week," Bor suggested, watching Vasek. "Are you?"

"That depends on my schedule here," Vasek said crisply, and walked away.

Never relaxes, Bor thought angrily; everyone kept running at his command. Seems to have settled down, though. How did he really feel about being sent to Prague? Was it a demotion from Moscow? Can't tell from that fellow—but he's more than a press aide or public-relations man. What's his real job? KGB? In what department? Never a hint—he's too important, is he, to talk to me? Well, I've done my duty and watched him, and there's nothing out of the ordinary to report. He has a reason for everything. It's curious, though. My orders were only passed through Prague—didn't originate here. In Moscow? Curious . . . He was sent here to inspect our work. So I thought. Does the inspector need inspection, too? That's Moscow's style, all right: always looking over each other's shoulder. What can you expect when they don't trust themselves? Oh, well—now it's time to find Engel and give him the kid-glove treatment. Why the devil can't Vasek find the time himself to deal with those damned journalists? It was his idea to send them away happy; I'd let them go with a handshake. They'll only insult us when they get home—capitalist lies, that's all they'll write.

Bor looked at his watch, wished he could delay some more, but headed for the likeliest spot to find Engel. These Western journalists avoided the public lounge like the plague. His annoyance evaporated when he reached the bar. The American was sitting with the Frenchman and the German. She looked tired and nervous, had scarcely touched the drink before her. This could be an excellent moment, most opportune. "May I have the pleasure of joining you?" He smiled and bowed, and sat down before anyone invited him. He concentrated on the American. "You had a pleasant talk in the garden?"

She stared at him, said, "Quite pleasant, thank you."

"Talk with whom?" Duvivier asked.

"With Mr. Vasek."

"Really?" Engel was suddenly amused. "You didn't tell us about that. Holding out on us, Karen?"

She shook her head. "He was just being polite to me."

Duvivier said, "I've been trying to corner him for three days. How did you manage it?" He, too, was much amused.

"We just met. By chance."

That's her first little lie, Bor thought. This might indeed be the moment. "What did you talk about?" he asked most innocently, curious but friendly.

"Acid rain." It seemed to Karen that there could be disappointment in his eyes, but he joined in the laughter around the table. "It's true," she told Duvivier and Engel.

"Ah, yes," Engel remembered, "you didn't get much of an answer on that subject yesterday. Better luck today?"

"Well, he did listen to my questions and gave me a long description of acid rain's effect. He didn't do too well on its cause, though." Yes, Bor was definitely disappointed. She glanced at her watch. Still five minutes to wait, heaven help her.

"Of course," Duvivier said, "mining is one of Czechoslovakia's chief moneymakers. Their heavy industries burn a lot of coal. Don't they?" he prodded Bor.

"No more than French or American factories use," Bor said.

He was helped, inadvertently, by Engel's natural curiosity. "Anything else you picked up that was interesting?" he was asking Karen.

"Nothing for any headlines. But I did get a promise that he'd make sure I stayed at a central hotel on my next visit here."

"Next visit?" Duvivier shook his head. "Yes, there are advantages to being a woman."

"Chauvinist," Karen told him lightly.

"No 'male' attached?"

"Always unnecessary. Redundant." She looked at her watch, rose abruptly. "I'll be late," she said in consternation. "I'm being collected at the front door in twenty minutes. Good-bye all." The men were on their feet, shaking hands. Bor's bow was brief.

"My card," Engel said, producing it. "Look me up in Hamburg if you are ever there."

"You still have my telephone number?" Duvivier asked.

"Most definitely." A warm smile for him. She liked this middle-aged, saturnine Frenchman. And he had helped her out on acid rain: Bor had been put on the defensive; no more questions. None of his business anyway, she thought as she hurried toward the lobby. Or was it?

The elevator was slow. It was quarter past four by the time she reached her room. Her envelopes lay on the desk, neatly tied into a bundle with heavy black tape. And a seal to declare it inviolate.

She could riffle through the corners of the envelopes, though, and check their numbers. All present. Including *Tuesday: Village Visits*, coffee stains and all. She hesitated. She couldn't extract that envelope without risking a loosening of the tape, even a break in its seal. Better leave it virgin-pure until she reached Vienna; it looked a nicely official package as it was. Censors' approval had even been stamped on the lower left-hand corner of each envelope.

She still hesitated. *Don't look inside that envelope.* Why? The less she knew, the safer she would be? And yet—she ought to know what she was carrying out of this country, she ought to know, even for the sake of a possible story. She was torn three ways: responsibility as a journalist; responsibility as a citizen (*You will be helping your country, too*); responsibility to a human being (*My life is in your hands*).

But was all that really true? How would she *know* if it was? Only a quick reading of the letters—and were they letters?—could tell her the real facts.

She didn't have time to find out. A knock at the door, a maid waiting to take down her luggage, ended all temptation. For the time being, certainly. Hurriedly, she locked the envelopes into her briefcase, reached for her white tweed jacket in the wardrobe, shouldered her purse. "One bag, one typewriter," she told the woman. "No, not the briefcase! I carry that myself."

With a sigh, she inspected herself in the mirror. She

looked perfectly normal. A good thing that the beating of her heart didn't show through her Chanel-type suit. You'll do, she told herself. She wished at this moment that she hadn't thought, quite suddenly, of Tony Marcus. Her hand tightened on her briefcase. Inwardly, she flinched as she entered the crowded elevator and found two uniformed officials jammed close to her. Outwardly, she seemed oblivious to any attention paid to her profile by the men, to her clothes by the women, accepting their stares as she always did.

She saw Vasek in the distance, pretending not to notice her safe departure. It was exactly half past four and the car waiting.

"What's the difference between Switzerland and Czechoslovakia?" she asked its driver, who would no doubt see her loaded right onto the plane, making sure she had no quiet conversation with any stranger or accepted any package.

He shook his head, looked blankly at her as if he were lost in the woods they had now left behind.

"There, the trains run on time. Here, the people run on schedule."

It took him almost a minute before he said stiffly, "We are efficient. You have noticed?"

How could I help it? "Most efficient," she assured him. And what about Switzerland?

He relaxed into a smile. Lucky I had the sense, she thought, not to say "people are made to run on schedule." I nearly did: it was tempting. And now, on the straight highway, she was being given an explanation of such efficiency. It was because of their education, the best there was. No illiteracy, here. In his third year of elementary school, he had even started a foreign language—obligatory.

"Russian?"

He nodded. "Later, we have German or English—often both."

In that case, with all those linguists walking the streets,

why did I need to have an interpreter as my escort? But she was on her best behavior, resisting all temptation, and the journey to the airport went without incident. Her passage through the checkpoints was without incident, too. Fortunate, she thought, that all these X-ray machines did not register her dry mouth and racing pulse.

4

A SUMMER AFTERNOON IN VIENNA, A SUCCESSFUL MEETING completed with a most likely candidate for high political office, and now a peaceful hour or two to sit at a café table and relax. Karen Cornell's mood was improving. She slowed her pace to enjoy the enticing shop windows, the people strolling as leisurely as she was, listening to their voices, watching faces and gestures—no strain here, no tensions. Kärntnerstrasse was a quiet and colorful street where people talked and discussed, even disagreed openly, or read from a choice of varied newspapers (foreign as well as Austrian) as they slowly drank their coffee. No pressure, no hurry. The background to this leisure, this life-as-it-should-be, was only the soft sound of shoes on the pavement. Yet a few years ago, long-time visitors like Hubert Schleeman had told her, Kärntnerstrasse had been cobbled, had trolley-car lines and heavy traffic. But some visionary had the sense to wave a magic wand and presto! Café tables with sunshades on a smoothly surfaced street, window boxes and giant planters overflowing with flow-

24

ers, traffic banished, pedestrians everywhere. Yes, her mood was improving. And yet memories of last night kept edging back.

Strange it was, when she was safely in bed in a free city (no interpreters or escorts, no overscheduled programs), that she had lain awake, too troubled to sleep. Although she ached with physical exhaustion, all her busy mind could think of was Vasek, Vasek and that envelope, Vasek and his somber predictions of world disaster. Over and over again, she had recalled his words, his phrases, his tone of voice; and her eyes—refusing to close and let her forget—had stared at the ceiling's shadows and saw the garden, the terrace, Vasek, as if they were all part of a staged scene and she were in a front-row seat.

Had it been a scene staged for her benefit? She no longer believed that. Until she had boarded her flight to Vienna, she had doubts mixed with fears. But no one had detained her, no one had led her away for questioning like Tony Marcus. She was free, and with her uncensored material intact. Vasek had not been trying to entrap her. Whatever he had been or had done in the past, at this moment in his life he was being honest. The garden scene was no myth; staged, perhaps, with careful planning, but real. Desperately real.

She had plunged suddenly into sleep as dawn tried to steal through the red velvet curtains in her room, and lain oblivious to everything until eleven. After coffee and a brioche, Austrian version, she had washed and begun choosing her clothes for the interview. But her thoughts were on her briefcase. Half-dressed, she pulled it out from under her bed and flicked its coded numbers to unlock it: 0615—the month and day of her wedding to Alan Fern. A safe enough sequence: who would have thought that Karen Lee Cornell, a widow of four years, would be such a sentimentalist? We all have our weaknesses, she reminded herself sadly, and Alan was mine.

What would he have been advising her now, if he were here? Probably, he'd laugh and say, "Just forget about

Vasek and that damned envelope. How the hell did you get mixed up in a business like that anyway?" Yet, remembering Alan, she wondered if he wouldn't have got mixed up in a business like that, too. Vasek had really played unfair, telling her that his life was in her hands. She wanted no more feeling of guilt over a death. Hadn't she enough sense of remorse over Alan's?

She had sat, without moving, looking down at the neatly taped package of Manila envelopes in her briefcase, thinking of Alan's last evening in New York. Both of them were ready to leave for a first-night play, to be followed by a party at its author's house. Alan hadn't wanted to go: he was tired, dispirited—he had been working too much, his third novel (after two spectacular successes) was almost half-finished, but he wasn't happy about it, was threatening to scrap it and begin something new. A night off the chain would do him good, she had urged. And looking at her expectant face, he said, "We'll go. You look like a million dollars, love. You'll slay them all." So they went. And attended the post-theater supper; too much food, too much drink, too much talk, too much everything. At three in the morning, they returned home. At nine, awakened by the alarm clock to let her catch the New York flight to Washington for her usual three-day visit to the *Spectator*'s offices, she left their bed to wash and dress. Alan seemed still deep in sleep when she came to kiss him a light good-bye and found his eyes staring, his mouth fallen open, his face turning to stone.

"Oh, God," she said now, right in the middle of Kärntnerstrasse. And damn Vasek, she added silently. She hadn't opened that envelope as yet, had left it intact even if she had pulled the black tape off the bundle. On impulse, she had wrapped the coffee-stained envelope in some tissue paper from a folded dress, bound it into a neat parcel with the tape minus its seal. Now it was in the Sacher Hotel safe, while the rest of the envelopes lay in her unlocked briefcase. Probably an unnecessary precaution, possibly stupid. She stared at her reflection in a polished shop window, regained her composure. And then she saw the man.

He was standing across the street, not much more than thirty feet away, and he was watching her. The same man—she was almost sure of that—yes, it could be the same man she had seen as she had passed through customs at the Vienna airport yesterday evening. Then, he had followed her out to the taxis and taken the cab after hers. She had glimpsed him early this afternoon as she left the Sacher. But he could be another hotel guest, couldn't he? Or had lunch there. Or something. Coincidences did happen.

She swung around to face the other side of the street to have a clearer look, let her eyes drift along Kärntnerstrasse as if she were undecided whether to walk to its end. Just as quickly, he turned his back on her, became absorbed in the window in front of him—ladies underwear, black and red lace in abundance. Without a second glance at him, she retraced her steps, keeping to her side of the street, searching for an empty table under a bright umbrella.

All were occupied. She would have to go indoors, choose a café with wide windows open to the sun-warmed air. She found a likely place, cool and dark inside, and chose a seat to one side of the central window's frame that would half hide her from the street. She saw the man again. Yes, he had followed her; and now—at this moment—angry and uncertain as he searched through the outside tables. Her entrance into this almost empty room had been abrupt. She relaxed as he walked on slowly, trying the next café. Given up, had he? She ordered coffee with whipped cream and a slice of Linzer torte from a glass-covered counter filled with the most delectable cakes. Why not? She was celebrating.

Too soon, however. The man, middle-aged, gray-haired, dressed sedately in brown, hadn't given up. He was just outside her window box, his pace steady. Had he noticed her blue dress before she had drawn back? She lifted her cup, sipped her coffee through its floating mound of whipped cream, kept her eyes looking straight ahead at the mirrored wall on the side of the room. It gave a clear reflection of what lay behind her back: entrance doorway, cashier's desk, patisserie display. The man entered.

She bent her head, concentrated on the coffee, and when she risked another glance at the long mirror she saw him in front of the cakes and tarts, speaking with the white-uniformed girl who presided over them. Choosing a slice of Sacher torte? No. The girl pointed her silvered tongs, not an éclair or napoleon, but in the direction of a side corridor near the end of the room. There, a discreet notice proclaimed TOILETTEN, and a red arrow pointed the way.

Ah well, thought Karen, and smiled. She could blame her amusement on her white mustache of cream. She wiped it off, brought out her lipstick to repair the damage.

The man reappeared. That was quick—barely two minutes by her watch. A record, surely. She watched him leave, walking briskly. Over the window box at her elbow, blue and pink and purple petunias spilling toward the sun-filled street, she saw him hurry on his way down Kärnt-nerstrasse, looking to neither right nor left. That's all he had been, a man in search of a toilet. She shook her head over her suspicions. And then amusement ended. She frowned as she replaced the lipstick in her shoulder bag and slung it over the back of her chair. A moment more of disturbing thought, and she hailed her waitress. "Tell me, please—are the washrooms over there?" She pointed at the distant sign.

"Yes. Straight along the corridor, then down the stair-case."

Down a flight of stairs? Then up? That could take almost two minutes. "Is there a telephone?"

"Just around the corner."

"In the corridor itself?"

"*Jawohl*," the girl said again. And when Karen didn't move, she asked, "The lady wishes something else?"

The lady is an idiot. She'd better straighten out her mind before she walks out into the street. "Another cup of coffee, please. No cream."

The pink-cheeked face became rounder in astonishment. The yellow curls shook in disbelief. "The lady didn't like the cream?"

"It defeated me. I need more practice." More practice in everything, Karen decided as the waitress hurried off with a puzzled look in her china-blue eyes. If she didn't understand my last remarks, she is at least sure about the coffee. My German can't be too bad. Travel . . . how simple it seemed until I stepped through Vasek's door.

She studied the street. What inconspicuous man had been summoned by telephone to wait for her out there? But if he was assigned to dogging her footsteps, how would he recognize her? According to the movies, the brown suit should have been hovering outside to identify her quietly. They'd hardly work that angle right in this room where she would notice the two of them together even if they tried to keep apart. She leaned forward to see as much of the street, of the tables outside, as possible. The brown suit had definitely left, had made no contact.

The coffee came, a pot of it no less. Perhaps her German hadn't been so good after all. But the strong black brew was welcome. She stopped watching the street, asking herself quite another question. If I am being followed, then why? Is Vasek under suspicion? Is anyone who talked with him automatically under surveillance? Even *here*— in Austria? Why? Suddenly, she felt chilled. And afraid. Thank God she had left the envelope secure in the safe of a reliable hotel. She might very well have followed her first idea: don't leave it behind, keep it close to you, tuck it into your handbag with your passport and other valuables.

A purse snatcher? she wondered, thinking once more about the brown suit. A foreigner, a woman by herself, a bag slung over her shoulder—if she had walked into a quiet lane or been jammed by a crowd, would he or an accomplice have attempted a snatch? It was a common practice for women traveling alone to carry jewelry in their handbags. She relaxed slightly, sipped the coffee. Perhaps that was all the little man thought of her—a likely quarry who wore good clothes and could afford the Sacher Hotel. (He wouldn't know about expense accounts or that her gold necklace, bracelet, earrings, and wedding ring were all she ever traveled with.)

A movement and laughter at the entrance caught her attention. She looked at the mirrored wall: three people— two men and a girl. "Well, look who's here!" one of the men called out and left the table he had almost chosen to come forward to hers. She set down her cup in astonishment.

The last time she had seen Sam Waterman was in Hubert Schleeman's office at the *Spectator*. Five years ago? Yes, almost five, and Waterman hadn't been in such an amiable mood then; he had just resigned on the spot. She had been given the job he had expected to have—he had been two years writing about Washington personalities for Schleeman; she had been working only a year on that column. He had stormed into the office to say he was quitting. It was an embarrassing moment for her, a nasty one on all counts. But at this moment, with his smile and friendly voice as he shook her hand, he seemed to have dropped any grudge against her, any feeling of bitterness and anger. His violent interruption of Schleeman's discussion with her about her new responsibilities was obviously something he wished forgotten. She would be glad to comply. She always felt a twinge of guilt whenever she thought of him; not guilt, exactly—something more like regret. He had been good at his job, certainly as good as she had been. He could have done VIP interviews with considerable success. He was a most personable man—as long as he didn't rage into an office—tall, a rugged face that other men seemed to trust and women liked, frank brown eyes, a firm handshake.

Introductions were being made: Andreas Kellner, most serious and proper; Rita, his girl, definitely adoring and slightly in awe. Very pretty, of course, and casually dressed in tight jeans and an oversized shirt. Kellner, by contrast, wore a prim outfit—a three-piece navy-blue suit that seemed inappropriate for an afternoon of café hopping in Vienna. It was also a tight fit, but he showed no sign of acknowledging its heat, didn't even loosen his collar and closely knotted tie, although his round face was pink and his broad brow damp. Sam Waterman was a compromise in his dress: blue jeans, too, but with tie and white shirt (a drip-dry that had been wrung out too tightly and left with creases) and a wrinkled seersucker jacket slung over his shoulders. Possibly he had been traveling. As for Kellner, perhaps he was traveling, too—he was a journalist from Bonn, she was told—and living out of a suitcase, as most of us do, with little choice in clothes. As for Rita— all giggles and gurgles, and not one show of intelligence so far.

"Now you can start your interviews on us," Waterman told her. "That's the way she works," he explained to a round-eyed Rita. "First, she surveys the field; then she reaches for her notebook. Right, Karen?" His voice was disarming, his lips smiled. "Hey, you need something better than that to drink. Scotch?"

"Too early for me." Instead, she lit a cigarette.

He ordered for the others and himself: beer, beer, and vodka for Rita. And went on talking. Rita had her little interruptions, all of them nitwitted. Kellner kept silent, simply sat like a redfaced Buddha with a benign smile hovering around his lips. Karen, wondering how soon she could leave without obviously taking flight, answered the questions that came her way. Yes, she had been in Prague at the Convocation for Peace. No, nothing new had been decided—just what could be expected. Yes, the usual crowd was there: World Peace Council, World Federation of Trade Unions, World Federation of Democratic Youth, and of course the World Council of Churches.

"You must have met so *many* interesting people!" Rita exclaimed. "Oh, how I envy you."

"The most interesting among them were two women."

"Who?" asked Rita. She pushed a strand of her blond shoulder-length hair back from her cheek.

"I never met them. They were ejected from the hall when they suggested adding a criticism of the Soviet nuclear—"

"Booted out?" interjected Waterman with a wide grin. "Just like Tony Marcus?"

"My, my—news does get around." Karen stubbed out her cigarette. Like the other two in the ashtray before her, it was half-finished. "Somehow American cigarettes never taste the same when you buy them abroad." And my turn to ask some questions, she thought. "I wonder you weren't at the Convocation in Prague, Sam. Or were you there and avoided the crowd?"

"I've been on holiday for a change."

"A European jaunt? How nice." He was now a free-lance journalist, with articles and reports occasionally appearing in the major papers in New York, Chicago, Los Angeles. He also had a steady job, news gathering for UPI. He hadn't done so badly, she thought thankfully.

"Poor old Tony Marcus—he'd have fared better to take a holiday, too. Did you hear the details about him?"

"Just that he forgot to submit all of his material to the censors."

"Forgot? That's a laugh." Waterman's voice lowered as he glanced around the room and saw that a neighboring table was now occupied. "He was trying to smuggle out a document. A complete no-no." He studied Karen's face. She looked at him blankly. "A manuscript by a Czech writer."

"How on earth did he get hold of it? We were thoroughly supervised."

"The Czech passed it to him in some café. All prearranged. But stupid."

She calmed a sudden fear. She kept her voice normal. "Planted material, do you think?"

"No. It was a real effort to circumvent the law."

"Oh—a banned book by a banned writer? Have you got his name?"

Waterman laughed. "You do your own research, Miss Karen." He shook his head. "But it just goes to prove that newspaper guys—and dolls—have got to be damned careful. Can't go smuggling out sensitive material even if we're tempted. Sure, it would make a good story but—" He shrugged to complete the sentence.

Her alarm was growing. How did Waterman on holiday pick up such information? It was little more than one day old. And not even known in detail by journalists like Duvivier and Engel who were right on the scene. She had a feeling that this whole conversation was being aimed at her. She mastered her nervousness. "Too bad about Tony. Will this compromise his work? Where is he now—in London?"

Kellner broke his silence. His English was halting. Perhaps that was why he hadn't spoken so far, Karen thought. Embarrassed at his difficulty with accent and words? Kellner was saying, "He will be soon. A few days. Do not worry. He will not suffer."

But the Czechoslovak writer would. "I hope not."

"Did you know him well?"

"Not exactly. I smiled at his jokes, though. He had a nice turn of phrase."

Rita said, "Why—I thought all you journalists would be so close together—really friends. Of course, perhaps you were too busy talking with other people. Didn't you meet any Czechoslovaks who were interesting?"

Karen looked at the large inquiring eyes, so appealing, so innocent. "There were only officials of one kind or another at our hotel. They were polite and very efficient."

"But weren't they interesting? I would love to talk with some of them—really talk and find out what makes them tick. Isn't that what a reporter does?"

She's not such a nitwit after all, Karen thought. She may be American, but even that is deceptive: something about her accent that is just a touch foreign. "Are you a reporter?" she asked. If so, she works outdoors. That perfect tan wasn't acquired in an office.

"I'd *love* to be one. Travel—meet important people."

"Seldom, I'm afraid. Certainly not when you're starting your career."

"That's right," Waterman said. "Listen to the successful journalist, Rita. You fight every inch of the way, aim for the jugular. But then you get a town house in New York and an apartment in Washington."

Karen's eyes blazed in anger. "Not true, and you know it!" A house that Alan had bought when he was affluent—years before he had married her—and converted into three apartments as his writing dried up and his money melted. She still lived in the top flat and leased the others to cover the house and caretaking expenses. The apartment in Washington was the spare bedroom off the living room in a friend's place.

"Now, now," Waterman said. "Just kidding, Karen. But you haven't done so badly, have you?"

He had managed to rattle her, put her completely off balance, damn his eyes. She looked at her watch. "I think I must—"

"Let me order a drink, no?" Kellner interrupted with a smile for Karen and a sharp look at Waterman. "You must forgive Sam. He has been—been on a journey all night. His jokes are not so good as your Tony Marcus makes them. I do want your—how you say?—your view on foreign news."

"I'm not an expert on that." And where can this be leading? "No, drink, thank you."

"I have read your writing. I think you know much of the—" He looked at Rita. "How do you say it?" he asked in fluent German.

"Much of the background."

"Much of the background to what happens in the news.

You pick it up as you visit, no? You must. But difficult, I think. I, too, am journalist. Today, everything is mixed up. A real farrago, would you not say?" The bland eyes watched her. "Excuse my English—did I not pronounce it in the right way?"

"Farrago?" she heard herself repeating. How did anyone who spoke English with difficulty ever use such an uncommon word as that? "That's new to me. What does it mean, do you know?" she asked Waterman.

"A mix, a lot of bits and pieces."

"Then I don't think farrago is a strong enough word. I'd say that the international scene is a mess." Lord, I'm well out of that trap, she thought. But they interest me, these people. I'll stay for five minutes. Then I'd better get out of here before I meet more trip wires. "A complete mess," she added decidedly, and pulled a cigarette out of her pack.

Kellner held out his hand with his lighter ready. Either he had a painful muscle in his arm or his sleeve was too tight. She had to bend over the tabletop to reach the extended lighter. It flicked and failed. He tried again. This time there was a brief flame. Once more, and he produced an adequate light as a woman leaving the neighboring table walked past. She stumbled slightly as she reached Karen, regained her balance, excused herself, walked on.

Karen's cigarette was lit at last. What we have to suffer for politeness' sake, she told herself as she sank back in her seat. She could have lit that cigarette herself in half the time. Suddenly, she was aware that her shoulder blade didn't feel the customary bulge of leather straps against her spine. Quickly, she looked down at her side. Her handbag was no longer anchored to her chair. In panic, she raised her eyes to the mirrored wall and saw the woman reaching the entrance. "My bag!" She rose to her feet, dropped her cigarette.

Kellner was quick, moving rapidly to the door, saying, "I catch her."

"He will, too," Waterman said reassuringly as he

gripped Karen's arm.

She wrenched it away from his grasp. "It's *my* bag!"

"Didn't you notice that woman?" he was asking Rita, whose mouth was open in astonishment. "Nor did I. Pretty damned quick, wasn't she?" But Karen was already at the door.

She paused outside, looking wildly around her at tables and umbrellas. "It's gone," she said aloud in despair. "We'll never find her in this crowd."

"I found it," Kellner said behind her. "But not the woman. She dropped it on a chair when she saw me. She ran." He handed her the bag. "It is yours?"

She nodded thankfully. "I'm grateful. Very grateful."

"Come inside," he said. "People are too curious. They stare. And you must examine your purse. She may have stolen something. They are cunning and quick, these thieves."

Karen let herself be persuaded. Her gratitude was tinged with suspicion. Do they want to see the contents of my bag? she wondered as Kellner guided her so politely back to their table. Let them: nothing inside that shouldn't be there, no coffee-stained envelope stamped with a Czechoslovak censor's mark of approval. Or was she being too ungrateful?

Waterman and Rita were visibly relieved to see her, handbag clutched in both hands. "Good for you," Waterman told Kellner. "All safe and sound?" he asked Karen.

"We'll see. The fastener was undone." She lifted the flap of the bag, pulled it wide open, then shook its contents onto the table. "Passport, thank heaven. And wallet, with money and charge plates intact. Driver's license, too. A book of traveler's checks. Room key. Cosmetic purse. And my notebook—*am* I glad to see that!" It was small and black, could conceal nothing. She picked up her pen, pencil, eraser, package of Kleenex, all the small items that didn't need to be enumerated, and returned them safely to her bag with her cigarettes and matches. "Everything is here," she said and began replacing the other items.

"What about the zippered pocket inside?" Rita asked. "Was there anything valuable there?"

"Emergency cash—dollar bills. And my airplane ticket home." She unzipped the pocket and emptied it, too. "Okay," she said as she checked and found everything as it should be. The notebook was the last to be returned to her bag. "Today's work," she told Waterman, who had been eyeing it with interest.

"An interview?"

"Really an informal meeting, but he allowed me to jot down some notes." The small book dropped into the bag. "Read all about it in next month's issue," she said and gave him a very sweet smile. She snapped the bag's fastener and hoisted its straps over her shoulder. "Must go. Tomorrow, I have an early start."

As she rose, Waterman said, "I was surprised to hear you were in Prague. Lectures and speeches aren't in your line." He grinned, added teasingly, "Sure you didn't get any interview, too?"

She didn't have to act out any disappointment. Her lips tightened. "No interview. Oh, I thought there was one arranged, but it didn't work out. Some snag or other. Never put your trust in a wink and a nod from any embassy, Sam."

"Never did," he told her with an easy salute. Rita beamed her good-bye. Kellner got to his feet and shook hands. "A pleasure, Miss Cornell."

"Good-bye, and thank you once more." She could feel three pairs of eyes watching her progress to the door. The air outside was warm, but she took a deep breath and rejoiced in its sweet smell of safety.

Tonight, she decided, she would open that envelope. She must. Because if it had been stolen from her handbag today, who in Washington could ever have learned what threats it contained? Yes, Josef Vasek, clever, clever man, you didn't think of that, did you?

* * *

She entered the Sacher with her confidence restored. Tomorrow at 7:10 A.M. she'd take the TWA flight (the only one) for New York. No direct route to Washington, alas. But she'd do the next best thing—a TWA flight from Kennedy at 3:59 P.M., arriving at National by 5:04. Between planes she'd be able to get through customs, grab a sandwich, telephone Hubert Schleeman to expect her that evening in his office around six. Expedite was one of his words. Okay, Hubie, I'm expediting. I will have to delete any mention of Vasek's letters meanwhile—even his name, and that may be tricky in every sense—but in the end you'll have such a story, Hubie, that all will be forgiven. I hope.

5

THE WASHINGTON SPECTATOR *HAD TAKEN OFF FOR THE* weekend. Only Hubert Schleeman was still in his office, its door open and waiting for her. Karen walked through the large empty room with its cubicles silenced—no night desks needed there; no hectic last-minute rush of a daily newspaper. A monthly periodical was a fairly peaceful place until the week before publication, when hell, in the best traditions of the press, could break loose.

Schleeman, in shirt sleeves, was marking a copy of the proposed layout for next month's issue with scores and arrows and question marks in thick red ink. He glanced up as she entered, waved her to the chair in front of his desk, put down his pen, removed his heavy glasses. Sitting, he seemed big: broad shoulders, burly, large head, formidable brow heightened still more by increasing baldness and the close cut of what remained of his graying hair. On his feet, he was five feet five and quick-moving. His eyes, brown and sharp, studied Karen. He said nothing.

"I'm sorry I'm late. Friday traffic. Also," she admitted, "I miscalculated—it took ten minutes to phone from the airport and make sure I had a bed for tonight and a quiet place to work on my notes this weekend." Mary Dunstan's apartment could be a swinging place on Friday nights. Karen rushed on. "I'll have everything in shape and on Jim Black's desk by Tuesday." That would give Jim time to edit and argue with her over a fine point or two; her typescript (with some sentences deleted or added) must be ready for Schleeman's inspection on Thursday. She would just make that deadline. If she hadn't opened Vasek's envelope last night, hadn't been thoroughly shaken by three sheets of paper that she had read with growing apprehension and dismay, she could have blocked out the Vienna interview on the plane. It would almost write itself.

Schleeman poured a glass of water, pushed it toward her. "Take it easy." She was flustered and nervous, talking too much about small details he didn't need to hear. Not Karen's usual style. What put her so much on edge? "About Prague—what happened to that interview? You didn't give the details when you phoned from Vienna." He watched her take a long drink.

"There was none to give. It just didn't take place." Her voice was almost normal again.

"Why?"

"I don't know. I did nothing to antagonize anyone. I was on my best behavior. Truly." She drained the glass and put it back on the desk.

"I believe you," he said. She relaxed visibly. "We were never meant to have that interview. Why did they want us there?"

"Us and eight other Western newspapers. All pro-NATO. I don't know whether we were being softened in our views or whether they wanted to use us."

"What about the far-left press?"

"The Eastern bloc was in our hotel, but it seemed to be avoiding us. There were several of the anti-American

Germans—*Der Spiegel*, *Stern*, *Rundschau* among them— staying at another hotel. They sought us out at the meetings, lectured us. Germans do that a lot, I think. But why they, of all people, should believe the Soviets are blameless and we are responsible for everything that's wrong in the world—that really is a bitter laugh. Don't worry: I restrained myself. I didn't even say, 'So helping you recover from a war *you* started, was that wrong? Or the Berlin airlift?' I just kept telling myself that most Germans don't think like their newspapers. Not yet, at least. But how long can you read papers and magazines and listen to broadcasts without having the anti-American bias affect you? I think that's what bothered me the most about that week: the power of the press and what it can do to ordinary citzens."

She has recovered, Schleeman thought; that's more like the Karen I know. "Now you see why I've always warned all of you working here to keep your political opinions out of your writing. Sounded dull advice, but let the readers make up their own minds about events as they are reported fully and honestly." Time to probe a little deeper, he decided. "You had quite an education in Prague, I think. What about Vienna?"

"Good. I hope you'll like my piece."

Was that all she had to say? "We'll run it in the space we held open for the Prague interview. What about your week there? You gathered some material, didn't you?"

"I'll describe it as it was." She gave her first smile as she added, "No cover-ups, but no slanting, either." It was a direct quotation from him, presiding at the last staff meeting. "I'll get a column out of it, at least."

"More than that goddamned monkey at their embassy deserves." Suddenly, his usually guiet voice rose. He cursed himself for being fooled, he cursed the press aide. Then his anger subsided. He noticed Karen's startled face, said grimly, "You should have heard me Wednesday night after you called from the Sacher. Well, now—" He looked down at the layout and picked up his pen. "If we advance the Vienna interview to next month, we'll have to come up with something to fill the gap in the following issue. Do some thinking, will you? Give me your ideas on Monday."

The meeting was ended.

Not yet, thought Karen. "I *have* been doing some thinking. On disinformation. I could write two articles at least on that subject—if I had some solid facts as a basis."

"Disinformation?" That had caught his attention. He dropped the pen back on the desk.

"It's important—something we all ought to be aware of. Most of us don't really know the difference between misinformation and disinformation."

"But you know now—since Prague?" He was amused but interested. "Give me an example of that difference, Karen. No fancy language: just a simple explanation that any ignorant layman—like myself—can understand."

He is challenging me, she told herself. All right, let's show him this isn't just a Prague-inspired notion. "The scene is Paris. An attempt to shoot Mitterrand as he was entering his car. The actual facts are that he wasn't hit, his driver was wounded, and the two assailants escaped.

"An early press report of the incident said that Mitterrand was wounded and his chauffeur was killed; two, possibly three terrorists had done the shooting. That report is a case of misinformation.

"Another press report starts appearing. It says that an attack on Mitterrand took place; he wasn't hit but his driver was wounded. The two assailants have been identified as gunmen used in previous killings by a West German intelligence agency. A reliable source states that the assassination of Mitterrand was to have been followed by a right-wing coup, establishing in power a French general favored by fascist elements in Germany." Karen paused. "And that report is pure disinformation."

She knew what she was talking about. Schleeman nodded his approval. "It includes a fact or two to make a story credible, then adds the distortions." And people fell for it: the riots in Pakistan four years ago, the burning of the American Embassy and two Americans killed—all the result of skillful disinformation. The lie that had lit the fuse? The Americans were responsible for the seizure of the Grand Mosque in Mecca, the CIA being the villains. "Yes," he said, "That's not a bad idea of yours. A slight change of pace, but that may be all to the good." He looked at his watch. Almost ten to seven. "Let's have a bite to eat. We can talk over dinner. Oh, don't worry about me. I've given up any idea of a weekend. This damned layout—all wrong. Not what I suggested."

You'd think he hadn't any editors who could take charge: nothing was ever perfect unless the boss supervised. But the *Spectator* was his baby. He had taken it over when it was a mewling infant that wasn't expected to live. He had nursed it along, feeding it with money and talent, and watched it grow in the twenty years of his care to respectable strength. A rich man's hobby had become a serious career. Karen's fleeting thoughts ended. She concentrated on her words. She began, "Before we leave—" and stopped.

He was tidying his desk: everything in order for tomorrow's work. "Yes?" He glanced up, noted the tension on her face.

"There's something important—a favor I have to ask. You know Peter Bristow. I must get in touch with him. As soon as possible. Would you help me? Would you try to reach him, either at home, or perhaps in his office?"

"What? Now?"

"Yes. Now. Please."

"What's important about Bristow? Disinformation? Surely that can wait." He was terse, annoyed, and hungry.

"That can wait. But what can't wait is—" She hesitated, drew a long breath. "In Czechoslovakia, a man approached me. Secretly. He needs Bristow's help. He wants to defect."

"Bristow doesn't deal with defectors—he's an expert on tracking disinformation. Analysis and evaluation, that's his line."

"The man knows that. But he said he could trust Bristow."

"Meaning?"

"Bristow is not in KGB pay, and so won't betray him."

"And who is this would-be defector?"

"All I know is that he plans to escape soon. He needs help. And secrecy. His life depends on it, he said."

"You really believe—" Schleeman began incredulously.

"Yes. So many strange things happened to me in Vienna that I do believe him. Once he is safe here and been accepted, you'll have the biggest story you've ever published."

"What's that about Vienna?"

A mistake, she thought in dismay: I should never have mentioned Vienna until later, much later, when I can tell him everything. "I was under surveillance. But first of all—please, would you try to contact Bristow? Would you, Hubert?"

He frowned, glared at the telephone, but he dialed Bristow's number at Langley. Someone answered his query, and he listened. "Thanks. I'll call back." He replaced the receiver. "He has gone out for something to eat, lucky fellow. But he is expected back any minute. He's working late. In the meantime, start explaining. What the hell have you got into? I've always told you not to get mixed up in politics."

"Not even to save a man's life?"

"What does he do—what's his job?"

"I don't know. But once I give Bristow the message, he will understand just what we're dealing with. He will be able to explain to you."

"Off the record," grumbled Schleeman, "and not much

of that." He looked once more at his watch. "I'll give you his number. Call him—"

"No! I'm sure he doesn't remember me, and I can't risk saying anything important over a telephone. He wouldn't listen to some strange female who gave no details, only said she had to see him at once."

That was true enough. "What do you want me to tell him?"

"No name. No mention that I write for you. Just tell him it's urgent. Arrange a meeting with me for tomorrow morning, a quiet meeting—as if by accident. Perhaps I could drive past his house or whatever and pick him up. I'll recognize him all right." Her cheeks, pale today, colored at that admission. "He knows you. If you say this is something urgent and that I'm to be trusted, he will listen. Please, Hubert!"

"You flatter me."

"But no name. Don't let him question you, either—not over a telephone."

Schleeman had to smile at that. "Don't teach this old dog how to play games. Before you were born, I was sending cryptic messages back to London from Nazi territory. Ever heard of the OSS?"

Her eyes rounded in astonishment. "You were with the OSS?" He could only have been fresh out of college, if that. His smile broadened, changing his face from its usual severity. A prominent nose, a determined chin, thin lips held tightly made him appear more unapproachable than he actually was. At this moment, he seemed years younger as he dialed once more. This time Bristow was at his desk.

Schleeman didn't identify himself—Pete Bristow knew his voice. He didn't name Bristow, either. "Got a minute? I've just heard an interesting piece of news. Thought you'd like to hear it, too. I think you should. I'm pretty busy tonight, but what about meeting me tomorrow morning? A quiet meeting—it shouldn't take long. . . . Eleven o'clock? I'll pick you up just south of your block—easier to park there if I'm early. If I'm delayed, I'll send my secretary to drive you to my place. A reliable type. Knows you by sight. No problem." He ended the call as abruptly as he had begun it.

How many other hidden talents does he have? Karen wondered, her amazement increasing.

"Well?" he demanded. "Did that fit your specifications?"

"You took my breath away."

He pulled on his jacket. "Play it loose, Karen. And stop worrying. The fate of the world isn't in your hands. He's just another defector. This story you've been promised—don't bank on getting hold of it soon. It may take weeks, months, before you can write about it."

"I know." Her voice, her movements, were slow. She rose to her feet, reaching for her briefcase, but Schleeman lifted it before she could. "I'm tired, I guess. I can't really face dinner. A sandwich and instant bed is about my level tonight. I'm sorry."

"Sorry but wise," he said. He had hoped a good dinner with a bottle of Château Latour might induce some answers to several questions he had in mind.

"It's been a long day." She was still excusing herself. Up at five-thirty this morning, thousands of miles away . . .

"I'll see you on Monday morning. Ten o'clock sharp."

Karen managed a small smile. "And hear how I was followed in Vienna?"

"And the reason why." He dialed again, this time for a taxi. Then he locked his office door, and they could leave at last.

She walked quickly through the staff room, halting at her desk, where she had left the rest of her luggage. Schleeman picked up the heavy bag and typewriter, giving her the lighter load. He noticed how she seized the briefcase with relief and held it tightly. He almost said, "What have you got in there—the crown jewels?" But he restrained his sense of humor, which was always heavy-handed at best.

As they waited for the elevator in an empty corridor with only the distant clatter of a cleaning woman's bucket to break the silence, Karen suddenly spoke. "Sam Waterman was in Vienna. He brought a couple of friends to sit at my table."

"How was he?" Schleeman couldn't care less.

"Outwardly friendly, but inwardly—" She shrugged. "I think he still believes I did a neat hatchet job to get what he wanted. Or did I?"

"No. He did the hatchet job himself. Where the hell is that elevator?"

"Why did you choose me and not him, Hubert?"

"That's none of your business," he reminded her. The elevator arrived, and he could follow her inside without the embarrassment of further questions, for there were other passengers, late leavers from the floor above, who groused about overtime on a Friday evening.

Karen's cheeks had colored. "Sorry. You were right. Not my business. But it was so strange—the way he seemed to—" She gave up. An elevator car was no place to give details.

Schleeman struck a bargain after they reached the hall and waited at its entrance for the cab. "You tell me all about Vienna, and I'll tell you about Mr. Sam Waterman. Agreed?"

Tell what I can about Vienna, she emended silently. She nodded an indeterminate promise, looked wan and miserable.

"Get a good night's sleep," he said by way of goodbye. He'd find out from Bristow what she wouldn't tell him. Or couldn't?

"I will. And thank you. Thank you for everything. I don't know what I would have done if you hadn't— Oh, nearly forgot. What is Peter Bristow's address?" It wouldn't be in the telephone directory: an unlisted number.

He told her and watched her intent face as she repeated

it. He said nothing more as he helped her into the cab. He stood there, looking thoughtful, watching the taxi disappear from view. Must be one hell of a story, he thought as he headed for his club.

6

IN SPITE OF TIME SPENT IN RENTING A CAR, IN SPITE OF circling around a few blocks and driving down this narrow street to make sure of the right number on a doorway, Karen was still ten minutes early. She could have borrowed Mary Dunstan's car for this morning, but it was a Firebird and a flaming red; safer to settle for a less obtrusive gray Plymouth from Avis. Bristow's address might be pleasant enough, but it was nothing imposing: an apartment above a quiet bookstore, with its own separate entrance. Was it on the second or third floor? Or were there more than two apartments? These Georgetown houses were deceptive, often stretching deep into their backyard, and this street with three-storied buildings of white clapboard or red brick, all narrow-fronted, all closely packed, would be no exception.

There were trees in full leaf spaced along the sidewalks, and Karen had parked under a patch of green shade, natural air conditioning to bolster the car's own system; this morning was typical August in subtropical Washington.

She was about fifty feet away from the bookstore's window—her eye always calculated short distances from the length of her New York living room, and that was twenty-five feet—and on the opposite side of the street. Her plan was nicely worked out. She'd wait for Bristow to appear, let him start walking south. She'd follow, and stop just ahead of him, opening the passenger door as a signal. He was bound to notice—he was on the alert for a car, wasn't he? Then all he would have to do was to cross the narrow street and get in.

If he came... She had had brief spasms of worry about that, and now this waiting brought on another attack. What if he appeared and she missed her cue because her view of his doorway was blocked by a slow-moving truck, like this one now edging past her, feeling its cautious way down a mostly residential street where it shouldn't be allowed in the first place?

Eleven o'clock. No one at the entrance to 27A Muir. A woman at the bookstore window; two men, dark-haired but the wrong height, walking slowly past. As the woman left, Karen saw him emerge. Not from 27A but from the bookstore itself. He paused on its front step, glanced up and down the street. Peter Bristow? Definitely Bristow, although his Saturday clothes were very different from the tailored suit worn at a cocktail party. Hair dark, height almost six feet, well-proportioned body, good profile shown clearly by the quick turn of his head. Now he strolled south: a well-controlled walk—no slouching, no lumbering. (She always noted people's movements: body language, in the way they walked or sat, was suprisingly revealing about attitudes of mind.)

"Everything according to plan," she told the automatic shift, changing from *Park* into *Drive*, and congratulated herself. But before she could draw even with the man in the tan trousers and dark-blue sports shirt, he had crossed the street, hoisting a green cloth book bag over his shoulder, and looked squarely at the Plymouth's driver. He's seen me, he's seen me all the time, she thought angrily s her stratagem crumbled. She had been so damned smart, nd now she felt like a six-year-old.

She pulled up just ahead of him, noticed two auto-mobiles about to overtake her, traveling too close to the Plymouth to let her open the passenger door. She opened ers instead, remembered to set the car at *Park*, scram-led over the barrier of automatic shift, hauled her pre-ious bag with her just as he slipped into the driver's seat, ropping his own bag behind him with one hand, closing he door with the other. Within seconds, the car was noving farther south to join a busier street and lose itself n traffic.

For a moment, he had stared at her as he entered the ar. Now he looked at her again, this time concealing his urprise. "Smooth. Very smooth." There was amusement n his eyes. "Did they teach you these little tricks at the Columbia School of Journalism, Miss Cornell?"

She recovered from her own surprise—he not only emembered her, he even knew something about her background. "All part of the curriculum—how to deal vith covert assignments. And did Harvard give you your asic training, Mr. Bristow?" She glanced pointedly over er shoulder at the green book bag lying on the rear seat. An affectation, she thought, and something she hadn't xpected from him. All right, Peter Bristow, we're even: et's start again. "I'm thankful you came. I wasn't sure f you would."

"When Schleeman passes the word, I listen."

Don't we all? she thought. Except for last night when evaded his questions. He will blow higher than Mount St. Helen's when he hears the full truth. But that's another roblem for another day.

"We'll drive around, and you can tell me whatever you old Schleeman. Sorry to take over the wheel of your car, ut it might have been difficult to give your information nd drive through traffic."

She hadn't thought of that. "Especially in a strange ar."

"You borrowed it?" She really was being security conscious, perhaps overmuch. Or did she think he'd expect it? He could only wonder at the strange notions the public could entertain about his work.

"Rented it this morning."

"Where?"

"At the airport."

He shook his head in amazement, repressed a smile. She's serious, damned serious about all this, he thought. "Why don't you begin?" he asked quietly and kept his eyes on the traffic.

"There's a lot to tell—the way things happened, how it was done."

"Give me the main points."

"I've just come back from Czechoslovakia by way of Vienna. On my last afternoon in Prague—actually just before I left—a man contacted me."

"And that day was?"

"Wednesday."

A day in Vienna, a day traveling home. "You got Schleeman to phone me as soon as you arrived here?" She nodded. He said, "Sorry. Go on."

"The man's name is Josef Vasek. A Czech, an intelligence agent, high-placed. He wants to defect. He asked me to alert you."

"Vasek... Vasek... Never heard of him." But he knew me, Bristow thought worriedly.

"It's a recent alias. He said it possibly wasn't recorded—as yet—in the file you keep on him. Disinformation. That's his special field."

Bristow's frown deepened. "He didn't give you one of the other names he has used?"

"He said they were numerous, a mixture. You know him by the label you put on his file: Farrago."

The car almost swerved. There was a long silence. And how the hell did Vasek get that information? Few know about that Farrago file: six people in my unit; the head of our section; the top brass, of course; and no one else.

So how did its name get into the hands of an enemy agent? Someone planted by the KGB? A mole? But surely not one of my people—we've worked together for years. He stared at the traffic, both mystified and alarmed.

She had opened her shoulder bag, was drawing out an envelope. "I was to give this to you. Only to you. No one else. Urgent, he said."

Bristow roused himself. "What's it about? D'you know?" His glance veered back to the stream of cars, saw a street corner ahead of him, edged the Plymouth toward the outer lane to be ready for a right turn.

"Samples of his work—as insurance that you'll help him. They are to be issued to the media as soon as the assassinations take place." She held out the envelope.

He negotiated the turn into a side street with little traffic and enough free space to park by the curb. "Assassinations? In the plural?" he asked incredulously as he switched off the engine. He looked at her: blue eyes, large and beautiful, were completely sincere.

"Yes. Two of them."

"Whose?"

"He didn't know. Date and place still being decided. He predicted wide protests, riots, the end of the Western alliance and of NATO. He foresaw a world war."

Bristow took the stained envelope, handled it carefully. The censor's stamp of approval caught his eye at once. The partly blotted inscription at the top of the envelope puzzled him: *Tuesday: Village Visits.* "Your envelope?"

She nodded. "One of several."

"You risked using it to carry—" he began almost sharply.

"No! I didn't put the letters there. Farrago did. But that's another part of my story."

He eased the envelope's flap loose—it looked as if it might have been opened and resealed—and pulled out three sheets of heavy paper with embossed letterheads, held them by their edges. His lips tightened, his jaw went rigid. He finished reading the three short missives. He drew a deep breath as he replaced them in the envelope. "Excellent samples of Farrago's talent," he said bitterly. He recovered. "And what else did he have to say?"

"Farrago had no idea—"

"Forget that name," he told her. "At least, don't use it." Then his voice softened. "Sorry—my fault for calling him Farrago. But he used so many names that it became simpler to give him the one on his file. Go on! He had no idea—?"

"No idea that the letters would be used to back any assassination."

"I wonder." Or had he really been following someone's suggestions for these letters' contents? Highly unusual for him: Farrago was the source of ideas, not their echo.

"I think he told the truth. Defection is the strongest protest he could make, isn't it? He is a Czech and a Communist, but he is in total disagreement with the use of these letters."

With their use, Bristow wondered, or with something else? Such as a demotion under the Andropov regime? Strange, though. "He's Russian, not Czech," he advised Karen. "KGB from away back when." He looked at her startled face. "What's the other part of your story? A lot to tell, you said. I'd like to hear it." If she hadn't known about Farrago, he wouldn't even have listened to her. Whose side was she on? Her story might make that clearer.

"All of it?" She glanced at her watch.

"All. But first, we'll have to get this envelope into safe hands—can't go carrying it around with us all afternoon." He reached for his book bag and loosened the drawstring around its neck, presumably to slip the envelope out of sight. But he had second thoughts and handed the envelope back to her. "Less chance of damage if you keep it." She noticed the hard bulge of a heavy object inside the green cloth covering: books tied together or some massive tome? He dropped the bag on the rear seat once more, became aware of her silence, said, "You *are* free, aren't you?"

She thought of her own work, her notes ready and waiting on her bedroom desk. "I'm free," she said.

"Good. See that mom and pop paper shop just ahead of us? I can telephone from there, won't take five minutes. Hang onto your bag."

As he left the car, he saw her reach across to lock its door behind him. She had locked hers, too. This time he didn't smile at her precaution: he had his own problems on security to work out.

The telephone call had taken considerably more than five minutes. Bristow had made three calls, but he wasn't explaining. Two had been to Langley—the first one in search of the Director, with an urgent request to be given him when (and if) he reached his office this afternoon: highly sensitive material to be read and discussed as soon as possible; this evening or night preferable; tomorrow early morning at latest—if not too late. (I stuck my neck out there, Bristow thought, but I don't request many urgent interviews.) The second call to Langley was brief—Fairbairn, his good right hand, was at work today and would take his car, drive to a gas station that was the most easily reached from Langley. No name given, but Fairbairn knew which one. He'd be there at twelve-thirty and wait if necessary. "Emergency." Bristow had said without any details. His third call was briefer yet. He had to cancel that tennis game this afternoon; sorry, Diana, but his shoulder was acting up again; he'd keep in touch.

Karen had the car door unlocked as he returned. There was a newspaper under his arm, two candy bars in his hand. That accounted for the delay, she thought as he tossed them into the back seat. She refrained from saying, "I was beginning to worry," and only said, "All settled?"

"The best I could do." There might be a chance that the Director would be in his office this evening—he worked erratic hours and kept all his subordinates hopping. It was a piece of luck about Wallace Fairbairn, though. It might have been Denis Shaw, always full of questions; or Jan van Trompf, who—like a lot of sticklers—could be something of a ditherer when the unusual came up. Susan Attley was on leave—she'd be back at her desk next Wednesday. Bob Reid took Saturdays off, definitely. Manuel Domingus was punctual with his work and it was good, but he never kept an appointment on time.

They drove in silence for the next ten minutes. He's probably making up his mind what to tell me, Karen decided. "When do we eat the candy bars? I'm hungry." Breakfast had been at six that morning.

"You'll spoil your lunch."

"We lunch somewhere?" she asked in surprise. "Then I'll wait." She hadn't wanted a candy bar anyway; it was just a small ploy to break into his thoughts without appearing to be the inquisitive reporter. That, he would shy away from, even if his manner was now easier, his voice friendly.

"We'll pick up some food at a sandwich place. Okay with you? And I'll hand over the envelope to—to one of my friends. I'm meeting him near the quick-food joint." The gas station that Fairbairn often used was right next door to the cafeteria.

She recognized the road they were traveling. It could take them toward Langley. "The envelope is open," she reminded him.

He reached into his trouser pocket, produced a small roll of Scotch tape. I'm beginning to believe her, he thought in surprise. There was a directness about her, a frankness that was appealing. Or perhaps it was just those sincere blue eyes. Careful, he warned himself.

"Mom and pop's novelty counter?" she asked.

"You're pretty quick, aren't you?" But his tone was bantering: no barbed wire laced around it. She smiled and shrugged. "Here!" He handed over the tape. "Seal that envelope so no one can open it. Not this time," he added.

Her smile faded, her hands froze on the fastener of her bag. Then she released its catch and extracted the envelope, began pulling the tape out of its container. She seemed thoroughly absorbed by the job on hand.

He let her finish it. "Was it you, Karen?"

The use of her first name calmed her slightly.

"I hope it was, and no one else," Bristow added.

"No one touched this envelope except me. And Farr— and Vasek warned me not to open it." She hoped that would close the subject.

"And that was a challenge in itself, wasn't it?"

"No!"

"I wouldn't be surprised if you did open it—there was a big story inside. Impossible to resist."

"It wasn't that!" Not altogether, at least.

"Besides," he went on smoothly, "the American public ought to be told. Your first duty is to them."

"Will you stop inventing reasons for me?" She was angry enough to hit him with the truth. "If that envelope had been stolen, who would have known what it contained? What help would that have been to you? What good would that have done Vasek? Yes, I opened the envelope—after I had a scare in Vienna."

"Vienna?"

"I think I was under surveillance there, even more than in Prague. A very odd thing happened—" She broke off. "Well?" she demanded. "Was I right to open the envelope?"

"You have a point there," he conceded. "I'm sorry I needled you. I had to make sure that no one else had tampered with it." Doesn't she realize that, if all this is true, she may have put herself in jeopardy? "Vasek warned you not to open the envelope. Did he give you a reason?"

"He said it could be dangerous to me."

And how right he was. But why hadn't he given her a concrete example of the risk she would run? Or at least explained that the less she knew, the safer she was. "It could very well be."

"Why? The dangerous time for me was between picking up that envelope from my desk in a Prague hotel and reaching the Austrian frontier. Which I did with no trouble at all."

"That was the first hazard you faced. The second was in Vienna, wasn't it?"

"And the third? Any prediction on that one?" She was half serious, half-mocking.

It all depended on whether she had indeed come under suspicion. But he wasn't going to add to the sudden fears that she was trying to hide. "I'm no oracle," he said with an encouraging smile. "How could I make even a guess until I hear the full story? Do you remember the details, what was said and how it was said?"

"I remember," she said tensely. "Couldn't forget them. Thanks to a sleepless night," she added, lightening her voice.

"Can you give them to me in sequence? From the moment Vasek met you?"

"From the moment I was waiting in my hotel room for my envelopes to be returned by the censors, and the telephone rang."

"By phone—he made the first contact by your room telephone?" My God, thought Bristow, she could be in danger. "Okay, okay," he added, easing his voice, trying to allay any alarm his startled question might have aroused, "I'll be patient. Just don't forget a thing, Karen. Thank heaven we have a trained ear and eye to give us the particulars."

"Can that actually be praise for journalists?"

"Actually, yes." Ahead of them, on a stretch of land that had flattened out and been robbed of its trees, he could see two square shapes of whitened concrete huddled together. The gas station was the nearer building, drawn off the highway, its red pumps standing at attention under a string of stiff bright-colored pennants. Beyond it were the blue and yellow neon lights of the café.

Bristow lessened his speed as they passed the side road on his left that slanted into the highway. What he could see of it, for trees still lined its narrow curve, gave no glimpse of Fairbairn's green Buick heading for their rendezvous. Not to worry, he told himself. Fairbairn won't be late; we are early.

They reached the gas station and parked on its free side in a small one-time field, now bare of grass, partly filled with two old trucks and three cars in need of repairs. "We still have seven minutes to wait," Bristow said. "Sorry about the view." They were facing a blank wall.

"Better than gas pumps and stiff little flags. Is that where you'll meet your friend?"

"Just around the corner. He'll probably be buying some gas."

"And then," she guessed, "you'll wander into the washroom, and he will follow, and you'll give him this." She presented the envelope.

"Perfect," he said as he noted the elaborate crisscross of tape on its back flap. No one could risk opening it without pulling away some of the envelope, too.

"A nice tangled mess," she agreed. "But how will you keep the envelope out of sight?"

He had foreseen that small problem and had already opened his book bag. He was now lifting a dictating machine and some cassettes out of its depths. "Much too heavy," he told her with a grin. "We can't have them bruising and crumpling those nice flat sheets inside the envelope. How did you manage to keep them without a fold or wrinkle?"

Karen just kept staring at the machine.

"Well, you know now. Do you mind?"

She shook her head, tried to look nonchalant. She could see the good sense of having her story on tape. "Recorded for posterity—I'm flattered. Do you always come prepared?"

Not prepared to meet anyone like you, he thought. Beauty and brains—it was a devastating mixture. "I use these gadgets for accuracy." His voice was stilted, embarrassed, and he knew it. "My memory isn't as good as yours."

"I wouldn't like to bet on that."

"What about this?" He was looking at the book bag critically. "Too noticeable?"

"Eccentric—for a gas station."

He replaced the machine and its cassettes in the bag. "In your care," he told her.

"Why don't I get the sandwiches and something to drink? It would save time."

He hesitated for a moment, looked at his watch. It would take them at least half an hour to reach the place he had decided to tape her story: a secluded spot, no one to wonder at them—or intrude—and a spreading tree for cool shade. Time wasn't for wasting this afternoon. "Okay. Beer for me—doesn't matter what kind. Anything liquid. Here's your expense account." He found a ten-dollar bill in his pocket, tucked it under the strap of her handbag. "Better leave now. And stay inside the café until I pick you up. Okay?"

She nodded, and then broke into a laugh as he pulled up his shirt and flattened the envelope against his diaphragm, anchored it there by tucking his shirt back into his trousers.

"All set," he said as calmly as if he did this every day before breakfast. "Let's go."

She glanced back when she reached the corner of the gas station: he was locking the car's trunk, presumably with his book bag stowed inside. Why not use the *Washington Post*, lying beside two candy bars, to cover the envelope? Ah, yes, she realized suddenly as she saw a station wagon at one of the gas pumps: man enters washroom, newspaper under arm, second man follows; first man exits with no newspaper, second man comes out holding it. That old bromide, she thought; too obvious. But she was wondering, as she took a shortcut behind the gas pumps to reach the circular driveway in front of the café, why so much security? Then she smiled at herself. After all the precautions she had taken, who was she to cavil at his? And it was proof, perhaps, that he was taking her seriously. Or the envelope. Or the Farrago name.

Unexpectedly, a brown Honda left its parking space in front of the café and—taking its own shortcut—skimmed past her to reach the gas station. She flashed the driver and his companion an angry glare, but it had little effect. Manners, she thought bitterly, whatever became of good manners? Or perhaps some men just liked to see the ladies jump, an old tradition—hadn't Papa Haydn used that phrase with glee when he inserted a loud bang in the middle of a placid sonata? But before the driver glanced away as if nothing had happened, he had a damned good look at me. Somehow, that troubled her.

Bristow was later than she expected. It was with relief that Karen saw him driving up to the café. She was out of its door, a bundle in each arm, as he halted the car.

"Sorry," he said, his face tight, his dark eyes angry. "Ten minutes wasted." He lifted the packages into the car as she climbed on board. She was barely settled before they had reached the highway and swung round to follow the direction they had taken earlier.

"Your friend was late?" she asked.

"No. My fault." *And blast me for an idiot. There I was, leaning against the Plymouth's trunk, congratulating myself that I'd have a clear view of Fairbairn's Buick tooling along the highway, then suddenly wondering if he had misheard me over the phone and chosen another route to reach the gas station. And when I walked to the corner of the building just to check, there he was, gas already pumping into the car. Not the Buick. He had been given a lift in Shaw's little number when his own car developed a flat tire, and Shaw was there, too. Shaw, the perpetually curious.*

"Your fault?" she asked disbelievingly.

"He arrived on time, but he took another road—one I hadn't expected. Just a misunderstanding. No harm done. Envelope safely transferred and now about to be stashed in the safest of safes." But not in our file room. I made that clear. It raised a smile from Fairbairn, as if my super-caution was a touch comical, but he said nothing. Nothing, too, when I specified its destination—in Blau's special security vault, but accessible for immediate consultation. Which meant a record of delivery, time of deposit indicated. Miriam Blau was meticulous about that. Anyway, I've made sure it won't lie on a desk for some unauthorized eyes to note the Czech censor's mark. The stamp itself caused a tightening around Fairbairn's lips for a moment, but he will hear the details tomorrow or the next day, once the top brass decides how we handle them.

"Well, you took every care," Karen said. Why blame himself for someone taking the wrong route? She smiled, remembering the envelope safely hidden under a sports shirt. "Did your friend have to hide it your way?" Or perhaps he had carried a useful newspaper.

"No need." Bristow's voice had dropped its worry. "His idea of dressing for summer is a seersucker suit. The jacket hid the envelope nicely." We're making good time, he thought, even if I'm keeping to the speed limit. No risk of being stopped by a traffic cop, no more delays.

Something jolted Karen's memory. "Was he in that Honda? A brown Honda? It nearly sideswiped me on the way to the café. Who was the driver—is he usually so wild?"

"Erratic sometimes. But why say 'usually'—he didn't do it on purpose, did he?" That wasn't Shaw's style. He was eager, yes, but never aggressive.

She shrugged, didn't mention that the driver had stared at her; the other man, too, but less obviously. Instead, she said, "They must have arrived too early and parked, and then suddenly noticed the time and came rushing out."

"Early?" Bristow fastened on the word. Fairbairn had been on time; no mention of having to wait.

"They were in that parking space when we pulled off

the highway. I noticed the Honda because it was the only car with two people just sitting in it and going nowhere."

"I didn't see—"

"You were busy navigating," she reminded him.

Yes, the approach to the field at the side of the gas station had been full of ruts and bumps. Bristow looked at her and smiled. If he had needed corroboration that her testimony this afternoon would be accurate enough to be trusted, he had been given a small demonstration. "Acute," he said. "You really notice."

Is he making fun of me? "Not always. It is just that today I'm slightly—well, on edge. That envelope really has a powerful effect. At least," she added, "I'm rid of it."

But I won't be rid of it, he thought, not for a week— two weeks—three—how many?

She misjudged his silence. "It wouldn't matter if your friends did add up two and two and put us together, would it? Or didn't you want to be seen with me?" she added as a small joke.

He didn't share it. "The other way around. I didn't want you to be connected with me." Or connected in any way with the delivery of those letters.

They had left the highway and were now following a narrow road, tree-lined, almost a country lane. Then they passed a gate to enter a curving driveway. Bristow stopped there. Ahead of them, through a screen of bushes, Karen could see a house; not large, but two-storied, with a steep slope of roof.

"Yours?" she asked. And why not drive up to its door?

"A friend's. He's in Spain right now. I have the use of the house on weekends. So don't worry. No trespassing charges will be lodged against us. Either we can go inside and have a comfortable chair in a hot room, or we can sit on the grass under a tree. Your choice."

"Grass."

"Good."

He led the way across the lawn, carrying the green bag

and the packages. It was a short distance through a screen of trees to a half-acre field with a large maple at the edge of a small pond. On its other side, more trees. "Seclusion complete," Karen said with approval as she sat down in the maple's shade.

"No mosquitoes until five o'clock, no bullfrogs until dark," he promised her.

"Birds?"

"I've never seen or heard any around here at this time of day. I guess they've had lunch and are now resting. They do that at three-hour intervals, I've heard. So what about *our* lunch?" He had sat down beside her and was opening the brown paper bags. "No wonder that one was heavy! How many cans of beer?"

"Only four. The ginger ale is for me." How natural this all seems, she thought as she watched him unwrap the sandwiches and offer her first choice. I was scared of him—yes, scared—when we met on Muir Street. And then I forgot to be either scared or nervous, and we've been talking ever since as if we had known each other for years. For a moment, she allowed herself a touch of cynicism: it could all be a matter of technique. His was certainly a good one—he had put her completely at ease. Then she accepted that. Gratefully. She began to concentrate on the facts she would give, once the picnic was over and a cassette was catching every sound. Everything must be clear, unequivocal—places, times, who appeared on the scene, who said what and how it was said. All part of the picture, and no room in it for anyone to misapprehend. Even if I look stupid and ignorant, she thought, I'll give it just as it was.

It was almost two o'clock. "Ready?" Bristow was asking. The first cassette had been inserted, the machine waiting with the hand microphone attached. He held it out with an encouraging smile. She took the microphone, kept it at the required small distance from her lips, and began speaking. "Last Wednesday afternoon, I was waiting in my hotel room for my notes to be returned by the

Czechoslovak censors. It was ten past three, and I was due to leave the hotel for the airport at half past four. The telephone rang."

She's off and running, Bristow thought with sudden relief. He lay on one elbow, his eyes on her face, and listened to the calm, clear voice.

The journey back to Washington was a silent one. Karen was more exhausted than she'd allow. Bristow had his own thoughts to mull over.

They approached Muir Street, where he had asked to be dropped off for a quick change of clothes—he could be at Langley till midnight or later. Then he had told her he'd take the cassettes and have them locked away with the envelope. They'd be secure. Her name wouldn't even be attached: just Prague and Vienna as identification labels. And no one would read the letters or listen to the tapes until they had been seen and heard by the Director and his second-in-command.

That was the only available route for Bristow at this moment: Menlo, who headed the section that unraveled disinformation and oversaw its various units, such as Bristow's, wasn't available. Menlo had taken a ten-day leave last Wednesday and would now be angling for salmon in Nova Scotia. So Bristow was going straight to the top with this one: no intermediaries, no wading through channels. He might be sticking his neck not just out but way out. Yet this was not only an emergency but also a potential crisis. "I'll try to see the top brass as soon as possible," he said. It sounded simple, but it wouldn't be. A weekend, of all times, to contact anyone ... And how would he go about it? Begin by introducing himself? *Peter Bristow, European Disinformation. It has come to my attention* ... Not bloody likely. Just say, *This is something that concerns the President, and it's urgent.*

Karen studied his face. It was tense, even if his voice had seemed normal. "And after that?" she asked quietly.

"Possibly a select group of experts, a very small group. A lot of verification."

"Can you ever tell me what happens?"

He had no answer for that, not at present. "But I'll be in touch. I promise you that. Give me your address and phone number."

She gave him both—New York and Washington—and watched his face as he memorized them. Will I ever see him again? she wondered as he said good-bye. As he prepared to step out of the car, he said, "Get rid of this Plymouth fast. Leave it at the Statler garage and give the keys to Conrad. Got that name? He'll have it delivered to Avis and take care of the bill. The receipt is in the glove compartment?" The book bag was over his shoulder, the car door half open.

"Yes. Are you trying to keep me out of sight?" she asked lightly.

His first smile since they had started the journey back came to his lips, softened his eyes. "That would be hard to do. But if anything worries you, however small it seems, call this number." He gave it to her, watched her jot it down in her notebook. "It's an answering service, very reliable. Just say you can't lunch with me—if you need to talk to me. If we need to meet, say you can't have dinner. No name. I'll know who it is. And I'll be in touch. At once." He held her hand for a few moments longer than necessary. "Thank you," he said, and left.

She took the wheel, watching him start the walk up Muir Street toward his apartment. He's back in his own world, she thought, and no room for me.

7

IT HAD BEEN FORTY-EIGHT HOURS OF INTENSE ACTIVITY since Saturday evening when Peter Bristow had reached Langely. There, to his great relief, was the Director on a quick visit before a dinner engagement. Bristow delivered letters and cassettes; the quick visit became hours long, and dinner was a sandwich on a tray. What happened after that, through Sunday and well into Monday, was only Bristow's guess. Telephone calls, scrambled; discreet visits to high places? Careful selection of experts to examine paper, type, ink, and study the forged signatures?

Now, at five-fifteen on Monday afternoon, six men were about to gather at a semicircular table in a room that was soundproof and bug-free. Windows were closed, shades drawn, lights on, and air conditioning almost noiseless. No paper or pens in front of each chair; only ashtrays, carafes of iced water, and tumblers. So, Bristow thought as he surveyed the scene prepared for a very select committee, before this meeting was over a decision would be made: how to deal with three calumnies and two assassinations. A tall order, but an urgent one. Their discussion would be reported back to their chiefs by tonight, and their recommendations either accepted or rejected. Accepted, Bristow hoped; delays were becoming dangerous. The men who had been chosen to come here were capable and responsible, quite aware they were representing high offices. (It was obvious that the heads of State, Defense, Intelligence could not risk meeting in the Oval Office themselves. Such a conference—and it would have been a lengthy one—would have sparked rumors and the inevitable speculations, mostly wild, some disastrous.)

Time they started arriving, Bristow thought as he stood at one side of the small room. They had all read Vasek's three letters; now, they would listen to the Prague cassettes—the background information on how the letters reached Washington in the first place. And then he'd have to explain Farrago—and answer some questions. But that was why he was here, to be seated at a separate table which—to his embarrassment—was centered to face the semicircle of chairs. He supposed it was the logical place—the table held cassettes and player. Surely, time wouldn't be wasted on questioning the cassettes?

The room door opened. Menlo, his ten-day leave interrupted, was the first arrival; a tall, spare man of sixty-odd years, more grim-faced than ever, preoccupied with nightmare thoughts—he had studied the letters that morning and was still in shock. He nodded to Bristow, took a chair at one end of the crescent, and was lost in a cloud of depression.

Martin Kirby, National Security Agency, entered next. He was an affable man with a ready smile, effective disguises for a steel-trap mind. Today he looked wan and worried, and older than his sixty-two years. A polite look was cast at Bristow; a friendly nod to Menlo although he chose a seat at the other end of the table. His modest manner was disarming; few who met him guessed he belonged to an agency that was the biggest, and most secret, of all branches of United States Intelligence.

Drayton followed quickly. He was State Department, fifty-five years old and on his way up, a specialist in East European politics. The letters had alarmed and angered him, but he hid his emotions as usual and gave Bristow a warm greeting. "I hear you have more surprises waiting for us, Peter."

Bristow smiled back. "Just some clarifications." He was thinking, I've got one friend at least among this bunch. As the bearer of ill tidings, he wouldn't be exactly popular around here. That and the fact he would probably be the youngest in the room—he was thirty-nine and feeling it at this moment—put him into the lower league of less experience.

Next to come was Robert Schlott, a brisk sixty-one in age, erect in bearing, smart in movement as a retired general should be. He was acting today as the eyes and ears for the Secretary of Defense. A nod to the room, a sharp glance at Bristow and then at the equipment on the table, and he sat down beside Maynard Drayton.

Frederick Coulton drifted in, a mere forty-eight-year-old to be the expert he was in forgeries. He was attached to the State Department's Bureau of Public Affairs, whose scope was wide enough to include serious study of Soviet "Active Measures" (in Russian, *aktivnyye meropriyatiya*), one of the KGB's most flourishing endeavors. It masterminded political operations, from economic blackmail, forgeries, disinformation, manipulation of front organizations and cultural exchanges, to attempted control of foreign media. The Bureau of Public Affairs gathered the facts (many of them furnished by Central Intelligence officers like Peter Bristow) and even published some of them. The CIA published nothing. It was the old conflict between silence to protect agents' identities and disclosure to alert the public. Bristow's personal opinion was that facts not actually dangerous to security could be published; and should be. But he didn't make policy.

Coulton, his desultory stroll taking him to the central chair, was reminded just before he sat down by a word from his State Department colleague that the seat was reserved for the President's special observer. Coulton shrugged, allowed his annoyance to be directed at Bristow in a brief stare. I know, I know, thought Bristow; you are wondering why the hell the letters were delivered to me and not to you. But you'll learn, once you listen to Karen's clear voice detailing the events in a hotel garden on the outskirts of Prague. One thing you won't learn, though, will be her name. It is something better left unidentified, even in this roomful of eminently important people. Sufficient that it has been made available to the Director, the Secretaries of State and Defense, and the President. They need to know; you don't.

Unobtrusively, the special observer came into the room—Abel Fletcher, a wily old bird, with seventy-four years behind him and forty of them spent in public service: lawyer, congressman, ambassador-at-large, presidential commissions; you name it, he's done it, thought Bristow as he left the wall against which he had been standing and took his own seat once Fletcher had sat down, and waited. It was now exactly five-thirty. The Secret Service men had been left outside to disperse themselves in the long hall. Security was tight but low in profile. This meeting was supposedly on new problems in Guatemala.

Fletcher began by placing a small recorder in front of him. "The President would like full details of our arguments," he announced. "Any objections?"

There were none. Bristow repressed a smile. How many had a microrecorder tucked away in either a wristwatch, a tie pin, a cigarette holder, or a cuff link? Menlo, for one, most certainly had; Kirby of National Security, too. Schlott of Defense—possibly; Drayton of State, perhaps. Coulton? He just looked bored. All in all, it was a first small breach in tight security, but Abel Fletcher had achieved one thing: there would be no high-flown rhetoric, no unnecessary comments, no wasted time. He looked around the table, peering at each man through heavy glasses. "Of course," he stated, "*any* recording of this meeting must be guarded with greatest care until it is heard by our chiefs. Then it will be destroyed. Agreed? Now we'll begin our discussion. I, myself, will merely give a categorical denial. The President has never written such a letter. Nor has he ever discussed such matters. Nor has he ever made one small comment that would lead me to believe he had such ideas in mind." With that, Fletcher lapsed into silence.

Drayton and Schlott agreed that the same could be said for their Secretaries. The letters were blatant forgeries. But clever, Drayton pointed out. They could, probably would, deceive most people.

Clever? They were dynamite, all waiting to be exploded, thought Bristow. The letters were brief. One, supposedly from the Secretary of State to the President, advised caution in solving the threatening problem in West Germany, but agreed that covert action by the CIA operatives was the most suited for immediate success. There was every indication that a one-time chancellor of West Germany was seeking a return to power after nine years in limbo and could be successful. He was now increasingly pro-Soviet in his views as he adopted the current anti-American crusade in the German press. His election would be disastrous for the United States.

The second letter, again to the President and dated a day later than State's, was a succinct statement from Defense. Necessary military support could follow the projected covert action to eliminate, once and for all, the constant source of danger in the Caribbean area, which over the years had been a permanent threat to anti-Communist governments.

Two days later, the President's supposed letter was written to the Secretary of the State Department. He agreed with the need for immediate action in both of the projects which had been discussed at length five days ago in the Oval Office. He was sending Defense a similar statement of his support. He advised them to coordinate their plans with Central Intelligence without delay.

And judging from the letters' dates, Bristow thought, that reference to "five days" could very well have meant a discussion on West Germany and Cuba.

The talk in the room was still focusing on the acceptance of these forgeries by the press and general public. "They would seem authentic," Menlo predicted. Tests made by Central Intelligence had proved that the stationery used was correct, from seals and letterheads down to the weight and color of paper. The ink was correct, too. The machines' typefaces were similar to those used in the three offices, and the initials of the typists involved were all in order except that the owners of these initials had no record of having typed any exchange of letters between Secretaries and President on these respective dates. "But that's no proof of forgery," Menlo ended. "The cynics will say that the women were ordered to destroy and forget any such records."

"We have one proof in the date used for the Secretary of State's letter. It couldn't exist," Drayton said. "He was at a secret meeting in Saudi Arabia that lasted three days. It was completely hush-hush—he traveled as an oil executive in a private plane. The second day of that meeting was the date on that damned letter. So it's impossible he could have signed it."

"And can you publicize the hush-hush meeting now?" Kirby asked. "Or is it equally impossible—like that signature?"

"Probably," Drayton conceded. "It's all extremely sensitive."

"My main challenge to the authenticity of the letters is simply this: who in their right senses would dictate such letters, have them typed? Even if they were clearly marked *Highest Security*?" Kirby shook his head. "A few quiet meetings, a verbal agreement surely. But a letter?" The National Security Agency would never be so careless in its methods, his raised eyebrows suggested.

Schlott came smartly to the aid of Defense. "We take no serious action without definite orders. A verbal agreement would not be enough for an investigating Senate committee."

Abel Fletcher said, "Gentlemen, gentlemen! We know the letters are forgeries but proof seems difficult. What about the signatures, Mr. Coulton? You are our expert on that branch of intelligence."

Coulton was flattered enough to sit up straight and talk frankly. "I was baffled, to tell the truth—couldn't decide at first. The pens used in the signatures were identical to those used by the writers—the supposed writers, that is." A quick smile as he added, "Stolen from the various offices, of course, like the paper that was used; possibly the typewriter ribbons, too. The machines could easily be doctored to duplicate the authentic action of the originals, provided you had been given the correct information on their makes and models. There's always someone who'd like to earn extra dollars."

"Or someone blackmailed," Menlo said. He had just dealt with a nasty case of blackmail for political purposes.

"Or," Kirby suggested, "someone who is a devoted party member and has kept his allegiance secret."

"Are you saying, Mr. Coulton," Abel Fletcher asked, "that you have made no judgment on these forgeries?"

"No, no. I now think they are forgeries. But in a court of law, you would find the experts split on their testimony."

"We will be before a court of world opinion, Mr. Coulton. And you say there will be disagreement among the experts about the validity of these signatures?"

"Yes. They are excellent imitations of the originals."

"Well, gentlemen," Fletcher said evenly, "we now know what we have—three examples of expert disinformation. The problem is: how do we deal with them?"

Schlott said, "The best defense we have is attack."

"A confrontation?" asked Drayton worriedly. "How?"

"Immediate disclosure to the press that three forged letters, fabricated by the KGB's department of disinformation, have come into our possession along with a serious warning that two assassinations have been planned to take place. The letters, we have learned, will be produced when the assassinations have occurred—as proof that the United States is the guilty party." It was the longest speech that Schlott had been known to make. "What's wrong with that?" he demanded.

For several moments, there was silence. Bristow straightened in his chair; it scraped loudly in the quiet room.

"Yes, Mr. Bristow?" Fletcher asked.

"There's not much wrong with it—it may be our only option. But—" He hesitated.

"Yes, Mr. Bristow?"

"The man who sent us both information and letters wants to defect. If he hasn't managed to escape before we release our news to the press, he's a dead man." And what about Karen, who carried the letters out of Czechoslovakia? Once Vasek was arrested and interrogated, his breaking point could come within a matter of weeks. If he held out that long.

"A possible defector?" Fletcher looked around the table in surprise. They all shared his astonishment.

"The cassettes will explain," Bristow said quickly.

Coulton said, "A defector—what's that to us? They come a dime a dozen."

"He is bringing more information."

"Any indication of its value?" Coulton wanted to know.

"He intends to name a name—someone in my unit or with access to it."

There was a shocked silence.

"That," agreed Kirby, "could be highly valuable information."

"But not as valuable as the safety of our country," Abel Fletcher said. "We'll listen to the recordings, Mr. Bristow. You said they would explain. I hope so."

Bristow switched on the cassette player and let Karen's voice take over.

As the playing ended, Abel Fletcher said, "You were right, Mr. Bristow. The cassettes explain a great deal."

"And raise some questions," Coulton added. He frowned. "What if Vasek doesn't defect? He used an American woman to carry out his plan."

"What plan?" Bristow asked, not concealing his rising irritation.

"To make us look like fools to all the world if we publish this story. The Soviet propaganda machine would start turning out its own denunciation. We would be charged with fabricating the letters to aggravate the Cold War. And your unit, Bristow, would be accused of creating some expert disinformation of its own. If no defector arrives in Washington to give credence to these cassettes, where would you stand?"

Bristow mastered his anger. "We do not create disinformation, and you know it."

"Of course not, of course not," Coulton hastened to appease Menlo, who was glowering at him from the other end of the table. "Just playing devil's advocate, Bristow. Someone has to. Can't just accept peculiar happenings because a pretty voice sounded so sincere. By the way, is she one of yours?"

"No," said Bristow.

"An amateur?" Kirby asked, eyebrows raised. He was nervous about amateurs.

"A journalist," Menlo said.

"We gathered as much." This was Coulton, unable to resist scoring a point. "Her notes were somewhat delayed by a censor, weren't they? But why? No reason given. No names, either, beyond Vasek and Prague. A hotel lobby was mentioned, a garden and its terrace well described. But exactly where? Why all the mystery? It makes her less credible."

Bristow kept his mouth tightly closed.

Menlo said brusquely, "She is a journalist and a good one. I know her work." He stopped there. "Recognized that voice," he told Bristow.

"A TV reporter?" Coulton guessed. "Oh, that explains how she could face a microphone without stumbling over a word. Can follow any script, I imagine."

Menlo explained to the row of wondering eyes, "She writes all her own material. Very perceptive, too. We can trust her not to be easily fooled."

"Good to hear," Coulton said. "I apologize to the lady. But the big question remains—is Vasek, whom friend Bristow lists in his files as Farrago, now sitting in his office wondering if we are rising to the bait he has dangled before us? Menlo, you're an expert on defectors, like my colleague here—Drayton. What's your opinion on Farrago?" Menlo was silent.

"He could be an authentic defector," Drayton said.

"Like Menlo's recent triumph—the defector we call 'Gregor'? Three—almost four—months since he was given refuge in a safe house, and what have we got out of him?"

"That's none of your business." Menlo's voice was sharp.

"I agree. But there is talk that Gregor's statements are not always provable, and I'm like everyone else around here—I can't shut my ears when rumors abound. I'm not saying that he isn't authentic, just that he's been a disappointment."

Kirby said quickly, and with some interest, "When did Gregor contact you, Menlo? You brought him in. Was it during his five-year assignment to their embassy here?"

"No. He went back to Moscow, took a year to decide—"

"Acquired a taste for democracy, had he?" Coulton asked.

Menlo ignored that. "And then left Russia," he continued. "With our help."

"You're too modest. With *your* help. He was a diplomat you liked when you met him in Washington—"

Drayton said swiftly, "A diplomat who was a KGB general."

"Gentlemen!" Abel Fletcher broke in with considerable annoyance. "We aren't here to discuss other defectors; only one possible defector, who is in Prague." He looked over his glasses at Menlo. "Is he still there? Has he made any move—dropped out of sight?"

"We've alerted our station. Its reports should be coming in," Menlo said. He was ruffled by the gossip that Coulton had mentioned. Gregor was invaluable, a source of excellent information. If his stay in a safe house was prolonged, it was only for his own safety. Coulton, like other know-it-alls, knew damn little of the true facts.

"Not enough time?" Fletcher asked sadly. "Not enough time for anyone. Mr. Bristow, you've studied Vasek, or should we call him Farrago? What is your estimate of the man? Briefly."

"His career has been varied, traveled a good deal. But for the last three years he has held a high position at KGB headquarters in Moscow. He never belonged to any particular clique. There was antagonism between Brezhnev and Andropov, but Vasek kept clear of that. Recently, he was reported absent from Moscow. Now he has turned up in Prague, a demotion, obviously—could be an incentive to his defection. Some may say"—Bristow glanced at Coulton—"that is all part of a grand deception but—"

"No, no!" Coulton interjected with a laugh. "I wouldn't say it *is* a part. I'd say it *could* be a part."

"But," Bristow continued, "we heard Vasek's own statement: he admits he is still a Communist. That was honest enough. He could be honest, too, in his rejection of war. World dominion won't be achieved by any military power in a nuclear age. And eventual world control is the aim of all Communists. So Vasek would be likely to see war as a useless means for world dominion."

"He would still accept political means," Kirby said, but he had found sense in Bristow's reasoning. "You will have to keep a close eye on him when he arrives."

"We always take chances with defectors," Bristow admitted.

Schlott's impatience burst out. "Do we go public on this? Do we disclose the letters, print the facts? What other options are there?" Angrily, he looked around the table. No one answered.

Bristow drew a deep breath and ventured a suggestion. "First, the President could phone Andropov, advise him that we are sending an immediate delegation to Moscow. It must be received without delay—its information is vital to Russia's interests as well as ours. Andropov must hear it himself."

"And then?" Fletcher prompted.

"Our delegation shows Andropov we know what his Active Measures has planned. We tell him we will publish, reveal the full facts and let the KGB be damned—if it isn't brought under proper control."

"He's got the power," Kirby said quickly. "All final decisions on Active Measures are made in the Politburo of the Communist Party Central Committee. He can void its previous permission to the KGB."

"That might work," Menlo agreed. "Provided, of course, that Farrago is not in their hands. Their Department of Active Measures never risks possible failure—not knowingly. Exposure is the last thing it wants."

Coulton repeated Menlo's phrase, "Provided Farrago is not in their hands. . . . But what if he isn't in ours? His escape could take time—might be weeks before he reached here. If he does."

Schlott said irritably, "What the hell does it matter if we haven't got him? We could be guiding him out, couldn't we?" He glared around the table. "Perhaps we are! The Russians won't know whether we are in touch with him or not."

Menlo nodded. "Provided," he said again, "that not one leak gets out of here."

"If it does"—Kirby's usually benevolent face was cold, forbidding—"one of us will be held accountable." There was silence as that hard fact was accepted.

Abel Fletcher looked around the table. "Then we are agreed on sending a delegation? There will be, of course, complete urgency in carrying that plan out. The minimum delay." He was addressing Drayton now. "The State Department might also warn the possible victims of assassination and communicate its intention to do that to Mr. Andropov if he is a little slow in believing we actually mean what we say." He paused, waiting for any further suggestions. There were none. He nodded, pocketed his small recorder, and rose.

As they all began to move toward the door, Kirby was saying, "I don't think Castro would be flattered by the KGB's intentions."

"Why Castro?" Coulton asked. "That's the most ridiculous part in this whole setup."

Kirby cut down that argument. "Castro's assassination could be a calculated failure. Castro unharmed, but the apparent attempt on his life would ignite a giant fuse."

"Or," Drayton suggested, "one martyr for the revolution. We'd be sure losers in Central and South America. Can you hear the Mexicans on our perfidy?"

Schlott said, "Perhaps the Soviets are tired of paying him three million dollars a day." That raised a brief smile. They began to drift into the hall, one by one.

Abel Fletcher was slow in leaving. He halted before he reached the door to look over at Bristow, who was packing cassettes into his briefcase. He said, "I understood there were four cassettes, Mr. Bristow. We heard only two of them."

"The others did not deal with the letters." Bristow glanced at Coulton, who was still at the door.

"They didn't concern the young lady's meeting with this Farrago fellow?"

Carefully, Bristow said, "Everything he told her was in the Prague cassettes." And thank heaven that Coulton was now entering the hall. "The others recorded later incidents in Vienna."

Satisfied, Abel Fletcher took a few steps and then halted again. "Your section doesn't try any disinformation on its own?" He was simply curious, all judgment suspended until he heard Bristow's reply.

"We track down disinformation; we don't invent it."

"Track?" Fletcher prompted.

The old boy was definitely interested. Disinformation was something he hadn't known in his younger days—at least not as it had been perfected and brought to a fine art in recent years. Bristow responded as fully as he could. "We try to spot it as it appears in foreign newspapers and makes its way across the Atlantic. Arab radio stations are another source—they seem to specialize in rumors that are broadcast as facts. Then we analyze, try to forestall any lies, disprove them as quickly as possible. Any delay and we have myth accepted as truth."

"Your Farrago file suggests that you must also trace the inventors of these lies and keep a watch on their activities."

"We try."

Abel Fletcher gave Bristow one last searching look. "Good hunting!" he said, and smiled, and reached the door. Another pause. "Who invented that hideous word 'disinformation'? Not any of you, I hope."

"Not guilty. Blame the men who could think up the phrase 'Active Measures.' Or a phrase such as 'Wet Affairs' to describe the blood spilled by their death squads."

Fletcher shook his head, pursed his thin lips, and went out to join his escort of Secret Service men.

Bristow checked the cassettes again. Only the ones dealing with the Prague incidents had been necessary. They were vital to the committee's final decision; the two Vienna tapes were not. Of interest to Menlo, yes, and other selected officers of Central Intelligence, but not to the deliberations that had gone on—and on—in this room. He could imagine Coulton's amusement over a woman's imaginary fears, an amusement that neither Bristow nor the men upstairs shared. But Coulton had never been part of any intelligence gathering. His career had begun in the Treasury, then developed into being their expert witness in forgery cases; after that, he was attached to the Bureau of Public Affairs, but not as a regular State Department official. Drayton, the career diplomat, had once confided that Coulton was neither fish nor fowl, which probably contributed to his carping and pecking.

Bristow locked the briefcase, his thoughts now branching off to his suggestion for dealing with the letters. He found no pleasure in its acceptance by the committee, only anxiety that he had or had not been on the right track. There would be a few days of delay in putting that suggestion to work, while Schlott's idea of going public could have happened tomorrow. But did they have a day or two to prepare for a Kremlin meeting? The assassinations could hit anytime. And yet, his hope was still the same—the hope that Farrago had started his journey to safety before the Politburo could be confronted. Everything depended on that: the charges made by the United States would not hold up if there was no Farrago as witness to their truth. Farrago and truth? Ironical.

Yet, as a Communist, he believed that truth was whatever was good for Communism, just as a lie was anything that was bad for it. And he obviously saw now that world chaos would not—in the long run—be good for Communism. Conquests were not successful or long-lasting if they had only ruins to dominate. A new Dark Ages, that's what he was afraid of; and weren't we all? It took Europe almost a thousand years to climb back to sanity and civilization once Roman law and inventions and culture had been ravaged by hordes of barbarians. In a new Dark

Ages, we'd all be lost—Communists along with the res
of us. It took centuries to put civilization together agair
once it had been smashed.

Yes, everything depended on Farrago's escape—
including Karen Cornell's own security. We'll get the FB
to keep a close watch over her, Bristow decided grimly
and even if that most independent lady didn't like it, h
wouldn't be too far away, either. He had still two weeks
leave due him this year. Once this crisis was over—n
one would drag his feet on this Kremlin meeting—onc
the threat was obliterated, he would have every logica
excuse to take a couple of weeks off the chain and con
centrate on Karen's safety.

He walked smartly into the hall, met two unexpecte
escorts to accompany him through the miles of corridor
to that safest of safes. They weren't Secret Service, jus
two from his own unit: Denis Shaw and Wallace Fair
bairn.

"Hey!" Fairbairn said, noting Bristow's face. "Eas
up, old boy." To Shaw he said, "He's probably hungry.'
It was almost eight o'clock. "A good meeting?"

"The usual talk. Words, words, and more words."

Shaw's eyes widened with excitement. In a whispe
he asked, "Was it really about Guatemala?"

"It's in one hell of a mess."

"Isn't everywhere?" Fairbairn asked. "Where do w
go for dinner?"

Bristow looked at Fairbairn's face, handsome as always
but too expectant as he waited for acceptance. Damne
nonsense, Bristow told himself—since when did he star
guarding his answers to someone who was an old friend
Since that old friend had seen him together with Karer
last Saturday and never even cracked a joke about it
"Not tonight. What about tomorrow?" And no evenin
stretching before him now, with questions coming at hin
like bazooka shells from Shaw.

"Tomorrow and tomorrow and tomorrow," Fairbair

said with resignation. "Okay. Denis and I can take a hint. See you in the slave pen in the morning."

"See you." Bristow walked on. Their departure had been abrupt; his fault, he blamed himself. Too edgy, too quick to question small reactions that were as innocent as they always had been. If he had dinner with anyone tonight, he would have opted for Karen Cornell. She would be the right companion for the end of this day.

8

Ten o'clock on Monday morning, and Karen Cor-
nell was waiting at her desk in the *Spectator*'s staff room,
ready for her command appearance in Schleeman's
office. He was there but on the telephone. A call from
Italy, his secretary told Karen; please wait. Twenty minutes later, he had another call. And another. This time
she was given the message: Mr. Schleeman has several
scheduled appointments, and he is running late; he would
like to see you at five o'clock. "Of course," Karen had
said to his white-haired secretary, overweight by fifty
pounds and permanently bent from the shoulders by too
much sitting over her desk. The humpbacked whale, the
younger staff members called her, but only when she was
well out of earshot. Her hearing and eyesight, like her
work, were exceptionally keen.

The Austrian interview with a possible chancellor had
been written yesterday, so Karen's morning was spent on
working over her notes on Czechoslovakia with occa-
sional breaks—everyone had questions about Prague

which she fended off without rousing extra curiosity. Lunch was a sandwich with Jim Black. He also had questions about her trip, but she could give him the Austrian interview to edit and that diverted talk about the Czechs she had met.

As five o'clock approached and the staff room gradually emptied, she began to worry over quite another set of questions that faced her. Vienna, she kept thinking, how do I deal with Vienna? Hubert Schleeman was a bulldog once he bit into a subject. Vasek's name must not be mentioned. Nor the letters. Oh, Peter Bristow, why aren't you here to help me out? And what are you doing at this moment? Persuading the high brass that I'm really quite a credible witness even if I am a writer, and one of the Fourth Estate at that? They probably think we all belong to the second-oldest profession, if not kissing cousins to the first.

The humpbacked whale, poor old dear—did she never exercise beyond walking to the bathroom?—announced in her frostiest manner, "Mr. Schleeman is available now, Ms. Cornell." She even opened Schleeman's door with a flourish. (God, how can he stand her? But the answer to that was efficiency: the woman had never misfiled one letter or forgotten an instruction.)

Karen entered.

"Sorry for this delay," Schleeman said, and pointed to the chair in front of his desk.

Karen took heart. He was in excellent humor, or else there would have been no hint of apology. She waited for Vienna to raise its head. Instead, Schleeman began talking about quite another subject.

"I had a phone call from Rome this morning. You've met Aliotto, haven't you?"

"Aliotto? Oh, yes—Luigi Aliotto." He had been one of the Western group of journalists in Prague. "I met him once or twice. Briefly."

"What d'you think of him?"

"A good reporter, I heard. He's attractive, lots of charm.

Even the tight-faced females from the Eastern bloc suc
cumbed to it."

"I've been checking up on him today. He is a free
lance reporter who is published in several reputable papers
He's good, as you said. How would you like a week i
Rome?"

She stared at him, blue eyes incredulous.

"Yes, Rome. It would be your first trip there an
worthwhile, I think."

Not her first visit. After their honeymoon in Venice
Alan and she had traveled back to New York by way o
Rome. She sat very still, realizing that this was the firs
time she had thought of Alan in days, feeling a stab o
wonder along with that small shock. She recovered an
paid attention to Schleeman's rapid words explainin
Aliotto's morning telephone call to the *Washington Spec*
tator.

Aliotto had been offered the opportunity, along wit
three other Italian journalists, to attend a private sessio
with two terrorists of the Red Brigade. There had been
lengthy trial, and now—after two years in jail—they wer
sentenced to twenty-five years in prison. Suddenly, the
had decided to talk. Aliotto had the idea of inviting a
American to be present when the talking began. The pris
oners had no objection, possibly wanted their views t
be known to a wide public; the authorities had no objec
tions, either—the more that was known about the histor
(and mentality) of two young terrorists who had bee
connected with murder and arson would strengthen gen
eral support for the government's firm action. Aliotto ha
suggested that Schleeman send one of his reporters an
thought Karen Cornell, whom he had met, might be a
suitable choice.

"An interview?" Karen sounded doubtful.

"Not exactly. There will be questions and answers, o
course. Aliotto's idea is that it would be interesting fo
you and him to write your separate accounts of the tal
session. Yours would be as a foreigner sees it; his woul

be as a journalist closely involved with the terrorist scene in Italy. Both your columns would be published side by side in *Domani*, a magazine he writes for, and in the *Spectator*. Appropriately translated, of course." Schleeman laughed. "I think he wants to outdo the three other journalists: his idea of two reports—one from the American point of view, one from an Italian who has had to live with constant terrorism—is original enough to make their newspaper columns seem run-of-the-mill. But whatever lies behind his proposal, it's still a first-rate idea." Schleeman studied her expression. It was indecisive, slightly doubtful, even troubled. "Well?" he asked sharply to force a reply.

"There are just so many things happening at the moment—" she began, thinking of Bristow and the cassettes and what would their result be? And had Vasek been accepted as a defector? So many things she wanted to hear as soon as Peter Bristow could tell her. His phone call could come next week; or would it be two weeks, three? "When would I have to go to Rome?"

"Why not on Wednesday? The session with the terrorists—a young man and his girl, by the way—is scheduled for next Monday. But a few days earlier are always useful. It lets you have a chance to soak up some background." She always liked to do that before approaching any strange assignment.

"*This* Wednesday?" She was aghast.

"Now what have you got to do here that can't be done by Wednesday?" he demanded. Schleeman was definitely in favor of Aliotto's idea. It was too good to let slip to some other magazine or a daily paper. "Jim will have both your pieces by tomorrow, won't he?"

She nodded. Jim Black already had one of them, and Schleeman knew that.

"What's so important to keep you in Washington?"

The whip was cracking: she could hear it sing around the room. "Not Washington. New York. I haven't been here for two weeks, and there's war between one of the

tenants and Max. He's the caretaker, handyman, genera
factotum. I'd never run the place without him. I had hir
on the phone yesterday, threatening to quit. I told hir
I'd be at the house on Wednesday if he'd just be patient.
And remember his ground-floor apartment with the yar
behind it as his own private garden. Karen sighed. "I'
straighten out the quarrel. Oh, Lord, why don't I sell tha
house anyway?"

The whip had stopped cracking. Schleeman was look
ing at her with a touch of amusement. "Why don't you
Get rid of it. Settle in Washington in a place of your own
Easier for everyone."

"I don't know why." She met his eyes. "Yes, I do
That house holds a lot of memories." Good memories tha
had kept her going when she was engulfed by loneliness
In spite of work, of travel, of a hundred acquaintance
and a dozen friends, there was always that swamp c
loneliness ever pulling her into its depths. Not even fou
affairs along the way gave any escape. She had broker
them off after a week or two of high hopes that ended ir
disappointment and anguish. No one she had met in thes
last years seemed able to replace the happiness she onc
had known.

"Memories," Schleeman said quietly, "can make yo
a prisoner, Karen. Don't let them tie you down." He an
Jim Black had talked about that: her five years of marriag
to Alan Fern shouldn't close out the rest of her life. He
work hadn't suffered, in fact it had improved, but a youn
woman with Karen's astonishing good looks who sud
denly cut off promising affairs with marriage proposed—
it wasn't right, it wasn't fair. Indeed, it was a complet
waste. "Well," Schleeman added, suddenly brusque
"when do you leave for Rome?"

"Friday?"

"Thursday evening it would have to be: night flight
only. You'll be there Friday morning. Good. I'll aler
Aliotto, and he can book a room for you at the Imperial
Might as well be comfortable. That will give you three

days to get the background from him. Enough?" Three days would be sufficient. She was a quick study.

"Possibly."

"Of course, I could send someone else from the *Spectator*, but Aliotto seemed intent on you. Perhaps a woman would be best—might help put the girl more at ease, loosen her tongue. Seemingly, it's the young man who has been doing most of the talking so far. She just follows along."

"As she did when she killed with a machine pistol? Or was it a grenade?"

That's better, that's much better, thought Schleeman, watching Karen's eyes. "You'll do a good job. By the way—how's your interest in disinformation coming along? Did Pete Bristow give you any leads?"

"I don't think he can. No more than has been already published."

"I expected that, but you can give it another try when you come back from Rome. What was his reaction about the defector? Interested or indifferent?"

"Interested."

"That all?"

"Well, we talked about several things."

"Prague, of course. Vienna, too?"

So I'm not escaping so easily, Karen thought. "Vienna, too."

"You said last Friday night that you were followed. Were you being serious?"

"Yes."

"But why?"

"Perhaps anyone who was seen in contact with that defector was put under surveillance. But it has stopped now—I haven't noticed any quiet little man following me around. So I'm in the clear. Don't you think?" she added nervously.

"First, tell me about the surveillance. I'd be a better judge then."

So she told him about the middle-aged man in a brown suit who had followed her into a café on Kärntnerstrasse.

"He left after he telephoned?"

"And saw I was settled at a table, meeting no one. Not then, certainly. Later, Sam Waterman and two friends— a man and a girl—drifted in." She had kept her voice light, so as not to worry him, which in turn would have stirred up more of her own anxieties. She paused. He kept silent. "Now it's your turn, Hubert. You made me a promise."

"I did, didn't I?" He wasn't eager to keep it.

"I really would like to know why you promoted me instead of Waterman. He holds it against me, you know."

"Did he show it when he joined you in the café?"

"There were several poisoned darts flicked in my direction."

"Brush them off, Karen. He's the one to be blamed if he didn't get the job you have now. This is between us, you understand. I don't add to his troubles."

She nodded. What troubles? Waterman had seemed carefree. If he could travel abroad, he certainly had enough cash flow.

"Sam Waterman used his own name to write for us. Then I discovered he wrote as Steven Winter for the *People's Incentive*, a Marxist weekly spawned in northern California. It's virulent, full of polemics, and far to the outer left."

"Steven Winter?" She was astounded. "I never knew!"

"No one was supposed to know. A well-hidden secret. That's why he never got the job he was aiming at. Of course, I don't think he expected me to accept his resignation—he made an effort to apologize two days later— but he saved me the task of telling him he wasn't wanted around here. That could have been a problem. I couldn't fire him without disclosing what I knew. Couldn't give away my source of information, could I?" There was a brief smile. (Menlo, for once, had been in total agreement with that. He had his own source to protect: an FBI agent had infiltrated the *People's Incentive*, and his safety would be at stake. Menlo had been alerted because Winter's articles were a constant pipeline for disinformation.) "There was no other choice: I had to get rid of him. I trust no man who hides his politics so carefully when he has the power to influence minds."

"How on earth did you find out?" she asked in wonder.

"Pure luck—a luncheon conversation about disinformation, actually, with an old friend." Schleeman shook his head over that memory. There he had sat, stating firmly that any publisher or editor with his wits about him would know if any of his reporters were outlets or conveyor belts for twisted information, only to be asked, "What do you think Sam Waterman is doing when he's writing as Steven Winter?"

Karen's eyes were speculating. "Was it—"

Schleeman looked at her. "No, it wasn't Peter Bristow who dropped that bombshell, although he must have heard about Waterman. It was an OSS friend, now a senior officer with the CIA, and one of the sharpest and most intelligent men I've met. He knows what he's talking about." Menlo certainly did: he had been eating, breathing, sleeping for the last thirty years with the problems of national security.

"Has Waterman discovered that you know what he really is?"

"Were there any of his poisoned darts sent in my direction?"

"No. He was concentrating on my life-style and working methods." He really threw me off balance, too. She sighed.

"I'm sorry about that Karen." And he meant it.

"Well"—she smiled—"we have to protect your sources, haven't we? And as long as I know the reason why he didn't get this job, I don't feel I'm responsible. So all's well that ends—" But it hasn't yet ended, she told herself. "That encounter in the café was no accident, was it?" Peter Bristow hadn't thought so. She remembered the sudden turn of his head as she named Waterman and the reporter called Andreas Kellner, the alert look in his eyes as he asked for every detail—even about a girl named Rita who spoke almost-true American. As for Kellner's use of the word "farrago"—that had created a brief moment of complete astonishment. Bristow's lips had tightened. He made no other comment.

"Not an accident, I think. It's an old pattern. We used it back in 1942. Some things don't change." But Schleeman was puzzled. Waterman, if he hadn't graduated into actual espionage, was being used by forces he wouldn't even believe existed. "What did they want from you?" What could they have wanted might be the right question, but he refrained from pressing it.

"The girl—I heard her first name, Rita—kept gushing about how she'd love to be a correspondent who traveled abroad, I must have talked with so many interesting people in Prague, didn't I meet any Czechs and get to know them?"

"You were supposed to be flattered." It always was a good method to draw out a confidence and learn of some unusual incident. "But I gather you didn't mention the defector. And what did Bristow have to say?"

"The same as you," she said carefully. "More or less."

More or less. "Are you holding out on me, Karen?"

She flushed. "I don't know everything myself. I'm sure Peter Bristow will tell you—and me, too—whatever can be told. He owes us that, doesn't he?"

"He takes you seriously?"

"I believe he does."

"And he's taking action?"

"He is. I hope."

"I'll have to be satisfied with that, I suppose."

There was a small silence.

Yes, decided Schleeman, she could tell more, but someone or something has locked her tongue. This story may be bigger than I even guessed. "What did you think of Bristow?"

"He was easier to be with than I had imagined."

Schleeman was amused. He had known Peter Bristow ever since he went to Harvard with his son—they had roomed together at Eliot House. Both had served, after graduating, in Vietnam. There, Bristow had been tapped by Military Intelligence to join a unit dissecting enemy propaganda, and that had led as a natural step into a CIA section that countered disinformation. "Never found him unapproachable. He was a history major, you know. Contemporary history. Almost became a college teacher after the war. But, as he told me, instead of lecturing on current events, he now deals with them in a more practical way." Schleeman noticed Karen's interest. "Too bad you can't do an interview on him. He'd make good copy."

"That's the last thing he'd want. Remember your party for the Brazilian ambassador?"

Schleeman reflected. "Oh, yes—about two years ago. What of it?"

"I met Peter Bristow there. Very briefly. The moment he learned who I was, he made an excuse and left. You saw it, didn't you? You were standing behind him."

Sharp memory she had: it always surprised Schleeman. "He left not because you were a reporter who'd note everything he'd say. He had just seen his ex-wife enter the room with a Colombian millionaire. A damned gatecrasher, too, and her current lover. The divorce wasn't even two months old. I'd say that wasn't the happiest time in Bristow's life." Not all memories of past marriages were good ones, Karen. Some were downright bitter—like his own when he recalled his first wife, which he did as rarely as possible.

"Why was there a divorce?" The question, involuntary, had escaped.

"He didn't make enough money or have enough spare time for all the things she wanted. A beautiful woman—outwardly, that is."

"But surely she knew the money he made or the time he had for a social life before she married him."

"Washington and its parties can go to some women's heads," he reminded Karen. "So now she's got her rich Colombian and all the emeralds that came with him." Schleeman pushed a manuscript into the desk drawer and rose. "She was a damn fool, if you ask me. Now, what about an early dinner tonight? I'll give you some background on Rome. I lived there for a couple of years. Or are you too exhausted again?"

"No. I'd love something to eat." And no more questions about Prague or Vienna. She laughed as she added frankly, "I'm starving."

Starved for what? he wondered. "Look out for Aliotto," he said. "I hear he's quite a wolf."

"I've handled wolves before."

Much too well, Schleeman thought as he locked his office door behind them.

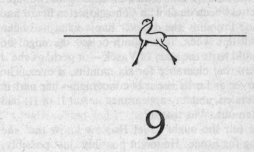

9

Thursday evening arrived and found Karen about to leave New York. The outbreak of hostilities at her house on 49th Street had been settled to the satisfaction of superintendent Max. Birney, the second-floor tenant who had planned to add French windows and a balcony to the back of his living room (at his own expense, and surely Miss Cornell would see he was adding to the value of her property), hadn't listened to the suggestion that his balcony would overhang the one sunny area in Max's backyard where tomatoes, lettuce, and zinnias grew. He did listen, however, to the fact that, if her property values were improved, then taxes would be higher and his rent would have to be much increased. That prospect brought capitulation. Birney knew quite well that his present rent was far below today's rates. So with all that settled, and thin dresses packed for Rome's end-of-summer heat, and her column on Czechoslovakia along with the Austrian interview all edited by Black and reviewed by Schleeman, she could take the evening flight from Kennedy with her mind at rest.

Except for Peter Bristow. He hadn't tried to reach her. What was happening? Had Vasek escaped—was he safe? Had the letters been dealt with? The cassettes heard and acted upon? Probably she'd never know what had been going on all this week. In a month or so, she might be told she could write the story of Vasek—or perhaps she'd not be given that clearance for six months, if ever. The play was over as far as she was concerned—her part in Act I was ended, and any appearance in Act II or III had been written out. Was that it?

Yet she felt she ought to let Bristow know that she was leaving for Rome. He might possibly, just possibly, want to reach her in Washington or New York to make sure everything was normal and under control. It was something she had been arguing with herself since she had started packing. She was supposed to word any telephone message in the code he had suggested; the trouble was that it didn't fit. Yet without "lunch" or "dinner" appearing in her call—no name, he had said—how would he know who was leaving the message?

It took her the taxi ride to Kennedy to make up her mind about contacting Bristow. She shouldn't mention Rome; "traveling" might be enough. All she was trying to do, she persuaded herself as she at last stood before a telephone at the airport with the required coins in her hand (so easy to charge it to her New York number, but this way was safer), was to keep Peter Bristow unalarmed if he found she was unreachable.

Her message, after three rehearsals, seemed passable enough to her. Bristow's answering service (a man's voice) was attentive. Karen spoke slowly, clearly. "I'd love to have lunch or dinner with you, but I must cancel all engagements for the next few days—I'll be traveling. I'll call you when I return."

Not her best composition, but adequate, she hoped. She had ten minutes left to catch her flight.

* * *

Bristow reached home and checked with his answering service for the second time that evening. It was accustomed to his constant calls. Normally, they were around five hours apart; since Saturday, three hours and sometimes less. There had been no message from Karen. Tonight, there was one. He heard it, asked for it to be repeated. "When was it made?" At six-forty this evening, he was told. It was now just after nine o'clock.

He went over Karen's message again. Traveling where? A holiday in Vermont, a jaunt to California, where? Schleeman would know; and then again he might not. If she was taking a short vacation, no one at the *Spectator* would know how she was using it. Perhaps that woman who had the Washington apartment where Karen roomed? Mary Dustan. He phoned her several times, reached her eventually. He was a friend of Karen's, he explained and stayed nameless. Did Mary know where he could reach her? Mary didn't know; only that Karen wouldn't be in Washington next week. "Thank you," he said, cutting off what was about to become an interested conversation. It was now eleven o'clock.

On Friday morning, he telephoned Menlo as soon as he reached his office, something he rarely did and only in emergencies. Menlo was senior enough to call you and not you call him. Bristow found him about to leave for a meeting, but he was sufficiently interested (Menlo had unbent a great deal since the six-man conference last Monday) to ask, "Anything special?"

"Have you heard from Aitchison?" Aitchison was Menlo's particular friend at the FBI who had obliged Menlo with someone to keep a watch over Karen. As Menlo had said, she was their secondary witness: she could back the statements made by their first witness to the truth—Farrago. Menlo even dubbed them "Senior" and "Junior" as a safe method of discussing their activities over a telephone.

Menlo asked quickly. "Is Junior in trouble?"

"No. Just traveling."

Menlo didn't like that, either. "Where?"

"I thought Aitchison might have heard."

"I'll check. I'll call you. This meeting won't take an hour."

A short but important meeting, judging from Menlo's haste and an excitement in his voice that couldn't be disguised. Bristow replaced the telephone, tried to concentrate on his own work.

Menlo's call came fifty minutes later. "See you in my office. Bring the file on *Blitz*, will you? I'd like to discuss its recent editorials on Lebanon that are being quoted in Europe."

Bristow retrieved the bulky folder on *Blitz* from the file room—a newspaper, written in English, published in India, financed and directed by the Soviets. It initiated much of the disinformation that appeared later in Pakistan, the Middle East, and soon afterward in Europe. As he was leaving, Wallace Fairbairn entered, glanced at the bulging folder with a tape tied around it that could barely hold it together.

"Who the hell wants that old turkey?" Fairbairn asked. "Menlo? What does he hope to find there now?"

"Whatever it is, he'll find it."

Fairbairn dropped his voice. "Heard anything about that envelope we delivered?"

"Not a murmur. We'd be the last to hear anyway."

Fairbairn could agree with that. "How did you get hold of it?"

"It was handed to me. Simple."

"And no explanation—that's odd. If I know you, Pete, you had a look-see inside."

"Too well sealed. Couldn't risk it," Bristow said. "Or did you chance it?"

Fairbairn shook his head. "Scared me off, too. Wonder who's dealing with it?"

"No doubt the computers." They laughed and parted.

Bristow found Menlo alone in his office and waiting

with a touch of impatience. "Sorry to be late. I met Fairbairn, who wanted to know more about the envelope."

"Oh?"

"Natural curiosity. I gave it to him to deliver here. The envelope was well sealed." And its delivery had been prompt, receipted with the exact time of its arrival. There had been no slip-up there.

"So I noticed. Your work or Miss Cornell's?"

"Hers. After I had read the letters."

"I've news about them. Have a chair, Bristow."

Good or bad? Bristow wondered as he sat down to face Menlo across his desk.

"We met with the Soviets. At first, there were some denials. Then protestations of ignorance. Then well-simulated anger against our attempt to slander the Soviet Union. But they kept talking, two whole days of sharp argument. In the end, there was an agreement. The letters would not be used in any way by either side. Abel Fletcher requested and received a written statement to that effect, signed by Andropov. In turn, the Soviets received an identical statement signed by the President."

"As easy as that?" Bristow's disbelief was plain. "It's too simple."

"The arguments could have dragged on for weeks. But Bob Schlott was there, with rows of ribbons on his chest, stating that we were making the letters public on Friday—today, that is—if no agreement was reached. And Drayton, at his diplomatic best, observed that such a revelation about disinformation was necessary to place full blame on the men who had concocted these letters for any assassination they had planned." Menlo paused, imagined that scene, smiled. "Must have been quite a session. Our representatives are now on their way home. Their report reached us just two hours ago."

Bristow said, "What made the Soviets listen? Has Farrago escaped and they haven't found him?"

"He's out. They haven't found him. We haven't, either, but they don't know that. What they do know is that these

three letters are missing. We have one of our agents'
word on that. He was present when the Czechs found
the letters were gone. They had been sent there, I
gather, so that Prague could disseminate them and keep
Moscow's name unsullied by the whole dirty business."

"So he's out and in transit." Bristow was thoughtful.
"How did he manage it?"

"Our agent reports that Vasek was scheduled officially
to leave for Rome this past Monday—a special assignment. He advanced his visit by four days on the pretext
of an emergency and left last week. He used his travel
pass and all his credentials to fly to Italy in comfort."
Menlo was much amused. "He arrived there and vanished. He's entirely on his own. Where—we can't even
guess. We are looking, though. But with the greatest discretion—we can't alert the Russians that we haven't got
him. They are searching, too, although they were forced
to assume we must be in touch with him when our delegation arrived so quickly and were so sure of their facts."

Bristow was thinking about Vasek's timing. Advanced
his Rome visit by four days . . . "Then he left Prague one
day after Karen. When were the letters discovered missing?"

"Quite soon after he had gone. But not in time to have
him arrested at the Rome airport. Cool as they come,
your Farrago. Must have planned everything for weeks,
even months."

Bristow continued his own line of thought. If Vasek
had left early on that Thursday and the disappearance of
the letters was discovered a few hours later, then the
Vienna incidents around Karen's handbag—along with
Rita's questions and Kellner's probe—proved she was
under suspicion as one of Vasek's last contacts. Even
with the problem of the letters resolved in the Moscow
agreement, she could still be in bad trouble. As long as
the KGB was looking for Vasek, she was in danger. "If
they could link Karen with the delivery of the envelope,"
he began slowly, and halted.

"Did anyone see her deliver it to you?" Menlo asked.

"No one saw her actually hand it over. That took place in a car she had rented. She took every precaution."

Something was still worrying Bristow. Menlo said sharply, "Did anyone see you together last Saturday? Anyone who knows you?"

"We weren't together—I made sure of that—when I handed the envelope to Fairbairn. Shaw was with him, but he stayed in the car."

"Could they have seen her at all?"

"They drove pretty close to her—she was on her way to the cafeteria. They were parked there, waiting for me to appear. They were early. They could have seen us arrive."

"And Fairbairn also saw the Czech censor's stamp on that envelope," Menlo said, speaking the words that Bristow had avoided. "So could Shaw, for that matter. He probably noticed its markings, too, when Fairbairn brought it back to their car."

Why the hell had Shaw accompanied Fairbairn? They were friends, sure. But it wasn't necessary for both of them to be there. Unless Shaw didn't allow anyone else to handle his car. Some men were like that.

"Vasek told Miss Cornell he had a mole to name when he talked with us," Menlo said smoothly, but the furrows on his brow deepened. "Someone who knew the name you had given to his file. Someone in your unit, Peter."

I've been promoted. Peter...But Bristow's growing depression didn't let him take any comfort in Menlo's unexpected thaw. "I'm aware of that."

"Ease up, Peter. Suspicion is an ugly business. The quickest way to end it is to find the truth." He hesitated, then made a decision as he watched Bristow's troubled face. "We have to realize that the KGB doesn't accept assumptions permanently. They'll search for Vasek until there's no doubt left; either he is safe here or dead. If they can terminate him, we have no witness, only Miss

Cornell's word that he did pass her the letters, that he did say he wrote them. And then—"

"I know," Bristow said. Then Karen might be eliminated, too. Might? Damn Vasek to bloody hell; he had given the letters to Karen, hadn't taken the risk of carrying them himself. That's something I'll never forgive him for, thought Bristow. He controlled his voice. "We had better find Vasek before they do."

Menlo nodded. Bristow, he was thankful to discover, knew exactly what could be at stake. "I have learned of Miss Cornell's destination. Aitchison's men followed her taxi to Kennedy yesterday evening. One tailed her inside the airport. She made a telephone call. And then she took the flight to Rome."

"Rome. What the hell is she doing there?"

I agree, thought Menlo. Vasek should be far from Rome by this time, and yet—I wish I didn't have the feeling that the pot has only been simmering and is now reaching boiling point. He said nothing.

Bristow was on his feet. "I'll see Schleeman. He must know." He glanced at his watch. "Too late to meet him for lunch. Better make it for dinner or a drink." Not a visit to Schleeman's office—too unusual. Not questions over a telephone, either. No alarm sounded. Play it loose.

Menlo approved. "Here's my number. I'll be at home. Call me anytime between eight and midnight. Let me know why she's in Rome." He was scribbling on a note pad as he spoke, handed the page to Bristow.

"One thing I'd like to know—and perhaps your Prague agent could find out. What other foreigners were contacted by Vasek just before he defected?"

"You think they could be under suspicion, too? We can't go looking out for everyone, Peter."

It was an admission, thought Bristow, that Menlo had Karen on his mind. "Another thing—my leave. I'm due two weeks. I'd like to take them."

"Starting when?" Menlo sounded casual.

"Tomorrow. Can that be arranged?"

"I'll see to it. Here—don't forget this!" Menlo lifted the *Blitz* folder from his desk, hefted its bulk. "We are thought to be a little eccentric in keeping our files in steel cabinets. But how do you computerize the kind of data we gather and manage to compare twenty newspaper clippings simultaneously?"

Once Bristow had thought Menlo's insistence on old-style files was more than eccentric, but after working in disinformation, he had changed his mind. There was only one way to examine a variety of news reports and articles: spread them out, side by side, on a large flat surface where a paragraph, even a sentence, and sometimes only a phrase could be collated, crossreferred or contrasted, and traced. The human eye, backed by instinct and memory, was still a necessity, and thank God for that.

Menlo had a parting word for him. "Remember—anytime between eight and midnight."

He's more worried than he admits, Bristow thought as he closed Menlo's door behind him.

Bristow entered the file room and met Fairbairn shepherding Frederick Coulton out. All three were equally surprised.

"Just showing our forgery expert where we slog out the day," Fairbairn said and waved vaguely in the direction of the other offices. "He doesn't believe we do much work. I told him he shouldn't judge conditions by the two hours we take for lunch."

A nice allusion to the emptiness of the rooms, thought Bristow. "Occasionally, we do some work," he told Coulton.

Coulton glanced back at the steel cabinets lining the small file room. Each held four deep lockers with its own combination for opening them. "You're strong on security, I see. Impressive. But"—his eyes were now on the *Blitz* folder—"what happens when you run out of space?"

"Menlo will find some more," Fairbairn said with a

laugh. "Where's Shaw, for God's sake? He's been giving Coulton lunch, and now he's making some phone call." He looked along the corridor impatiently.

"Why not use the computers?" Coulton asked Bristow. "Or d'you think some hacker playing around with his two-bit machine will obtain access?" He spoke with amusement.

Bristow only smiled. It had been done, but not by hackers.

"Anything that simplifies work," said Fairbairn, "is detrimental to the brain. That's Menlo's dictum."

"Which reminds me," Bristow said. "We'd better have a session this afternoon, Wallace. That Athens editorial you analyzed last week seems to have had its origins in *Blitz* last month."

"Well, I'm free once I deliver our friend to Shaw."

Coulton said, "Sorry if I'm holding up any momentous decisions. Why don't I find Shaw and let him escort me out? Or simply make an exit by myself—if I don't lose my way in this labyrinth."

"Here he comes," Fairbairn said as the young man trotted down the corridor. "Get ready for some more questions, Coulton. Shaw," he added in an aside to Bristow, "has discovered the fascinations of forgery."

Shaw, annoyed and breathless, said, "Sorry, Freddy. It was a wrong number—didn't find out for several minutes—some crank at the other end of the line—a real foul-up."

Freddy . . . Bristow had never seen Frederick the Great with Shaw before. Chummy, he thought as the two of them left for the elevator. To Fairbairn he said, "Give me forty minutes. Once I dump this folder, I'm going to lunch."

"Thought you'd given up the habit. How was Menlo?"

"Admonitions and advice."

"As usual," Fairbairn said with another of his easy laughs. "See you later, Pete."

"See you." Bristow went into the file room and locked up *Blitz*. He could find no sensible reason why he should have waited until Frederick Coulton had left. Except that Coulton had no business here, even if young Shaw had been trying to impress his visitor from State. As Menlo had said, suspicion was an ugly business, but he still wondered why Coulton was wandering around the file room.

He didn't use the telephone in his office but called Schleeman from the cafeteria. Schleeman was at his desk; a lot of work to clear up, he explained, before he left for the Maryland shore this evening. That forestalled any dinner invitation. "I'd like to see you," Bristow insisted. "Can you manage an early drink? Somewhere near your office?"

Schleeman considered that. "Something important to discuss?"

"I'm taking a vacation and thought I'd talk with you before I leave tomorrow."

Talk? Schleeman was interested. "It will be a very short drink—my wife is giving a party tonight, got to be there this time. Meet me at my club. Five-thirty."

"Five-thirty is fine. But at your club?" Bristow had doubts about that. A private meeting was what he needed.

"We'll probably be the only people around at that early hour. Besides, it's dead in the late summer—everyone out of town. See you at five-thirty. You know the routine if I'm delayed."

"Yes. I wait for you in the visitors' room."

"And don't you be late or it's my head on the block." Schleeman ended the call with a short laugh.

Bristow had a quick sandwich and coffee, now wondering how he'd break the news to Fairbairn and the others about the leave he was taking. They shouldn't be too surprised—he had postponed it twice since June. Rome, he kept thinking, why had she chosen Rome?

10

To enter Schleeman's club at this time of day in
late August was like stepping into a church in midweek:
space abounding and no one to fill it. There was the same
hush, a silence surrounded by pillars, a ceiling that soared
over frescoed walls, a marble staircase leading not to a
pulpit but to dining room and bar. There was little sign
of life, with Congress in recess and bureaucracy at half-
staff. No one was in the entrance hall except the porter
behind his mahogany desk and another guest who was
early—like Bristow himself—and waited alone in the visitors' room, its wide doors permanently open. The stranger
was thin and tall, with thick brown hair and dressed in a
light-colored gabardine suit that hadn't been sitting in an
office all afternoon. That much Bristow's quick glance
had told him. The man's equally quick glance veered away
in disinterest as he walked to a chair, picked up a magazine, and began leafing through its pages.

Bristow went to the desk, introducing himself as
Schleeman's guest. "Not much business tonight," he

added, and stayed where he was. He'd rather remain here than face another guest, be caught in a polite exchange of chitchat.

"No, sir. But it's early. Later there will be a few—the gentlemen whose wives are in the country."

Or, to quote the old adage, when home became intolerable there was always the club. But better not say it aloud. The porter, correct to the last button, might see no humor in his club being merely an alternative to the sound of TV or hot rock played at fever pitch.

"Perhaps you would care to join the other gentleman in the waiting room?" the porter suggested, as elderly and dignified as the vaulted ceiling above him. "His name is Mr. Jones."

Bristow had another unobtrusive look at the lanky figure, who was discarding one magazine for another. Waiting seemed to make him impatient. "I don't think he's much in the mood for conversation."

The porter dropped his voice. "He has been waiting ten minutes, and he will probably wait ten minutes more. Mr. Coulton is usually a little late. Now your host, Mr. Schleeman, is always on time. I take it you were a little early tonight?" he asked anxiously.

"Five minutes." That relieved the porter. His Mr. Schleeman had not been guilty of keeping a guest waiting. "Is it Mr. Frederick Coulton who is usually a little late?"

"Yes, sir. A recent member. A very pleasant gentleman. Is he a friend of yours?" The porter's rising curiosity was cut short as he looked at the front door and saw Schleeman mounting the half-dozen steps that led up into the hall. "I think Mr. Schleeman is now arriving, sir."

"Exactly on time, too."

The porter nodded approvingly and then allowed himself a brief stare. Schleeman had glanced toward the visitors' room as he reached the hall. He stopped abruptly, whirled on his heel, retreated down the steps, and only then—well hidden from the guests' waiting room—signaled for Bristow to follow him and made a rapid exit into the street.

The porter looked at Bristow, who said as casually as possible, "There seems to be a change in plans." And with a parting nod, he followed Schleeman. A last quick glance at the stranger in the empty room showed nothing changed there. The man was still thumbing through the magazines.

He found Schleeman waiting just outside the club's entrance. "The quickest drink I've ever had," said Bristow, trying to relieve Schleeman's definite agitation.

Schleeman, his face set, took Bristow's arm in a firm grip and urged him to increase his pace. "My car is around this corner. We can talk there. My God, Pete, did you know who that was?"

"Someone you want to avoid."

"Someone I don't want to see you with me. Did he spot me, d'you think?"

"You were pretty quick on your feet."

Schleeman's excitement was still high. "Can you imagine it? Sam Waterman, all spruced up, sitting in the waiting room of the most conservative club in town."

Bristow almost halted. He stared at Schleeman. Sam Waterman meeting Frederick Coulton?

Schleeman said irritably, his anger beginning to break. "Sam Waterman also Steven Winter also heaven knows who else."

"I've heard of him." And seen his record, too.

"You've never actually met him—he didn't recognize you as Bristow?"

"We both drew a blank. What's his persona tonight—Waterman or Winter?" For the porter's register, it had been Jones. For Coulton?

"He's the same, whatever name he uses." They reached the Mercedes. Schleeman's anger made him fumble with the lock, but at last they were inside. Schleeman closed all windows, turned on the air conditioning. "Can you beat it?" he was saying. "Infernal impudence! Who invited him, I'd like to know. Pity we couldn't stay to see."

"Dodging behind a pillar. We're better off here."

"Wonder if his host knows whom he's entertaining."

So do I, thought Bristow. What brought these two together? As for Coulton, who held a highly sensitive position—good God, important and trusted enough to have taken part in Monday's high-level meeting—Bristow had never heard him speak well of journalists. The forgery expert had suffered at their hands on his court appearances as an expert witness. "Let them revel in their ignorance" was the phrase he used when a newspaper misquoted his opinion.

"You think I'm prejudiced against Waterman?" Schleeman asked, misinterpreting Bristow's silence. "I hate that guy's guts—not only because of the way he deceived us at the *Spectator*. I don't like the part he played in Vienna. Something damned odd there. I think he has moved into politics in a heavy way."

"Could be. Karen told me about that meeting in Kärntnerstrasse."

"She did, did she?" Schleeman looked at Bristow with a new surmise. "You must have got on nicely, you two."

"I did, at least. That's why I called you today. I had hoped to take her to dinner tomorrow, but she isn't in Washington. Or New York. Is she on vacation, or did you send her traveling again?"

"She's in Rome. And it's a job none of us could turn down. Much too good an opportunity to let slide."

"What's the assignment?"

"Aliotto—Luigi Aliotto, a journalist she met in Prague—called me last Monday—he writes for *Domani*." And Schleeman launched into a full explanation.

Bristow listened, made no interruptions, no comment at the story's end.

"What's on your mind, Pete? Come on—out with it!"

"Just planning a little holiday in Europe."

Is he indeed? "Rome?" Schleeman asked, and began to wonder.

"Why not?"

"Karen is still under suspicion, is that it? She isn't in danger, is she?"

"Only from me dogging her footsteps."

Schleeman's alarm faded. He studied the young man: a strong face with good bones, a steady gaze, dark eyes that met Schleeman's with a smile. "Don't go keeping her mind off her work. She has a job to do in Rome, you know."

So have I. "Where is she staying?"

"At the Imperial."

"Have you heard from her?"

"She arrived safely, hasn't met Aliotto yet. He's been nursing an attack of twenty-four-hour flu." Schleeman looked at the clock on the dashboard, thought of the questions he had wanted to ask. Damn Waterman for chasing them out of his mind.

"Better not be late for your wife's party." Bristow unlocked his door.

"Before you leave for Rome, see my old friend Menlo. He has been interested in Waterman."

"I'll call him as soon as I reach a phone." Bristow avoided noticing the telephone in the car, looked over his shoulder at the quiet street with its rows of impressive buildings. "Not a café or drugstore in sight."

"Try this," Schleeman said with amusement and reached for his car phone. Young fox, he thought—did he imagine he could outrun an old one? Could be an interesting conversation with Menlo. Bristow in Rome must mean something more than chasing a girl, even one so damned attractive as Karen. Schleeman made his identification with the Exchange and handed the receiver to Bristow.

"Thanks. I'll possibly still find him at the office." He asked for that number and reached Menlo. "Could I see you at home this evening?"

Menlo, who had been about to leave, said without much enthusiasm, "Is it urgent?"

"I'll be heading for Rome tomorrow."

"Did you find the reason for Junior's travel urge?"

"I did. There's too much to tell at the moment." Bristow could sense Schleeman's disappointment. "I'm using a car telephone. My friend beside me has an urgent appointment, so I have to keep this short."

"It can't wait until tomorrow?"

"Better not."

"All right, all right. I'll see you here."

"In forty-five minutes." And Menlo would be in a pretty disgruntled mood. But there was one big advantage in meeting him in his office. The computers at Langley might come up with something more than Aliotto's name.

Schleeman replaced the receiver. "He's actually seeing you at his place? That's a new one on me. Menlo's home is his castle: drawbridge up, portcullis down."

"And barracuda in the moat? I won't have to risk them. He's waiting in his office." Bristow stepped onto the sidewalk. "I'll be in touch when I get back. We'll have a longer session."

"I'll hold you to that."

Bristow nodded and set off at a rapid pace in the direction of his parked Camaro.

There was always something to occupy Menlo's attention: he was up to his elbows in work when Bristow arrived earlier than expected. "You must have driven like hell." He pushed aside a map of Italy along with lists of freighters sailing in this last week from Genoa and Naples.

"The traffic wasn't too bad, either."

"Sit down, sit down. What's it all about? Why did she take off for Rome?"

Bristow gave him the information exactly as he had heard it.

"It sounds reasonable. What worries you? Apart from

the location itself, and the fact that Aliotto was in Prague for that convocation."

"The timing of the invitation worries me."

"It could be purely accidental. And I'm now less perturbed about Rome. Vasek isn't likely to hang around a city where he was last seen. He will be avoiding airports, of course. A freighter out of the Mediterranean is his best bet. He could break the voyage at Algeciras or Lisbon or Tangiers—some place where he could risk taking a plane or shipping out on another freighter."

"He never does the expected. That's why our file on him consists of bits and pieces." Aliases, disguises, sudden appearances and disappearances; the Farrago record was full of inexplicable gaps and surprises. "Before he specialized in disinformation, he was a fully trained agent in the field. Even there, he managed to stay mostly anonymous. We recognized him more by his actions and style than by the man himself."

Menlo thought over that, registered it, and went on to Luigi Aliotto. "Ever heard of this Italian journalist?"

"Not known to us."

That was a good sign, Menlo thought: Aliotto was not listed as a pipeline or outlet for disinformation. "And have you ever read *Domani*? It's a monthly, I think. Right?"

Bristow nodded. "A serious periodical and reputable. Small but important. Published in Milan. Its articles are often reprinted abroad. So Aliotto is possibly okay. Schleeman must have checked before he sent Karen to Rome."

"We'll make our own check." Menlo swiveled his chair to face the small table behind him on which his computer stood. A tap of the key to activate it, and the Smart Modem took charge as he typed. First name and password, then his command: information on Luigi Aliotto, journalist, based in Rome; correspondent for *Domani*, published Milan. With that on the monitor, he pressed the Execute button. The monitor went blank as the search started. "Now we wait," said Menlo. "It's usually quick,

but an unknown journalist in Italy may take a little time."
He rose, a lanky figure in loosely fitting shirt and pants—
his clothes always seemed too big for his long thin frame—
and stretched his back. "Damn that disk," he said, rubbing
his lower spine. He began the customary slow stroll around
his office. "How are you going to handle Miss Cornell in
Rome? Personally or keeping in the background? I'll alert
Levinson to expect you. You'll find him at the embassy."

"Personally. I'm there on vacation."

"Will she accept that?"

"Perhaps she'll raise an eyebrow and think I'm overreacting. But she would find more to puzzle her if I was
in Rome and made no effort to reach her. Schleeman will
certainly pass the word that I'm there on holiday. We'd
better keep everything normal. There's no good in stirring
up her fears about some possible danger. So, unless I
sense some trouble brewing, I'll meet Karen as if I hadn't
a care in the world. But I'd like to tell her that the problem
of the letters has been settled. Just that," Bristow added
quickly. "Not a detailed account."

"Keep it to one sentence if you think that would relieve
her mind."

"I know it would."

Indeed? wondered Menlo. "There may be no danger
at all. This whole visit of hers to Rome could be only
another bloody coincidence. I'll alert Levinson all the
same. No protests about that, Peter. He could be helpful
in many ways. One of his girls can book you into the
Imperial."

"Nice, but too rich for my bank account." With the
traveler's checks he had bought and the emergency money
he had drawn out of his savings, he would probably have
to hock his Camaro to stave off bankruptcy.

"Enough cash on hand?"

"For the next week, probably yes."

"I'll instruct Levinson to see you get an advance on
your expense account. You may be acting on a personal
basis, but you are definitely reporting to me. So you're

on the payroll. No one in Rome will know that except Levinson, and any contact you two make will be discreet. As for the Imperial, it couldn't be handier: it's practically adjoining the embassy. And if you're keeping a close watch on Miss Cornell, then you don't stay at some other hotel that is several blocks away. She's too valuable to put at risk."

Bristow said nothing. Doubtless, Menlo would have one of Levinson's girls or boys watching from the background. And only this afternoon, when he had signed the traveler's checks, he had actually thought he was vacation-bound. A quaint notion. He studied Menlo, wondering how many other surprises were going to hit him.

Menlo eased himself into his chair. "Can you be ready to take off at twelve-thirty? Yes, tonight. There's a flight out of Washington with some NATO personnel and two members of the Senate. Space is available. I've reserved it for you. You'll be arriving at an airfield not too far from Rome—no fuss, no customs, no KGB or Czech or Bulgarian agents disguised as porters or travel guides watching incoming or outgoing traffic to the United States. Lookout for the Bulgarians. In the last few years, the Czechs have concentrated on Austria, the Bulgarians on Italy. So make that flight if you can."

"I'll make it." Or else I won't reach Rome until Sunday morning. Bristow glanced at his watch, looked impatiently at the computer, and said, "Before I leave, I've got an unexpected footnote to add to Sam Waterman's file."

"Waterman-Winter?"

Bristow nodded, quickly described the strange incident at Schleeman's club.

"Coulton was meeting him there? Coulton?"

"So the porter said."

"Coulton is a member of that club?" Menlo's disbelief grew.

"A recent member."

"Must have cost him a third of his year's salary." A

pause, and then sharply, "What kind of car does he drive? New?"

"I've no idea." Bristow's sudden amusement faded. It had better not be a Mercedes or a Jaguar, unless Coulton had a rich aunt who had just bequeathed him her stash of tax-free bonds. Strange the direction Menlo's mind had taken, while Bristow had only wondered how Coulton could be such a damned fool.

"He could have consulted us before he started playing host to that bastard. Or checked with the Bureau of Public Affairs' info on Waterman. But no, Coulton wouldn't. He thinks security precautions are mostly for idiots and he's not one—"

The monitor flashed its signal, and Bristow pointed. Menlo whirled around to face the small screen. Angrily, he typed, "Why delay?"

"Translation required. Now completed."

Menlo said under his breath, "Then execute, damn you." He hit the button hard.

The printed words were displayed on the monitor in steady rhythm, line by line by line. We've hurt its feelings, Bristow thought as rapid information came flooding out, and much of it unnecessary.

Luigi Aliotto, born in 1932 Milan, educated Padua (dates and degrees), resides in Rome (address and telephone number). Newspapers and journals to which he contributes (all named along with places of publication; all major articles by Aliotto dated). Unmarried. Politics, indefinite. Religion, unknown. Travels widely: France, Switzerland, Russia, Britain, China, Japan, Hungary, Germany, recently Czechoslovakia. Popular in varied circles.

The long list ended.

"Varied?" queried Bristow. "Not various?"

Menlo typed the questions.

The reply came back: "Translation accurate. Varied."

"That puts you in your place, Peter," Menlo said and switched off the computer.

Bristow laughed. "The first time a machine ever read

my mind." Then he turned thoughtful. "Interesting...
Does Aliotto play both sides against the middle?"

"That's how he gets his material. Politics, indefinite.
Religion, unknown. He hurts no one's feelings, arouses
no animosity. A smart fellow. Relax, Peter, relax! What
more do you need to know?"

"Did Vasek talk with him in Prague? Were they seen
together?" If so, Aliotto could have come under suspicion, too.

"We haven't been able to make contact with our agent
there. Not since yesterday." Menlo paused, lost himself
for a moment in that additional worry. "If he can answer
your questions, I'll let you know. Through Levinson. And
keep me informed."

Through Levinson, no doubt. Bristow said, "Do I pick
up travel orders on my way out?"

"Everything ready and waiting. Get a move on, Peter.
There won't be food served on that flight."

Bristow nodded thanks for the hint. He'd brown bag
it if necessary or stay hungry all the way to Rome. He
said good-bye and left.

Menlo rubbed his forehead, ran his hands through his
thinning gray hair, wondered if their agent in Prague was
still in place and functioning. He could see a long evening
ahead of him, and it wouldn't be at home in a reclining
armchair with Bach for company.

11

On Friday morning, Karen along with other slightly disoriented passengers stepped off the plane at Leonardo da Vinci Airport. An eastbound journey from New York was always a trial. The extra six hours for Rome's time zone made it seem as if breakfast was just ahead, but she felt as if she had been awakened—as indeed she had been—in the middle of the night. Bless Hubert Schleeman for insisting that his travel agent order a car and driver to meet her. A taxi, her own suggestion, would only have added to the hassle of arrival at any giant terminal. Porters were scarce on this sun-filled morning already threatening a midday broil. She found a cart, once she had hauled her bag and suitcase, typewriter and briefcase away from customs (more clothes than she had taken to Prague, blast her idiocy as she had packed; but in Rome she'd be surrounded by pretty dresses), and began pushing its load toward the main entrance.

A string of hotel touts, a sprinkling of drivers holding high their expected clients' names boldly inscribed on pieces of cardboard, clusters of anxious relatives, a press of waiting friends—all formed a guard of honor to welcome the stream of arrivals. The noise level was as high as the confusion.

A polite voice, a hand on her arm, stopped her slow progress. He was young, neatly dressed in collar and tie like the other chauffeurs, with a wide smile but no card displayed. "Miss Cornell—*il signore* has his car waiting. This way, please." He elbowed a path free through the tight knots of people. "Please," he repeated, urging her on.

"*Il signore* who? Mr. Aliotto?"

"Yes. Mr. Aliotto. We must hurry. The car is parked where it should not be. It waits near the front door."

She hesitated, looking around for her name on a card, and saw it (misspelled Cornel) waving high in the air. That would be the driver from Brent Travel Agency, hoping she would identify him wherever she was. She must tell him that she no longer needed his services. "One moment." She halted, pulling her arm free.

"But the car—"

"I know. It's waiting." I may be tired, I may want to be rescued from this mob scene, but I'm not yet completely stupefied. "Mr. Aliotto is in the car?" And why doesn't he have the grace to welcome me here himself? It wasn't Aliotto's way to be so ungallant. She looked at the shock of black hair (no cap on that head), at the heavy black eyebrows now slightly frowning, at the black mustache above a white smile that seemed to be permanently held at the same wide stretch. "Is he?"

The young man's hesitation ended. "No. He is not well—a bad cold. He will be better tomorrow. He sent me to take you to the hotel."

And how did you pick me out of this scene so easily? she wondered. A photograph? Not from my luggage labels. He hasn't even noticed them, hasn't even offered to take charge of the cart. He leads and I push, I suppose. "Give Mr. Aliotto my regards. Tell him that I already have a

car." She raised an arm, waved wildly. "Cornell! Over
here!" It was almost a shout.

Brent's driver heard her. He might have slightly misspelled the name, but the pronunciation was the same.
What if she were called Cholmondeley? she wondered.
No need to ask this middle-aged man what he was doing
here or why: the name Brent Travel Agency was over his
breast pocket. "Miss Cornell for the Imperial? The car is
near. Permit me." He placed his card on top of her suitcase, took hold of the cart, and they were on their way.
The young man was nowhere in sight. Not until they
reached the street. As she walked toward the limousines'
parking area, she saw that mop of thick black hair about
to duck into a gray Fiat drawing up beside him. Odd, she
decided; she might have acted out of pique, but that whole
incident was definitely odd. And unsettling. Disturbing,
in fact.

The drive up the curve of Via Veneto's hill was enough
to chase doubt away. Karen eyed the little shops, the
cafés that lined the avenue's sweep, and thought with
amusement as the limousine reached the Imperial that she
was, this time at least, in a central hotel. Now, the street
was quiet. Almost. Once noon arrived, the sidewalks would
be crowded, the traffic boundless, and people would start
filling all those outdoor tables in all those upper-avenue
cafés.

She followed her luggage into the grand hotel with
expectations restored, hope renewed, and plans for the
next few hours already complete. First, a shower and
breakfast in her room. Next, a call to Aliotto to find out
when they would meet. Then three hours of beautiful
sleep. By one o'clock, she would be sitting at a table in
front of Doney's watching the constant parade of chic
girls and handsome young men. And by four, she'd be
calling Washington, reaching Schleeman at the start of
his morning in the office.

The disappointments began. Her room was on a lower

floor, and its two windows faced a tight courtyard, their
long curtains completely drawn to block out the nonview.
It was spacious enough, adequately furnished, but definitely what the French called, with their apt turn of phrase
"the mother-in-law's room." It was certainly silent apart
from the air conditioner—its corridor seemed set off from
the central part of the hotel. She investigated a possible
fire exit nearby, a comforting presence, but it turned out
to be the service staircase. However, the telephone-shower
in a giant bathtub worked once she learned to control it;
the croissants and coffee were excellent.

She was still annoyed by the drawn curtains when she
put in her call to Aliotto. And more annoyed when there
was no answer. She checked the number that Schleeman
had given her with the telephone directory. No mistake.
She decided to try later. And later. And later. In disgust
she went to bed for those three hours of sleep. She managed two in a kind of drifting wakefulness. At last she
gave up and dressed—but left her suitcase unpacked and
her bag relocked for early removal from this room—and
called Aliotto for the fifth time. A woman answered in a
brisk young voice, changing from Italian to English when
she heard Karen's name. Her accent was heavy, but not—
to Karen's ear—that of an Italian: her natural language
must be less liquid in vowels and thicker in consonants.
Her message was brief. Mr. Aliotto was not well; he would
telephone Miss Cornell on Sunday evening.

And what happens to my briefing on the two terrorists?
Karen thought in dismay as the woman replaced her
receiver and she was left with a dead telephone in her
hand. Annoyance gave way to anxiety. She did not know
Aliotto well, yet enough to sense this was not his style.
He would have telephoned her himself or sent her a brief
résumé of the names, ages, crimes, prison sentences of
the terrorists, perhaps directed her to the official who was
in charge of their appearance on Monday. Aliotto was a
professional, not a fly-by-night reporter. As of now, she
knew nothing, not even the name of anyone to contact

for information on some of the background for Monday's meeting. Her anxiety turned to anger. She picked up her shoulder bag, didn't even glance in the long mirror to check her appearance, and took the long walk to an elevator for the front lobby.

There was a lull in its usual restrained bustle—a contradiction in terms but a definite goal for any luxurious hotel that was also popular. At this hour, with guests at luncheon or out on the town, there seemed to be more bellboys standing around than inhabitants. No customers at the porter's impressive desk. Karen checked there first, in case a note from Aliotto was waiting and as yet undelivered. Nothing. But there was a giant basket of flowers. "Just arrived," the porter said. "We shall have them sent to your room."

"Not immediately. May I see the card?" But there was no card tucked away among the mass of chrysanthemums.

The porter said, "It must have fallen out when the messenger was bringing it here." He shook his head in disapproval.

"Of course."

"It would be much better to have the flowers sent to your room directly. The maid will add water—most necessary."

Karen didn't argue with politeness. The basket will just have to be moved along with my luggage, she decided as she smiled her thanks and left for Reservations.

The junior clerk was perturbed by her request. "Madam does not like the accommodation she has been given?" He turned for help to a senior clerk. The senior clerk was equally perturbed, low-voiced, and incredulous.

The assistant manager, summoned from his office, was puzzled. "I remember distinctly that madam requested privacy and quiet."

"I didn't make the reservation," Karen said with equal politeness. "I believe Mr. Aliotto did that on Monday or early Tuesday."

"Let us see." The assistant manager, handsome and

immaculate, signaled to the junior clerk, who searched in the filing cabinet and produced a card. "Yes," said the assistant manager, "Mr. Aliotto did make a personal visit last Tuesday and—" He hesitated, frowning. "The room he requested was changed yesterday evening to your present accommodation—at your wish for privacy."

"Was changed? By whom?" Karen was wide-eyed. "It couldn't have been Mr. Aliotto. He knows I like sunshine in a room. At present, I have none." Nor daylight.

The senior clerk ventured an interruption. Mr. Aliotto hadn't made the call changing the room; it had been his secretary who had telephoned.

The woman who had made excuses for Aliotto? "An unfortunate misunderstanding. I'm sure she meant well."

"He," corrected the junior clerk, and, in embarrassment at his temerity, averted his admiring gaze from *la signora* with eyes as blue as the heavenly skies and a complexion of carnations.

"He?" A girl as Aliotto's secretary could be a euphemism for mistress. But a man? Not Aliotto's life-style. Most definitely not. She reached into her handbag and produced Hubert Schleeman's business card, handsomely embossed with his name and that of the *Washington Spectator*—complete with telephone, Telex, cable directions—noted in a lower corner. "I believe Mr. Schleeman, who is my publisher, stays here when he visits Rome each year."

The effect was immediate. "Yes, indeed. One of our most valued guests." And Hubert's brief sentence on the back of the card—*Please extend to Miss Cornell your usual courtesy*—along with his signature was scarcely to be ignored. "A change of rooms will be difficult, of course. Be assured, Miss Cornell, we shall do our best. You may not find so much privacy in your new location but—"

"Some more sunshine?" Karen retrieved the card and replaced that little ace in her bag. "I'll return by—" she consulted the desk clock: one forty-five; she was running late—"by four o'clock, when Mr. Schleeman will be expecting a telephone call from me. I'll tell him how helpful you have been." She gave a warm smile to everyone as she accepted the polite bows and made her way to the street, a neat figure in her mid-blue linen suit (a Chanel copy, right down to its black braid and gold buttons) and her high-heeled black sandals. Luigi Aliotto, she was saying silently, I am no longer upset by you—I am worried.

"Sunshine?" the senior clerk queried as he watched the swing of Miss Cornell's hips. His own preference was a room completely darkened by closed shutters.

"Perhaps she comes from California," the junior clerk suggested hopefully. It was one of his far-off dreams.

"New York," the assistant manager corrected, "and start juggling the rooms on the fourth floor." His door closed. End of the Cornell episode.

In Via Veneto, Karen was greeted by a blaze of light, a dazzle of brilliant colors on the broad sidewalk, a screech of gears and brakes from the clutter of cabs and cars. But no blare of motor horns, she thought thankfully. Her walk up the street was slowed to a saunter by the pace around her, but it was only a brief distance to Doney's. There, by two o'clock, she might find one outside table where someone was not lingering over his coffee under the shade of a small tree. But no one at Doney's was in any haste. So she strolled on.

Even if she did find a less fashionable table at another café, she wouldn't be sitting there, as she had hoped, to watch the Romans. The foreigners, not just from Europe but from the whole wide world, had followed Julius Caesar's example: they came, they saw, they conquered. Or at least, if they hadn't conquered—judging by the aloof tolerance of the surviving Romans—they were most certainly an army of occupation. Their variety wasn't so marked by differences in dress except for those few who were determinedly ethnic in their costumes. It was their voices, speaking in twenty or more strange tongues, that made them noticeable. The city was becoming universal rather than eternal, she thought as she reached a side street and prepared to cross it to continue her way. So far, no luck in tables. Soon she would come to the end of Via Veneto where it met the Roman wall that had once guarded the ancient city. Beyond that were the vast grounds of the Villa Borghese: an abundance of umbrella pines and magnificent gardens, but no café for a mile or two within that enormous park.

She hesitated at the curb, changing her mind about crossing the side street, turned and collided with a venerable priest who had been right at her heels. She had seen several priests around, and some nuns, too, all of them black-skirted and serious, ignoring the prostitutes of both sexes dressed either in brief low-necked dresses or in skin-hugging pants who strolled with the crowd. A priest was no surprise, but this one, white-haired, shoulders bent with age, caught her hand as if to steady himself.

Her astonishment changed to shock as he slipped a card into her palm, closing her fingers over it. "Careful, Miss Cornell," he was whispering in English, his lips scarcely moving, his arms already dropped to his sides, his eyes meeting hers in that brief moment. "*Non c'è di che*," he said aloud and limped across the street, his head bowed in contemplation, his hands clasped behind his back.

"Don't mention it," he had said, as if she had just excused herself. Or a double meaning? she wondered, retracing her steps down Via Veneto. The small card was still hidden in her hand as if the sudden shock had glued it to her palm. It can't be, she kept saying, but it is. It is. I know those eyes: pale gray, intense. I know that voice— the deep-throated way Cornell was pronounced even in a whisper. It's Josef Vasek. It can't be—that priest is thinner, older. But it is.

At Doney's, an elegant middle-aged blonde was gathering her purse and French poodle. Her escort, young and handsome, six feet of masculinity and as expensively clothed as his mistress, was on his feet to help her rise.

The waiter was bowing and thanking *la Contessa* as he pulled back her chair. The minute it was freed from the Givenchy dress, Karen slipped onto it with a smile of thanks in general, of relief in particular, forestalling a most respectable German and his wife from taking possession.

She ordered an omelette, white wine, and coffee. Only then—once the waiter had left and the German couple had departed—did she risk slipping the small card into her handbag as she took out cigarettes and lighter. She had not dared to glance at it; reading would have to come later. She relaxed a little, lit a cigarette, ignored the admiring glance of a man at a neighboring table, and seemed absorbed by the passing scene. She counted two more priests walking leisurely, three hurrying nuns, and—a study in contrasts—another prostitute. Also a Hollywood director, three TV stars from America, a French couturier, a rock-and-roll millionaire. Also a host of other people she couldn't identify, all out to eye and be eyed—the favorite pastime on this section of Via Veneto. She thought of Josef Vasek, Mr. Farrago himself, and almost smiled. Prague had been nothing like this.

She finished lunch and reached into her bag, rummaging in its depths for her wallet. For a second, she tilted the hidden card so that she could read its message: *Capuchin Church, 4 P.M.* She dropped it back in place, found the wallet, and began calculating the tip she would leave. Dammit, I'm scared, she thought as her hands fumbled with the outsize Italian notes. She reasserted her will power and paid her bill, even calmly applied some lipstick as she waited for change to be made. Her watch said quarter past three. The Capuchin Church was somewhere down Via Veneto, below the American Embassy—not a far walk, but she'd take it at a saunter in the prevailing style. No one seemed to hurry in this city. As for her telephone call to Schleeman—postponed for an hour or so. If only she could somehow manage a discreet message to be passed on to Peter Bristow.

It was hot, the sun high in a cloudless heaven, with

streets half-empty: the wise had long since disappeared into their bedrooms for a siesta behind closed shutters. Some tourists were braving the temperature with cameras and guidebooks in hand. Karen slipped off her linen jacket, took out her own little guide to Rome from her handbag, stopped occasionally to consult it and look briefly around her. She could read snatches of information about the Church of the Capuchin Monks. Founded in 1624 as St. Mary of the Conception; now with friars around, conducting tours of the subterranean chapels with more than three centuries of their predecessors' bones and skeletons on display. She blanched at the idea and pinned her hopes on the ground-floor church and chapels: they should be secluded enough for any private meeting.

She followed the curve of the street in its sweeping descent to the church and found she was twelve minutes early. Better to enter now than loiter around. She drew on her jacket to cover her arms and low neckline—Italian churches had their strict rules about exposed skin—and pulled a silk scarf from her bag to drape over her head once she was inside. Her legs were bare but deeply tanned; they might pass muster. She began walking the short distance from the street to the church steps and felt more reassured when a friar in his coarse brown gown roped around his waist, hoodless, bearded, bare feet (not especially clean, either) in leather sandals, his naked ankles clearly displayed under his sacklike habit, hurried past her with giant strides and never a glance of censure. A similar friar, bearded too, with black tonsured hair and of heavy build, descended the steps almost at a run. Hefty fellows and quite unlike any monks she had ever seen. Even if their bellies weren't with rich capon lined, they were filled with spaghetti.

She entered a place of deep shadows, made darker by contrast with the street's glaring light. As her eyes became accustomed to the shade, she could count about twenty or so worshipers as well as a handful of wanderers being guided around the ground-floor chapels by a friar, whose booming voice echoed among the pillars as he recounted the story of St. Francis. She chose a wooden bench, far removed from the women kneeling before the altar, but tied her scarf around her head to follow their example and felt suffocated by the heat that had been trapped under a seventeenth-century roof. At least, the scarf hid the color of her hair: one must suffer to avoid attention.

Movement beside a distant pillar caught her eye. The brown-robed friar (and how could they bear the touch of heavy rough wool in this heat—one must suffer to be holy?) was not gathering a few people around him. They were all talking, and in Italian. A priest was joining them, a black-skirted figure she hadn't even noticed until he moved forward. His hat in his hand revealed his straggling white hair; his limp was definite.

So I follow, she thought, rising, walking down a side aisle to join the little group. The friar asked in a quick flow of words, so quick that it mesmerized Karen, "The lady understands Italian?" She stared at him. His deep bass voice rumbled on, "This tour is for those who speak the language. No translation available. The lady must wait for a later visit to the subterranean chapels. German at four-thirty. French at five. English at—"

"If the lady speaks French," the white-haired priest interrupted with an apologetic smile, "I could translate. Madame," he inquired in French, "do you understand?"

Understand that he doesn't want to be identified as knowing any English? *"Mais oui,"* Karen said and added her thanks in a few phrases, which might be criticized by those who had learned their French accent in Tours, but neither the two Italian teen-age girls, nor the family speaking Portuguese to the children and Italian to the friar, nor the English couple with a *History of Rome* noticeably on view showed anything but impatience to start the tour.

It was only logical that the obliging priest should walk beside Karen as they began a steep descent into the nether regions. Reasonable, too, that his limp made them the last in line, and even let them drop back a little from the friar's brisk pace. Vasek *has* lost weight, Karen noted; no more spreading waistline.

They entered the first subterranean chapel and were silenced. It was dark, with a few weak bulbs to show them the path they must follow; and cool, almost cold; and still. At first glance, it seemed that rows of slender pillars, closely packed, touching one another, were built against the walls. Then, as Karen passed a bleak light, she saw them more clearly. Skeletons all, standing erect, their gaping mouths grinning from white skulls at those who still lived. She flinched. The silence was broken by gasps and screams. She looked at Vasek, who had neither flinched nor gasped. There was a suspicion of a smile around his lips. The friar, leading the way, was giving the details: more than four thousand holy men had been gathered here to rest in peace. Vasek's smile broadened. And as the English couple—following the friar closely with questions about the extraordinary purity of the air—disappeared into the second chapel, Vasek seized the moment.

In English, his voice so quick and low that Karen had to slip the scarf away from her ears, he was asking, "You delivered the envelope?"

"Yes."

"To Bristow?"

"Yes."

"Has action been taken?"

"I think so. I've been told nothing. Security is tight."

That relaxed Vasek slightly. "Can you send him a message?"

"No."

"When will you see him?"

"I don't know."

"But you *must* see him!" He eyed the straggling line ahead of them, buzzing with exclamations and smothered shrieks as still more details were noted—some skeletons white, others partly draped by fragile remnants of brown tattered wool. "Tell him I was delayed in leaving Italy—

an accident—I twisted—" He stoped there, broke into French and a normal voice. The Portuguese mother had darted back to pull her twelve-year-old son away from touching a skeleton's hand and hauled him into the second chapel.

Karen and Vasek followed. His limp seemed to have intensified. Their progress was slow. The friar was beginning to lead the way into the third chapel. "I was delayed," Vasek said hurriedly. "No matter. I'll arrive in Washington. In two weeks. Tell him that."

"You'll find American territory only a few minutes from here," Karen reminded him. "Just walk right in and wait for Bristow to come and vouch for you." If that, she added silently, is what you need. Ridiculous caution.

"And how do I leave your embassy? Take a flight back to Washington with Bristow?" he asked sarcastically.

They were entering the third chamber. Vasek, his face still tense, spoke a sentence in French as the friar looked back.

"You must keep up, brother," the friar called to him.

"Yes, yes. My leg—"

The friar nodded his understanding and began urging the group into the fourth chapel.

Vasek looked at Karen, his lips tight. "I intend to reach America alive."

"You would be guarded on that flight. You'll be safe."

"Hunted men have been killed whenever they were known to be in transit. Their guards along with them. A bomb in a car, a bomb in a plane. The only safe journey is anonymous, unknown to anyone. No whispers, no rumors, no reported movements, no discoveries. *That* is safe."

They entered the last chapel: a major display of bones arranged into careful patterns. "Be careful with Aliotto. A good man. But under difficulties."

"Was it he who told you I was in Rome? At the Imperial?"

Vasek judged it wise to speak some French, even if

the rest of the group were all lost in fascination of the bones. But he was still speaking of Aliotto. "Yes. I phoned him. Last Tuesday."

"I think," she said very quietly, "that a lot has happened to him since Tuesday."

"What?" Vasek asked sharply.

"He never met me, hasn't called me. Others do that— in his name, they say."

"Be *very* careful with him," Vasek said, his face somber. "Your warning was unnecessary, but I thank you."

"Do you think I will be meeting him?" She had her doubts. Another fiasco, she was thinking, another assignment from Schleeman that never took place.

"Yes. If it is useful to them, he will meet you."

"Useful to whom?" she asked in alarm. "And why—"

"Blackmail. He's vulnerable."

They joined the rest of the group. The teen-agers had graduated from little shrieks and tears to silence. The Portuguese were subdued. The Englishwoman was talkative. "Interesting, isn't it?" she asked Karen.

A quick glance from Vasek reminded Karen. "Intristing?" she echoed slowly. *"Intéressant? Oui, madame. C'est bien intéressant. Incroyable."* She turned to Vasek to thank him for his excellent translation. The others began to dip into purses and pockets for donations as the friar seated himself outside the chapel's door at a table with a slotted box on its top. All contributions welcomed.

Quietly, Karen asked Vasek, "Were you waiting for me near the hotel today? Or did you have a doorman phone you as I was about to leave? A hefty tip and a tall story can always work wonders." She began searching in her wallet. "Was I the runaway wife of your dear brother?"

He actually laughed. At her, not with her.

"You should wear colored lenses," she couldn't resist telling him. And one up for me, she thought.

"I do. But today, how would you have known me so quickly?" He bowed and said good-bye. The friar refused his offering and hoped the French lady had understood everything. "Everything," Vasek assured him. He stood aside to let the others start climbing a long flight of stone steps to the outer world. Karen was already on her way, keeping close to the pretty young Italians, who, as daylight drew nearer, were now in a state of giggles.

Vasek reached Via Veneto, turned downhill to Via del Tritone, a crowded street at all hours of the day. A bus from the Corso nearby would take him close to the depot, where a large tourist bus would leave this evening, packed with one-day trippers. His seat there had been booked six weeks ago on his last visit to Rome. A battered suitcase—with change of clothes, hair, make-up, new papers and passport—was waiting for him in one of the depot's lockers. Aliotto's arrangements for passage on a freighter out of Genoa had been a useful subterfuge. Now they would think he was stranded temporarily, and the search in Italy would intensify. But, luck holding, he would be in Switzerland by tomorrow morning. Luck? No. Preparations, thorough and farsighted, made your luck.

His limp lessened, but he'd keep it until he was joining a pack of tourists out for a cheap jaunt to Zurich. Two weeks, he had told Cornell—a pity to practice a little deception on her. She could be trapped, though, like Aliotto; and that was a risk he would not take. Her risk? A pity, he thought again, but necessary.

The city bus was packed, but he welcomed the jam of people. The more, the safer. A motherly woman offered the limping priest her seat. He took it with thanks and a blessing.

12

KAREN AWOKE IN HER NEW ROOM WITH STREAMS OF SUN-shine slanting in through the windows. Last night, she had been so tired, bewildered, too, that she had forgotten to close the shutters. The maid, of course, had latched them securely when she had turned down the sheets of a most comfortable bed, but Karen had opened them again to let her see the lights in the street below as company for supper in her room. She hadn't been able or willing to visit the restaurant downstairs, far less explore Via Veneto again. There were three little bruises on her left hip where she had been quietly nipped as she walked back from the Capuchin Church. Apart from that (indignity or compliment?), she had suddenly felt swamped by loneliness after her brief call to Schleeman was over.

She made little of Aliotto's nonappearance. "Nursing a cold," she had told Hubert so as not to alarm the old boy or make him order her back to Washington. He would, too, if he tried to phone Aliotto and got a sweet run-around from an evasive "secretary." She couldn't leave for two reasons. First, she wanted this interview with two recanting terrorists. Second, there was her pride: no more fiascos. This time around, she'd accomplish what she had been sent to do—produce a sound article for the *Spectator*. She did tell Schleeman, though, about the mix-up with her room (no blame attached to anyone; everything kept light and amusing), and the new accommodation was a suite, no less; all that was available until Saturday, and the one which he usually occupied, according to the assistant manager. If the thought of a mounting expense account had fazed Schleeman, it was shown only by a slight pause. Then he said, "Keep it. Better hang up now. These phone bills are monstrous. Call me Monday once the interview's over." She hadn't been able to give him a message for Peter Bristow. All the way back to the hotel from the Capuchin Church, she had tried sentence after sentence, and found none that was both informative and discreet—an impossible combination when you wanted to say, "He's here in Rome. Vasek himself. Help!"

Now, with the sun's rays strengthening, she rose and partly closed the shutters, turned up the air conditioner, ordered breakfast for eleven. By then, she would have bathed and dressed and forgotten the last snatches of her nightmare. It was fading fast, thank heaven. Not four subterranean chapels but forty . . . Her feet dragging over the smooth sanded floor, Vasek limping heavily by her side . . . "Could we rest?" she had turned to ask, and saw Vasek's face as a grinning skull, his body a white skeleton draped in his long black gown that was tattered, thinned, and dust-covered with age. She was running, the friar trying to stop her with a smile—Aliotto's smile, Aliotto's clean-shaven face, Aliotto's carefully waved hair. She was mounting the steps. Somewhere, a woman singing a Portuguese fado. Somewhere, young Italian voices rising in laughter . . .

At least it had ended in laughter and not in screams. She switched the air conditioner to a less chilly blast— it was too strong a reminder of that subterranean air. In the warmth of the shower, she thought of the message she should have sent to Peter Bristow: *Having wonderful time. Wish you were here.* And she began to laugh.

She was ready to leave her room by ten past one. Lunch where? she wondered. Damn you, Aliotto: you should be giving me luncheon and talking my ear off.

The phone rang. Aliotto, she thought, and forgave his neglect. She picked up the receiver. But it wasn't Aliotto's voice. "Peter? Peter Bristow! You?"

"In one piece. Are you free for lunch? If not, cancel him and come with me."

"Peter!" she said unbelievingly. "And what on earth are you doing here?"

"I'm on holiday—two weeks doing nothing but enjoying myself."

"But where—"

"I'm at the Imperial, just checked in. Give me time to get the travel grime washed off. I'll meet you in the lobby at one-forty. Okay with you?"

"Yes. Yes. Oh, Peter—I'm so glad you are here."

"I've missed you, too." The call ended.

Missed me, too? That was only for the benefit of any listener in the lobby—judging by the background noise he had probably been calling from there. Checking on me even before he reached his room? Worried about me? Two weeks ago, she would have been indignant that she couldn't manage by herself, thank you. Now, she was admitting, as she quickly changed her dress and brushed her hair, she was happy that someone did worry about her. And in particular, she admitted further as she found her bottle of perfume, Peter Bristow.

He was ahead of time and nervous. There was no sign of that, outwardly at least, or that he had arrived little more than half an hour ago from an all-night flight and a journey by car. A shower, a shave, a change of clothes, and he was ready to face Rome. And Karen. She stepped out of the elevator, saw him, and came forward with a smile that dazzled him. My God, she really is glad to see me, he thought, and met her with outstretched hands. He grasped her firmly. His nervousness vanished.

She said in a murmur. "Do I look affectionate enough?" She reached up and kissed his cheek as he hugged her. "After all, I have to give everyone a reason why you called me as soon as you arrived."

He released her. She had put everything on a neat businesslike footing. "You're quick," he told her. "Thank you for making things easy." He took her arm, guiding her toward the restaurant. "I thought we'd lunch here—there are some empty tables." And not crowded together, either. They could talk safely. "Tonight, we can have dinner out."

"My constant companion?"

"Almost right. You forgot to add 'willing.'"

She dropped all pretenses. "Peter—I really am so glad to see you. Yesterday, I thought of a dozen messages I might give Schleeman to pass on to you, but they were no good."

He was suddenly serious. "A lot to tell me?"

"Yes."

"Then we'll find a very quiet table."

He did. And once their drinks arrived—white wine for Karen, a Scotch highball for him—he suggested to the captain that the menu could wait meanwhile, and they were left in peace. "To you," he said and raised his glass.

She raised her glass to him. "Thank you for being here."

As bad as that? "Tell me."

"The important thing first." She lowered her voice. "Vasek."

Bristow sat quite still. "Go on."

"He's in Rome. Was in Rome yesterday, that is."

"Go on," Bristow repeated, and listened intently as she described the strange encounter in Via Veneto and the meeting that followed. She kept it brief and clear, concentrating on what Vasek had said. His appearance

and manner were also described, as well as his little stratagem to let her accompany him into the subterranean
chapels. The people around them, her own reactions,
weren't mentioned.

But Bristow could fill in those details for himself. He
had once taken a tour of the chapels. "Bastard," he said
under his breath; but a clever one. "I need another
drink. So do you." He signed to the captain. "We'll order
now. And have some real food," he told Karen with a
smile. "You didn't eat much yesterday, did you?"

"No," she admitted. Half an omelette, small to begin
with; and for supper, a third of a chicken sandwich. She
chose medallions of veal; he ordered a steak from the
grill. With a bottle of Soave Bolla, it was a very pleasant
meal. The talk, which he kept far away from problems,
was very pleasant, too. It ended. And once the waiters
had removed themselves with the plates and the last
crumbs brushed off the tablecloth, they could linger in
peace over small cups of filtered coffee. Bristow said, "So
that was the important thing first. What comes second?"

"Aliotto."

"Oh?"

"There's a lot of small details—just incidents." She
looked at him, hesitating.

"I'm listening, Karen," he said with an encouraging
smile. He stretched out a hand and covered hers as it lay
beside her coffee cup. "Come on," he urged gently. "And
remember I'm the guy who likes every detail."

"Even the possibly stupid ones?"

"Even those."

"And you won't laugh at me?"

"Laugh with you. Never at you."

I believe that, she thought as she looked into his eyes.
She relaxed, and he could withdraw his hand. She began
talking: the airport, the room, the telephone calls, no direct
contact with Aliotto until tomorrow evening. "And," she
finished, "the meeting with the terrorists is scheduled for

the next morning—Monday. Perhaps it has been canceled. Or has Schleeman been misled again?"

He pieced together the information he now had about Aliotto, a man popular in varied circles; friendly with Vasek, enough to have Vasek phone him last Tuesday; since then, certainly since Karen's arrival, an enigma. A change in Aliotto? Natural or compelled? He was vulnerable, Vasek had said. Bristow ended his brief silence. "I know someone who probably has a friend at police headquarters. I'll find out through him if the meeting is still scheduled."

"Time and place. And do the authorities expect me? I need to know all these things."

"We'll find out." I'll get in touch with Levinson as soon as possible—he was the type who believed in cooperation, whenever feasible, with the police top brass in whatever friendly country he was stationed. "Do you intend to be at the Monday meeting even if Aliotto is not available?"

"Yes. That's why I came to Rome."

"Dutiful, aren't you?"

She raised her eyebrows. "*You* are telling me about duty?"

When he signed name and room number on the bill, he was imagining Menlo's sour amusement; expense account and Levinson were two suggestions that originally had roused little enthusiasm in Bristow. Now he was finding them both necessary and all within his first two hours in Rome. Yes, Menlo, would have more than smiled. That craggy face would have split into a wide laugh.

As they were bowed out of the restaurant, he said, "Why don't you show me the room with so much privacy—its location, at least?"

Her confidence was restored enough to let her say lightly, "Why not? But I am beginning to feel just a little ridiculous." Somehow the room, after a good luncheon and company to match, began to seem unimportant.

It was on the second floor, down the long corridor she had described. He noticed the doorway at its far end and checked to see that it did open onto a service stairway. As they returned past the room, he halted abruptly as he saw its door lay slightly ajar. His eyes traveled to the lock. Something was wrong there. It had lost its grip. Before he could examine it more closely, a maid appeared from the pantry area and came hurrying to intercept them.

"*Signorina*," the maid said as her sharp dark eyes recognized Karen. Relief showed in her face, and then a touch of anxiety. "You left something behind in your room? But I saw that everything was moved safely. Nothing remained."

"Everything was perfect," Karen told her.

"We just wanted to thank you with this," Bristow said and slipped sixteen hundred lire—the rough equivalent of a dollar—into a willing hand. "What happened here?" He pointed to the lock. "Did someone forget his key?"

The maid's eyes became guarded. "It will be repaired on Monday," she said stiffly.

"I think someone lost his temper," Bristow went on jokingly. "Or a thief perhaps?"

"Oh, no. No, *signore*. Nothing was taken. I assure you. Ricardo and I—we saw them. And they ran." She gestured to the service stairs.

"Both of them? Or were there more?"

"Oh, no, *signore*. Just two. Dressed as kitchen help—we thought that is what they were, at first. But of course they were not employed here."

And either didn't have access to any keys or tried one that didn't work. Bristow said, "Of course not. Too bad they ruined the lock. It looks new."

"It was. Now it will have to be changed again." She shook her head. "People nowadays—"

"That's right," Bristow said with a parting smile. And to Karen, as they walked along the quiet hall, "Are you feeling just a little less ridiculous?"

The maid hurried after them. "*Signorina*," she called,

"I forgot to add water to the flowers. Have you remembered?"

"No. Thank you for telling me."

"*Mi dispiace molto*," the maid apologized. "They were so beautiful."

"I'll do it right away," Karen assured her.

Bristow took her arm and pulled her toward the elevator. "I know she's lonely and likes to talk with the pretty *signorina*, but what flowers?"

"Someone sent them to me. I don't know who. The card must have dropped out."

He looked at her, shook his head. "I'll see you to your room. Which floor?"

"The fourth."

"Good. We'll be almost neighbors." Thanks to Levinson, no doubt.

The elevator was empty. She said slowly, "Those two men—kidnappers?"

"Probably they were after your typewriter or watch." But, he thought, they wanted much more than some easily sellable items.

"I wonder," said Karen.

They reached her suite. "Cosy," said Bristow. The sitting room was agreeable and elegantly furnished. The bedroom, larger, was enticing. "You'll be comfortable."

"Poor flowers," Karen said, looking at the basket with its profusion of drooping heads. "I'll get some water. Oh, Peter, would you order up some drinking water for me? And white wine? And Scotch for you? Not for us now," she added. "Perhaps later? Sometime?"

"Might as well make use of the refrigerator," he agreed, opening its wood-paneled door. "A lot of little bottles inside," he reported, and shook his head at the array of sweet liqueurs.

He investigated the television set, also disguised as a piece of furniture, and at last came over to the table on which the basket of flowers had been set, watching Karen as she parted the drooping stems to let a tumbler of water pour onto their roots. He caught her hand, put a finger to his lips, and pointed.

She looked more closely, then stared at him in horror. He studied the miniature device that nestled so unobtrusively under chrysanthemum leaves, but he didn't touch it. It might transmit, reach some place not far distant from this room. Or it could record and have its microtape collected daily. In either case, best leave it undisturbed and its discovery concealed. We'll get rid of it, but not too quickly. He said, "I don't think you'll have much luck with these flowers—they look dead or dying. Too bad."

"Perhaps some aspirin in the water?" She hoped she sounded natural. She set down the tumbler as her hand trembled.

"Could always try it. But I think it's useless." He was over at the phone now, calling room service with an order for drinks as he gestured to Karen to leave for the bedroom. He joined her there, closed the connecting door, switched on the radio, turned on the television near her dressing table.

She was sitting on the bed, looking suddenly woebegone and helpless. "The phones?" she asked. "Are they all right?"

"Everything is all right except that damned basket. Don't blame the hotel. Someone is playing games with it and with us."

With me, she thought. "But it's senseless. If they wanted to kidnap me—as perhaps they've kidnapped Aliotto—why go to the trouble of bugging my room?"

"To have a record of anything you said over a telephone or to a visitor in your room." Before they snatched you, he thought.

"Was that tiny gadget powerful enough to reach in here?"

"If you left the door open and didn't have a radio playing and the television going. Look, Karen—I hate to do this. But I have a phone call to make and a man to see. The sooner I do that, the better."

"I'm all right. Really. How long will you be away?"

"With luck—if my friend is in his office—about an hour."

"Then the very best of luck." He was looking at her with such real anxiety in his eyes that she gave him the most reassuring smile she could produce. It had some effect.

"Just stay here. Don't go sightseeing. We'll do that together. Right?" He glanced at his watch. "I'll see you by five—or five-thirty at latest."

"Peter, stop worrying about me. I'll be—"

The telephone rang. She reached its receiver on the night table. "Who?" She sat up erect, stared over at Bristow. "Sorry, I didn't quite recognize your voice. This *is* Luigi Aliotto? How glad I am to hear from you! How is your cold? Delighted you are better. . . . Dinner tonight?"

Bristow shook his head.

"No. I'm sorry. I've already accepted an invitation. I thought you couldn't meet me until tomorrow evening. . . . No, I can't change my plans. He's a very dear friend who is visiting Rome." She listened as Aliotto talked on about the many things they had to discuss. "Meet you for a drink before dinner? Well—"

Bristow nodded.

"At half past five?" She kept her eyes on Bristow. He shook his head, held up six fingers. "Half past five is a little early. I could manage six, I think." Bristow pointed in the direction of downstairs. "Why don't we meet here, at the Imperial? I could easily manage that by six. My friend will expect me by seven, though. You do understand, Luigi? . . . Yes, he is most attractive. . . . All right, I'll meet you in the lobby. Six o'clock."

Slowly, she replaced the receiver. "So he wasn't kidnapped," she said. "Lord, what idiotic notions I sometimes have!" She dropped back on the bed, drew a deep breath. Those two sneak thieves had been after only her typewriter or watch as Peter had said. "At least, I hope so," she added uncertainly.

He was still watching her and concealing his own doubts. "I'll be in the bar, too. Or near there. Not far away, I promise." Suddenly, he knew of one piece of news to leave her smiling. "We can relax about Vasek's letters. They've been dealt with."

"The letters?" She sat up, eyes wide with surprise. "So soon?"

"A confrontation in Moscow. A joint agreement signed by both. No use of letters by either party." Unless Vasek was caught; or dead. Then our case would seem one big bluff, and God only knows what Soviet reaction would be. It wasn't the first time they had disregarded a signed agreement.

"And no assassinations." She was smiling, her relief increasing. "Incredible how quickly an agreement was signed—usually it takes weeks of argument, doesn't it?"

"We threatened to publish." That was the limit of what he could tell her. He had gone beyond Menlo's one sentence, but the results were good: she had put aside her fears. "Get rid of that basket, Karen."

She nodded, followed him into the sitting room, thinking of the letters. "We really must have sounded as if we meant it," she said.

That had been Menlo's explanation. Bristow hadn't quite believed it then, and it still puzzled him. Too easy, too simple. To sound as if we meant it—was that really enough? "See you later." He opened the door to the hall to face a startled boy with a laden tray. The goddamn drinks, he thought, and more minutes passing. Levinson could be leaving his office before I even telephone him.

"I'll sign," Karen said. "This is on Schleeman." And now she wasn't just smiling, she had begun to laugh.

13

Bristow CALLED MICHAEL LEVINSON FROM A PUBLIC phone in the hotel lobby, relaxed when he heard that husky baritone he remembered too well. As usual, Levinson was nonchalant. "Heard you were around. I'm stuck here at the office, but drop over and see me. Use the shortcut. I'll have Giovanni meet you. When?"

"Soon. And Mike—I need to make a call to my boss; there's a business deal he's considering, and I think he'd better have another look at it. Can I use your phone? It could be a long chat." And a nicely scrambled one.

"Okay. Always liked the old geezer. Can't have him losing his shirt on a bad investment. I'll let him know you're calling."

"Be seeing you."

Satisfactory, Bristow thought as he left the lobby and had the doorman call a taxi. He could have walked the short distance to Levinson's domain in five minutes, but caution was needed. The brief interchange between them had been discreet enough to please Levinson and fit his present assignment, too: he was specializing in tracing the clandestine purchases of American classified technology by so-called friendly foreigners who then resold them at a handsome profit to the Soviet Union. Old geezer... Menlo might not appreciate the description, but it suited his eccentricities admirably.

The cab arrived. Bristow directed it up Via Veneto, then right; then after a short distance, right again until they had circled a few blocks. No one followed. Bristow dismissed the cab a little distance from the street which led—if he walked its full length—back to the Imperial and Via Veneto. But Levinson's doorway would be reached just before Bristow approached that end of the street. Circuitous, careful, and probably necessary, even if the roundabout journey irked him. He set out at a leisurely pace. Nothing urgent ahead of him, it must seem.

As for what he would tell Levinson, he'd leave most of that to Menlo's discretion. Levinson would probably know about the defection of a KGB colonel called Josef Vasek, but he might not be involved in the actual search here in Italy. He certainly didn't know about the three letters. No one knew except the people who had been involved with them: seven men at last Monday's meeting, two Secretaries, a Director, the President, the KGB of course, and Karen herself.

Karen... She had been as surprised as he had been at the speed of the Moscow government. "We threatened to publish," he had told her. "We really must have sounded as if we meant it," she had replied. But, he kept thinking, was that really enough? And he kept saying, "No. It damned sure wasn't." So what else could have made the Kremlin listen? Not have the suspicion that it was mostly bluff? Unless—unless the KGB had discovered that there were two small pieces of evidence: the date of the Secretary of State's visit to Saudia Arabia; the sworn statement of three typists that their initials had been used on letters they had never typed. Still not enough. The Soviets would rely on the secrecy of that Saudi visit to prevent the Americans from using it publicly; and the typists, of course, they would dismiss as paid lackeys.

So what the hell prodded the Soviets into an agreement? What if—what if the KGB had uncovered more than the two small pieces of evidence we had? The contents of the Prague cassettes? Vasek's words relayed to Karen, an admission of his authorship of the letters, of their future use, of his intention to defect. Yes, that was something that wasn't any American bluff. The KGB would be the first to sense the full weight of evidence against them—one of their own, able to verify Karen's account of that Prague meeting. But how, Bristow wondered, had the KGB been able to discover the contents of the cassettes so damned quickly? Only a matter of days. Not even long enough for whispers to start or the inevitable guesses that were endemic in Washington.

His thoughts ended abruptly. Ahead of him was the door to Levinson's shortcut set into the high wall that encircled the embassy grounds, a door that was narrow and heavy and no doubt guarded inside. The street was quiet. A few parked cars, apparently empty; no traffic now; only one pedestrian—a good-looking blonde, elegantly dressed, walking a white French poodle not far from the door. On the opposite side of the street, an imposing row of houses, and a black Ferrari standing before one of their entrances. Yes it all seemed safe enough, except for that blonde. She was dawdling, letting the poodle take charge of her; she looked at Bristow as he passed her, appeared to be amused—perhaps an apology for her pet's whims. He decided to walk on and reach Via Veneto before he turned back. At that moment, a quick movement from the Ferrari caught his eye. A young man had slipped out and was already halfway across the street, heading for the door. Bristow was ready to enter as the stranger—tall, dark, and definitely vigorous—turned his key in the lock. The blonde paid no attention.

"Bristow? I'm Giovanni." He closed the door behind

him, nodded to a couple of gardeners who were studying Bristow from the shade of the nearest tree.

"How did you recognize me?" Bristow asked.

"Saw you check into the Imperial." Giovanni's voice was pure American; in looks and dress, he was completely the well-heeled Roman. "You know the way from here?"

"I can make it."

"*Ciao*," Giovanni said in his nonchalant way. He gestured to the door. "You just pull it hard when you go. Self-locking." He left with a cheerful wave and an exchange of quick and authentic Italian with the gardeners. They were capable-looking types and still watching Bristow carefully as he followed the path to a small annex. The guard inside its door was equally capable, even if he was dressed like a janitor. Bristow was expected but had to show his CIA identification and wait until a phone call to the second floor let him pass.

Levinson's office, unlike the man, was understated. Barely comfortable but with all the necessary furniture and its walls placarded with maps. The desk was near the single window, allowing Levinson to have a clear view of the entrance from the street. He had probably seen Bristow being ushered through by Giovanni.

Bristow looked out at the garden, said, "Don't tell me a bell sounds here when that door is opened."

"Why not? Here and downstairs, too. Lots of surprises if you had been trying an unauthorized entry."

"There was a blonde outside, attached to a poodle, who paid me too much damned attention."

"*La Contessa?*" Levinson laughed. "She wanted to put a face to a name. You'll find her around with Giovanni—her present escort. A good team."

"Italian?"

"She was Maggie O'Brian from Milwaukee, with a fortune made by her father in beer. She married an Italian. She had the cash, he had the title, but they were happy. Until he got killed in a racing-car smash-up. That was five years ago. Since then—" Levinson hesitated briefly—

"she has dedicated herself to good deeds. As for Giovanni, he's a Brooklyn boy, studying music now and again at the American Academy. On his off-duty days, you'll find him in blue jeans and tee shirt over in Trastevere, where he has a pad and a wild collection of young friends. Okay?"

"Untrained agents? How do you get away with it, Mike?" Bristow shook his head.

"Giovanni is well trained, believe me. One of us. As for *la Contessa*—well, it seems to me most women don't need much training—just comes naturally. All the world's a stage."

"Okay," Bristow agreed reluctantly. "And they'll be our watchdogs?"

"None better." Levinson had turned abrupt.

"Okay," Bristow said again and soothed some of Levinson's annoyance. He was a man in his early fifties, solidly built and adding extra weight from good Italian dinners; outwardly full of self-confidence, inwardly watchful of any criticism of his team, which meant—in his judgment—a reflection on himself. But he was first-rate at his job, and Bristow only hoped a countess and her escort in his silk shirt and carefully tailored suit were as adequate watchdogs as Levinson believed. "Sorry to press the matter, but there's a sticky situation that could develop. Miss Cornell seems to be a target."

"Oh?" Levinson was fishing. "Anything to do with that meeting of journalists with terrorists on Monday? I heard she was invited—"

"Is it still on schedule? Where, when? Can you find out? She needs your help on that one."

"I'll make an effort. What's going down, Pete?"

"That's what I'd like to know. I'd better call Menlo. Where do I phone?"

"Feel free." Levinson rose from his desk, pointing to a telephone on a small corner table, and lifted his sand-colored jacket from a peg on the wall. It matched his sand-colored hair now receding from a bold brow and his sand-colored complexion in process of losing its holiday tan. "Just pick up, identify, and you'll be through."

"Efficiency."

Levinson ignored the compliment. "How long will it take?"

"Ten minutes or so." And you'll know damned well when the call ends, Bristow told him silently.

"I'll see you then." Tactfully, Levinson left, his amber eyes—completing his natural color scheme—without the smile that appeared briefly on his lips.

I know, thought Bristow as he picked up the receiver and identified himself, I'm just another pain in the butt that Menlo has added to his aching back. Levinson never had much use for—how did he used to put it?—for "the boys who sit in offices, poring over documents and blue-penciling newspapers like a bunch of college professors."

Menlo's voice was at Bristow's ear. "Well?" he demanded. So Bristow told of Farrago's appearance, his contacts with Karen, and the messages he had sent.

Menlo cursed, paused briefly, recovered himself. "So he means to go it alone," he said with resignation. "Hell, doesn't he trust us?"

"He doesn't trust the man who has stepped in as a substitute for a chauffeur or as replacement for the fourth gardener who has suddenly been taken ill or for a mechanic at the airstrip."

"Got you, got you," said Menlo impatiently. "I'll figure out the details for myself." He relented. "How's Junior?"

"Shaken, but she has a lot of grit. There have been other things to alarm her, too." Then followed bare details about Aliotto, the room with a broken lock, the basket of flowers.

"Not good. Get help from Levinson, I think."

"I agree. What else do I tell him?"

"Difficult. If you mention Senior, Levinson will wonder why he knew Junior, and how, and what. Too many revelations at the moment. Tell him I'll call him at five-thirty, Roman time."

"Talking about revelations—remember my objections to the quick solution of our letter problem?"

A slight hesitation. "You said it was too easy."

"Could there have been a piece of information delivered by a KGB agent that added weight to our threat to publish? Such as Senior's statements in a hotel garden?"

"Delivered by someone who had heard those cassettes?"

"If so, they'd know we weren't bluffing."

"One of us at that Monday meeting? KGB, you think?"

"Or who was in contact with one of their agents, or who just talked too much."

Menlo reflected. "If a report was sent to the KGB, it happened damn quick. They weren't too surprised in Moscow when the President made a phone call on Tuesday and said a delegation was on its way." There was another pause. "Which one of us? Our devil's advocate?"

Coulton—yes, at present he seemed to be the likeliest suspect. "All we have to do is prove it." And finding proof wouldn't be easy: giving dinner at his club to a doubtful acquaintance didn't make Coulton a traitor. "Perhaps Waterman should be more closely examined," Bristow said tactfully.

"I've already started along these lines." Menlo's voice was somber. Coulton and Sam Waterman—the combination had haunted him too much to let him neglect it. "Keep me posted. Take care of Junior."

"I'll do that. And thank God we didn't play the Vienna cassettes."

"They are both locked away in the cabinet that contains the Farrago folder in your file room. And they are marked. If anyone tries to remove them, they'll be traced."

In alarm, Bristow said, "Someone got into that file before."

"But not with guards stationed around the clock in the corridor. Anyone entering or leaving the file room will be noted."

"Anyone could slip the cassettes into his pockets."

"And will be stopped by the guard. He has a device that can detect any cassettes. They've been treated as well as marked—they'll be discovered."

Bait, thought Bristow. Damn his eyes, he is hoping someone does try to remove the cassettes. "You've got what you needed from those tapes." And identified Waterman's Vienna friends: the man, a Czech agent; the girl Rita, a courier. "Why the hell don't you destroy them?"

"We never mention the word 'destroy,'" Menlo said with mock severity. "How could you think of such a thing?" And with that, he ended the call and left Bristow in a strange mixture of anger and concern.

He controlled his anger. Professionally, Menlo was right. Bait could produce a definite lead, and it was much needed. But Bristow's concern remained. If real danger developed for Karen, he thought, I put her there. I asked her to make the Vienna cassettes, give every detail however small. If they ever got into the wrong hands ... Then he thought, They won't. Menlo's precautions were good. He didn't agree with them, but he had to admit they were more than adequate. Some would say they were excessive. Even so, his concern grew.

The door was flung open, and Levinson burst in, filled with energy and enthusiasm. "What's the news?"

"Menlo will call you at five-thirty."

"Fine." A quick glance at his watch told him he could have fifteen minutes with Bristow. "All right, Pete. Solved one problem for you. If you have doubts about the two terrorists appearing in public, discard them. The meeting is definitely on. Haven't heard where or when as yet. That's being kept secret until an hour before—the reporters participating will then be told. Just a matter of preventing a mob scene of other journalists and photographers outside the meeting place. It won't be at police headquarters for the same reason—too conspicuous; could draw the wrong element. It will be well guarded, everyone authenticated, probably searched. Now, have I answered your questions?"

"Almost. How many people will be there? Apart from police, detectives, and other precautions."

"About ten journalists and—"

"Ten? That's risen."

"It always does. The PR fellow who's responsible for the whole idea had his arm twisted by some publishers and their pet politicians."

"Some secrecy! Who else will be allowed to enter?"

"Two relatives of each prisoner—the explanation being that they can see for themselves that neither terrorist has suffered at the hands of the police. Another PR idea, of course, but it's a good one. Too easy for *Avanti* to publish later that the victims showed signs of inflicted brutality."

"One last question," Bristow said as Levinson glanced again at his watch. "How do I get in?"

That jolted Levinson. "You mean to attend?"

"I mean it. Someone accompanying Karen. Could you vouch for me with your friends at police headquarters?"

"Accompanying her as what? A secretary—an assistant—what?"

"As an interpreter," suggested Bristow. "She may need one. There could be a rush of talk—you know how Italians can pour out their words."

"Sure you could follow it all yourself? How's your Italian? Oh, I forgot, you're one of those linguists we keep in Washington."

"Just a bunch of college professors poring over foreign newspapers and documents," Bristow said blandly.

Levinson looked at him. "You've a long memory, Pete."

"Can you manage to get me inside as an interpreter?" And as Levinson brooded over ways and means, he added, "I knew you could do it. Thanks, Mike."

"I can try. That's all I can promise."

"Good enough for me." Bristow prepared to leave. "Menlo will be calling you in six minutes. Tell him about our chat. He'll approve." That could have been the clinching argument.

"Damned if I don't get myself invited, too. Why not as an official observer?"

"Why not? After all, one of those terrorists was involved in kidnapping an American colonel."

"Yes, she was, wasn't she?" Levinson said. "Good to see you, Pete. Anytime. But remember, if I do turn up on Monday—and it's doubtful; I've got a meeting at noon with a Swiss businessman who runs a front corporation in Rome for the reselling of American machinery to Russia. And that's a must, can't miss it, took months to run him to earth."

"If you do turn up?" Bristow reminded him.

"We've never met."

Bristow nodded, made his good-bye. Levinson really must take me for a bloody fool, he was thinking.

"If I don't show," Levinson added, "I depend on you to give me a complete rundown. Agreed?"

"Agreed." So that was his chief role: stand-in for Levinson. He had been neatly jockeyed into it. Bristow had to smile.

"It's only a public-relations brain wave. You know that, Pete. Why even bother with it?"

For my own peace of mind, Bristow thought. "Menlo put me in charge of Karen Cornell."

"A target, you said. For what?"

The telephone rang. Menlo's call was early. Thankfully, Bristow closed the door behind him.

He chose a convoluted route back to the hotel. A direct walk from Levinson's office would have barely taken five minutes, but he had reentered a world where nothing was direct.

He wasn't altogether a stranger to it. At the outset of his career, he had soon learned that self-preservation depended on caution. And on wits. The broadening of that education had, at first, been a concentration on the basics for his future field of interest (primarily Western Europe, although it led naturally, and unavoidably, to Eastern Europe, too): a year all told of concentration on contemporary history as he had never learned it at Harvard, and on languages. French he knew—it had served him well in Vietnam. German, half-known, was mastered; Italian and Spanish learned. Then came the more interesting basics—a year in Western Europe to observe the scene, make friends and recognize the unfriendlies among writers and politicians. Good God, the newspapers he had read, wading through them often with the help of a dictionary! Part of his job, now as before, was to keep his ear and eye open to the trends—people's behavior and beliefs—innocent usually, but always lethal when political violence was their gospel. People... Without seeing them behave and listening to what they had to say, a study of language and history was academic. Admirable and enjoyable, of course. But what about language as it was used, what about history as it was being made? What about distortions that could end as apparent facts, be accepted as established truth? There had always been that danger: the victors wrote the history books. But today—with the far reach of television and radio, of instant news—future victors wouldn't even need to win a war before they wrote the history books. They'd manipulate minds and emotions, outsmart an unwitting world.

He reached his room by ten minutes to six. As he changed his shirt, he phoned Karen. It took four rings before she answered.

"Are you all right?" he asked quickly.

"Yes. I was just telling the maid to take away those poor sad flowers."

He relaxed. "Ready to leave?"

"Almost. By the way, Aliotto called again and suggested we go out to Doney's."

"That's original." A sarcastic comment, but he didn't like the idea. There might be the problem of finding a vacant table with a view of Karen and Aliotto. "I'll be around, even if I have to sit inside. By the way, Karen, don't you think it would be useful to have an interpreter beside you on Monday morning?"

"I've thought of that," she admitted. "There have been some bursts of Italian when I caught only one word out of three." The Capuchin friar and his racing sentences had been difficult to cope with. "But are interpreters allowed?"

"This one, possibly."

"You?" She was incredulous. "Sitting beside me? Can we really pull that off?"

"Just passing on the idea so you can prepare Aliotto."

"And what is this interpreter's name?"

"Why not—simply—Peter? Give me five minutes, and I can be in the lobby when you arrive. Take care, honey."

Honey. Was that real or part of the act? In any case, it sounded good. She checked her appearance in the long mirror, found her lace wool scarf to cover bare shoulders when she went dining with Peter—an open-air restaurant meant falling dew, she remembered, and a cough in the morning; indoors, there was always throat-cutting air conditioning. She added a touch of perfume for Peter's benefit and was ready to meet Aliotto.

14

BRISTOW STEPPED OUT OF THE ELEVATOR AND HEADED
for the porter's desk—his best bet for a few minutes of
unobtrusive waiting until Karen came downstairs. And
there, also putting in time as he studied a poster of opera
performances at the Baths of Caracalla, was the elegant
figure of Giovanni. Without his Contessa, though. Pure
accident, wondered Bristow, or has he been tailing me?
Bloody hell—it proves that I'd better keep my mind on
business instead of brooding over the course of history.
Either Levinson thinks I need a nursemaid or he's just
damned curious about my movements.

He picked up a folder detailing the delights of Sardinia,
but glanced around the lobby. It had its usual six o'clock
flow: people returning from a day's outing, others leaving
for an evening on the town, and some just standing and
waiting. And Aliotto? There were two likely candidates,
both in their early fifties. Which one looked as if he could
charm the ladies? The blond, smooth-featured Italian

probably from the north, or the gray-haired, overdressed Lothario with the wandering eye?

Karen appeared, and the fair-haired man hurried to greet her with a warm smile and a kiss on her hand. Bristow replaced Sardinia, picked up Capri. "Miss Cornell," Aliotto was saying, "can you forgive me? I was desolated I was unable to meet you on your arrival."

Giovanni, at the sound of Karen's name, looked in brief astonishment at Bristow. Bristow caught the glance, nodded. Relax, Brooklyn. All is under control; there are some things that even Levinson doesn't know about.

Karen, closely followed by Aliotto was coming over to the porter's busy desk, her voice now audible. "That sounds delightful, but I must leave a message for my friend. He expected to meet me at Doney's. Where did you say we were going? Armando's on Via Ludovisi?" She halted in dismay, suddenly realizing a small problem. How did you leave a message for someone the porter knew who was barely eight feet away? "Too long to wait," she said, and the group in front of the desk with their endless questions made her excuse seem credible. "We'd have the shortest visit on record to Armando's. Why don't we keep to the original idea—go to Doney's?"

Aliotto said quickly, dropping all his formality, "Armando's is only a minute's walk from here—just across Veneto. I'll have you back at Doney's in time to meet your friend." His English was perfect, his accent attractive.

"In time?" Karen asked. "Definitely?" She began walking toward the hotel's doorway.

"No more than five minutes late," he promised with a laugh. "And I'm sure your friend will gladly wait ten, twenty, forty minutes to have your company."

Bristow dropped the Capri folder on a chair, followed. Armando's... why the change? More privacy? Hardly. Armando's as he knew it two years ago had been an expensive hangout for the beautiful people. Aliotto must have adequate spending money. And, more important,

Aliotto was hell-bent on taking Karen to Armando's. Bristow's questions sharpened.

He paused near the door to light a cigarette and give Aliotto and Karen time to start crossing Via Veneto. Giovanni slowed his pace as he passed Bristow and paused on the front steps to light a cigarette, too. As Bristow reached him, he said without raising his eyes from the flickering lighter, "Where?"

"Armando's."

"I go first. You follow." Giovanni left.

It was an old dodge in surveillance. Suits me, thought Bristow as he walked down the steps.

Giovanni had decided not to wait for a taxi and was now hastening to catch the pedestrian flow before the white-uniformed policeman, from the heights of his traffic-control box at the juncture of Ludovisi and Veneto, would bring it to a halt. Soon, Giovanni—hurrying like all the other late arrivals at the crossing—was right behind Karen and Aliotto; then he overtook them and drew well ahead. Bristow was already at the intersection and just made it across Via Veneto before its traffic started. He veered to his left, taking the opposite sidewalk from the one that Aliotto was using as he escorted Karen along Ludovisi.

Twice, Aliotto glanced over his shoulder, but no one walked behind him except an elderly woman leading a granddaughter by her hand. He didn't look at the other side of the street, where Bristow, some distance back, was following two young couples with arms linked around waists. Giovanni, his stride as smooth as the cut of his suit, had reached Armando's and was now entering. A few seconds more and Aliotto guided Karen inside. Bristow didn't increase his pace, walked on for a short distance before he stopped at the curb, let two cars pass; and only then—no one had been following—did he cross Ludovisi and approach Armando's restaurant.

He stepped through its handsome glass doors, mounted a few steps, and was in a cramped foyer so small and filled with urns of flowers that the few people clustered there made it seem crowded. They were talking, laughing, oblivious to everyone else; obviously old acquaintances meeting after their summer out of Rome. With difficulty he made his way through them, thankful that Giovanni was already inside the bar to keep an eye on Karen. *I take it all back,* he told that expensive young man: *you're as good as Levinson said.*

At this hour, the restaurant was empty and would stay that way until ten o'clock. The bar was, so far, only half-filled. It was a vast stretch of wall-to-wall carpet, divided into a few broad alcoves by a series of see-through book-cases that reached the ceiling. But the teak shelves had not been installed for books. Very wide, very deep, they displayed collectors' items of Venetian glass. The arrangement was artistic, well separated, no clutter, and the general feeling was of space and lightness. The total effect was attractive—mirrored walls and Venetian chandeliers set the rows of crystal gleaming on the small counter that lay in one corner of the room. No stools, no customers there; only a man with an air of intense dedication fixing the drinks that the red-coated waiters ordered. Voices were held low, laughter muted. Even the background music—Respighi, of course—was gently played.

From the bar's entrance, Bristow couldn't see Karen and Aliotto. Or Giovanni. So he walked up the center of the room to note who was sitting around the low coffee tables enclosed in each alcove—or section or recess or whatever they liked to call it. The first enclave had its squat armchairs mostly occupied. The second had two tables occupied and one free. He might take it once he made sure where Karen was. But just then he caught sight of a tall man slouching in an armchair in that second alcove. The man's back had been toward the room, his face unseeable until his head turned to order a drink from a waiter. It was Sam Waterman.

Bristow walked on. Sam Waterman. His companion had been facing the room: young, thick dark hair, black mustache, gray suit, lemon-yellow tie, and unknown to

Bristow. Sam Waterman ... He gets around, thought Bristow as he recovered from that shock, including crossing the Atlantic as fast as I did. How? Not by the usual overnight flight to Rome from New York; and there is none by day. He was at Schleeman's club in Washington around five-thirty yesterday. Must have had private transportation, either with Soviet help or in a jet owned by some millionaire who dabbled in far-left politics. Anyway, Waterman's here and—Bristow's thoughts stopped dead. In the very next alcove were Karen and Aliotto.

Karen could see him as he strolled past, but she couldn't have noticed Waterman—her low armchair was backed against the teak divider between his section and hers. Aliotto, facing her across their coffee table, had a full view of both Waterman and his friend. Fortunate that Karen hadn't been offered Aliotto's chair. Or was it not a matter of chance but of arrangement? Bristow went tense, took the first vacant table he saw in the fourth alcove, sat down to face Karen, but his view of her was partly blocked by a sea-blue vase shimmering with flecks of gold. He glanced around at the tables near his and suddenly realized he was sitting, damn fool that he was, next to Giovanni's. Yes, he admitted now, he had been really shaken. Waterman and Karen in Vienna; and now, Waterman and Karen in Rome.

He ordered a Scotch and tried to find the answer to the questions that raced through his mind. There *was* an answer to be found—if only he wasn't feeling so goddamned bewildered. Jet lag beginning to hit him? He hoped it was that and not premature senility that clogged his brain. Why, he kept asking himself, why was Waterman so speedily in Rome? Was he in control of the search for Josef Vasek—or the link between a Communist sleeper in Washington and a Communist cell here? Did he bring information or instructions to Rome? Unanswerable questions, Bristow decided, and a sign of his exhaustion that his mind had even posed them. He made himself relax, lit a cigarette, kept his eyes on what he could see of Karen.

Giovanni's secret amusement, when Bristow had chosen a seat without making sure who his neighbors might be (a C minus to you, Bristow), turned to sympathy. Bristow had reason enough to be worried even if he knew only half of this little drama. Giovanni, first to arrive, had seen the whole play of events. By good luck, for which even Giovanni could not take credit, Aliotto had chosen the alcove adjacent to his and made quite sure that the American girl would sit where she did. And then the two men, one known to Giovanni, one unknown, had followed Aliotto almost directly—they must have been loitering in that small crowd in the foyer, for they hadn't been visible on the street—and chosen the alcove where they could watch Aliotto. Deliberate selection. The two men had halted as they caught sight of Aliotto's blond head and veered toward the nearest vacant chairs. Even this meeting had been timed well. By seven o'clock, the fashionable hour for cocktails, every seat would have been occupied. Yes, Giovanni decided; deliberate, and very smooth. Now let's do some playacting of our own.

Giovanni took a cigarette from his silver case. Giovanni's lighter failed. Giovanni looked around for a matchbook and could find none. (Naturally enough: he had pocketed the one on the ashtray as he waited for Karen and Aliotto to enter the bar.) Giovanni, in flawless Italian, could ask the man at the next table to oblige him with a light. And as Bristow flicked his lighter, Giovanni could lean over to draw on his cigarette and ask quietly in English, "D'you know the guy who's with the Bulgarian?"

Bristow froze.

"Yellow tie, black hair. Who's the other?"

"Waterman, a.k.a. Winter."

"Thanks, pal." The cigarette was lit. Giovanni drew back to his own table. *"Grazie."*

"Prego." Bristow's drink arrived. He sat unmoving, haunted by Menlo's warning that Bulgarian Intelligence had moved in on Italy. What the hell was one of them

doing here with Waterman? He drank some of the Scotch, slowly in an agony of waiting. At ten minutes to seven, Karen was rising to her feet.

"No," she was saying, her voice carrying clearly as she smiled down at Aliotto's protests. "I really must go. I have to get back to the hotel before I meet my friend at Doney's—I forgot my lipstick. Can't face an evening without that, can I? We'll have to hurry." And hurry she did.

So she saw me, Bristow thought—she spoke for my benefit. Bless her quick wits. Now I won't need to meet Aliotto tonight. I'll trust her to leave him flat in the Imperial's lobby. He dropped the price of his drink and a twenty percent tip beside the saucer on which his tab lay as he rose from his table. Take it easy, he warned himself, slowly does it. Giovanni was already on his way to the door. Waterman and the Bulgarian were about to follow Karen, but their path was blocked by Giovanni, who was practically on her heels. Aliotto, lagging behind, turned his head to look at the Bulgarian; a brief glance, but definite. Bristow was sure about that. Then Aliotto hurried to catch up with Karen, who was being escorted into the foyer by a gallant Giovanni.

Bristow could increase his pace. He walked smartly past Waterman and his friend, didn't look at them, reached the street. Just ahead were Karen and Aliotto, and in front of them Giovanni. Bristow dropped caution, followed closely. She was well guarded, front and rear. If any Bulgarian had hoped to pull her into an automobile on this darkening street, he thought, as a car almost stopped beside her and then drove on, two able-bodied witnesses were certainly discouraging.

He kept Karen well in sight, all the way back to the Imperial.

In the lobby, Karen had her hand kissed once more as she made a quick but friendly good-bye to Aliotto. The Italian didn't even notice Bristow when they passed each other: his face was a study in despair. Something, decided Bristow, was much further wrong than an evening cut short by a beautiful woman. His attention turned to Karen, now entering the elevator with a group of French visitors, and he managed to reach it before its door closed. On the fourth floor, he followed Karen into the corridor. "Ten minutes to find your lipstick," he told her as he saw her safely into her room and could leave for his own at the other end of the long hallway. I'm too damned far away from her, he thought as he walked its length, and added that worry to all the others he had collected today.

Quickly, he washed and changed into the one complete suit he had managed to pack. Saturday evening, and what do we do? A pleasant drive, as he had planned earlier, through the Borghese Gardens to the Casino Valadier, where a dining terrace looked down on Rome from the heights of the Pincio? Good food, a magnificent view of a brilliant sunset, then night and an abundance of stars. But the events of the last hour made him want to cancel the whole idea. He couldn't, though. Karen, in her pretty dress, was not to be disappointed. Overreacting about that car on Via Ludovisi? But Giovanni, too, had heard its slow approach; he had stopped, looked around as if he were about to cross the street while Bristow directed an intense stare at the two men in the car—one at the wheel, the other in the back seat. Suddenly, the car speeded into a more normal rate of travel, disappeared into the mass of traffic on Via Veneto. A gray Fiat, Rome plate and number.

With his tie still unknotted, Bristow went over to the telephone. He'd risk a call to Levinson's office—it was the awkward choice between the need to know and security—but the phone rang just as he was about to lift the receiver.

"That was quick," Giovanni's voice said. "I've requested a trace on that car. Okay?"

"Very much okay. And would you ask the office to make copies of any newspaper items they have on file dealing with terrorists in Italy for the last four years or so?"

"Doing your homework?"

"It's much needed. By the way, did you know either of those two in the car?"

"Kissing kin to Yellow Tie. I suppose you'll need that material by tomorrow?"

"Soonest possible. And get your boss to call mine. Waterman's in town. Important!" Bristow ended the call, stood grim-faced. He drew a long breath and dialed Karen's number. "What about dinner?" He tried to sound cheerful. "Ready to leave? I'll collect you in another five minutes, if that's all right with you."

"I'll be waiting." Her voice was excited.

"See you," he said and left the phone to unlock his bag. From its hiding place he drew out his small Beretta, neat enough to slip into his jacket pocket. It had been a long time since he had stepped out for an evening with a pistol as company.

Karen had the door open as soon as he knocked. Bristow said, "You'll have to learn to ask a visitor for his name before you let him in." To soften the warning, he touched the side of her cheek for a moment and brought a surprised look to her eyes. He dropped his hand. Careful, he told himself, still aware of the soft feeling of her skin: no emotional complications, not at this time. Concentration was needed, not romantic involvement. And a damned hard effort it would be. "All set to go?"

She had been ready, with purse and scarf in her hand, but as she looked at him and noted his face was strained and tired, she tossed purse and scarf onto a chair. "It would have been lovely. Only—I think we could talk better here. Why don't we order supper now? D'you mind?" Thoughtless of her to think he really wanted to take her out for a Saturday night in Rome. He was more than tired; he had to be exhausted. Since he got off the plane this morning, he had been constantly on the move—

not a minute to himself. She knew she had guessed right as she saw his relief.

"Suits me." This would be the safest place to spend an evening; to spend tomorrow, too, although she would probably rebel against the idea. "I'll fix the drinks. Sure you don't mind staying here?"

"I'd like a rest—for a change. Armando's was bewildering. The bar itself was extraordinary. Rather nice to relax there, if you had the right company."

"Aliotto seemed pretty attentive."

"When he was being himself. A mixture of charm and warmth. Then—" She hesitated.

"Then what?"

"He became nervous. On edge. Scared, in fact. Then once again he made an effort and everything was natural. He is a nice man, you know; kindhearted, even sentimental."

"How often did that switch occur?"

"It's probably silly, but I thought it happened when he looked past my shoulder."

"At the next alcove?"

"You're clairvoyant, Peter." She took the glass of wine from him, smiled her thanks. Her face turned grave. "A man with a black mustache and dark hair had been sitting there—I recognized him as I was leaving. He was with another man whose face I couldn't see, but taller, older than the other, I thought." She frowned, trying to place the tall man who had bent down to pick up something he had dropped. "Odd, really odd," she said.

"A dark-haired man with a yellow tie?" Bristow prompted. "You knew him—how?"

"He met me at the airport instead of Aliotto." She saw Bristow's lips tighten. "No coincidence that he should turn up at Armando's, was it?"

"No coincidence," he admitted.

"So that's why he was there—to remind Aliotto to ask me the right questions. And I suppose it was he who had Aliotto take me to Armando's."

Bristow said nothing. She was right on both counts, although the instructions might have come originally from Waterman. Unlikely that Waterman could confront Aliotto openly himself.

"You know, I have the odd feeling that the tall man was no stranger. Have you an idea of who he—"

"What hold have they got on Aliotto?" Bristow asked. He didn't expect an answer, but he had slid the conversation away from Sam Waterman. "Gambling debts? Compromising photographs with an important politician's wife? Important enough to have Aliotto's career smashed—no more publication in reputable papers?" He sounded as if he were joking. "Just guessing. But they've got to have some hold."

"His mistress."

Bristow stared at her. "And how did you get on to the subject of mistresses?" he asked in disbelief, sat down to face her.

"Only one mistress. He adores her. We were talking about—" Karen stopped, embarrassed.

"About what?"

"You. He was teasing me, you see. He's quite sure that the dear friend who has been monopolizing me ever since he arrived in Rome must be—oh, well—anyway—He was teasing me, and then quite suddenly he was serious, sad, talking about finding the right woman, the right man, the only thing that really mattered in life. I asked him, 'Why haven't you married, Luigi?' And it poured out. There was a woman, the most beautiful of women, but her husband wouldn't give her a divorce. She left him, came to live with Aliotto. I said I would like to meet her. At that, Aliotto almost broke into tears. 'She's a prisoner. No one can get near her.' So I said, 'What about the police—can't they help?' He shook his head; if he told the police, she would be killed. He must do what they wanted. They were determined men. And then he fell silent. And I said nothing. You see, I had thought it was the husband who had arranged her abduction." Karen stopped. She was upset.

"And after that?" Bristow asked gently.

"He said he shouldn't have told me, hadn't meant to, but it was a relief. Now I would understand why he had behaved so strangely: the strain was unbearable. I asked if her husband could really have her kidnapped—was it quite legal? Not her husband, he told me. 'For money?' I asked—a stupid question; how could a journalist have enough money for a ransom? 'Not money,' he said almost in a whisper. 'Not money.' Then, abruptly, he changed the subject."

Bristow could understand the scene: Karen, her beautiful blue eyes filled with sympathy, would elicit any man's trust. "Aliotto was sending us a message, I think." As much as he dared, at least. Poor bastard, they had his neck in a noose.

"Perhaps he was," Karen said slowly. "He changed the subject to Josef Vasek."

"Just like that?"

"Just like that—after he looked past my shoulder."

"What about Vasek?" Bristow asked quickly.

"Had I seen him? He was in Rome, certainly as of last Tuesday, when he had telephoned Aliotto. I looked astonished. It was no act, Peter. I was absolutely dumbfounded. I said I scarcely knew the man. Then I did some changing of the subject on my own. Was it true, as Duvivier and Tony Marcus believed, that Vasek was KGB and not a press aide at all? And had Aliotto heard anything more about Tony Marcus? Was he safely back in London?"

"Did Aliotto have any more questions about Vasek?"

"No. He merely tried to bring him back into the conversation, saying he was worried about the man. Aliotto had arranged passage on a freighter from Genoa, but Vasek had never taken it."

"And you, Karen—what was your reaction?"

"I was amazed. I said, 'Don't tell me a democratic man like you, Luigi, has been helping KGB agents in their secret missions.' Aliotto spent a full minute persuading me he would do no such thing. Vasek was a friend who was defecting. And I registered plain old astonishment again." She looked at Peter. "Was that all right?"

"Very much all right." Bristow had begun walking around the room. He was restless, trying to make up his mind. "Wouldn't you reconsider that meeting on Monday with the terrorists?" he asked at last. Just get her home as quickly as possible, that was all he wanted.

"But everything's arranged. I have my official permit—it's in my purse. I persuaded Aliotto to give it to me because there was no need for him to collect me at the Imperial and take me to the place. My translator would be with me, and we'd arrive together."

"No objections to a translator?"

"He didn't think one was necessary—I understood his Italian, didn't I? I said there might be other accents that weren't so easy to follow. No more argument—I sounded quite decided. I rather think he didn't want a translator's voice interfering with his concentration. But we can whisper, can't we?"

"The mildest murmur," Bristow said. "Now, what about a rare steak? Some salad and cheese?" And from now on we talk about ourselves and no more bloody politics.

"Wonderful," Karen said. And please stop worrying about me, Peter: I am worrying enough all by myself. "After dinner—tonight—Peter, would you object to staying here?"

He looked at her.

"This couch is firm enough, and long, too. Sorry to ask this, but it's just that . . . well . . . I'm a little nervous." She tried to laugh. "There! The emancipated woman has admitted it. She needs company." And she's scared, damned scared.

"I've slept on a couch before this," he told her, watching the relief in her eyes. Businesslike, that's us. She had set the tone; he'd better keep it. He picked up the phone and requested room service. "What about some Bordeaux?" he asked her and added it to his order.

"Poor Hubert Schleeman," she said.

"Not tonight. My expense account this time."

"It's all because of Vasek," Karen said as Bristow left the phone. "They—whoever 'they' are—want to control me as they do Aliotto. But why did they attempt to abduct me last night from that isolated room? They must have intended it, or else they'd never have changed my original reservation. But *why*?" she demanded, her anger breaking out. "Because Vasek talked with me?"

"With you and with Aliotto. They got something out of him—probably the details of the Genoese sailing. But Vasek never showed, so they're using Aliotto now to get to you. They may think that you know more about Vasek's plans than anyone. In a sense, you do: you met him yesterday in Rome."

"And they could learn that? Make me talk?" Her voice faltered.

"Karen, please—"

"No, tell me the truth. I can face it. It's not knowing what is the truth that makes me afraid."

"They would make you talk," he said very quietly.

"But I can tell them nothing important!"

"They don't know that."

"But a—a—an amateur like me? They must be crazy to think a professional like Vasek would send messages by an amateur."

That had puzzled a lot of people, he thought wryly. "Except that Vasek never did what was expected. It's his kind of deception." Bristow paused, considered, and then said, "If I hadn't asked you to make the cassettes, you wouldn't be in this danger. My fault—"

"No!" she said sharply. "It's Vasek's fault for choosing me. And I made the recordings willingly. They did help, didn't they?"

"Yes. Without them, we'd still be arguing in circles—or have taken action that could have been desperate. The

Vienna cassettes weren't played to that meeting at Langley—they have been heard in secret by only three people besides us. Because they could identify you. The Prague tapes identified only a woman's voice."

For a minute, she said nothing at all. Then, in a surprise question which only proved to Bristow that Vasek hadn't been stupid in his choice of his amateur, she asked, "If you had played the Vienna cassettes, would I ever have reached Rome?"

No, he thought; probably not.

"Who was the other man in Armando's? The one who dropped something so conveniently under the table?" As Bristow hesitated, she said, "The truth, Peter: you recognized him, didn't you?"

"Sam Waterman."

"Waterman . . . So he is after Josef Vasek." She managed to smile, said, "Well, you'd better keep me safe, Peter."

That I will, he promised silently.

Room service arrived, and they began talking of other things.

It was approaching eleven and the sitting room was at peace. The waiter had wheeled away the dinner table; the maid had brought in fresh towels for the bathroom and turned down Karen's bed. Both beds, actually, either from custom or assumption or from her sense of symmetry— like the way she had displayed Karen's nightdress with waist tucked in and skirt spread out over the coverlet and Karen's slippers neatly together on a little foot rug. With warm wishes for a good night, she slipped out of the room.

"Nothing seems to astonish her," Karen said with relief.

Except when she sees I slept on that damned couch, thought Bristow. But tonight he'd have slept on the floor with pleasure. Anyone who slipped through hotel security, and it was tight since the attempted "robbery" on the second floor last night, would have to face him before Karen was reached. At this moment, he was feeling at

ease. A good dinner, excellent company—a cure for most
troubles if you didn't let yourself brood on them. He
watched Karen as she entered her own room to pull off
the extra coverlet and pillow from the unused bed.
Typically, she concealed her nervousness by being completely practical. "I have doubts about your suit," she
told him as she returned to drop pillow and coverlet on
the couch. "How many did you bring?"

"One."

"What's amusing you? You'll look as crumpled as a
dishrag tomorrow. And you know what I'd like to do
then?"

"What?"

"Visit the Forum. I bet you'd make the most wonderful
guide. You're a historian, after all."

"Was," he reminded her. "Contemporary history, too.
Not Roman."

"But you've visited Rome before—and Athens."

Yes, he thought, in the last three hours we've discovered a lot about each other's early lives.

"And so," Karen said, as she arranged pillow and bed-
spread to her taste, "you would be bound to learn what
Rome and Athens meant. That's you, Peter: you don't
spend time anywhere without knowing what happened
and when and why."

"That's me, is it?" In a way, she was right about Rome
and Athens: their history had fascinated him. The source
of Western civilization, and what were we doing with that
legacy? Heading for ruin and chaos if we let the barbarians
take over—the repeated pattern of ancient Athens and
Rome. A walk through the Forum was a necessary warning for all of us, classicists or not. But not for Karen
tomorrow. "I don't know if it's such a good idea to go
there now," he began. "Let's wait and see the Forum
when—"

The telephone rang. They looked at each other. "It
might be Schleeman," Karen said. "I ought to have called
him—just forgot." She picked up the receiver, showed

amazement. "For you, Peter. How did he know you were here?"

"Who?"

"A man. Sounds young. And amused."

Bristow took the receiver. It was, of course, Giovanni. "Knew where to find you," he said triumphantly. "Sorry to disturb you, but you've two visitors about to enter your own room. Beat it there. Important."

Bristow replaced the receiver, deciding what to tell Karen. "I'd better change this suit you were so worried about."

Karen studied him. A next excuse, but for what? "How long will that take?"

"I'll be as quick as possible." He was already at the door. "Don't let anyone inside. Not even the maid."

"And identify yourself," she reminded him, "if you don't want to stand out in the corridor."

"Three long knocks, two short." He still hesitated to leave.

"Don't worry about me. I'll make my call to Schleeman."

Reassured, he left.

No one waited outside his room. Bristow opened its door, his free hand in his pocket ready to grasp his Beretta. Two men were inside: Levinson and a stranger. Middle-aged, gray hair, deep tan, and remarkable dark eyes, Bristow noted.

"Just thought I'd drop by with this," Levinson said and handed over a bulky envelope. "Five years of newspaper reports. Enough?"

"Splendid. And thank you. A great help in several ways."

"I wanted to introduce you to my good friend," Levinson went on. "We were having dinner together, and I told him about your problems—as much as I've been told," he added pointedly. "This is Chief Inspector Alberto Tasso."

Tasso—a distinguished name. "A descendant?" Bristow inquired politely as they shook hands.

"I am afraid not." Tasso's English, like his dark-gray suit, was impeccable. His deep-set eyes studied Bristow with interest. "We shall meet on Monday morning, and I shall escort you inside the room. As a translator, I believe." Almost a smile touched the severe mouth. "You are qualified?"

"More or less."

Tasso seemed pleased with that answer. This, he was thinking, is one of those Americans who deal in understatement as much as any Englishman. Never underestimate such men. But he only nodded and retreated into his customary silence.

"Inspector Tasso," Levinson explained for him, "has been attached in recent years to Rome's special antiterrorist force. So he is involved in Monday's proceedings. They should go smoothly. The place is in—" he looked at Tasso, who again nodded his approval—"a branch police station, now unused; moved to another location. It's north of the main post office, a small street surrounded by a lot of other small streets—no open piazza fronting it for any pro or contra crowds to gather. The narrow streets can easily be cleared if any terrorist sympathizers try to protest there. You'll find the exact address inside the envelope." Levinson looked again at Tasso. "That's all, I think."

Tasso added, "I'll be inside the entrance at ten-thirty."

"We'll be there," Bristow said. They shook hands again.

Levinson said, "I sent your message to Menlo. He was—well, let's say a little surprised." He enjoyed that memory. Menlo wasn't easily confounded. "Good luck, Bristow. No trouble is expected, so it will be pretty routine. From what I hear, the events this evening at Armando's all circled around Miss Cornell. We'll keep an eye on her, come Monday. That is—" he corrected himself quickly—"Inspector Tasso's men will watch out for her."

Tasso nodded and opened the door, and Levinson, with a one-finger salute for Bristow, followed him into the corridor.

Bristow only glanced inside the envelope. The pile of newspaper clippings would be studied at leisure. The address of the meeting place—Via Borgognona—was also there. He relaxed. Quickly, he changed out of his clothes into his old wash pants and sports shirt—he never wore pajamas, didn't even own a set of them—and replaced his socks and shoes with loafers. He looked more like a casual day at the beach than a man about to sleep on a couch. The Beretta was a problem. It couldn't be hidden in a tight trouser pocket. So he found his toilet kit, made of thin leather, shapeless but concealing, and slipped the pistol inside after he had removed his hairbrush. But he managed to find space for razor, comb, and toothbrush.

With the kit and envelope securely in hand, he strolled along the corridor. Any hurry would have roused more stares than he did encounter from a party-dressed group of late revelers.

Karen had just ended her call to Schleeman. She looked with a moment's astonishment at Bristow. "Modest," was her amused comment, "but definitely more comfortable."

"Definitely. The best I could do. I travel light." He threw the toilet kit onto the couch, handed her the envelope. "Tomorrow's cram course."

She pulled out the sheaf of newspaper clippings, and her eyes widened. "Peter! Background material—this is what I hoped Aliotto would give me. How did you manage it?"

"Friends in the right places. No, honey, don't start reading now. We've got all of tomorrow."

"No Forum?" She picked out the note with the Via Borgognona address, glanced at it.

"Another time."

She half smiled.

"I mean that," he said.

She looked at the note. "Borgognona. So that's how

it's spelled. It's somewhere between the Corso and the Spanish Steps—just north of the main post office. We'll reach it within half an hour at most, wouldn't you say?"

He stared at her. It was hard to remember that anyone who was as beautiful as Karen was also sharp as a needle. "You know your Rome."

"I managed to get that out of Aliotto," she admitted as she tucked the note back into the envelope.

If Aliotto knew, then so did Sam Waterman and his Bulgarian friends. "The best-kept secret." Bristow hid his alarm. "Reminds me of Washington." He glanced at his watch. "Time for some sleep." He noted that she had left open one of the doors in the sitting room. He walked over to check if it led to a closet or communication with another suite and found a small bathroom. Tactful, he thought. "All the comforts of home." Almost. He shook his head, returned her good-night wave. I'm beat, he admitted at last.

But he made sure of the lock on the room door, unzipped the toilet kit, and placed it close to his hand as he dropped gratefully on the couch. A lot to think about, he told himself: Aliotto had found out Monday's address in advance—why? Natural curiosity? Or perhaps he had been instructed. He was being played like a damned Yo-Yo, the poor bastard. Then quite suddenly exhaustion hit Bristow. Thoughts drifted, ended, and he was asleep.

15

TEN MINUTES AHEAD OF TIME, THEY ARRIVED AT VIA Borgognona. (As difficult to pronounce as it was to spell, thought Karen.) They left the taxi at the street's corner, both of them interested in the surroundings but for entirely different reasons. Bristow noted with approval that each end of this block had been shut off to traffic: one had four men at work on its pavement, the other had a water department truck and three men seemingly surveying a problem with its main. Pedestrians were scarce. And the restaurant they passed, just before entering the disused police station, had MONDAY CLOSED posted on its door. Karen was studying the setting—the narrow street, the low old buildings—that would probably start the first paragraph of her article. She was back in her own world, with yesterday's cram course on terrorist activities giving her a feeling of confidence in the background of the two young people she was about to meet. With her blue linen suit and smoothly brushed hair she was as attractive as ever, Bristow considered, but definitely the professional.

She had scarcely spoken since they left the Imperial, and he had kept silent, not intruding into her thoughts. He had plenty of his own. But security on Borgognona was good; he relaxed a little. Now for the interior itself.

They entered directly into a rectangular hall, brightly lit but bare and shabby, with worn wooden floor and peeling plaster on its walls, stretching to the rear of the building. Halfway along its length, a staircase on its right had been roped off. The floor above looked as if a demolition project had begun and was abandoned for this morning. At the foot of the stairs, a table had been set up along with a metal detector of the type used at airports. Beyond that point, as the hall narrowed, there was a wide doorway on its left wall which must lead to the meeting room. It was guarded on either side by uniformed policemen. The rest wore civilian clothes—one checking the list of visitors along with their credentials; two at the detector; two more (one a woman) at the table where contents of shoulder bags and pockets were being examined. There was a thin line of people passing slowly through these checkpoints. Where's Tasso? Bristow wondered, his eyes searching the small group of officials who stood near the staircase wall and watched the slow traffic at the table. Tasso was there, half-hidden by the large bulk of a detective.

"We wait," Bristow advised Karen. Tasso had seen them and was coming forward.

"How many journalists? I thought there were to be only five of us." She could count eight right now. Some had cameras and tape recorders, too. "I didn't think those were allowed," Karen said.

Tasso had heard her. He shook hands with them both, expressed his pleasure in seeing her here, and then said, "All cameras—if small—are examined most thoroughly. Larger cameras are not permitted. The same procedure applies to tape recorders. You brought none, Miss Cornell?"

"I just wasn't told." She tried to hide her chagrin.

Dammit, she thought, Aliotto should have warned me. A recording would be really useful.

Tasso said, "No need to bring one here, Miss Cornell. We are taping all the proceedings. I will make sure you have a full transcript by this evening. Believe me, it will be much more accurate than these small gadgets"—he waved a hand at a cassette that was being removed from its machine with protests from its owner—"can capture at a distance."

Bristow watched the policewoman replace the cassette with one she lifted from a supply under the table. "I wondered about that," he told Tasso. "Your precautions are good."

What were they expecting? Karen looked from Bristow to Tasso and decided not to display her ignorance by any question.

"Security is tight," Tasso said, not displeased with the American's compliment. He nodded in the direction of the tall and massive detective. "He is responsible."

He definitely was, thought Bristow, conscious that the chief of Security had twice eyed him thoroughly.

Tasso guided Karen to the table. "You will have to empty your handbag, Miss Cornell. No contraband?" The grave face almost smiled.

"Only my notebook, pencils, and pen." She opened the shoulder bag and let all its contents fall on the table's surface. Bristow held back, remembering Security's sharp look as he thought of the machine waiting to signal that he carried a pistol tucked into his trouser belt.

Tasso returned. "Something to declare? In your pocket perhaps?"

"Under my jacket. In my belt."

"How big?"

"A Beretta."

"I think you should hand it over now. To me."

There was no arguing with that voice. Bristow slipped his hand inside his linen jacket, quietly freed the pistol. Tasso grasped it, slid it into an inside pocket of his suit.

It was quick and unobtrusive. "No need," Tasso said, "to carry that around."

Bristow looked over at Karen. "She's my responsibility."

And perhaps something more, thought Tasso. "It will be returned to you. I suppose you have a permit for it?"

"In the United States, yes." Complete honesty, Bristow had decided, was the only policy with Tasso. "I have no permit to enter as Miss Cornell's translator. Don't I need one?"

"Unnecessary. You are my guest. We shall enter the room together. No problem, Mr. Bristow. I have already explained your presence to Security. This way."

They walked through the detector. It registered briefly as Tasso passed its alarm, but that only raised smiles from the men in charge. Karen was already through, watching with some astonishment as a young couple, well-dressed, were undergoing further search by expert hands.

Tasso said, "These are the boy's relatives: brother and sister. The girl's relatives haven't yet arrived. Her cousins, I believe."

The young couple was cleared, their small camera was returned to them ("With a new spool inside," Tasso murmured to Bristow), and they entered the room. Tasso nodded to the two guards as he followed with Karen and Bristow. "Where do you want to sit?"

"Not in the first row," Bristow said. Aliotto was already there, in a front seat, partially hidden by a group standing around him, engrossed in conversation. "Toward the back of the room perhaps?"

"Wise," said Tasso and led the way.

"No objections?" Bristow asked Karen.

"Not if it's wise." But she was puzzled.

"I like to see all the room, not just sit facing a stage."

"Not a bad idea for me, too. The audience is part of the scene." And she would see the stage clearly enough—a narrow platform running along one end of the room—for there were only four well-spaced rows of chairs set out to face it, with six chairs to each row. Not too many were expected, but more than she had thought. And as Tasso, hurrying off to talk with another journalist, left them alone, she could ask, "Relatives, Peter? Why on earth relatives?"

He told her, as he led her to the last row of chairs and selected two on its far end with the emergency exit close by. "Sure this is all right?" he asked as they sat down.

"Fourth row? Perfect. Clear view and all the reactions to watch."

And nothing behind us except a blank wall, Bristow thought. The room, he estimated, was less than forty feet long and about twenty feet wide. The chairs formed a central island, leaving broad aisles on either side. In front was the long platform backed by another blank wall with a high row of small windows, almost at ceiling height, slanted open for ventilation but barred on the outside. The platform had two wooden chairs separated by a small table, powerful overhead lamps along with a dangling microphone, and a lectern at a front corner where a plain-clothes officer was adjusting his recording machines. Only two doors: the entrance on the right side of the room, the emergency exit on the left. A simple place for a compli-cated morning, and one big headache for Tasso and his colleagues. When they had agreed to this meeting, it was to be only a rather cosy little affair for five journalists and two recanters who could have twenty-five year prison sentences for murder, kidnapping, kneecappings, and bombings reduced to five for their cooperation. Now, the front row held four journalists; the second row had its full complement of six. The third row had the two young relatives sitting directly in front of Karen and Bristow—but the girl was no taller than five feet and blocked no view—and next to them were two somber-faced men and then two empty chairs. Presumably, guessed Bristow, for the late-arriving cousins.

"Comfortable, I hope," said Inspector Tasso as he returned.

No one would fall asleep on these wooden seats, thought Karen and smiled as an answer.

"You seem troubled," Tasso said to Bristow.

"No. Just speculating. What's outside that wall behind the platform?"

"A courtyard. Well guarded. The prisoners will arrive there."

"And where does the fire exit door lead?"

"Into a corridor, with two men on duty."

"And the corridor's entrance?"

"It is on the street. A narrow door. Cannot be opened from the outside—like the fire exit on your aisle. Everything has been checked—table, lectern, chairs, walls, floor, and ceiling. The inspection ended at ten o'clock this morning. You approve?"

"Very much. You must have had major problems to face."

"We still have, my friend. No, thank you, I won't sit down. I like to move around." Tasso noted Bristow's second glance at the somber-faced man who sat so silently in the row in front of him. "Lawyers," Tasso said. "One for each of the criminals. They brought the suggestion for this meeting to our public-relations department." He spoke with distaste.

"So they were the link between the terrorists?" To Karen, Bristow said, "I wondered how those two got together on this idea—they weren't likely to be in the same cell."

Tasso almost smiled. "Not even in the same prison."

"There's Aliotto!" Karen exclaimed as the Italian rose to look around the room.

"He arrived early," Tasso said. "Insisted on that seat."

It lay on the right-hand side of the aisle, a front-row seat as Bristow had noted, with an empty chair beside Aliotto, presumably for Karen. But no chair reserved for any translator—Aliotto's last word, no doubt.

"I never saw him when we came in," Karen said. She had been too absorbed by a terrorist's relatives—obviously a well-to-do family: it wasn't poverty that had induced his taste for violence.

"I did," Bristow acknowledged, "but he seemed occupied with some other journalists." A poor excuse, perhaps. How else did he say that the less Karen saw of Aliotto the better?

Aliotto caught sight of Karen, waved, gestured to the empty seat beside him. She rose to wave back and shook her head. Out of custom, Bristow got to his feet, too.

Tasso seized that moment to slip the Beretta from his own pocket into Bristow's. With a side glance at Karen, who was now signaling her refusal of a front-row view, he murmured, "As you said, your responsibility." Then he moved down the aisle toward the platform, taking out his small transceiver.

Aliotto stood irresolute for a long moment, gave up with a small wave, and sat down.

"Perhaps I should have gone over and explained," Karen said as she and Bristow resumed their seats.

"He damn well should have come here and talked with you," Bristow told her. Aliotto hadn't wanted to risk leaving that front-row position. *Insisted on that seat*—Tasso's words. It had puzzled Tasso, as it now puzzled Bristow. His attention switched to the doorway, where a janitor was carrying in two extra chairs. Behind him, a young helper brought two more. "Are we packing more people in?" Bristow looked at his watch; the meeting ought to be starting any minute.

Quickly, the janitor placed one chair at Aliotto's right and the other behind it. There was still ample leeway for movement on that aisle. But Tasso, on the other side of the room, disagreed. And vehemently. He broke off his talk on the transceiver to shout, "No, no! Out, out!" Then some report was being sent him, important enough to hold all his attention, and he was listening intently with a hand over his free ear to blot out the buzz of comment around him.

The janitor's helper obeyed, carrying his chairs back

into the hall, standing aside as two latecomers entered—
young, dark-haired, of medium height, and dressed in
faded U.S. Army field jackets. They sat down in the nearest available space, which was logical enough. The janitor
shrugged his shoulders—the extra chairs were now occupied—and left. The young men seemed to realize they
were not in the section that had been allocated to them.
The one beside Aliotto rose, stared down at the journalist
and then at the empty seat on Aliotto's left, frowned as
he retreated to the third row. The other had bent down
to pick up something he had dropped; then, straightening
his back, with his hands deep in his pockets, he followed
his friend. They paused before they sat down on the chairs
next to the lawyers, surveyed the curious journalists with
a truculent scowl. The frown was still deep on the first
man's face; it cleared as his eyes rested on Karen.
Bristow, studying them covertly, felt his spine stiffen.
They both took their seats with a quiet phrase exchanged,
and the second man turned his head slowly to glance over
his shoulder. He looked at Karen, only shifted his gaze
when Bristow returned his stare. What had caught their
interest—a pretty face, or a woman journalist? Or what?
Bristow's tension grew.

"The girl's relatives, I suppose," Karen was saying.
"Why the glowers and the hard looks? They seem to be
prepared to dislike everyone. But they'd better take off
those heavy jackets—it's warm in here." She removed
hers and wondered why Peter, who helped her ease her
arm from its sleeve, made no comment. Today, he was
strangely silent; quite unlike yesterday, when they had
stayed in her room most of the time and worked and talked
and laughed together. A good day, she thought, a wonderful day. And tomorrow, she thought, we'll be separating. I will go back to Washington, and he will start his
vacation. And I'll hate that, she admitted, and felt suddenly desolate. She busied herself with her notebook,
propped it on top of her bag on her knees. With pencil in
hand, she said, "Well, I'm ready for Martita and Georgio.

She's the meek one, Schleeman told me. Just follows Georgio in everything he does. And did." Their past record was appalling. Yesterday, when she had studied the detailed accounts of their exploits, she had been horrified. Brazen cruelty, senseless violence, obscene delight in destruction; and all to be forgotten, a thing of the past. Repentance and forgiveness instead of hate and vengeance.

"Here they come," Bristow said as voices and footsteps mingled in the hall. He grasped Karen's hand for a moment, gave her a smile that reassured her: not her fault if he had seemed so buried in this thoughts. He worries too much about me, she decided, and was both pleased and distressed by the idea.

All heads had turned toward the entrance. First, two uniformed guards appeared, armed with machine pistols, and halted at each side of the doorway. Then came a young girl—slender, with long brown hair falling straight over her shoulders—flanked by two middle-aged women in uniforms as solemn as their faces. The trio walked past Aliotto, mounted the narrow steps that led up to the platform. White blouse and wide gray skirt, Karen noted; hair held in place by a red band worn low on her forehead; a pretty girl, looking even younger than her nineteen years, fragile and helpless, almost angelic as she sat down and clasped her hands on her lap. So this was Martita, who had shot a Milanese newspaperman in both his knees after he had fallen helpless to the pavement with a chest wound. Her two guards, tall and heavy by comparison, took their posts against the wall. And, thought Karen, there wasn't a man in this room who didn't notice the contrast and feel his sympathies tilt away from law and order. Except for Inspector Tasso and those few who had read the detailed facts of Martita's past achievements. If I hadn't, she reminded herself, my sympathies would have tilted completely.

Giorgio and his two guards, capable-looking males in uniform, had entered almost unnoticed. He was tall and thin, with closely cut brown hair and a neat beard. A handsome young man, erect and smart in his walk; a decided young man, Karen thought as she watched his brusque movements; and confident. He sat down, reached over the small table to touch Martita's hair and smile encouragement. As his guards assumed their positions against the wall, Giorgio straightened his shoulders, began speaking. For both of them, it seemed.

He gave their names, their occupations (Martita had been a movie extra; he had been a philosophy student), and outlined their association with a group of five other dedicated revolutionaries—a section of the Red Brigade. He spoke of their beliefs, their hopes; even listed some of their deeds. But now he admitted they had been wrong in such action. In prison he had come to the conviction that violence was no solution, would not further the cause of justice for the poor. When released, he and Martita would marry and return to a normal life. They still believed in their opinions. It was the methods they had used, along with their comrades, that were wrong. He was convinced that only peaceful means could bring a better future for everyone.

"Do you need translation?" Bristow had asked as this speech began, and Karen had shaken her head. Giorgio spoke clearly, at a measured rate, easily understandable even for her Italian. Besides, she thought, how can Peter translate when he keeps watching the relatives—not the brother and sister directly in front of him, but the two cousins at the other end of the row? "I'll have the transcript," she whispered back, and bless Inspector Tasso for that privilege.

Giorgio's speech was ended. Martita sat without moving, her Mona Lisa smile in place. The questions began and chaos broke loose. Tasso, over by the door, shouted, "Gentlemen, gentlemen! One question at a time! Each of you in turn—and keep your questions to three minutes. We begin with the front row." He pointed to Aliotto. Sanity having been established, he ascended the steps and stood behind the lectern to survey the room.

So now, thought Bristow, we have Tasso and the recording expert at the lectern, a couple of male guards within reach of Giorgio, two female guards to the rear of sweet Miss Silence, two men with machine pistols at the door, the door itself safely closed, and God knows how many men in the hall and the street—not to mention the two armed men in the corridor outside the fire exit. No one can say Tasso didn't take precautions—he worries more than I do. Strange, though, the difference in the reactions of the two pairs of relatives.

Giorgio's brother and sister listened intently. The girl needed comforting, wept, was quieted by her brother even if he seemed about to give way to tears himself. Martita's cousins were bored; they sat slouched and unmoving, eyes straight ahead and unseeing, kept a stolid silence. The one who had frowned was now expressionless, held with obvious disinterest a small cassette recorder that he probably realized was useless to catch any words beyond twelve feet away. He ought to have stayed in that front-row seat beside Aliotto. The other had both hands deep in his pockets, ignoring the heat of the room as well as its voices. With their family connections, Bristow would have expected these two to be the more emotional pair: Martita came originally from south of Naples—an Italian father, a Spanish mother. Giorgio was from the north—his people lived in Turin.

Yes, thought Bristow, a strange contrast in their reactions. And his sense of unease deepened. There was some peculiar logic in the behavior of Martita's cousins. They had entered this room quick and alert, their eyes interested in every detail. For a brief minute they sat on the two extra chairs at the front and then, still observant, moved back. Too observant, he was convinced. He glanced around the room—everything was normal, everyone was engrossed by the questions and answers that were calmly spoken—and felt his uneasiness growing.

Suddenly, in the street outside, there was an explosion. The room shook, the ceiling lights trembled. All heads turned in alarm, all voices silenced. From the street again—staccato bursts of rapid fire.

It has begun, thought Bristow. Not here, out there. Quickly he grasped Karen and looked toward Martita's cousins. The man with the small recorder no longer slouched—he sat erect, the cassette recorder held in both hands, his thumb raised, his eyes on the platform. The second man was rising. Martita's arm shot straight up, her fist clenched.

At once, the man brought his hand out of his pocket, aiming his pistol at Giorgio and fired. Giorgio fell as Martita leaped sideways, leaving a clear field for the second and third bullets to strike her two guards, and jumped down from the platform. The extra chair beside Aliotto exploded violently.

Flames and smoke, a shaft of fire along the front row of seats, shouts changing to screams. In a matter of seconds, hell had broken loose.

As Giorgio fell, Bristow shoved Karen face down on the floor, dropped on one knee. His Beretta was out as the assassin swung around to take aim at Karen. Bristow fired first, caught the man's chest, sent him staggering back, his wild fourth bullet buried in the ceiling. His companion hurled his only weapon at Bristow—the bogus recorder with its remote control—and made a bolt for the entrance, was lost in a spreading cloud of black smoke. Bristow dodged—a bad moment when he thought it could be a grenade—and hauled Karen to her feet, pulling her toward the fire exit. Martita was already there, thrusting the door open, the hem of her skirt lifted to cover her mouth.

Screams were mixed with moans, shouts with yells of command. The foul-smelling smoke that engulfed half the room was spreading. So were the flames from the front row of chairs. Bristow, gripping Karen's wrist, saw Martita disappear into the corridor. Two armed policemen out there, Tasso had said. Martita would have the shortest

escape on record, he thought grimly, and shouldered the
door open.

In the corridor there was another kind of smoke, a
haze: gas of some kind. Two policemen lay motionless
on the floor, weapons gone. Bristow, shoving his pistol
into his pocket, clamped a hand over Karen's mouth.
"Hold your breath!" He held his own as he urged her at
a run toward the street's exit. No door was left, just a
gaping hole where the first explosion had taken place.
Shots were still being fired out there in heavy bursts. So
he halted just inside the demolished doorway, removed
his hand from Karen's face. "We can breathe," he told
her. And choke and cough, as the fresh air cleared their
lungs.

The firing ceased. They could step out into another
small scene of bedlam. He looked around. No sign of
Martita, but two young men in jeans and loose shirts were
stretched at the doorstep of a *trattoria* across the street.
Like most restaurants in this quarter, the *trattoria* had its
CLOSED MONDAY notice displayed, now dangling from a
shattered window. It had been the way of retreat for two
of Martita's comrades, the unlucky ones abandoned to
die on the sidewalk—perhaps the place where they had
gathered to set off the first explosion and then attack the
corridor with gas grenades. On the street itself, three
men—probably detectives—were scattered over the
pavement, wounded and bloody, moving feebly. A fourth
lay as dead as the two terrorists who had covered Martita's escape. Sweet, helpless Martita had managed it.
Managed it in more senses than one, Bristow thought.

Karen took a few unsteady steps and slumped against
him. He caught her, held her, looked for a place to let her
rest. The curb and sidewalk were littered with shattered
glass and splintered wood; jagged fragments lay on a pane-
less window sill behind them. But there he could sweep
the shards aside with his sad-looking jacket. With his arm
supporting her, they sat on the edge of the sill. Her face,
like his, was smoke-streaked. She had lost her jacket. Her

shoulder bag had twisted its strap around her bare arm, cut into it painfully, making her wince as he freed her. Tightly held in her other hand was her notebook. She raised it, said in a small voice, "I can't let go. Peter—" He eased her fingers loose. That's the wrist I gripped, he thought. He rubbed it gently, wondering when the bruises would start showing.

"Sorry," he said. "I guess I was desperate." He looked up from the wrist to find her watching him. He tightened his hold of her waist, his other arm went around her. He kissed her gently. She didn't draw back, didn't resist. He kissed her again, long and hard.

Other survivors were stumbling out from the hallway's entrance. The first ambulances and a fire truck arrived; police swarmed around, cleared the street of people who were now venturing out, sent them back inside their houses and shops. Karen's head rested against his shoulder, his arms still enfolding her.

For almost half an hour they watched the turmoil as it gradually decreased into businesslike movements, commands, trained efficiency. "We'll soon be out of here," he told Karen. And he thought, as he looked at the smudges on her cheek and felt the grime streaking his own face, it was one helluva place to give your first kiss to the girl you damn well intended to marry. Then his lips tightened. I nearly lost her, he thought, I nearly lost her.

A voice said, "Thank God, you're safe! Should have known." It was Giovanni, elegant as ever, relaxing into a wide grin. "Levinson sent a car. Come on—can you walk?" he asked a startled Karen. "If not, we'll carry you. The car's just beyond the roadblock." He gestured to the end of the street, where the curious were already gathering behind a barricade.

"News does get around," Bristow said, eyeing the crowd. He handed his jacket and Karen's bag and notebook to Giovanni, renewed his firm support of Karen. "We'll make it."

You certainly have, thought Giovanni. A hundred

questions he'd like to ask. Later, later . . . He began clearing a path for them through the groups of worried officials, of journalists still in shock, dodging the hurrying stretcher-bearers, steering clear of the injured, avoiding the fire hoses, and hoped that Karen hadn't noticed the burned remains being carried in body bags out of the hall.

16

They entered the Imperial by a rear door, Giovanni guiding them through a labyrinth of corridors. "Levinson suggested this," he told them. "Thought you could do without a grand entrance through the lobby." Karen nodded gratefully. She hadn't spoken on the journey back to the hotel—none of them had. She was in shock, Bristow was buried in thought, Giovanni was tactful. She felt chilled, even in the midday heat with the warmth of Peter's arm around her.

"Where's Levinson?" Bristow demanded when they had reached Karen's rooms. "Still with that businessman?" He was bitter and didn't disguise it.

"A big fish. Levinson hooked him in midstream and is now playing him into the bank. He'll be netted soon, another hour or so. It took us five months to make the catch." His explanation ended, Giovanni turned on the TV and chose the most comfortable chair. "I'll wait here."

Bristow, at the door of Karen's bedroom, said sharply, "Not necessary." Then he added, "Sorry. Thanks for what you've done, Giovanni. A great help." My nerves must be a bit shattered, he thought. Levinson might not have appeared himself, but at least he kept us in mind.

Giovanni settled deeper into the chair. "I'll wait," he repeated as Bristow left. A lot of questions to ask, and Levinson would want to hear the answers.

In the bedroom, Karen stood paralyzed before the long mirror. "Look at me! Just look!" She gave a shaky laugh. "And you kissed a face like this!"

Bristow caught his own reflection in the glass and shook his head over the picture he, too, presented. "A pretty pair, aren't we?"

Karen's laughter was breaking into tears. "You saved my life."

"You'd have made it out yourself. The exit was near enough." And was it her gratitude that had let him kiss her?

His brusque reply steadied her. "You chose to sit there. You wouldn't let me take the chair I was supposed to have. Beside Aliotto." She shuddered. Her voice weakened. "Those men—those poor men! I don't remember—not much—not now. Just the noise, the screams. Oh, God, it was hideous." She began to weep. "Without you, Peter—" She broke off, tried to regain control.

"We'll clean up," he said gently, "and then we'll talk. Have a shower, Karen. Or a bath." Play it cool, he warned himself. Gratitude was not enough. Yet, in that shattered street, suddenly safe together, he had felt as he drew her close that she, too, knew the swift, overwhelming emotion that had mastered him. But he had been wrong.

She turned away from the mirror. "A shower," she decided, then stood irresolute.

"Steady enough?"

"Almost normal. Just slow-thinking and freezing."

He pulled the quilted cover from a bed, dropped it on a chair near the bathroom door. "Wrap yourself in that when you come out of the shower. I'll find some brandy and leave it on the dressing table. Okay?"

"Peter—" She looked at him.

"Yes?"

She touched his shoulder, slid her arms around it. Then she reached up and kissed him. "I owe you two," she said softly, and kissed him again.

"Look," Giovanni said when Bristow returned to the sitting room, "I've questions to ask and then a call to make. Levinson wants to know."

Bristow took his room keys from his jacket's pocket and tossed them over. From the other pocket he drew out the Beretta and placed it on the desk. The jacket, after a last glance at its black stains and wrenched seams, he dropped in the wastepaper basket. "Fetch me some clothes from my room after you have your talk with Levinson, will you? Pants and shirt will do."

"What's your report for Levinson?"

"Tasso will give him that."

"He's in the hospital. He was thrown by the explosion, broke his shoulder. Minor burns, too. Would have been worse if he hadn't been blown flat on the platform. How did it happen? Everyone was searched, weren't they?"

"We were. Thoroughly. I thought about that, all the way back to the hotel."

"Come up with anything?"

"Two chairs were brought in by a janitor just before Martita's 'cousins' arrived. One was placed in the front row, on the aisle, and the other behind it. They were near the door. The cousins sat on them. Briefly. Then moved farther to the rear."

Giovanni nodded: the scene was fixed in his mind.

"The gun must have been taped under the chair in the second row and picked up by the man who did the killing. The explosive device was beneath the seat of the other chair, set off by the second man."

"Remote control," Giovanni said. "How?"

"Concealed in a small cassette recorder he was carrying." Bristow was searching through the refrigerator's stock of miniature bottles. He found two with brandy, picked up a glass, and headed for the bedroom. He halted at its door, pointed to the Beretta. "Had to use it. Trouble ahead, I guess."

Giovanni stared openly. "Did you smuggle it into the room?" How? What about the search?

"Tasso did that for me. Thank him, will you?"

"But you didn't kill the man."

"Chest wound. The other escaped by the main hall."

"Attempted to escape. He was shot dead."

"Pity. He might have talked. Eventually."

"A terrorist talk—after Giorgio was killed as an example?"

"Terrorists . . . I wonder. I'm still puzzling out that one. Two questions for Levinson. When did Martita's lawyer suggest that meeting to the police? When was the suggestion accepted? A timetable is what I need. Can you get it?"

"I'll try." Giovanni was astounded. "If not terrorists, who else?"

Bristow said nothing, carried the brandy and the glass into the bedroom, and returned within a minute to start stripping off his shirt. Giovanni was on his feet, but not ready to leave. He had poured out a stiff Scotch for Bristow, placed it beside the Beretta.

"Thanks," Bristow said. He took a long draft; it had as much effect as water. "Guess I was three drinks below par," he admitted.

"Who else?" Giovanni insisted.

"That's for you and your friends to find out. I've no facts. Just guesses from what I saw."

"They'd be useful to us."

"All I can tell you is this. The bomb was carefully placed to hit the first row where Aliotto was sitting. And Karen should have been there. Her empty chair puzzled one of the men. He moved back to the third row, caught sight of Karen, spoke to the gunman, who looked her way, marked her position on the fourth row. After three rapid shots at the platform, he swung around and took aim at her. I spoiled it." Bristow finished his drink. "That's what I know now. Hindsight's invaluable, isn't it? Pure twenty-twenty vision. At the time, I couldn't figure it out—just sensed something odd, menacing." Bristow's anger increased. He slammed the empty glass back on the table. "I had all the small pieces of the puzzle, couldn't fit them together and prevent the killing."

But no one else had put the small pieces together, hadn't even noticed them, thought Giovanni. As for the killing—it would have taken place. Not Giorgio's perhaps, but possibly Bristow's. And Tasso's. Giovanni could see these two, trying to outflank the two "cousins." Which brought him sharply back to the question that needed an answer. "So you ask, would terrorists have a reason to kill Aliotto and Karen? And your reply is a loud 'No!' Right?"

"You've got it." Bristow was discarding trousers and shirt on top of his jacket. "Now get the hell out, Giovanni. And remember that timetable!" He was into the small bathroom, turning on its shower as Giovanni closed the sitting-room door. The cold water felt good, cleared his thoughts.

There was yet one question, perhaps unanswerable: why Karen? Aliotto could have been eliminated because he was useless: no more information on Vasek was obtainable. And dead men could bear no witness. But Karen?

Twice, ineffectually, the Bulgarians had tried to abduct her. She was still a source of information—their only source—so why kill her? Senseless murder was the terrorist's way, but a trained hitman did not strike at random. So why Karen?

He scrubbed himself clean, toweled himself briskly. His body felt fine—a stiffness in one shoulder where he must have wrenched it and God knew when, and little enough—but his mind had bogged down in that question. He could find no solution.

*   *   *

It was fully two hours before Giovanni returned and found Bristow relaxing on the couch with softly played music from the radio and a tray of sandwiches and coffee on the table beside him. "Thanks," Bristow said, taking the gray flannels and checked shirt from Giovanni. He dropped the towel tucked around his waist and pulled on his clothes.

"How is she? Asleep?"

"Deep into it. Didn't even stay awake for her sandwich."

"Haven't had my own lunch. D'you mind?" Giovanni lifted a sandwich, watched Bristow as he finished dressing. With respect. He had been right about several things, the young man thought, and I hope I look as fit as he does when I'm his age. "How d'you keep in shape?"

"Worrying," Bristow said with a grin. "I'm a world champion in that department. So what's new?"

"A lot. But first, your boss wants to have a chat with you. Scrambled, of course. So be in Levinson's office at five o'clock. On the nose. Can't keep a call from Langley waiting."

Menlo... "Then you'll have to stay with Karen." I'm not leaving her alone, not for Menlo or anyone else. "Who'll see me through Levinson's gate?"

"The Contessa will be airing her dog at four-forty-five. Okay?"

Bristow glanced at his watch. "I'll leave here at four-thirty. That gives us about half an hour."

Between bites on a second sandwich, Giovanni began. First, the timetable Bristow had wanted. The lawyers for Giorgio and Martita had made the suggestion for the meeting three weeks ago when the two terrorists (Giorgio already beginning to talk, Martita concurring with everything he said) had been brought together in Rome for further questioning. Together, because that is what Martita stipulated. She would give no testimony without Giorgio beside her. It seemed logical—they had been lovers for three years and were still in love. When they were together in Rome, the lawyers argued, why not let them face a few carefully chosen journalists? The prisoners had already agreed, so why not use this opportunity for good public relations? Giorgio and Martita would be seen to be in excellent health, contrary to rumors, and make their statements freely, not under duress. Ten days ago, the authorities had consented. Four Italian journalists had been approached, and at the request of one—made last Monday, a week ago exactly—an American journalist was also given permission to attend in his company. A good idea, public relations had decided: foreign coverage, particularly in the United States where there was a large population of Italian descent, was always important. "That's it," Giovanni ended. "Any help?"

Bristow nodded. The initial plan had been made long before the two lawyers had approached the authorities. Ten days ago, their suggestion was accepted. Last Monday, Aliotto had phoned Schleeman with his invitation for Karen. The call had been genuine, probably; made in good faith. But by Tuesday, Aliotto was intimidated, his mistress held hostage by the Bulgarians. For on that day Vasek had telephoned him and sensed that something was far wrong. Why else had Vasek warned Karen about Aliotto? Vulnerable. That had been Vasek's word.

Giovanni repeated, "Any help?"

"A lot of help." As Giovanni waited expectantly, Bristow relented. "Originally, the plan was a terrorist idea and simple: kill Giorgio as a warning to others who'd like to talk, and explode a bomb to cover Martita's escape. Then last Monday, certainly by Tuesday, the professionals muscled in—someone talked about it, perhaps Martita's lawyer; who knows?—the Communists have their connections. The Bulgarians proposed a joint operation, bigger and better and with sure chance of success. Quick planning, but the professionals have been trained for that; they've money behind them; they've contacts; they've people they can use like that janitor. So Martita and her friends listened. The lawyers—one, at least—were the intermediaries. The Bulgarians added Aliotto and Karen to their target list. Everyone would believe they had died in another terrorist attack. Smart operators."

Giovanni sat very still. "A joint operation," he said at last. "That explains it. Four known terrorists took over the *trattoria* opposite the police station this early morning, just as its owner and family were closing the place. That outside explosion must have been prepared days before—they used plastic and remote control. They rushed the entrance, threw in a gas bomb while people were picking themselves up from the street. Two terrorists were killed covering Martita's escape. They've been identified—members of her old group, all Italian. The man who detonated the bomb inside the room had a passport as a Czech tourist who arrived on Friday from Vienna. The gunman you wounded arrived from Zurich on Saturday —his passport says he's a Bulgarian student. So international terrorism is now the accepted explanation. But—" Giovanni paused, his smile growing. "You and I saw the car that the Czech tourist had rented. On Via Ludovisi, just after we left Armando's."

You had it traced, thought Bristow. The car that had come too close to Karen as it had slowed. "Good for you, Giovanni."

"Just one thing—can't figure it—why were Aliotto and Karen targets for the KGB? That's what it boils down to, doesn't it? Czechs and Bulgarians are their surrogates."

"Have you heard of a KGB defector who was recently stationed in Prague?"

"Sure. Rumor is he's around—pretty near here, at least."

"The day before he got out of Prague, he spoke with Aliotto. And with Karen. They were there, covering the Convocation for Peace."

So Aliotto and Karen had been marked for questioning, Giovanni thought. And when Aliotto was no longer needed, he had been terminated to keep his mouth permanently shut. But Karen— "Does she have information about the defector?"

"Obviously they think she has."

"Then why kill her? Why not another attempt to snatch her?"

"That," said Bristow, "is the solid blank wall I've been facing for the last few hours." He looked at his watch— ten minutes before he must leave. He moved to the bedroom door, opened it quietly. Karen was still asleep, just as he had left her, with her head tilted sideways and her hair soft and loose on the pillow. The coverlet had slipped to the floor. He picked it up, discarded it—too warm now, he decided. He drew up a sheet to cover her from the air conditioning, stood for a long minute remembering the touch of her smooth skin, the curve of her breasts and hips. He resisted kissing her awake—sleep was what she needed. One hell of a day to discover you're in love, he thought as he closed the door behind him. "Tell Karen I'll be back here as soon as possible. Don't leave this room, Giovanni."

"I'll be here." Giovanni laid Bristow's room key on the desk. "Do you mind if I keep this near me?" he asked, picking up the Beretta. "Don't worry about the bullet they found in the Bulgarian. Levinson went over to the hospital to see Tasso. He'll get you off that hook." But there were others, he thought, watching Bristow's set face. "I'll guard her well," he said very quietly.

Near the small gate at the side of the embassy's grounds, the Contessa and her midget French poodle were having their usual battle of wills. She won. She coaxed it as far as the gate just as Bristow reached her, and had it open to let him step inside. "They know you by this time," she murmured, smiled sweetly as he closed the gate, and walked on with the poodle now straining toward the curb.

She was right. The gardeners let him pass with a friendly nod. He reached Levinson's office without delay. That came at five o'clock: Menlo had to postpone his call, they were told. He was in conference. Sorry. Six o'clock, he would be on the phone. Definitely.

"So we wait," Levinson said. Bristow's face was unreadable. "Something unexpected must have hit Menlo. The conference wasn't scheduled when I talked with him this afternoon. I told him what I had learned about today's bomb and bullet attack, which wasn't too much. Why don't you fill me in now, Pete? A useful way to spend the next hour."

For you, not for me. But I owe you. And blast Menlo, why couldn't he have phoned one sentence to me at the Imperial, said, There will be an hour's delay—just one small sentence, no security broken, and I could have waited at the hotel, kept watch? Menlo, Menlo . . . whatever your reason, it had better be good. "Okay," Bristow said and began his account of that morning.

At its end, Levinson asked the same question as Giovanni: "Why Karen Cornell?"

"That's plagued me all afternoon."

"The Bulgarian thug definitely aimed at her?"

"Yes."

Both were silent. "There's *got* to be a reason," Levinson said at last. "It was all too well planned."

Another silence. Suddenly, there was a glimmering of an idea in Bristow's mind. The Vienna cassettes—stolen from the Farrago file? "God," he said softly and prayed he was wrong.

"Yes?" asked the quick-eyed Levinson.

Bristow shook his head. "Probably nothing. I'm edgy, I guess. Always a bad time to make judgments." He looked at his watch, then across the office to Levinson's priority phone. Another five minutes to wait.

Levinson said, "Don't worry about your girl. She's in good hands."

"I know. Giovanni's efficient."

"Quite a surprise package?" Levinson asked with a grin.

Bristow nodded. "And useful. Are all your agents so cosy with the Rome police?"

"None of the others have Tasso for an uncle." Levinson enjoyed the momentary astonishment on Bristow's face. "And what's your impression of our Contessa?"

"She's trained her dog pretty well to fake disobedience on command."

Levinson's smile burst into a laugh.

"Why did she enlist with you, Mike? Or perhaps you co-opted her—useful connections like Giovanni. What motivates her, anyway? Must be something deeper than a widow consoling herself with fun and games."

"Much deeper." Levinson had turned serious. He hesitated. "Off the record, Pete—"

"Sure."

"I told you her husband was a racing-car driver killed in an accident. True. What I didn't say was how his car went out of control. It exploded. He was with Italian Intelligence. A Marxist-Leninist group got at him before he could nail them. The Contessa spent two years grieving and then enlisted with us. That's her motivation—the Irish have long memories and don't forgive in a hurry. But that's off the record, Pete," Levinson reminded him. "And so is the fact that Giovanni had a second uncle— a journalist in Milan. He was shot in the back as he left his home one morning by another far-left group. Italians have long memories, too." Levinson watched Bristow closely. "Does that reassure you? They have a lot in common, those two; they make one helluva good team. Last month, they—"

The telephone rang. It was six o'clock. Bristow was on his feet, the receiver in his hand, gesturing to Levinson to stay in the room. This could be a crisis call.

Menlo's voice said, "Peter? Listen—I want you back here. As soon as possible. Bring Miss Cornell with you."

No more talk of Junior? Bristow spoke quickly. "She's leaving tomorrow. The one daily flight to New York. I'll take it, too."

"No. Neither of you. They'll know her time of departure from Rome, arrival in New York. We've arranged other transportation—the same way you went in. Be at the airfield before midnight."

"What about travel papers? Permission?"

"You'll both be expected. Space is available. You'll be met at this end."

"So you know they tried to kill her today?"

"We heard about the explosion and Aliotto. Was there another attempt?" Menlo's voice had quickened.

"There was." Bristow's voice was hard. "So someone broke into the files, got away with that—that special material."

"You'll hear the details on your return and some—"

"How did it happen?" Bristow cut in.

"You'll hear. And there are some leads, too—could be good."

Nothing at this moment seemed good to Bristow. Controlling anger and frustration, he said, "We'll make that flight."

"And leave the hotel quietly," Menlo warned him.

"No need to tell me that," Bristow said savagely. Not with the Vienna cassettes gone. "When was the break-in?"

"You'll hear," Menlo said for the third time.

"When was it? I need to know."

"Saturday evening. Now, can you get hold of Levinson? I'll meet you at the—"

"He's here." And end of conversation as far as I'm concerned, thought Bristow, his anger mounting. He was out of the door before a startled Levinson could even begin speaking to Menlo.

17

EVER SINCE SATURDAY EVENING AND THE DISCOVERY THAT the Vienna cassettes had been stolen, Menlo had been a driven man. It was now Sunday afternoon, and he had many of the pieces of the puzzle fitted together. Not all. Just enough to give him an understanding of what had happened and how. But not even the fact that some important leads had been discovered could sweeten the taste of defeat. He had taken full precautions. He had been outwitted. He had failed.

Deeply depressed, he faced his desk, pulled the notes he had made in front of him, picked up a pencil. At hand were the recorders to play back the tapes he had made of today's interviews. He could recall much of them without benefit of machine—his anger had sharpened his memory—but a total review of events was needed, item by item, and in sequence. His notes required editing, must be ready for typing into a report which he'd deliver by Wednesday. He'd get them into good order, add some flesh to their bare bones, make the story as complete as

202

possible. And it was quite a story, he thought grimly as he began reading.

It had begun late Friday evening, just after Bristow left for Rome. Menlo called Doyle of Security, reached him at his home, requested an early meeting—most urgent—for next morning.

On Saturday, at 7:00 A.M., Doyle met with Menlo. The two Vienna cassettes were marked, treated for electronic response, placed beside the Farrago file in its locked cabinet, on which a notice was posted: OUT OF COMMISSION. Round-the-clock guards were arranged.

At ten o'clock, the first man on duty was installed outside the entrance to the file room. A small table and chair, a detection machine for any electronic signals, a telephone—and the guard, with notebook and pen and a Thermos of coffee, was all set for his eight-hour shift. Adequate precautions, Menlo judged. No cassette could be carried past the detector without the alarm sounding. But it was with some misgivings that he had used the original tapes instead of substitutions. If he were dealing with the Prague cassettes, he wouldn't even have considered the idea of using them as bait—they were Top Security. The Vienna tapes contained useful information, but of a lower grade. If stolen, they might put a young woman at risk, but they wouldn't endanger the United States. The clinching argument in Menlo's mind was of less importance except to himself—a vision of a thief being caught with only worthless cassettes in his pocket. The man would maintain he had taken nothing of value, and claim that blank tapes amounted to blatant entrapment. We'll give him something to steal, Menlo decided grimly, and he will be stopped dead in his tracks. The Vienna cassettes won't fall into enemy hands. No thief can pass the guard's table undetected.

Ten-fifteen. Menlo asked everyone in the European unit in his Section of Counterdisinformation to step into his office. Susan Attley, Denis Shaw, Manuel Domingus, Jan van Trompf arrived. Robert Reid did not work on

Saturdays. Wallace Fairbairn was due—so Denis Shaw reported—at noon. Menlo reassured them that they had no cause for alarm. Some precautions were being taken, a nuisance but necessary. What were they working on?

Each gave a brief answer. Except Shaw, who could never be brief, in either his questions or his explanations. He and Fairbairn were having difficulties in tracing the route of a lie, first published in India, then broadcast from Iran, next appearing in Lebanon, and making its European entry in Athens. From Athens it must have traveled through Central Europe—newspapers there yet to be identified—and arrived via Paris in London. (From the initial "It is reported" it had graduated into "It now has been confirmed.") It was the mid-European newspapers that Shaw and Fairbairn were busy trying to track down. "A long job," Shaw predicted.

Menlo had let him run on, even if the rest of the group were clearly bored. (Anything that Shaw or Fairbairn said was worth noting.) Then he cut short any more explanation from Shaw by saying that—judging from their stated projects today—they would not be inconvenienced by the precautions taken. None of them needed to use the fifth cabinet in the file room, which had been posted *Out of Commission*.

"That's one of the Eastern European cabinets," Shaw said. He looked astonished. The others were curious, too.

"Before Bristow left, some highly sensitive material was placed in that cabinet. Two cassettes, actually. I am making sure they will still be there when he returns. The precautions are an insurance against any unauthorized entry. So is the guard on duty."

"But none of us—" Attley began, highly indignant.

"None of you," Menlo agreed. "But there may be others who seek entry to the file room. So wear your identifications. That is all. I hope I have explained the situation and calmed any fears."

"There has already been some talk about the guard," Attley said. "Everyone's a bit upset."

"There was, is, and always will be talk. Speculation is part of your job. But keep it focused on your work. And"—he looked pointedly at the clock—"it is time to get back to it." As they trooped out, Menlo said, "Susan, will you tell Bob Reid about our security arrangements on Monday? And Shaw—you'll see Fairbairn. When?"

"At noon. We're lunching together, and then we'll—"

"Good. You inform him, will you?" And I bet you will—in full detail, thought Menlo, as the door closed.

It was now ten-forty-five. Menlo began reading, for the third time, the dossiers on Shaw and Fairbairn. Nothing there that was derogatory. Perhaps he was following the wrong trail. Both men had good records. Well-adjusted, no family problems, no indications of financial troubles, no drugs, no public drunkenness, no exceptional sex patterns. Work was good. Just two normal citizens devoting their careers to public service and getting more criticism than thanks for it, too. Which made Menlo's task all the more distasteful.

Hard to believe that either of them was the mole that Vasek had mentioned. Yet, there *had* been someone who had dug into the Farrago file and sent information to the KGB. Someone who had known Bristow was responsible for that file. How else could Farrago, a colonel in the KGB, have learned of Bristow's interest or been so certain that Bristow would recognize his name and value? An inside job obviously, someone working in Bristow's unit: the others in the section did not know about his interest in Farrago. If Fairbairn and Shaw had come under suspicion, it was for two valid reasons: they were the only ones in the European unit who knew that an envelope, with a Czech censor's seal, had been delivered by Bristow; they were the only ones who had seen Bristow when he was with Karen Cornell.

One of them could be the mole and the other innocent. A dupe. Who was directing the mole, controlling him? That was another question. First things first: the mole was the objective at present. Damned if I'll let one hide in my section, thought Menlo as he rose stiffly and paced around his room to get the circulation flowing. He could use his good standing here to make valuable contacts in other departments. I'll be twice damned if I let him tunnel his way into dangerously sensitive areas with my people as his cover.

The back pain had eased—either his walk around the room or three minutes of solid cussing had relieved the strain—and he could sit down in time for his prearranged call from Bristow, who had arrived in Italy. Bristow's news was definitely unexpected. Josef Vasek was in Rome, had contacted Karen Cornell. Vasek's estimate of safe arrival in the United States was two weeks. Two weeks for a mole to continue uncaught? That justified all Menlo's precautions. Relieved, he went to lunch.

And met Shaw leaving the cafeteria.

"No Fairbairn?" Menlo asked.

"He's here. Arrived at noon. Had some phone calls to make. We'll be nosing the grindstone for the rest of the day. Probably into the night."

"It's a hard life," Menlo said and watched Shaw hurry off. Some phone calls? To whom?

At two o'clock, Menlo checked with the guard on duty at the file room. His notes logged several visitors. Shaw had visited the room. But no Fairbairn.

Menlo wondered about that. Fairbairn had been here since noon. Wasn't he curious about the setup at the file room door? "Is this complete?" Menlo asked as he returned the guard's logbook.

"Mr. Fairbairn did stop by, but he wasn't in the room. Just exchanged a word or two. Didn't think I needed to mark it down."

"Note every visit to your post. A full record is what we need. Got that?"

"Yes, sir." But Menlo could almost hear the man thinking he was dealing with another mucking fusspot.

Four o'clock and all was well. More names were listed

on the guard's record. Shaw had signed out the Greek files. No appearance by Fairbairn.

Saturday's second shift began at 6:00 P.M. Menlo checked at seven. The new man on duty, O'Donnell by name, was carefully noting all activity. Susan Attley, van Trompf, and Domingus had each returned the files they had been using; all of them had left. Only Fairbairn and Shaw still worked on.

At nine o'clock, Fairbairn used the file room but took out no folders; a lengthy visit of twenty minutes. Menlo learned of this when he made another check with O'Donnell at nine-thirty. Quickly, Menlo entered the room and opened the cabinet containing the Farrago file. Nothing missing. And how could it be missing? The detector on O'Donnell's desk would have given warning if the specially treated cassettes had been carried in anyone's pocket. Annoyed with his overreaction, he returned to the corridor. Its traffic had ended; most people had gone home. Lights burned brightly, but silence enfolded the walls. Menlo decided to stretch out on the emergency cot in his office—forty minutes for a catnap before he made another check. (He was more tired than he had been willing to admit. Age, he thought angrily: even five years ago he could have gone without sleep for three nights in a row.) He took two more aspirin for the pain in his back.

Ten o'clock, and O'Donnell noted that Fairbairn and Shaw went into the file room to replace some folders. A friend from another department was with them but waited in the corridor. That was all O'Donnell had been able to write down. The rest of his report was made on Sunday morning when he had recovered enough to be able to answer Menlo's questions in his hospital room.

If O'Donnell's body was still weak, his mind was clear and his memory good. Menlo's probe was deep and exact. Between them, the events of Saturday night became alive.

At ten o'clock, with Fairbairn and Shaw in the file room, their friend waited for them about twelve feet away from O'Donnell's desk. He wore a label on his lapel, but that was unreadable from O'Donnell's chair. He didn't speak, seemed to be having a bad time with a summer cold; sneezed and blew his nose; didn't even look at O'Donnell, who was pouring his first cup of coffee. Just then, a call came from the file room (Shaw's voice), and Fairbairn was at its door to ask for O'Donnell's help. A cabinet had jammed. O'Donnell hadn't been more than a minute or two away from his post. He verified the lock on the Greek cabinet would not open. So he gave up, followed Shaw out of the room. Shaw had the files, placed them on his table. O'Donnell assured Fairbairn he'd call Maintenance and have the lock fixed. There had been no electronic warning signal as Shaw and Fairbairn were checked out. None. The three men walked smartly along the corridor; Shaw began to hurry ahead. He entered the elevator. The other two stopped halfway, decided to use the washroom.

O'Donnell began drinking his coffee before it cooled off completely. After that, he'd call Maintenance and start bringing his notes up to the minute. It was now seven minutes past ten. He was also intending to phone Menlo's office once the lock was repaired so that the files could be safely placed in their cabinet. He did none of those things except drink that cup of coffee.

An hour and fifteen minutes later, a team of cleaners arrived and saw O'Donnell slumped over his table at the far end of the corridor. One joked about it, but another thought it strange. He walked down the corridor, shook the guard. No response. Dead? The cleaner shouted the alarm.

Menlo had wakened at the shout. He reached O'Donnell, stayed with the man—and heard the cleaner's story—until Security arrived to take charge. Then he could enter the file room, cursing himself for having fallen asleep.

He should never have dropped onto his cot, never taken those damned aspirin, never let his eyes close.

The cabinet was locked. He opened it and his heart missed a beat. The Vienna cassettes were gone.

Sunday morning's hospital visit ended with a few clarifications about the previous evening. They were taped, of course, like O'Donnell's previous statements. He had no objections to being recorded. "Some additional questions," Menlo explained. And they were vital. "Do you always have coffee at ten o'clock?"

"Yes, it's midway through the shift. Coffee keeps me awake."

"You were drinking it when the three men arrived?"

"No, just poured the first cup."

"Had anyone remarked on that Thermos? Earlier?"

"Miss Attley made a joke, asked if I could spare a cup—she said it as she left. Mr. Fairbairn also joked. Said a coffee break was the right idea, thought he'd join me. I told him he'd have to wait until ten. He said he'd be having his own coffee break by that time."

"When was this?"

"Nine-twenty. At the end of his visit to the file room."

A twenty-minute visit. Twenty minutes to make sure the lock would jam later? Excessive, though. A few minutes was all it needed. "No complaint from Mr. Fairbairn about the lock on the Greek cabinet?"

"Not until they called on me to help."

"Did your coffee have any strange taste?"

"Needed more sugar. I thought the cafeteria had forgotten to add enough. The Thermos comes all ready."

Needed more sugar . . . "Bitter?" We'll have to check on the cafeteria handler who filled that Thermos, Menlo thought, but the man who had only twelve feet to cross, four strides would do it, and add knockout drops to a cup of coffee—that's the guy who really needs checking.

"Bitter?" O'Donnell was uncertain. "I thought it only wanted some sweetening. Could have been something I ate—I had my supper just before I came on duty. The nurses say it might have been food poisoning."

A reassuring euphemism for knockout drops, strong enough to have killed anyone with a weaker heart than O'Donnell's. But he preferred the idea of food poisoning: it seemed less his fault than letting his coffee cup be doctored. But it had to be the coffee. That lethal dose, if administered in O'Donnell's supper, would have felled him long before he reached his post. The cup was no help at all: rinsed and carted off by one of the cleaners. "What was the man like—the one who waited in the corridor? I know you couldn't see his face much. He was too busy sneezing and blowing his nose, you said. What about height, weight, hair?"

"Five feet nine or ten. A hundred and seventy pounds, I'd say. Hair was straight, brown—like Mr. Shaw's, but thinner. Needed a cut." O'Donnell was beginning to worry again. "Sorry, sir. I should have asked his name."

"Not necessary. Your description is enough." Menlo switched off the tape recorder. "What happened was no fault of yours. Get well. See you back on duty." Menlo left O'Donnell then. He looked relieved but was still a ghastly color. Who wouldn't be, after stomach pumping and injections and blood tests and analyses and X-rays and all the other miracles of modern medicine?

By nine o'clock on Sunday, Menlo had returned from the hospital and was eating a doughnut in his office with his breakfast coffee as he requested the State Department to locate Mr. Frederick Coulton and have him visit Menlo as soon as possible. Yes, he had to repeat, Frederick Coulton. Attached to Public Affairs. No, not regular Foreign Service: attached. Simpler by far, he thought, if two of Doyle's agents could have brought Coulton here. No go, however. A matter of protocol.

He corralled Shaw, however, pulled him out of bed to be at Langley by ten o'clock. Urgent business, was all Menlo said over the phone.

He had less luck with Fairbairn. His wife answered, seemed vague and harried. Wallace had left early to go sailing with some friends. She had no idea when he would return, but it would be late, very late—he always was when he spent a day on Chesapeake Bay. She was just about to drive the children to visit their grandparents—would Mr. Menlo excuse her? "Tell him I'd like to see him tomorrow at nine o'clock," Menlo said and had to be content with that.

He contacted Doyle once more. A quiet search should be made of Fairbairn's house when Mrs. Fairbairn and the children had left. An equally quiet search of Shaw's apartment was needed at ten o'clock. Also, phone taps should be installed and surveillance on both places around the clock. Doyle knew what to look for. Not that Menlo had much hope that the cassettes would be discovered in either place. They had been passed to Coulton, most probably, before he left the building last night. Yet everything had to be checked and checked and checked.

Or am I jumping the gun? Menlo wondered. He began playing over his recorded talk with O'Donnell once more. Then, just before ten, he had a surprise interruption. Fairbairn called; his sailing date had been canceled, he had phoned his wife and got Menlo's message. "Something urgent?" he asked.

"Yes. When can you reach here?"

There was silence.

Consulting with someone? "Fairbairn—where are you? At home?"

"No. At the marina. I'll try for noon, if Sunday traffic allows."

"See you then." Menlo's voice was definite.

At ten o'clock, Shaw arrived. At ten past twelve, Fairbairn. And Menlo learned that one of them was an expert liar.

One-thirty, and Menlo was still in his office, brooding over a sandwich and lukewarm coffee, while he jotted down estimations of this morning's interviews. First, of course, he had given Shaw and Fairbairn the reason why he had called them so early: the guard's seizure; concern over a possible security lapse; a report that he must make on the events of last evening. It would be easier for him, he had said casually, if the conversations were taped—just in case his notes were vague on some small point.

Suspicion, Menlo had told Bristow last Friday, was an ugly business. How ugly, he was now finding out on a bright and peaceful Sunday. He sighed, switched on his two recorders, played their tapes, changing from one to the other as he compared Shaw's answers with Fairbairn's.

Why had Coulton been here last night?

Both men gave similar explanations. Coulton had been visiting Langley to consult one of its forgery specialists. Nothing unusual about that: Coulton had visited here before. He had dropped in to see them on his way home and needed a lift—his Mercedes was garaged until a spare part arrived.

Whom did Coulton ask for a lift?

Shaw: Coulton had asked him. After all, Coulton was one of his friends. (Shaw was proud of that, definitely honored.) As to how and when they had met—Fairbairn had introduced them at a Georgetown cocktail party several weeks ago. Yes, he found Coulton interesting and informative.

Fairbairn: Coulton didn't ask, just said he would be grateful for a lift. Shaw had offered. It was only natural he should. They had been seeing a lot of each other recently, both interested in those fake Hitler diaries. How had they first met? Fairbairn had no idea. To Fairbairn, Coulton was only an acquaintance and a bit of a bore like his subject. Shoptalk was not exactly Fairbairn's notion of conversation.

Did they leave the corridor together?

Shaw: No. Coulton said he'd use the washroom, so why didn't Shaw find his car in its parking space and drive around to the front entrance? Coulton would meet him there. Made sense—time saved for everyone. So Shaw left at once. He had looked back along the corridor as he entered the elevator. Coulton and Fairbairn were already in the washroom, and the guard was drinking his coffee. Shaw checked out at the front door at ten-twelve, took about six or seven minutes to reach his car, found its door ajar and its interior lights on, so that the battery seemed weakened and gave him some trouble in starting the engine. He arrived at the front door to find Coulton waiting. Fairbairn had already left for home.

Fairbairn: They didn't leave together. Shaw suggested he would pick up his car and save time, meet them at the entrance. When Coulton and Fairbairn arrived there (after Coulton had surrendered his identification and they had been checked out), they could see no sign of Shaw. So Fairbairn left. It was almost ten-thirty when he reached his car. What about the guard upstairs? He looked pretty fit to Fairbairn. He had put down his cup, was reaching for the phone—no doubt to call Maintenance—as Coulton and Fairbairn entered the elevator at the other end of the corridor. "Too bad about the guard," Fairbairn added. "What caused that attack? Food poisoning? That's the rumor downstairs. True?"

Menlo made a decision. "False. Someone tampered with his coffee. Could have killed him. Then we wouldn't have only an investigation into a breach of security. We'd have the FBI dealing with a case of murder."

Fairbairn stared at Menlo. "But how—" He paused, frowning. "How long before the guard was found?"

"More than an hour."

"Plenty of time for anyone to enter the file room."

"Plenty." But it needed only a few minutes for someone who knew our system of locking to open the Farrago cabinet.

"You know who it is?" Fairbairn asked. And as Menlo said nothing, "Sorry. Not my business. But this is a bad show. Can't help feeling concerned."

"We are all concerned. Thanks for coming in, Fairbairn. I'll see you tomorrow."

Fairbairn nodded, rose to leave, said slowly, "If it's one of us—then what?"

"I'd say he would have four choices. Either get out of the country and end his life bumming around South America or the Far East. Or head for Moscow and permanent exile. Or brazen it out, play innocent, until it's too late for anything except prison. Of course, if his usefulness is over to the comrades and he's a danger to those who were conspiring with him—well, his future will be decided for him. It will be terminated. There will be no choice for him."

"Not a bright prospect any way you look at it."

"He could make it brighter if he set the record straight. That's his fourth choice."

"A turncoat? Not much future in that, either."

"His family might not agree with you. They've a stake in his choice, too."

Fairbairn shook his head. "You amaze me, Menlo. You've really thought it all through. What choice would you make?"

"Whatever I chose, I hope I'd feel some remorse. But I suppose an enemy agent never would. You remember where Dante placed traitors in his Inferno? In the lowest depths—the ninth circle of hell. Encased them in ice."

Fairbairn's astonishment grew.

"Symbolic. As deep frozen as their hearts when alive."

"You really do amaze me," Fairbairn said slowly. Menlo and Dante—what next? He smiled. "There could be a fifth choice. Suicide."

"For an agent who has been trapped, that's a matter of sheer necessity, a spur-of-the-moment reaction. No choice."

"I guess so." Fairbairn was no longer smiling. "Those who think long about suicide rarely commit it. Do they?" He nodded, opened the door, slowly closed it.

* * *

Menlo's notes were completed as far as Sunday had brought them. Tomorrow, Monday, he'd probably have additions to make before he typed them on Tuesday. By Wednesday, as arranged with the Director, his report would be ready. He slipped the four closely written sheets into a heavy envelope, sealed it, and locked it into his safe along with the tapes of three interviews.

There was still some business to settle before he left for home: arrange for Justice to secure a search warrant for a complete sweep of Fairbairn's house; of Shaw's apartment, too. (Doyle's men in their quick search had found no Vienna cassettes in either place, but there had been a lot of electronic equipment. Shaw's had been considerable; an unmarried man could perhaps afford expensive hobbies.) Then there would have to be some diplomatic prodding of Coulton's bosses. Today, no one at the Bureau of Public Affairs seemed to be available, Coulton included. But suddenly, Menlo felt his fatigue mounting. He would deal with these problems later.

He set out on the long walk to his car. Whatever I've accomplished this Sunday, he was thinking, I've brought the simmering pot to a bubbling boil. But better concentrate on a long hot tub, a change of clothes, a real dinner, my own bed, and time to think things through.

18

Monday dawned and found Menlo wide awake, eyes staring up at his bedroom's ceiling. Time to think things through, he had promised himself. But a hot and sleepless night had simply created more conflict in his mind. By half past five, he gave up. He left the disarray of crumpled, damp sheets and took a cold shower. A mistake: its coolness only stirred up his back pain. My God, he thought in disgust, do I have to live like a bloody orchid? He shaved, dressed slowly, ate a quick breakfast. He was in his office before seven.

Just as he was settling at his desk, a call came in from Rome. It was Levinson, speaking rapidly. A bombing had occurred an hour ago in the old police station on Via Borgognona. He had only the barest details—he was interrupting a lunch with a Swiss suspected of illegal trading and was calling without benefit of scrambler from a restaurant. Four dead inside the building; three in the street; some injured; some survivors, Karen Cornell and Bristow among them. No exact accounting, as yet. But he had sent one of his boys to the scene, would be able to give a fuller report around three this afternoon. Rome time.

That's 9:00 A.M. over here, Menlo thought as the speedy call ended. A new possibility raised its ugly head. Worriedly, he began comparing the differences in time between Rome and Washington.

The cassettes had been stolen shortly after ten o'clock on Saturday morning. They could have been played, their contents digested and radioed from Washington by midnight. Which was 6:00 A.M. Sunday in Rome. And who, over there, could have received that message? Unanswerable as of now. But one thing was certain. There was time enough to plant a bomb by Monday morning. And yet—a bombing might have been arranged long before the Vienna information reached Rome. No link between the two, perhaps. Not unless Karen Cornell had been killed by the explosion. But she was alive. So possibly no connection, Menlo decided with considerable relief.

Still, that was the crux of the matter. She had tied Sam Waterman closely together with Andreas Kellner and Rita, two known Communist agents. If Waterman knew about that, he'd have that evidence destroyed—tapes and girl. That son of a bitch had most to lose if the Vienna cassettes were publicized. Until now he had been accepted at face value: a left-wing writer who had been unfairly ousted by the *Washington Spectator* (whispers had circulated about Karen Cornell and Hubert Schleeman) and now worked free-lance. His hidden name of Steven Winter might be known by some intelligence officers, but their suspicions couldn't be circulated; another case, Waterman would say, of paranoia and harassment. Yes, he had the most to lose—he and the KGB, who had recruited him, aided him, cosied him, and made his cover story credible. Until Vienna.

Waterman was now in Rome, Menlo reminded himself—last seen here on Friday evening waiting for Coul-

ton. Waterman and Coulton . . . A case of who whom. Wa
Coulton merely an agent, recruited through either black
mail or money or politics? The real control was Waterman
both of Coulton and the mole—was that it? And tha
bloody mole—Fairbairn or Shaw? The evidence seeme
to point Fairbairn's way. Seemed . . . Not good enough
We have to be damned sure, Menlo told himself, an
opened his safe for a further reading of the notes he ha
completed yesterday.

They were intact inside the envelope. But he coul
swear it had been opened and resealed. One small corne
of its flap wasn't properly adhered. It had loosened it
grip. He opened the entire flap of the envelope—it fe
sticky, as if glue had been used. Imagination, perhaps
Two sleepless nights in a row played havoc with th
mind. He did, however, inquire who had been workin
in the European unit on Sunday afternoon. Both Fair
bairn and Shaw had still been on duty when he had le
for home.

Promptly at nine, the call from Rome came in. Lev
inson was back in his office and gave a fuller account o
the bombing. Bristow and Cornell were slightly the wors
for wear but unharmed. "An interesting note: a Bulgaria
arrived in Rome on Saturday with a false passport. H
was at the meeting this morning as a 'cousin' of the ter
rorist Martita. The police think that he and the Czech wh
accompanied him replaced the real relatives and used thei
passes to enter the hall. Looks as if the Bulgarians hav
an interest in Bristow's girl. One tried to meet her whe
she arrived Friday, and he was keeping watch on her o
Saturday evening at Armando's—along with an America
called Waterman."

"Sam Waterman with the Bulgarian!"

"Identified by Bristow. My boy was at Armando's, too
He identified the Bulgarian. Interesting combination
wouldn't you say?"

"Where's Bristow now?"

"At the Imperial, recovering and keeping close watch on the girl. She's an attractive piece, I hear."

"I'll talk with Bristow at—" Menlo paused, calculated. First, he must see what arrangements could be made to get Bristow and the girl out of Rome. Immediately.

"At when?"

"Give me a couple of hours. I'll call at five. *Your* time."

"Suits me," said Levinson cheerfully as Menlo ended the call and reached for pad and pencil.

Quickly, he scrawled a memorandum, heading it with a large question mark. *Waterman or Coulton as control? The mole—Fairbairn? Or Shaw? Incentives blackmail, money, ideology? Check.* Then he selected a fresh envelope, sealed the four pages of notes and the memorandum inside, and signed it Frank Menlo. As an afterthought, he wrote on its face, "To be collected only by me—or Peter Bristow." The addition of Bristow was instinctive, yet reasonable enough: he needed Bristow's quick eye to review these notes, and by tomorrow at that. And if it was yet another day to entangle him in phone calls, Bristow could collect the envelope and set to work without delay.

This time, he'd make sure of the notes. And the tapes of Sunday's interviews, too. He tied them into one package, the envelope on top, and placed it in his safe temporarily, after he had altered the combination lock. When he left for the day, he would leave the package with Miriam Blau, give her the instructions about Bristow. He was taking no more chances with a mole who seemed to have had some expert training in opening an office safe.

Before eleven o'clock and the scheduled call to Bristow in Rome, he was summoned upstairs for the conference he had requested. He had just time to postpone his call for an hour (the conference would be brief, mostly a matter of impressing the need for Bristow's and Cornell's safety; they must be found space for tonight's flight) and install a secretary in his office to type out some written

letters while he was absent. "Stay here. Wait until I ge
back," he told the girl, whom he knew well. She knew
his ways, too, and showed no surprise.

The conference was satisfactory. Menlo returned to his
office within the hour. "Have something to eat now," he
suggested to the secretary. "Come back at one-thirty. I'l
need you until three." That, he reflected, would let him
have lunch with Doyle as arranged.

At noon, his delayed call to Rome took place. The talk
with Bristow was more difficult than he had expected
and abrupt. But Levinson gave him the details of the
bombing. It was then he learned that a definite bullet had
been intended for Karen Cornell. And the man who had
fired it was a Bulgarian.

In black depression, he left his office in the secretary's
charge and met Doyle. They talked over a small table in
a large room that was now almost empty. The white-haired
Irishman, neat and compact in his light summer suit, stud
ied his old friend as he emphasized the need for extra
precautions tonight on Karen Cornell's arrival. They had
worked here a long time, Doyle thought, were due to retire
in the same month three years from now, had shared many
an emergency before this, but he had never seen Menlo
so much on edge.

"She worries me," Menlo was admitting, the food on
his plate scarcely touched. "Bristow can take his chances
like the rest of us, but she's vulnerable. We'll have to find
her a safe house for the next few days, but some place
that no one in my section has heard about. No one at all,
if possible. The less she can be connected with us, the
safer she'll be."

"A tall order—we haven't much time before she arrives
Two A.M.?"

"Pretty close to it—if I've calculated correctly. Damn
those time zones."

Doyle agreed completely. "Last June, my daughter
had to make a quick trip back from Paris. Took the
Concorde. Left at eleven in the morning, arrived at eight

forty-five A.M.—almost two hours earlier than her departure."

But Menlo wasn't even listening. He was saying, "We'll need two cars at the airfield: mine and one of yours. Bristow will leave with me. Your men can escort Miss Cornell to the safe house and stay on guard. Can't have her using her address in Washington—or in New York. Nor can she check into a hotel without being noticeable at that early hour."

"Surely you don't mean to be at the airfield yourself. At two in the morning, for God's sake." And the man doesn't like night driving anyway. "You'd be better in bed, see Bristow on Tuesday."

"I've a lot to discuss with him. I'm leaving an envelope and three tapes with Miriam Blau. He's authorized to take them out, work over them. But before he does—well, I'd like to give him some extra background. And admit," Menlo added slowly, "that I was wrong and he was right about using the cassettes as bait."

"How else get any leads?" And that was the truth, Doyle thought. No answer from Menlo, either. "Not easy to watch your suspects," he went on. "Fairbairn sometimes uses his Buick, sometimes his wife's station wagon. But Shaw's the biggest problem: that apartment house of his, six floors spreading out like a pancake mix. Four separate entrances and eighty families as tenants. It's one of those modern-style rabbit warrens. He uses his own car, but it's parked all around the place—often blocks away."

Menlo's frown deepened.

"Look—" Doyle said, "I'll meet Bristow and Miss Cornell this morning."

"I'm meeting Bristow." Menlo was determined.

"Then," said Doyle, equally determined, "I'll send a car and a driver for you. Pick you up at your place and get you to the airfield in plenty of time. I'll be in the other car with a couple of good men—they'll be assigned to look after Miss Cornell wherever she's staying. Agreed?"

"Unmarked cars."

"We'll rent them, if necessary," Doyle said with a wide grin. "We'll collect you at 1:00 A.M."

"Make that twelve-thirty."

"You'll have to wait at the—"

"Perhaps. Perhaps not. There may be a tailwind."

From east to west? Doyle didn't argue that point. Menlo was already on his feet and talking about the prospects of Australia in the America's Cup races as they left their table.

Menlo took Doyle's parting advice to shut up shop and leave for home. He locked his office at four o'clock.

Fairbairn and Shaw saw him passing their open door. He halted, nodded, and went on his way.

Shaw said, "He's early. A record." Fairbairn didn't share his amusement. "Briefcase as usual tucked under his arm," Shaw went on. "Probably sleeps with it. That package—did you notice? What's your guess, Wallace? Special homework for tonight?" Shaw laughed. "Could be that envelope holds all the notes he was taking down yesterday."

"Don't forget the tapes," Fairbairn said sourly.

"Why would he need them?" Shaw was astounded.

"To go over what we said. Word by word."

Shaw stared. "Why should he—"

"Why not? Someone got into the file room and stole Bristow's cassettes."

"We weren't told about that. How the hell do you know?"

"Why else were we questioned?"

"Then he does suspect us," Shaw said. His jaw tightened. "You or me?"

"I'll toss you for the honor," Fairbairn said bitterly and went back to work. That lasted only ten minutes. "I'm leaving, too. Can't get my mind settled."

"Why worry?"

"Don't you?"

"No, I'm not worried. I'm just damned mad. Tapes checked—what next?" Shaw's vehemence subsided into another laugh. "Shaved heads and numbers stamped on our forearms?"

19

KAREN CAME SLOWLY OUT FROM HER DEEP SLEEP. FOR
a few minutes, she lay oblivious to everything except the
comfort of this bed, the peace of this shaded room. But
where? Then she remembered. The Imperial, Monday
afternoon, and Peter—she raised herself on an elbow. No
one beside her. But near, she thought, and relaxed as she
heard faint music from the sitting room. She rose, drawing
on her dressing gown, and crossed to the windows, pulled
back the shutters to let sunshine stream in. There was
none. Just a bustle of evening traffic down on Via Veneto
and the sun dropping toward the west. It was still daylight,
but the street lay now in the shadow of the buildings
opposite. The neon lights were already in full brilliance
to welcome the coming dusk. Late—almost six-thirty—
what happened to this afternoon?

She opened the sitting-room door, saying, "Darling,
I—" and stopped in confusion. A dark-haired man sat on
the couch with his feet propped on a table. As he turned
his head, she recognized him: the young man who had

run such expert interference for her as she left Armando's on Saturday evening; the young man she had first seen with his beautiful if slightly middle-aged Contessa at Doney's.

He was rising to his feet as he said, "Not to worry. I'm a friend of Peter's. Left me here as your watchdog while he was away. He'll be back soon—a bit delayed—but that happens." He had a most engaging manner.

"I'll dress," she said, backing into the bedroom. "Just a few minutes. What's your name?"

"Giovanni."

Giovanni who? Peter had some extraordinary friends. She closed the door and dressed quickly. Her working clothes, she called the jeans and shirt she was pulling on. For tonight, there would be no partying in town. They'd be staying here, as they had done yesterday, avoiding people such as Sam Waterman. And she'd set to work, start writing an account of this morning's bombing while the facts were fresh in her mind. Hubert Schleeman wouldn't have the articles he expected, but he'd have at least something to fill two pages in the *Spectator*. Aliotto ... She had picked up her portable typewriter, ready to carry it to the sitting room, where there was a desk, sturdier than the thin-legged little writing table in here. Aliotto, she thought again, and wondered if she could ever write about today's events. She was too near to them, had been a part of them. It was one thing to be a reporter arriving at a disaster scene, observing, describing the horrors of a six-car smash-up on the Long Island Expressway—she had done that for the TV cameras. But it was something else to have been trapped in noise and smoke and flames, to have heard voices screaming around her, to have felt death reaching, spreading, engulfing ... She closed her eyes, set down the typewriter at her feet, and began to weep.

She forced herself to recover, wiped the tears from her cheeks; then at last she entered the sitting room.

Giovanni was quick to notice. "Are you all right?"

She nodded. "Just beginning to remember. Odd, isn't it? At first, I could think only that I had escaped, that Peter and I were alive. The rest was confusion in my mind. All I could feel was bewilderment—and relief. But now—" She broke off, walked over to the window, kept her back turned. "When did he leave?"

"An hour ago or so. No problem. Pete had to talk on the phone to Washington—in my boss's office. He won't be long."

"I'm really ruining your day." She came back to the couch, emotions under control. "But thank you for staying with me. Frankly, don't you think Peter is worrying too much about me?"

"No."

She looked at him in surprise. "But he has other things to think about. And I really can do my own worrying."

Giovanni studied her face. "Didn't you know that a bullet was intended for you?"

Her eyes widened. "This morning?" she asked faintly.

"This morning."

"When? When I was down on the floor? Yes—I heard two shots. Very close. At *me*?"

"One at you, the other at the man who fired."

"Peter shot him?"

"Yes." Giovanni hesitated. His voice softened. "I wasn't meant to tell you. But—"

"I'm glad you did." She was completely bewildered. "They actually tried to *kill* me?"

"Forget about it."

"Forget!" She was indignant.

"Well, don't think about it. Not now. Later, when it's farther away from you—"

"It will make an amusing anecdote?" she asked coldly.

"Well—we all like to tell an interesting story when it involves ourselves."

"We cast ourselves in the leading role, grab our moment of stardom?" She was on the defensive.

Giovanni only said equably, "We enjoy it. Don't we?"

Her annoyance vanished. "I suppose we do," she admitted. Listen to me, my friends, and hear how *I* escaped, how I felt, how I suffered. "Self-centered, all of us."

"Not all. Not everyone," he reminded her.

No. Not everyone. "How long have you and Peter been friends?"

"A couple of days. Since Saturday."

She began to smile. "You waste no time—either of you."

"Well, you can like—or dislike—at first sight. No explaining it. It happens."

Like love, she thought.

"What d'you want to drink?" At least the tears have dried and her smile is back, Giovanni thought. But where's Pete? That phone call from Washington was at five o'clock or wasn't it? Six-twenty now. Keep talking, keep her from watching the clock, keep her from thinking about that goddamned bombing.

Bristow found them both laughing over one of Giovanni's tall tales. "Sorry, darling," he told Karen. "There was a delay." And a circuitous route back to the hotel. His arms went around her as she came to meet him, and they kissed.

He wastes less time than I do, Giovanni thought with amusement as he drained his glass and rose. "Time to push off. I'm meeting Maggie—" he cleared his throat— "*la Contessa* at seven." He looked at Karen. "I think you saw us at Doney's."

"Yes. But you aren't what I thought you were."

"Were we that good?"

Bristow said, "I'd like your help, Giovanni. In fact, I need it. We're leaving tonight. Quietly."

"By NATO express?"

"Something like that."

"Do you have travel orders, papers?"

"I came away from Levinson's office in too much of a hurry. Think he'll provide something for us?"

"Will try. When d'you fly out?"

"Midnight."

"I can drive—"

"No. Better not. Just hire us a car, have it waiting around the corner—on Via Boncompagni. We should leave the hotel at ten, I think. But how do we get the bags down to the car? I'd like to have us walk out the front door as if we were going to dinner. I've paid the bills, told the cashier that we had an early start tomorrow so I'd square everything tonight. I'll pay cash for dinner when we have it in this room. Any ideas, Giovanni?"

"I'll get a bellhop to collect your bags at nine-thirty and have them packed in the car. I'll wait with it until you come."

Karen said, "I'm slightly bewildered." We don't sleep here tonight although it's all paid for. We don't use our Pan Am tickets tomorrow morning. "Why the rush, Peter?"

"A change in plans. Sorry to spring it on you. There's a small crisis at Langley. Menlo wants me back there as soon as possible."

"Menlo," Giovanni said, "is his boss. Never met him, but I hear that when he requests, you jump."

"Well," Karen said, "if we must look as if we're only going out to dinner, then I'll play the part. A sleeveless dress and my lace stole, I suppose." And I'll shiver to death on the plane, she thought.

"Night flying at thirty-five thousand feet can be chilly," Bristow said. "You've nothing warmer?"

"Just summer things. I packed for late-August weather in Rome."

"Wear what you've got on now. Add a sweater. We can say we're visiting Trastevere—there are plenty of little eating places across the Tiber. I'll look as casual as hell, too. Okay, Giovanni? You're the expert."

Giovanni grinned. "She might even look too chic for Trastevere—but she'll pass. You do have a sweater?" he asked Karen. "You can't arrive home with pneumonia."

"A thin cardigan. One with a beaded collar." That amused her.

"I'll find something," Giovanni said. "Leave it with your luggage in the car."

"Sorry about all this, but you know women." She began to laugh. "We never have anything to wear, do we?" She left them smiling as she went toward the bedroom. "I'll pack before dinner, Peter."

"Can you stay another five minutes?" Bristow asked Giovanni. "I'll get packed, too, and bring my bag along here." He was already at the door, opening it.

"Sure," Giovanni said as Bristow closed the door behind him. He thought for a moment, then phoned down to the bar, where *la Contessa* would be holding court with two businessmen whom Levinson was investigating. "A little late," he excused himself. "Can you find me a sweater, your size—bulky and droopy and warm? I'll meet you at nine. Your place. Okay?"

"Of course, dear boy. Simply delighted," Maggie said in her best Italian for the benefit of her table. "And just wait till I see you!" she added sotto voce in pure Midwest American.

It went as planned. Karen and Bristow made the midnight flight, with travel papers complete and the bulkiest of sweaters draped around her shoulders.

"How d'you like being a third-class aide's secretary?" he asked her as they found their allotted space.

"I thought they'd have made you at least a second-class aide. Aiding what?"

"Some agriculture department. Foot-and-mouth disease." Trust Levinson and his sense of humor, he thought as he shook his head.

She pulled on the sweater before she buckled the safety belt. "*Très* chic, *très* snob. I'm all set for Gstaad. Did you notice *la Contessa* walking her little poodle past the car as we were getting in? I suppose it was her way of saying good-bye."

"Or of having a look at the girl who was going to wear her prize sweater."

"I can't keep it, you know. Mail it back where?"

"We'll return it when we give her a dinner party in Washington."

"We are giving dinner parties?"

"Why else get married?"

She turned to face him, staring in wonder. "Married? You're rushing things, Peter."

"Not half quick enough." He leaned over and kissed her. "Damn this seat belt," he said and unbuckled it.

"Are you sure?"

He became serious. "Yes," he said. "I am sure." He looked deep into her eyes. "And you?"

"Yes," she heard herself say, "I'm sure."

This time, he could really kiss her properly.

As they drew back at last, Karen caught her breath, said, "I feel slightly—slightly delirious." And madly and truly in love, something I thought could never happen again. Peter, Peter—I adore you. Then she laughed with sudden joy, pressed his hand as it lay against her breast, held it there. Her head fell naturally on his shoulder.

"I've never been happier," he told her, and he meant it.

Someone behind them said he'd like to sleep. So they sat, hands tightly held, fingers intertwined, and talked softly. Not exactly what he would have planned for their first night together, Bristow thought. But she was safe. And homeward-bound. And he was the luckiest of men.

20

A BLACK MONDAY—MENLO KEPT THINKING ABOUT THIS day's bad news from Rome all the way home. It was past five o'clock now, and a long evening ahead of him before he met Bristow and Karen Cornell at the airfield. Must stop brooding—no future in that, he told himself as he neared his house.

It lay on a quiet street, was sheltered like its neighbors by hedges and trees. He turned his car into the short driveway, lined with azalea bushes, that cut across a stretch of grass to the small garage at one side of the neat little house, six rooms in all. Behind it, a meager backyard ending in an eight-foot wall that kept out any picnickers in the woods at the rear of the property. (Before it had been built, their discarded beer cans and paper bags had been an eyesore.) And that completed Menlo's three-quarters of an acre.

Not much but my own, he thought as he took a pre-dinner stroll around the front garden, a glass of bourbon and branch water in his hand. Garden? Only grass and bushes. When Peg had been alive, it had been different: flower beds, window boxes, touches of color everywhere. But everything was different now. You couldn't spend thirty-five years of your life happily married and not feel an emptiness that invaded every part of your home. It was more space than he really needed, yet he had gathered too many things here, and not just memories, to move into a couple of rooms in some new condominium. Books, music, the furniture that Peg had chosen, the small mementos they had collected on trips abroad. Besides, when did he have the time for an upheaval like a removal? He didn't even have time enough to water the grass, and it needed it badly. Later this week, he'd drag out the hoses and set up the sprinklers, trim back some of the bushes too. His friends said he had become addicted to overwork since Peg had died, almost ten years ago. Better that than becoming an alcoholic. Lonely drinking was no solution.

He turned back to the house. Minna, as long established here as the azaleas, would produce dinner in another fifteen minutes. Each afternoon, she'd shop for the food-stuff (the best part of her day, Menlo thought), clean, prepare dinner, and depart at eight for home and her TV. If he were late, she'd leave something for him to heat up. A makeshift arrangement, but judging from the amount of frozen dinners sold in the food markets, Menlo considered himself luckier in his domestic arrangements than most people these days.

The telephone was ringing. He hurried as he heard Minna shouting into it: the louder, the clearer was her belief. Her accent, too—Hungarian born, she still had difficulty with English—would only bewilder the caller more. Had to be a friend, he thought as he rescued the receiver from Minna. His home number was unlisted.

"Sorry," said a man's voice, young, apologetic. "I tried to reach you at your office. I hope it's all right to call you now. Mr. Bristow gave me your number before he left on vacation. For an emergency, he said."

"Who's this?" I know that voice, Menlo thought. Bristow's answering service, possibly. "Who are you?" he insisted.

"Joe Lampton," the voice said. "You left a message with me last month for Mr. Bristow. About canceling a meeting."

Menlo relaxed. "What's the emergency?"

"Well, it's more like—something strange. I took a call for Mr. Bristow—we're connected with his telephone, so it was his number the man used. Wouldn't give his name. Said it was urgent. He must speak with Mr. Bristow. I told him Mr. Bristow was out of town—couldn't be reached. Was this a business call? If so, I'd give him the telephone number of Mr. Bristow's office. Someone there could perhaps help him. He shouted, 'No!' He dropped his voice, said, 'No one else. Only Bristow.' He asked when Mr. Bristow was expected to return. A week or ten days, I told him. He swore. Not in English. Some foreign word, but I got the idea. Then he said, 'Take this message. I wait for his return. I arrived earlier than expected. Two weeks were not necessary. I shall call his number each day, half an hour later each day.' So I said, 'Later than what?' Later than this call, I was told. I asked for his name. He only said, 'Someone Bristow would very much like to meet.' He rang off then."

Surely not Josef Vasek. Farrago. And yet this stranger's words ("No one else. Only Bristow . . . earlier than expected . . . Two weeks . . . Someone Bristow would very much like to meet") all pointed to Vasek.

Joe was saying, "Mr. Menlo! Are you there, Mr. Menlo?"

"Still with you. You've got a tape of that conversation, of course." And that's what we need to study; let Karen Cornell hear it, too—she could identify the voice.

"Standard procedure." As if, Joe's hurt tone seemed to be saying, any telephone answering service could function without taping its calls.

"I'd like to have it."

"Mr. Bristow will—"

"Certainly. As soon as he returns. When did the stranger phone?"

"Five-forty."

"Then at six-ten tomorrow, put his call through to Bristow's office."

"Mr. Bristow's? He isn't—"

"I'll be there." And Bristow, too. "Any idea where the man telephoned?" Vasek, Menlo kept thinking, alone and safe out of Europe, traveling with no help—the man's confidence was startling. But the Farrago file said that was typical.

"A pay phone. Some public place. I heard traffic noises. He had to add coins, a lot of coins. Long-distance, I'd think. By the way, I hope you don't mind, sir. I told him to call collect tomorrow. That way, we might trace the place where he's telephoning."

"Good for you, Joe. Glad you called." And Joe was a good man, Menlo thought. His legs might have been blasted off in Vietnam, but he was still as capable as when he had been Bristow's driver. Bristow's and young Schleeman's driver. Schleeman's son had lost more than his legs by that road mine. Must call Schleeman, he reminded himself, see if he has any ideas about a safe house for Karen Cornell. His place in town? Empty until after Labor Day, with a reliable man as its caretaker. No, he decided suddenly, too risky. Schleeman was too obvious a choice. Waterman and his friends would investigate that house once they didn't find Cornell at her usual addresses.

At least, she was on that flight now. It had already taken off by this time. If she were on board. But Bristow would make sure. Of that, Menlo was certain. Bristow's girl, Levinson had called her. If so, pretty damn quick work. Not that he had anything against love. Just that love and danger didn't mix. Emotional involvement could blunt a man's judgment.

He saw Peg's photograph smiling at him from the mantelpiece. "I know," he told her. "We were engaged within a week, married in a month." He smiled, too. Minna's voice, calling from the hall, ended his memories. "Coming, coming," he called back, picked up a book to read as he ate, turned on his record player to let Mozart's D minor flow into the dining room.

He had planned on a three-hour sleep after dinner with a loud-buzzing alarm clock set for ten o'clock. But as he lay down, the telephone rang. Cursing it, he was back on his feet. It was Levinson from Rome. At one in the morning? Menlo's acute anxiety, nicely lulled by Minna's blueberry pie, surged back.

Levinson said, "I thought you'd like to know that they've left the hotel. Smooth departure. Couldn't be neater."

Menlo drew a long deep breath. "Thanks, Mike." And he was grateful, even if his digestion had stopped short.

But Levinson had another piece of news. "Remember the fellow that Pete knew?"

What fellow? Bristow knew hundreds. "Come again."

"The joint identification," Levinson tried.

Levinson's agent had recognized a Bulgarian, Bristow had identified Sam Waterman. Waterman . . . "Last Saturday?"

"Right. Well, I thought we'd try to locate him for you. So we checked the hotels—recent arrivals—just a chance—but we found his name on one register. He stayed for two nights and left this morning. He was flying over the Mediterranean when the big bang went off. Nice planning."

"Flying where?"

"To New York. Nonstop. Departure ten-fifty, arrival two-ten at Kennedy."

"Did you tell Bristow?"

"Only now verified the facts. Sorry to break into your dinner hour. 'Bye."

It took Menlo a full minute to recover and dial Tom Doyle's number, and found him in the middle of a family party. "Wife's birthday," Doyle explained. "Just a moment and I'll close the door." It banged shut, ending the sound of laughter. "The three girls are here, one husband, one fiancé. Quite a roomful. We're just about to sit down for dinner," he added as a tactful hint.

"Won't keep you long. We'll need special precautions, Tom. I've just heard from Rome that Waterman is here— we discussed him at lunch, remember?"

That sobered Doyle. "Here?"

"Reached New York this afternoon. Could be in Washington right now. So, special precautions. Right?"

"I'll see to it. I'll have two men collect you, as a starter."

"No need—"

"That's my department," Doyle reminded him. "Wish you'd reconsider—"

"No."

"I can bring Bristow to you."

"After you've settled the girl some place safe? Come on, Tom. That's your job. Right? Bristow and I have other things to do." Such as study the tape made by an answering service. "Good-bye."

Menlo had been half-amused, half-irritated by Doyle's concern. He wasn't the one who needed guarding. By this time, Waterman would have learned the results of today's bombing. Nice planning, as Levinson had said, to be well out of Rome when it happened. That, of course, explained why he used his own name at a hotel and with the airline; he'd have witnesses to testify when he had left. A false name wouldn't have cleared him, could have increased the height of evidence against him—if ever he were caught and brought to trial. He's an eel, Menlo thought, as strong and voracious, as cunning and quick as any that lurked in the salmon pools of a Nova Scotia river. Remembering his own battle with such an eel less than three weeks ago—it had swallowed his best hand-tied fly right down into its stomach in one gulp; no way of recovering it unless you could stamp a hold on its neck with your foot and slit its belly open. And even a firm hold didn't mean you could keep it still for just one moment. Menlo had cut his good line, let the eel twist from the bank back into the water—it also knew where to jump, that three-foot stretch of muscle—and now it was tearing young salmon to shreds with Menlo's prized fly in its stomach. Not, he thought as he went into his bedroom, his idea of fishing. He could use a couple of hours of it now. There was nothing like casting for trout in a cold rippling stream—slow rhythm and gentle sound—to calm your anxieties. He stretched out on the bed once more, and this time he slept.

Menlo was dressed and ready to leave, but there was almost forty minutes until the car would arrive to pick him up. He had already checked the back door and the windows in the other rooms; all bolted and secure. In the living room, they were still wide open to let the night air have full access; closed, the place would have been suffocating. Their locking would be the last thing he'd do before he turned on the alarm as he left the house. A necessity he disliked, but in the last few years there had been armed burglaries even in this quiet, sedate section of Fairfax County. Once, he thought with nostalgia, we could leave our doors unlocked and drive off to a movie. Something new has been added to our lives, a feeling of threat. It can't be blamed, not this kind of menace, on big bad government or heavy-handed bureaucracy. The lawbreakers have been let loose among us, the criminal activists, whether they're into small-time thuggery or into grand-scale terrorism. Two extremes of the same ruthless intent: do what you want and have no sense of guilt. These terrorists, for instance—the ones who bombed a group of journalists in Rome to let a comrade make her escape— they don't see themselves as political puppets. They are their own heroes, the advance guard, men and women of courage, risking everything for their beliefs. Who could be nobler? They'll find justification for anything they do, even for killing and maiming the innocent. If ever we let— Was that a car he heard?

They're early, he thought, glancing at his watch. Barely twelve yet. He rose from his chair, moved stiffly to the window. There was nothing to see, just darkness and black shadows; no headlights beamed along the road. The engine switched off. Must be a late visitor at a neighboring house, he decided, and walked back to his chair. False alarm. Unless, of course, Doyle's agents had overestimated their timing and arrived too soon, were now waiting in their car for twelve-thirty to approach. Punctilious they were, he knew from past experience. They'd appear at his door not a minute late, not a minute early.

He didn't sit down again. He switched off the Brahms Fourth he had been playing, stood debating with himself. He decided to start preparing to leave. He'd walk down to the gate and, if they were waiting for him in the car, he'd join them. They would arrive too early at the airfield, but better that than late. Better, too, than sitting around here, unsettled as he was. Strange, this feeling of tension. Too much strain recently, perhaps. Yet, stress didn't usually affect his mind, just his goddamned back.

He closed and locked the windows, drew their curtains together, checked the lights he usually left burning: here, bedroom, hall. One more thing—a flashlight. The porch, when he turned on its light, wouldn't be much help with the driveway, a dark stretch of gravel and the road not much brighter. Street lamps were few and far-spaced around this district.

In the hall, he picked up his jacket and was now ready for the usual hassle in setting the alarm system. First, he reminded himself, unlock the front door, activate the warning signal and be ready to get out and have the door shut again in forty seconds. Or else the damned thing will blast off. As he was about to unlock the door, he saw the lock wasn't secured. How was that? he wondered. Did he forget to twist its knob to the locked position? Did he sit and listen to Brahms this evening with an outside door ready to open? No, he had locked it as usual; the back door, too. And just then, he saw the handle turn. Gently, carefully. He wrenched the door inward. Two men stared at him. They were as startled as he was.

In that moment of paralysis, he could note one was young—tall, fair-haired, and armed. The other's face was hidden by a stocking mask—medium height and build—he was now straightening up from the lock, quickly side-stepping into the shadows to avoid the light from the hall. The unmasked man jabbed his revolver at Menlo's chest. "In! In!"

Suddenly, Menlo raised his arm, aiming the flashlight at the man's wrist. But he was even faster, struck Menlo on the shoulder with the butt of his pistol, sent him reeling back a pace and the flashlight clattering on the floor. Then a second blow, full strength. It caught Menlo on the side of his head, and he fell.

"Quick!" The man holstered his revolver, stopped to grip Menlo's shoulders and pull him away from the threshold. "Shut and lock that door! Then give me a hand." Together, they dragged Menlo into the living room. "Now where?" he asked his silent companion. "Over by the fireplace," he answered himself, and let Menlo's head drop on the raised edge of the brick hearth.

"Dead?" asked the masked man.

The other shrugged. "He had guts. But he has lost his speed." *More guts than you,* he thought, staring at the concealing mask. "You can take that thing off your face. No one to see you now."

The other hesitated but kept the mask in place. He moved to the desk.

"Afraid I'll know you again?" *The idiot put on that mask even as I stepped into the car, right make and color, at the right place and time. Right recognition signals—page five of today's* Washington Post *for me, page nine for him. Right exchange of fake names, too. Doesn't this guy trust anyone?* "Okay, okay. Sweat away. I wouldn't wear one of those damn things in this kind of weather. Washington!" He spat in disgust.

The masked man had examined a briefcase and was now opening desk drawers, his hands protected by surgical gloves. "Start searching," he said.

"The name is Barney for the next hour or so of your company. And you're Connie, I was told, for the next hour or so of mine. Easy, Connie, easy. There's no rush."

Connie pointed to the hi-fi player and the collection of records that lay on open shelves. "You know what to look for. Start there!"

"Not rigged for playing tapes," Barney said of the hi-fi set.

"Search!" Barney talks too much, the masked man was thinking. A sign he's nervous? Or he thinks he speaks the language so well that he wants me to believe he is actually American? "Wear the gloves!"

Barney drew them on reluctantly. "Too hot in here. I'm opening a window."

"Leave it!" Connie had completed his search of the desk. Nothing. He began pulling out the books that lined one wall of the room, felt behind them for an envelope.

"Only disks," Barney reported from the collection of records. "No tapes."

"Then start on the bookcases. Look for an envelope, too."

Barney swore. Sweat was on his brow, trickling down his back. He pulled off jacket and tie, threw them at the nearest armchair. The tie slipped to the carpet, fell beside the skirt of the chair's loose cover. He worked quickly. "Nothing," he said as he met Connie halfway along the bookcases. His manner was no longer easy, half-jocular, half-contemptuous. "Are you sure they are here?"

"Yes. He took them home this afternoon."

"You are sure?"

"Yes." Connie was now looking behind two pictures on the wall. No small safe was concealed. He was suffocating with the heat bottled up inside the room. He pulled the stocking up to his brow, breathed deeply. "They weren't in his office. I saw them yesterday in his safe, not today."

"You saw them? Why the hell did you not take the damned things?"

"I photographed the notes." Connie was angry. "If I had been stupid enough to take them, all hell could have broken loose this morning."

So he had passed over the photographs, and whoever had taken charge—Sam? but Sam took his orders, too—had decided notes and tapes must be destroyed. "Do you know Sam?" Barney asked.

Connie stared at him blankly. "No."

Whoever gives Sam his orders has kept him insulated, Barney thought. He said casually, "Just an old friend of mine in Europe. Thought you might have met him," he added as he followed Connie into the dining room. Connie pulled down the shades, switched on the lights, searched quickly. Only silver in one sideboard drawer, mats and napkins in another, crockery in two cupboards. Nothing hidden.

"You look upstairs," Connie said as they reentered the hall, and hurriedly opened the door of a grandfather clock, then a small drawer in the table, then the coat closet, where everything was in order and easy to see. Nothing.

Barney came running downstairs. Nothing to report. Two bedrooms, one unused and empty; the other simply furnished, its few drawers and closet held clothes. The bathroom was blank, too.

They reentered the living room. "They've got to be here," Connie said. "He took them home. I *saw* them, I tell you. In his hand."

"Sure they weren't phonies? Could have been a false lead."

"I made certain of that." Connie's anger mounted with his frustration. "I risked another look in his office safe. They weren't there. They—" He stopped. "Unless he left them—" He stopped again. Tell this goon where they might be, let him know they had put themselves in danger for nothing? No. Not bloody likely. He talked too much. Where had Coulton found this man anyway? Foisted on Coulton as he was on me? "Try the kitchen," he told

Barney. "He's a wily old coot. Could have used a vegetable bin—or the refrigerator."

"What's the hurry? We've rushed everything. Too quick."

That was true enough. Their search had lasted only half an hour—perhaps less. "I'll check in here again," Connie said. "It's the likeliest—"

They both halted, looked at the fireplace. Menlo had stirred. I know that voice, Menlo half thought as he tried to gather consciousness, to fight through the daze that blotted out his memory. He couldn't even guess where he was—two men at the door—where now? He moved his neck a little—something sharp and hard increasing the pain. Pain—it encircled his head—a band that drew tighter. He forced his eyes to open, saw two figures standing over him. Then his eyes closed again. "You," he said, scarcely audible.

"He recognized you," Barney said, and drew his revolver. "Caught you with your mask up."

"No firing! No sound—" Connie broke off in alarm as he heard a car approaching.

Barney slipped his revolver back into its holster. "What of it? Cars use this road." But he listened intently. His frown deepened. He moved to the window, parted the curtain half an inch. "It's turning in here. Come on! The back entrance." He picked up his jacket, took a step toward the hall and the kitchen beyond it.

"Finish your job," Connie said tensely.

Barney stopped, stared at him. "Why not you? It's your neck on the block." And if he hadn't stopped me firing one quick bullet, the job would have been over. Now, a shot would be heard. The car was in the driveway. "Sure," Barney said angrily as he reached the fireplace. He dropped his jacket, bent over and gripped the gray head, smashed it down on the hearth's corner. "Okay? He tripped and fell." But he was speaking to an empty room. Connie was already in the hall.

Barney swore as he snatched his jacket from the floor

and followed at a run. The doorbell sounded as he passed through the kitchen and found the rear entrance. He stood for a brief moment on a narrow stretch of grass, his eyes searching for Connie through the darkness. A movement by a wall that edged the yard caught his ear; his eyes saw a figure in deep shadow trying to scramble over it. He reached Connie, jumped to catch the top of the wall, hoisted himself up. He stretched down his arm to grasp Connie's upraised hand and pulled hard. Connie gave a small cry of pain as he made the top of the wall. "Nearly dislocated—" Connie began. "Shut up!" Barney said, and lowered himself down the other side. He was faced by a mass of trees. Behind him, he heard Connie stumble onto the ground, begin to follow.

Barney groped along the wall to gain the next house and its backyard. No wall there; just a tangle of bushes to push through and a light left burning on the back porch. They skirted the sleeping house, reached its front gate and the car they had left just beyond it.

Connie drew back. Between gulps for breath, he said, "They saw it. They must have. They noted its—"

"Then walk," Barney told him. "Walk all the way back to Washington." He unlocked the door, took the driver's seat, ripped off his gloves, thrust them into his pocket, dried his hands on his jacket as Connie joined him. He started the car and headed toward the highway. "The car's rented," he reminded Connie. "No trace to you or me. I'll leave you where you met me. And you ditch this crate before you reach home. Understood?"

Connie nodded, drew off the stocking from his head, took several long deep breaths, wiped the sweat from his sodden hair.

"There was no choice. He was getting too close to you."

"To the others, too." And he saw me. He saw me.

"Mission only half-successful," Barney said grimly. "No envelope, no tapes."

"I know where to find them."

"I hope you do." Barney's voice was ominous. Sam's instructions had been precise.

"I need a day—a couple of days."

"And some help." Barney's smile was derisive.

"No!" Never yours, never again.

In silence they reached the Potomac, crossed Chain Bridge into Washington.

21

"You'll be met," Menlo had told Bristow over the telephone. And there was Doyle of Security waiting near two cars at the edge of the airfield. His hands were deep in his pockets, his shoulders hunched, his face blanched and furrowed under the unflattering light at the corner of the hangar. He left it as he saw them, came forward to meet them in a patch of deep shadow. He shook hands, seemed stiff in his manner. "Miss Cornell, please wait in the first car. I'll escort you after I talk with Mr. Bristow." He signed to a man who had stepped out of the automobile. "He will take your luggage."

"Just a moment," Bristow said. "Who's in that Ford?"

"Two of my best men. Also two in the second one. Quick, Miss Cornell! Get out of sight." With relief, Doyle watched her obey. He turned back to Bristow. "Drop your bag here. It will be picked up. Now, let's walk." He avoided the lights, kept well in a stretch of darkness.

"Two cars—unnecessary." Bristow's voice was sharp.

He had guessed the reason: Karen and he were to be separated. Like hell we will be, he thought. "Whose idea?"

"Menlo's. He planned to be in the second car and talk with you. A lot to discuss, he said."

Past tense, Bristow noted. "Where is he?" he asked quickly.

"He's dead."

Bristow halted his slow pace, stared at Doyle. "Dead?"

"I sent a car with two men to collect him at twelve-thirty. They were punctual. Found him in the living room, stretched on his back, his head on one corner of the hearth. Body still warm, blood still flowing from the back of his head. My men contacted me at home—I was just about to leave for the airfield. I drove around—took me three minutes; my house is on the next road to his." Doyle paused, remembering that agonizing journey.

"Accidental death?" Bristow asked slowly.

"Did he trip and fall, you mean? But you trip forward, not backward. And how could he trip? No rugs, just a smooth carpet. He didn't drink much, either—a glass of bourbon before dinner. And there was no sign that he had poured a beer while he waited for the car." Another pause. "That injury looked as if he had been hit by a sledge hammer. Someone—" Doyle couldn't go on.

"Any sign of an intruder?"

"Some books on their shelves—not in their regular neat row. A quick search, I'd guess. A desk drawer had been forced open. The rest of the place was neat. There're a couple of men at work there now, searching for finger-prints. The garden will be gone over in daylight—the back door was unlocked, and there was a car parked in front of a neighboring house when my men arrived. They heard it leave, just as they were making an entry into Menlo's place—rang three times, no answer. They found a flash-light—Menlo's—on the hall floor near the door. Perhaps he was going to replace a bulb in the lamp on the porch. It was in darkness. Except, there was no bulb in the lamp. We didn't find any near the flashlight, either."

"Not much to go on." Bristow's face was grim.

"Except for a tie. It was found on the floor under an armchair. Not Menlo's taste," Doyle added bitterly.

"Why the search? Why the murder?"

"Could be he had found out too much about the theft of the cassettes. Worked all weekend, gathered the facts—"

"By himself? Didn't he call in—"

"Not yet. You know the old rule: clean out your own midden. If you can't, then get help. Menlo had permission to turn in his report and recommendation on Wednesday, so notes on the evidence he had gathered must have been ready. He left them with Miriam yesterday afternoon. And three tapes."

"In her vault?"

"Yes. Didn't trust his own safe, apparently. I'm thinking that whoever killed him was searching for those notes and tapes. He authorized you to work over them. So he said—lunchtime yesterday—I saw him and—" Doyle stopped, fought back his last memory of Frank Menlo.

Bristow said quietly. "Anything else he told you?"

"Over the phone this evening. Wanted extra precautions for Miss Cornell. Sam Waterman is back."

"When?"

"Arrived in New York twelve hours ago."

"Monday afternoon?" Bristow was incredulous.

"Yes. Rome passed the word."

Bristow turned toward the car where Karen waited, began walking. Doyle caught up with him, said, "Slow down, slow down. Menlo wanted her taken to a safe house, but that's impossible at this short notice. The only one available has been used a lot. It could be under scrutiny. In fact, we're about to sell it and find something more secure. And we can't take her to her Washington address or to Schleeman's house or to some hotel. Not at this hour of the morning. So, I'll put her up at my place until tomorrow. By that time—" He shrugged.

"By that time you'll still have a problem. And what

about your family—do they know you're bringing a guest?"

"I'll tell them tomorrow. They can keep a secret."

"How many vital secrets have you ever told them?" None, of course. Bristow's judgment was confirmed by Doyle's unhappy face. "Look—no one yet knows we've arrived in Washington except you and your agents. Keep it that way. It's dark for a couple of hours at least. Leave two of your best men with me for the next few days. They'll sleep in my spare bedroom and guard Karen. We'll smuggle her into my apartment before dawn breaks. And she'll stay there, out of sight."

"Your place could be searched like Menlo's."

"And there will be three men to face them by night, two by day."

"Menlo said—"

"Menlo would want me to finish his report. And that takes concentration. I need peace of mind, no extra worries. Agreed?"

"It's a risk."

"We've been taking risks for the last three days."

"It's your responsibility."

"It is." Almost as they reached the car, Bristow halted again. "That possibly unsafe house you mentioned—could you install one of your agents there? She should be approximately Karen's height and weight, dressed in jeans and white silk shirt—as last seen by the hotel porter in Rome. If she's a blonde, give her a dark wig. Leave two agents with her, and tell her to be only now and again visible. Okay?"

Doyle looked at him. "Okay," he agreed.

"I'll be at the office early tomorrow and start on Menlo's notes. If you've anything new on his death, come and see me."

"We'll probably pass out the word that it was an accident. Any objection to that?"

"Not if you find the murderer soon."

"We'll get him. Could have used that parked car. My

men noted its number, thought it was odd that it wasn't garaged or in a driveway. Cars don't often stand on that road by night."

"Could we keep the news of Menlo's death out of circulation for a couple of days? Until Wednesday at least?"

"That's tricky."

"Then you can do it," Bristow said. "If we're asked about his absence, we can say he's in the hospital." True, in a macabre and horrible way: an autopsy would start there tomorrow.

"You know all the dodges," Doyle said, and this time a brief glance of approval was forced out of him.

"We're up against a bunch of artful dodgers," Bristow reminded him as he opened the Ford's door. Karen was in the back seat. He spoke to the two men in front. "I need someone to drive my car."

The younger of the two said, "Sure."

"Okay. You'll find a blue Camaro just around that corner, in the parking area." He handed over its keys as he pointed and gave the plate number. "We'll wait here for you. Then follow us to Muir Street. Park it fifty yards or so from my door—27A—there's a bookstore at 27. Got it?"

"Got it." The man began an astonishing sprint.

To Doyle, both doubtful and impatient, Bristow explained, "I left it there Friday night. It will take him only three extra minutes. See you tomorrow." He got into the Ford. "As soon as the Camaro swings around the corner, start driving," he told the man in the front seat. "I'll direct you." The door closed.

He certainly will, Doyle thought, and turned toward the other Ford. Wouldn't leave her while he got his car himself. Wouldn't risk me making off with her, taking her to my house. And he was right about that. It will be a pleasure to work with him.

Doyle joined his men. "Change in arrangements. Back to Menlo's place," he said as he saw a blue car come into sight. The Ford with Bristow and Miss Cornell was already moving. He watched its taillights disappear ahead of him, the Camaro following closely, and traveling fast.

Their arrival at Bristow's apartment was inconspicuous. The tightly packed houses of Muir Street were asleep, the bookstore in darkness. The Ford was parked about twenty yards away from Bristow's door. The Camaro found space a short distance ahead of it. Too near, thought Bristow, but he hadn't heard any gears being stripped, and for that he was thankful: no one drove that car but himself. He locked the front door, and even to Taylor's critical eye— he was the older of the two men—security seemed good. So far.

He and his colleague, Hansen, made a quick tour of the third-floor apartment, noting any drawbacks and weaknesses. Karen, on her own tour, found it comfortable and definitely a bachelor's pad: outsize bed in the master bedroom; two divans in a room with TV and hosts of paperbacks in the bookcase ("Where my friends stay when they drop in for a weekend in Washington," Bristow said); a living room, with stereo and books everywhere, that lay between the two bedrooms. That was the front of the apartment. To the rear, across the long hall, was a very small study with a large desk and a typewriter, a bathroom, a kitchen with a dining section near the front door. Utilitarian, she decided, and was disappointed. Surely the furniture wasn't Peter's choice. It was a contrast to the pictures on the walls. They were good.

He caught that fleeting expression. "I've leased the place until its owner gets back from Singapore."

"Everything?"

"Except the books and the records. The pictures are mine, too." Then to the two men, who had just explored the back stairs, he said encouragingly, "A few days and you'll be sleeping in your own beds."

Hansen, a brisk thirty-five, was cheerful about the lack of space in the guest room. "Better than a motel," he pronounced with his ready smile. "Once spent ten days

cooped up with—" He caught Taylor's eye and ended
with a laugh.

Taylor said, "Who occupies the apartment below this?"

"The owner of the bookstore. She's old and very deaf."

"Reliable?"

"Mrs. Abel? She's the widow of a man who once worked
in Security."

Taylor accepted that with a nod of approval. "The back
stairs lead down to a yard?"

"Yes. Small. Walled at the rear from another back garden on the next street. But you'll see it better by daylight.
Why don't you—"

"Any exit from that yard?"

"Through a rear door in the bookstore."

Taylor frowned.

"I often use it to reach Muir," Bristow said, and Karen
marveled at his patience. "Now, why don't you get a few
hours' sleep? One of you be on deck by six o'clock. I'll
be leaving then—no later. And if we need more food,
Hansen can take the Ford and drive to some supermarket.
No difficulty there," he added quickly and cut short an
objection from Taylor. "I often have an old friend from
college visiting me for a couple of days."

And Taylor, who must be fifty, Karen thought, doesn't
look young enough for a college friend. He had relaxed
though, when he heard Peter was leaving by six o'clock—
work ahead, not just fun and games. It's me he disap-
proves of: he's been tight-faced ever since he saw the
sleeping arrangements.

The two men took Bristow's advice and left for their
room.

"I hope they can cook. I'm strictly short-order," Karen
said. "Peter—how much sleep did you get on the plane?"

"Plenty."

"Then let's have breakfast." She led the way into the
kitchen. "And we can talk," she added. "Or can't you tell
me what has happened?" Before we arrived at the airfield,
he was in high spirits. We laughed, we joked, we made

plans. Since he spoke with that man who met us, Peter had been depressed, has tried to conceal it, but every now and again I can sense something is wrong. He's troubled. And sad.

"I'll tell you as much as I can," he said. "After breakfast," he added. "You already know most of the background, darling."

Not troubled or depressed by something between us, she thought with relief, watching his face, listening to his tone of voice. "I'm starved," she admitted. "Bacon and eggs and hot buttered toast? I never get these things abroad to taste the way they do here." She opened the refrigerator. "There's enough food for a week, Peter! Hansen won't need to go shopping."

"Enough for one man," he said, breaking into a smile. "Not for three."

"Do you do your own shopping?"

"Mrs. Roscoe does it on Fridays when she comes in to scour and clean."

"And you manage all by yourself?" She was horrified.

"I'm out most of the time. Not the way I like to live," he admitted, "but at least I am free." He hesitated, then said frankly, "Free of memories. When a marriage turns sour, it's pretty bad—for both people."

But some get more out of it than others, thought Karen: Peter had his books and records and pictures; his ex-wife took everything else, along with emeralds and a millionaire husband. "Two eggs or three?" She began breaking the first shell.

"Make it three. Sandwiches at the Imperial seem a long way off." And he'd skip lunch. A busy day ahead.

"What would we ever do without sandwiches?" No bitterness in his voice when he had mentioned his marriage. And that was all he might ever tell her about it. Thank heavens, the outsize bed was rented with this apartment, she thought, and lowered the heat under the frying pan. "Do you know how they were invented?"

He had taken charge of the toast and coffee making.

"Sandwiches?" He repressed a smile as he watched her absorbed by the sizzling bacon, ready to remove the rashers and drain them of grease. "How?"

"There was an Earl of Sandwich who liked to gamble, never could leave the gaming table when he was playing. So when he got hungry, he called for his servant to slap a hunk of roast beef between two slices of bread, and he ate it while he—oh, damn, I nearly broke that yolk. Sunny-side up, Peter?" She looked at him, saw the amusement on his face. "You *knew* the story all along, didn't you? Really—"

"I liked the way you told it. Sunny-side up, if you can manage it."

"Help! This fork is no good—where's something flat?" She took the spatula he found for her in a drawer. At least he was smiling—something he hadn't done very much for the last three hours. Complete the cure, she told herself. "Just remembered a silly saying about sandwiches. Fourth-grade humor. Can you stand it?"

"I'll brace myself."

"If you want a sandwich, you go to the beach and pick up the sand which is there."

He hadn't heard that one in thirty years. "Do you do this often?" His smile broadened into a laugh.

"Only when trying to cook at five in the morning. Oh, see what I've done!" She stared at a broken yolk in dismay.

"It will run worse when I dig a knife into it. Come on, darling—"

"I forgot the orange juice!"

"We'll have it as dessert." Then, sitting across from her at the small kitchen table, he said, "Thank you, Karen."

She could only guess what he meant and hoped she was right. Whatever news he had heard this morning must have shattered him.

They finished eating, sat over their third cup of coffee, and she heard how bad the news was. The Vienna tapes had been stolen on Saturday night. Menlo had been investigating for the last two days. Menlo had met with an accident early this morning.

"He died?" Karen asked, watching Peter's eyes.

"Yes. But few know that yet. We're keeping quiet about it."

"Because it was murder? And the murderer has still to be caught?"

"First found, and then caught."

Suddenly, she was filled with foreboding. "Your job, Peter?"

"No. My job is to finish Menlo's report. So I won't be home until late, Karen. Sorry, but—" He shrugged.

"I'll stay here, won't show my face even at a window." The stolen cassettes would make her sure of that. They explained a lot: the bullet; the quick flight from Rome— "Well, we did escape from Waterman," she said. "I suppose he must have heard about the cassettes."

"He may even have listened to them. He isn't in Rome. He's back here."

"Here?"

"In New York, certainly."

And that means here. She set down her coffee cup as she felt her hand tremble.

"Darling—"

"I'm safe, Peter. You've given me two good watchdogs. And you did smuggle me in here most expertly. Could I borrow your little study, use the desk? I thought I'd keep out of Taylor's way. He doesn't approve of me, you know," she added with a good attempt at a smile. "I'll show him I work, too, for a living."

"You are writing about the terrorists?"

"Schleeman will expect some copy. And soon."

"Don't call him," Bristow said quickly. "I'll do that later this afternoon."

"And explain what?"

"Enough. He knows you escaped the bombing."

"He'll want to know the details. That call he made to

me last night—" and nearly caused us to be late in leaving
the Imperial—"well, I was rather brief."

"He'll put it down to shock. I'll talk with him, reassure
him that all is well. I like the old boy as much as you do,
honey. So stop worrying, darling. Will you?"

"All right. If you'll stop worrying about me, I'll stop
worrying about you. A bargain?" She rose to throw her
arms around him. "And this seals it," she said, and kissed
him.

He kept hold of her, eased her onto his knees. "No
telephone. Promise?"

"I won't even answer it."

"No calls will come in here. The phone is switched on
to the answering service." It had better be left that way
meanwhile. The apartment should seem as unoccupied as
possible. His arms tightened around her, and they kissed
again. And again. "I love you," he told her softly.

At the kitchen door, Hansen cleared his throat. "Five-
thirty, Mr. Bristow. Any further instructions?"

"I think you know the routine."

"Let me cook some breakfast for you," Karen said,
regaining her feet and some composure.

"I'll cook," Hansen said cheerfully. "Do it all the time."

"See you around midnight, Peter?" she asked as he
rose to leave. She was half-joking, half-anxious.

"Whenever. I have to finish a report and turn it in
tomorrow. If there's the least suspicion of an emergency
here—"

"Call your answering service?"

"No. Not you, Karen. Let Hansen do that." He gave
her one last kiss. To Hansen, he said, "Identify yourself
as an old friend staying with me for a couple of days."

"Won't even need to do it," Hansen assured him. "We
can reach Mr. Doyle anytime."

"Should have thought of that," Bristow admitted as he
reached the hall. He almost left, remembered additional
instructions. "Spare keys for front and back entrances in

my middle desk drawer. And—yes, better pull the desk well away from the study window." This time, he left.

Menlo was right, he told himself as he ran downstairs: love and business don't mix, make a man forgetful. And, thinking of Menlo, his pace increased. He reached his car. As he unlocked its door, he recalled his last words to Menlo, spoken in anger, something he would always regret. Goaded by that memory, he reached Langley in record time.

22

First, Bristow retrieved Menlo's envelope and tapes from the deposit vault. It was too early for Miriam to be there herself, but an assistant on night duty handed them over with a glance at Bristow's identification. Next, he reached his office and prepared to read the notes and listen to the tapes. Without them, he would have been blind and deaf. He knew only two facts about these last three days—the Vienna cassettes had been stolen and Menlo was dead.

With his door securely locked, and no one in the offices around him—he'd have two good hours before they started drifting in to their desks—he set to work. There were four closely written pages in Menlo's small neat hand, with abbreviations and jotted phrases to make everything compact, but the dates and times and sequence of events were all in good order. Menlo had gathered an incredible amount of detail, enough for circumstantial evidence. His report was almost ready to be typed and presented.

And yet—he hadn't named the mole. As if he still had

some doubts in spite of the facts he had gathered. What had prevented him? Some instinct—or some need to double-check? His brief memorandum on Waterman and Coulton—who was the control?—had only queries on the incentives of an unnamed mole. Possibly, he had wanted more investigation into the past histories of either Shaw or Fairbairn. They were certainly Menlo's candidates for the enemy agent who had infiltrated his section. And Fairbairn held the definite edge on that, Bristow had to admit against his will. He liked Fairbairn, had always trusted him.

His depression deepened as he played the two tapes and listened first to Shaw's words and then to Fairbairn's words as they answered Menlo's questions. It was obvious that Menlo was tending toward Fairbairn—why else talk at the end of Fairbairn's interview about the four choices a traitor faced when he was discovered? As if Menlo had been giving him a chance to admit his guilt. Menlo was right about suicide as no choice at all, but he had forgotten—or ignored—the real fifth choice. Murder. To save your mission. To save your own miserable hide.

But Fairbairn is no murderer, Bristow told himself angrily. That, I can't believe. Or is it prejudice that is prompting me to find him innocent? Yes, I'm prejudiced when it comes to judging a friend. So let's go over the evidence again, let's see if I am trying to ignore facts, let's discover any small gaps in Menlo's findings that should be explored.

He reread the notes, slowly, carefully, and marked a few points that might need more investigation. Pitifully few, he realized: Menlo had done a complete job. Still— for his own peace of mind, he'd check them out. And then he thought of the discrepancies in the accounts of Saturday night given to Fairbairn and Shaw. Check these, he told himself, check these thoroughly; trap the mole with his own lies. A long chance, he knew, but worth a try. Once more, he played the two taped interviews.

Voices in the corridor warned him: the beginning of

the day's work. He gathered notes and tapes and locked them in his safe. He left the office in search of either Fairbairn or Shaw.

Fairbairn was at his desk. "Hello!" he said in surprise as Bristow entered his room. "That was a short vacation. When did you get back?"

"This morning."

"Just in time for the bad news. Or is it good? Menlo's in the hospital. An accident, I've heard. Happened last night. Fell down in his own home, cracked his head. But if I know Menlo, he'll be up and around in a few days. He's on the warpath, Pete, and he won't give up until he's added another scalp to his belt." Fairbairn was nervous and tense. Bitter, too. He looked as if he hadn't slept much last night. "My scalp, I think. And God knows why. I didn't take those damned cassettes. I was there, sure, just before the guard was doped. But I swear to you, Pete—" He stopped. "You heard about the cassettes?"

"Yes. Menlo telephoned me."

"He probably gave you the story, too."

"Some of it. Why don't you give me the rest? Where's Shaw, by the way?"

"He'll be here this afternoon. He has a dentist's appointment at eleven."

"Did he call you about that this morning? Or was it a long-standing appointment?"

Fairbairn looked in surprise at Bristow. "Sure, he called. Reached me at home before I left." Then Fairbairn's surprise vanished. "Are you stepping in where Menlo left off? What in hell is so important about a couple of damned cassettes? Shaw couldn't steal a run at a softball game. I didn't take them, either. So why the devil are you—"

"Wallace—stop talking and listen, will you? Let's clear this thing up together. You and Shaw are in deep trouble, and you know it. All I'd like to do is prove you didn't take the cassettes."

"Prove innocence? And how do you do that?" Wallace shot back at him.

"By finding the man who is guilty." Bristow watched a struggle of emotions on Fairbairn's face: anger, anxiety, hope. Hope seemed to win. At least, Fairbairn calmed down. Bristow said, "But I need your help. Come on, let's walk in the fresh air. You can fill in some of the details for me."

"Do you think I have this office bugged? God, you're as suspicious as Menlo."

"Not bugged by you," Bristow said quietly and led the way into the corridor.

"I could use some coffee," Fairbairn said. "Didn't feel like breakfast this morning. The commissary's quiet at this hour."

And more private than being in public view. "Coffee sounds good."

There was no more talk until they had settled at an isolated table with a pot of coffee. Bristow studied his friend's face, a handsome face that appealed to a lot of women with its thin features, tanned skin, hazel eyes that usually seemed amused, fair hair that fell into a wave no matter how hard it was brushed. Today, Fairbairn's tan looked gray, his eyes were shadowed and didn't find life so comic, his hair was unkempt. Even his well-fitted seersucker jacket was crushed and dejected.

Bristow said awkwardly—this conversation would be as embarrassing for him as it was disturbing for Fairbairn—"Wallace—just give me straight answers, will you? Cut out the humor and your throwaway remarks and understatements. Give me the facts, even if they bore the hell out of you."

"But Menlo heard everything. There's nothing to add."

"I wasn't there to hear it," Bristow reminded him. "So let's get started—shouldn't take long—just a few points that puzzled me."

"I was clear enough, I thought." Fairbairn was annoyed.

"Then I'm stupid."

Fairbairn's laugh was forced. It broke off abruptly.

"Sorry. I guess you're right. I'll be dead serious. No flippancy. Okay?"

"Okay. For starters—you told Menlo you had no idea when Coulton and Shaw had met."

"But I have no idea. They knew each other before Shaw ever introduced me to Coulton."

Bristow's voice sharpened. "Shaw introduced you? When?"

"Must have been six weeks ago. A Saturday evening. Emma and I had been at a cocktail party in Georgetown and went on to dinner at a French restaurant in M Street. Shaw and Coulton were there. As we passed their table, Shaw rose and stopped me. I had to introduce him to Emma, and he introduced me to Coulton. But how long they had known each other, I haven't the foggiest notion. Never asked Shaw. Why should I?"

"No reason." Not until now, thought Bristow. "Was Shaw using the extra desk in your office at that time?"

"Oh, he had been dotting in and out for some weeks. Questions, you know. Always eager for my advice."

"When did he move in?"

"Last week, when we were working on the same problem but from different angles. It seemed simpler to me to have him there—it's a double office, actually, and his was only a cubicle."

"It seemed simpler to you. . . . Do you mean you suggested the change, or did he suggest it and you agreed?"

"I agreed. I was tired of having him bouncing in and out." Fairbairn was puzzled. "Just where is this getting us?"

"A little deeper into the picture. So tell me—when the cabinet in the file room jammed on Saturday night, you stood at the door and watched the corridor. Why?"

"No need for me to stay with Shaw and the guard. I thought someone ought to keep an eye on the corridor and on—" Fairbairn halted abruptly.

"And on what?"

"Coulton. I don't really cotton to the guy. I couldn't

understand why the hell he hadn't waited in our office until we had finished with the file room. In fact, he and Shaw could have left, let me handle the Greek files alone."

"Did he make any move while you watched the corridor?"

"None."

"Just stood there?"

"Just stood. I felt like an idiot. So when he wanted to find the washroom, I showed him the way—being extra polite to make up for my rudeness."

"Rudeness?" Bristow smiled. "Never heard you being rude to anyone in my life, Wallace."

"Well, I had a strange feeling about the guy—the way he arrived and needed a lift home and all that. I didn't say much on our way to the file room, cut him down a bit. What else is rudeness?"

So Fairbairn had a stirring of suspicion, but then dismissed it when he felt it was unwarranted. As most of us do, thought Bristow. "When the guard, O'Donnell, came out of the file room, did he go straight to his table?"

Fairbairn frowned. "He came out first—Shaw with him—I think."

"Come on, Wallace. You can do better than that."

"I spoke to him. Yes, I asked about getting the lock fixed and what did we do with the Greek files. Would I have to wait with them until Maintenance got the lock working?"

"And he reassured you he'd call Maintenance and keep an eye on the files for the time being?"

"That's about it. He'd phone Menlo and have him lock them up, once the cabinet was fixed."

"How long did you talk—a minute or two?"

"Could be. I joked a little."

"And where were the files? With Shaw?"

"Yes."

"And where was he? Standing at the table?"

Fairbairn stared at Bristow. There was a long silence.

"Yes," he said at last. Then, quickly, "Not Shaw—it couldn't be Shaw."

"Take it easy. We aren't saying it was Shaw who dropped something into O'Donnell's coffee cup." Until this moment, I thought—as Menlo had thought—it was Coulton who had that assignment. Then why was Coulton present? Just to receive the cassettes after they were stolen? He could have waited in the car park for that, never neded to show his face. Or was he there to give an appearance of complete innocence? Lurking around a car park where he didn't belong would be hard to explain if he were seen. Or was he making sure that the job of drugging O'Donnell was efficiently done—no hesitation, no mistake, no rousing of any suspicion?

"But there was only Shaw and Coulton and myself in that corridor. And Shaw was close to that table longer than I was. If it wasn't Shaw, then who—"

"Easy, Wallace," Bristow cautioned again. "We don't know yet. It's your word against his, and he may not have the same story to tell."

"But that's what happened!"

"Let's go back a little earlier. You visited the file room for twenty minutes that evening. Alone."

"I was consulting material from several files, but not in the Greek cabinet, if that's what you're driving at. I didn't go near it."

"Did Shaw know you were consulting other files?"

"Sure. We were working on the same problem—tracing that Athens-to-London route of the *Blitz* disinformation." Fairbairn's face was tense as he remembered another detail. "Later, when we both visited the room at ten o'clock, I left Shaw to replace the Greek files and went to the Austrian cabinet."

"Why?"

"Following a hunch—a vague memory. There's a Graz newspaper that might be a transmission belt from Athens to West Germany. It did act as that a couple of years back."

"So you opened the Austrian cabinet." And that was on the opposite side of the room. Fairbairn's back would be turned to Shaw.

Fairbairn nodded. "I had just found the Graz folder when Shaw called for help with the lock that was stuck. I closed the cabinet and went to help him."

Bristow lit his second cigarette. "Have one?" He offered his pack. "Or are you still refusing them?"

"Gave up the habit for good." Fairbairn watched him anxiously. "Well? Or is the jury still out?"

"Has to be until I talk with Shaw, too."

"His word against mine. That's what you said. Hopeless. Who can prove whose word is false?"

Bristow ignored that little outburst. Very quietly, he said, "Whoever removed the cassettes waited until you had left the corridor and O'Donnell had collapsed. Did Coulton stay with you all the way to the front entrance?"

"Yes. And Shaw left ahead of us—so that lets him off the hook, too, doesn't it?" Fairbairn was embarrassed. "Guess I was too quick to judge him," he admitted.

"You were defending yourself."

"At his expense." Fairbairn drew a long deep breath. "When you talk out of fear—well, you never make a pretty picture, do you?"

"Fear?"

"Fear of this shadow forever hanging over my head. But I have nothing to confess, Pete. Nothing. Except blindness, perhaps. There must be more involved in all this than just the theft of two cassettes."

"Much more."

"I feel I'm—I'm trapped. How or why, I don't know. I could lose my job—my career—my family. My whole life, in fact. Pete—what do I do?"

"Ignore it."

Fairbairn's laugh was short and sour.

"Say nothing to anyone. Talk to no one about our meeting today. Keep your cool, play it loose."

Fairbairn asked slowly, "Do you believe me?"

"Enough to try and find the whole truth."

"I'll settle for that."

"Let's get back to the office," Bristow said.

There was a considerable walk ahead of them, and Bristow used it to say, "By the way—a week ago last Saturday, when I phoned you to meet me and take an envelope to the vault—"

"I remember. When I went to get my car, I found it had a flat—must have been a slow leak."

"So you went back to the office to ask Shaw for a lift?"

"No, no. He was already in the parking lot. He was on his way home."

"He offered you a lift?"

"And I took it gladly."

"You arrived at the gas station ahead of time."

"Well ahead. Shaw's a wild driver. It would have been too noticeable to keep his Honda waiting in front of the gas station, so he parked it among some other cars close to the cafeteria."

"With a clear view of me when I arrived?"

"Yes. But I didn't notice you arriving—you weren't driving your own car, and I was watching for a blue Camaro."

"Did Shaw notice me?"

"Don't think so. Didn't say anything, at least."

"Why did he suddenly shoot out of the parking space?"

Fairbairn was baffled by that question. "Guess he was a bit speedy in reaching the gas station. But it was twelve-thirty, you know."

"He knew of our appointment?"

"I—I may have mentioned it. He was in the office when you telephoned." Fairbairn was embarrassed. "I suppose I talked out of turn. Sorry. Didn't think it was any state secret we were dealing with. You were pretty casual about that envelope, you know."

"Was I that good?"

"You fooled me."

But not Shaw, Bristow thought. And then wondered if

he were too quick in judgment. He'd have to talk with Shaw, too, hear his story.... "See you around," he told Fairbairn as they reached their floor. "And not one word about this discussion," he added quietly.

"Not even in my sleep."

He's recovering, thought Bristow as he entered his office. Did I give him too much hope? It is one thing to believe a friend, another to prove he is innocent. I'll have to do more than convince myself. And I doubt if I'm qualified for this job; I'm not objective enough. So why the hell did Menlo entrust me to take over his investigation? Perhaps I'd better choose someone to follow me—in case of an accident. Such as being eliminated as Menlo was.

Abruptly, he switched his mind away from that unpleasant idea. Shaw, he considered now—Shaw had longer access than anyone else to the guard's table and his coffee cup. But Shaw had left ahead of the other two, and Fairbairn backed Shaw's statement on that point. So where did that leave us—with some third party, who didn't belong to this unit and yet knew the combination of the Farrago file, knew that the Vienna cassettes were there for the stealing? Coulton? But the time of his leaving the building was definite. He accompanied Fairbairn out. Accompanied or escorted? To make sure Fairbairn was safely and quickly away from the corridor when the Farrago file was opened and the cassettes lifted?

I may have answered my question why Coulton was present on Saturday night, Bristow thought, but I'm still floundering around on the exact timing of his departure. Both taped interviews had been vague about that. There was one way to solve that problem: call Doyle and ask him to have Saturday's records checked on everyone who was signed out between ten and ten-thirty.

So he called Doyle.

"Yes, it's possible," Doyle said in answer to his request, but obviously thought Bristow was beginning to saw sawdust. "Give me until one o'clock. May have more to report by then. New developments. We've had a spot of luck."

We could use it, thought Bristow. "Also, would you check if anyone returned to this building after he had signed out?"

"A re-entry? That's a bit unusual."

"*Anything* unusual—that's what we want to know. Okay? One o'clock will be fine. See you here."

Bristow spent the next hour making his own notes on his talk with Fairbairn, comparing them with the earlier statements to Menlo. No divergence. Just more explanation, a clarification that changed the whole picture. Carefully, he went over his series of questions to Fairbairn. They had prodded, but they hadn't led. Why the hell hadn't Fairbairn been more explicit in the first place? But when Menlo had talked with him, Fairbairn hadn't thought it necessary to go into details or justification. He had assumed, in typical fashion, that everyone knew he could never be guilty of theft or treason.

There was still half an hour before Doyle would appear. Time to check in with Joe at the answering service, let him know he was back from vacation. Some vacation, he thought as he dialed Joe's number and relaxed at his desk with a cigarette.

Joe was astounded to hear his voice. "Then you can take the six-ten call instead of Mr. Menlo. He told me to put it through to your office."

Bristow swung his feet off the desk, stubbed out the cigarette. "What call?"

"Didn't Mr. Menlo tell you? I phoned him at his home yesterday evening. He said I did the right thing."

"Phoned him about what?"

"An urgent call for you at five-forty. A man. Spoke a lot, but wouldn't give his name. Said—"

"Play it back to me."

"Just a minute. Got your taped messages right here. You'll have to listen to all of them, Mr. Bristow. They're on one—"

"Okay, okay. I'll listen." A call puzzling enough to make Joe call Menlo, interesting enough for Menlo to thank Joe for having trespassed into his privacy—Bristow's tension increased by the moment as Joe's minute stretched to almost two. Finally, the weekend's messages came through. And the very last was one in a stranger's voice, speaking fluent American with a foreign inflection when his words rose in anger. The sudden oath was definitely Russian. The phrases "No one else. Only Bristow" echoed Vasek's words to Karen in Prague. "Two weeks earlier"—yes, two weeks had been his time limit when he spoke with her in Rome. "Someone Bristow would very much like to meet..."

"You bet I'd like to meet you, Vasek," Bristow said under his breath as the tape ended. "One more trick out of you, and I'll wring your bloody neck."

Joe was saying, "Okay, Mr. Bristow? Clear enough?"

"Clear and true. I'd like to collect that tape."

"I'll be here from five on. My brother—"

"That's right—he takes over for the afternoons. I'll drop around this evening—could be late, very late."

"Anytime until midnight," Joe reassured him. "Hope you had a good vacation."

"Just loafing around," Bristow said. "And Joe—tape all the calls for me for the next few days, especially the one that will be made at six-ten this evening, even though I'm taking it in my office. Got that?" Bristow replaced the receiver, thinking of Vasek. Farrago. The man who trusted no one.

How the devil had he managed it—safely out of Europe, across the Atlantic, into America, and playing everything alone? He had courage, plenty of that to match his self-confidence. A master of planning, of the unexpected, of deception, too. In his peculiar way, a genius. Was he proving that we need him more than he needed us? Establishing his superiority, even domination, before we met? If he ever learned what a mess we are trying to clean up here, he'd add one more tally to his conviction that Americans are nitwits, only to be tolerated when useful.

Then Doyle breezed in, and Farrago retreated into the shadows.

23

TOM DOYLE MIGHT NOT HAVE HAD MUCH TIME FOR SLEEP last night, but his step was elastic, his eyes gleamed with barely concealed excitement. "Some interesting developments," he began as he took the chair opposite Bristow at his desk. "We got—"

"First," said Bristow, "have you heard from Taylor or Hansen?"

"Every hour on the hour. Checked with Hansen just before I came here. Everything is quiet and under control at your place."

Bristow drew a deep breath of relief. "What's your news?"

"We got the car."

"The one standing last night near Menlo's house?"

"The same. Rented, of course. And abandoned in a parking lot at a bus stop on Wisconsin."

"Quick work!" There were many bus stops along that avenue.

"Well—we needed some help on this one," Doyle

admitted. "We had the police circulate number and description—two-door sedan, dark color, new model Ford possibly. A patrol car spotted it this morning when they were cruising around Friendship Heights."

Friendship Heights? That was near Chevy Chase, Fairbairn's district. God, no!

"It wasn't even well hidden. Standing in plain view."

Bristow stared at Doyle. "Friendship Heights," he said slowly, still aghast.

"About a couple of miles from Fairbairn's house on Cherry Lane." Doyle watched Bristow curiously. "He could have ditched the car and then hiked home. He walks a lot, I hear."

"I'd have thought he'd have his own car waiting in that parking lot—if he was abandoning the Ford there."

Doyle shook his head. "His Buick stayed in his driveway all night. Looked as if he never left home. But someone telephoned him around eleven. His wife answered. She said he had gone out for a late stroll."

"You mean—you've his place under surveillance?"

"Menlo requested it. Suggested a proper search warrant, too. I've hung back on that, but perhaps it's now time to get one and use it. We found a stocking mask lying on the floor of the rented car—slipped off the seat and was forgotten, no doubt. There were also a couple of cigarette butts—"

"Fairbairn doesn't smoke," Bristow interjected. A foolish clutch at hope, he realized. Fairbairn, under strain, might have gone back to his old habit.

"Then it could have been the other guy who does. We found his thumbprints on the steering wheel, but we can't identify them. The FBI has no record of them, either. The same thumbprint is on an outside panel of Menlo's front door and on his stereo." Doyle looked at Bristow with some impatience. "Two men did the job: one wearing gloves and the other a little careless about that. Perhaps because he knew he couldn't be traced in this country."

"Two men—are you sure?"

"At least two. If a gun had been used, one man could have dealt with Menlo. But there is no trace of a bullet fired. There is no trace of a fight, either, and I don't see Menlo being overpowered by one man without a struggle. Also, the search of the house was complete—a big job for someone working alone—upstairs, downstairs. They weren't ordinary burglars. Nothing was taken. Not radio or a camera lying on the hall table or silver candlesticks and tray or Menlo's supply of extra cash in his bedroom. The papers in his desk drawer—cleverly opened, by the way, and no fingerprints left—were jumbled. The bookcases had also been searched. My guess is they were looking for something like—well, these notes he made. And the guy who led that search must have known about them. How many in your unit could have known? The two who were interviewed by Menlo. Right?"

"What about Shaw's movements last night? You had his apartment house under surveillance, too, hadn't you?"

Doyle nodded. "Seemed to be spending the night at home. His Honda was parked in front—for a change, I must say—and the lights went on in his bedroom when the living room was darkened."

"That can be controlled with a timer."

"Yes. But there was a telephone call at midnight, and he answered."

"He spoke himself? Not a recorded message?"

Doyle took out a small notebook and consulted it. "He said, 'Yes? Shaw here. Who's speaking?' A man's voice answered, 'Carl.' Shaw said, 'Look, Carl, call me tomorrow, will you? That's a good chap. I'm busy right now.' And he hung up." Doyle waited for Bristow's reply, got none. "You're a hard man to convince," he said, shaking his head. "I'm thinking you don't find my news too welcome."

"To tell you the truth, it knocked the wind out of me. I spent a good part of this morning listening to Fairbairn, studying his answers. And," Bristow added wryly, "I found him innocent. A dupe, yes. Someone who was being used, set up to take the fall if our mole was in danger of being unearthed."

"Mole?"

"That's what it's all about. Didn't Menlo tell you? We've got one in my unit. He took the Vienna cassettes—Menlo used them as bait to catch him."

Doyle was silent. then he said, "A mole is a pretty expert con man. Clever, too. That car he ditched—" He broke off, looked at Bristow.

"Too clever to leave it anywhere near his own house," Bristow said, and Doyle nodded in agreement. "Shaw's apartment is right in Washington, isn't it?"

"M Street, west of Connecticut. But a long way from Friendship Heights early in the morning."

"Unless Shaw had someone waiting for him in the parking area to drive him home. Or almost home." Bristow thought over that and had a better idea. "If his friend was unwilling to be seen waiting there, what about a bus? Doesn't one of the Owl Routes run from Friendship Heights right down into northwest Washington?"

"From one until five A.M.," Doyle said softly. "Takes you down Wisconsin into Pennsylvania Avenue, ends at Seventeenth Street."

"Shaw wouldn't have to travel that distance. If he got off at Washington Circle—"

"Less than a mile to walk home. But what does that prove—unless we know he's definitely the man we want? Suppositions don't make a case."

"It proves that Shaw could have ditched the car at Friendship Heights as easily as Fairbairn."

"You have a point there."

And not much more, thought Bristow. "I'll talk with Shaw this afternoon. After that I'll have to get Menlo's report into shape, add what I can, turn it in tomorrow. It looks as if we'll have to let others continue the investigation. We won't look so good, will we? Menlo's section can't even clean out its own midden—as you so neatly put it."

"Just a moment. May I used your phone?" Doyle was on his feet. "It isn't bugged," he said reassuringly. "I had your office swept this morning." Then as Bristow looked at him, astonished, he added, "You're in charge here now that Menlo has gone."

"I wouldn't say that."

"You were close enough to him to raise questions in some minds. Right? So I was just making sure you weren't under *their* surveillance." He began dialing. "And I don't want you working late here. Alone. If you were thinking of bedding down in your office, forget it. Can't spare two more guards to baby-sit—" He turned his attention on the phone. "Jack? Any word yet from the lab boys?... No trace of hair oil or pomade? I see.... Two hairs? Is that all?... Yes, I *know* it's a cheap stocking sold in the millions, probably cut off from a pair of panty hose. Who wears stockings nowadays?" Doyle ended his call, turned to Bristow. "None of my three girls, that's for sure. Well— did you get any of that?"

"Most of it." Bristow repressed a sense of small triumph. "Fairbairn uses something on his hair to keep it in place. Smells of lavender, I'm sorry to say."

"He does, does he?" Doyle was a good loser. With a grin, he added, "The two hairs that were found on that mask are brown. Shaw's color. Right?"

"Pity you don't have that search warrant ready. Shaw isn't at home this morning—a dentist's appointment." Which could mean anything, such as a quiet meeting with Coulton to discuss where Menlo might have kept his notes and tapes.

"He hasn't left his apartment," Doyle said. "His Honda is still parked out front. Dammit all," he added in sudden temper, and picked up the phone again, dialed quickly. "Just trying to reach Shaw," he explained, and listened as he let the phone ring twelve times. "He's out, it seems. These blasted exits from that apartment building—four of them." He reached into his pocket for his small transceiver and contacted his office to send an immediate message to the two agents who were keeping faithful watch on the Honda. "He has left. Check first, then enter. Search thoroughly. Let me know as soon as you find anything. Look out for part of a panty hose or a nylon stocking. And check any recording machine that could be connected with the phone. Also time-set lighting. Got that?" He switched off his transceiver and said, "I'd better get back to my office. But one more thing—Menlo's death was no accident. The medical examiners say that force was needed, considerable force, to make that wound in his head. A fall alone couldn't have done it." And with that gruesome information as his parting word, Doyle— now grim-faced—made a quick departure.

Bristow found Fairbairn at his desk with a mess of papers around him.

"Don't feel much like lunch," Fairbairn said. He was trying to work, and failing.

"You should call it a day and get home. And stay home, will you?" And keep out of Shaw's way, Bristow thought. "Where did you go last night?"

Fairbairn looked at him.

"Emma said you went out for a stroll. Where?"

"I don't see this is of any importance to—"

"It is. Where?"

"I stayed in the backyard, walked around the flower beds, and then sat down on a chair. I do that on clear nights. Any objection?"

"How long were you there?"

"Returned indoors around midnight. And if you want to know what I was doing—I was trying to find an answer for myself. Just looked at the sky, plenty of stars to steer by, a clear moon—easy sailing if I could only get to Chesapeake Bay."

"That would have been the wrong answer."

"If I were alone—no wife, no children—it would have been the best one."

"For the opposition, certainly. That's what they'd like

you to do. Break and run, look guilty. It would save them the trouble of getting rid of you."

Fairbairn's blank look of astonishment gave way to anger. "Like hell they will."

"That's better. So stay at home until I call you."

"Watched by a couple of squares? They've been tailing me around for the last two days."

"Noticeable?"

"No. But I'm not completely stupid. Why else was I finding everything so damned hopeless last night?"

"Keep indoors," Bristow advised. "And be glad your watchdogs are there. They make a good deterrent—the opposition are not completely stupid, either."

"You really are serious?"

"Yes. They can play rough."

"Oh, come on! I'm not important enough to be—" He stopped abruptly. "Menlo—did they—"

"Beat it," Bristow cut in. Yes, Menlo. Aliotto, too. And a couple of other Italian journalists, a Roman policeman on Via Borgognona, one recanting terrorist and God knows how many maimed and injured.

Fairbairn took one look at his friend's face. "All right. I'm leaving."

Bristow watched him hurriedly clear his desk. "Keep indoors," he repeated. "You can do your stargazing from the backyard next week."

Fairbairn nodded, picked up his briefcase. "Don't worry. When you give a warning, you give it good."

Bristow watched him as he was about to enter the elevator and was met by Shaw, who was leaving it.

Shaw said, "Hello! Where are you going? Taking the day off?"

"Half a day." Fairbairn's voice sounded normal, and Bristow relaxed. "How's your tooth?" Fairbairn was stepping into the elevator.

"Took an hour to fill. I'm up to here with Novocaine. See you tomorrow?"

But the elevator door had closed. Shaw turned to face

Bristow. "He looks as if he could use some sleep—must have been up all night." Then Shaw suddenly remembered. "Hey, what brought you back from your vacation?"

"Menlo."

"Oh, yes. I heard about that downstairs. How is he?"

"As well as can be expected."

"He's tough. What happened, d'you know?"

"No one does. As yet."

Shaw's face, innocent and wide-eyed, was briefly thoughtful. "Better get on with my work. A lot to do, with Fairbairn off duty."

"Sure you feel well enough yourself? You look as if you could use some sleep, too." A low jab, thought Bristow—Shaw looked as healthy as ever, and not much like a man who had spent an hour under a dentist's drill.

"I'm fine."

"Good. I'd like to talk with you. Have you time?"

"Of course. Talk about what?"

"About what's been going on here. I need you to tell me—"

"I told Menlo everything."

"But he isn't here now. And I know little. So set me straight. Let's use my office."

"Didn't he leave you his notes?"

"His notes?"

"The ones he made as he quizzed me and Fairbairn. Haven't you talked with Fairbairn?"

"He'll be in a more talkative mood when he catches up on his sleep." Bristow stood aside to let Shaw enter his office.

His desk was bare of any papers or envelopes and not a tape in sight. The typewriter was covered. Shaw took a chair, said with a laugh, "Wish I could keep my desk as neat as this."

"It has been on vacation. Just give it a day to get back to normal. I suppose I'd better make a note or two as you talk. D'you mind?"

Shaw had no objections. "It's rather a mixed-up business. What do you want to hear?" He unbuttoned the jacket of his fawn gabardine suit to keep it uncreased as he lounged in his chair.

"Whatever you think is important."

So Shaw talked. And repeated the story he had given Menlo, in a voice that was forthright and earnest. Not a glib verbatim response but sometimes with a natural hesitation as Shaw tried to recapture the sequence of Saturday's events.

It was impossible not to be impressed, and favorably. If Bristow hadn't learned about two brown hairs trapped inside a stocking mask, he might have believed Shaw completely. And yet he realized, too, the evidence could be turned around: Shaw would protest that the hairs had been inserted to lead the blame to him; and if anyone had left the mask, in order to identify the car, he could also have faked proof of its supposed driver. Again, Bristow thought, it will be Shaw's denial against Fairbairn's. We need more than that before we level charges against one of them.

"No further questions?" Shaw asked. He was unconcerned, at ease, as innocent as he always looked. Then suddenly he was embarrassed. "I don't know whether I should mention this," he said hesitantly as he rose from his chair. "But Coulton told me yesterday—" He seemed to find it difficult to go on.

"What did he tell you?" Bristow's interest quickened.

"Well—he just mentioned it as odd. But it's worrying him. He has been asked some questions about Saturday, too, you know."

"I didn't know. I suppose everyone who was near the file room around ten o'clock that evening is being asked for details. Understandable. O'Donnell didn't drug his own coffee, and the cassettes didn't walk off by themselves."

"No," Shaw agreed unhappily. "Just our bad luck we were on the scene. Were these cassettes really so important?"

"Yes. What did Coulton find odd?"

"Fairbairn. But I don't want to—I mean, I can't believe he would have—" Words failed Shaw.

"Of course not. You're his friend."

"I thought he was my friend."

"What made you change your mind? Coulton?"

"Well, when O'Donnell and I were struggling with the lock, Fairbairn left the door for a few seconds and stood at O'Donnell's table, looked at his logbook. At least, that was what Coulton thought he did. But Fairbairn's back was turned and blocked Coulton from seeing anything else."

So that was Coulton's story. "Did you notice Fairbairn leave the doorway?"

"Only briefly." Shaw's admission was slow and painful. "And then, another thing troubled Coulton."

"Oh?"

"When he and Fairbairn were stepping into the elevator, Fairbairn remembered he had forgotten to lock his office desk. He left the elevator and told Coulton to wait for him downstairs. So Coulton did. They checked out together. When they reached the entrance, Fairbairn said good night and left. I found Coulton waiting on the front steps. Pretty annoyed, too, about all the delays."

That story could be damming. There was no way of proving that Coulton had or hadn't waited for Fairbairn— the hall by the elevator wasn't visible from the guards at the check-out point. And now it wasn't one man's word against another's. It was two against one.

"I'm sorry," Shaw said, watching Bristow's face. "I know you and Fairbairn are pretty close. But—what else could I do? I mean—I'm not to be blamed for Saturday night—I did nothing. I just wanted to set the record straight about that. Wouldn't you fight to prove your innocence, Pete? If you were involved?"

Bristow looked at Shaw, pleading, anxious, believable in voice and expression. "More than innocence in a theft is involved."

"More?"

"Murder—or attempted murder."

"Menlo's? But it was an accident. Wasn't it? And why should anyone—"

The telephone rang. Damn, thought Bristow as he picked up the receiver: Shaw had shown a touch of panic there. "This won't take long, Shaw. Hang around until I finish this call."

Doyle, at the other end of the line, said, "I get it—you have company. I'll keep my voice down. Okay?"

"Very well, thank you. And how are you?"

"We searched the apartment. No stocking or panty hose. But we did find a recording—with Carl's voice and all. That's something but not enough. A stocking would have nailed him—probably went out with the garbage. It's collected tonight."

"You will be working late, then."

"I have a yard-detail there now. Do you know how much garbage these apartments accumulate? And one more thing—that rental car has been traced to a girl who is Coulton's part-time secretary. Coulton said he needed it because his Mercedes is under repair. It was stolen, he also said; couldn't find it this morning outside his house. Had to taxi to the office."

"He reported it?"

"As soon as he reached his office. Smart man. By the way, we'll run tests on Carl's voice. Could be Shaw's, don't you think? Made the recording himself and had it play when some obliging friend—who didn't want to talk—phoned him around midnight."

"Could be. Glad you called me. Any time." Bristow replaced the receiver. Now let Shaw make what he could of that. "Sorry for the interruption. You were asking why should anyone—?"

Shaw's mind was slow. Or he was still trying to find some meaning in Bristow's telephone conversation. "Anyone?" Shaw collected himself. "Oh, yes, why should anyone try to kill Menlo? Perhaps he was there at the wrong time—when a burglar entered."

"Two burglars."

Shaw stared.

"There was evidence of two, I hear." And let him sweat that one out. "Well, I think we have covered Saturday night pretty well. Back to work, both of us."

At the door, Shaw said, "I hope I was of some help."

"A great help." More than you can guess, buster.

"I'm sorry I had to mention Fairbairn."

"It's all part of the picture."

"There must be some other explanation—can't believe he'd be guilty of—" Shaw hesitated—"of anything. Except chasing a pretty girl. It's just the life style that leads to blackmail." And as Bristow looked at him sharply, he said, "You don't imagine he goes sailing alone on Sundays, do you?"

Bristow kept his voice even. "I never asked. Have you met Mrs. Fairbairn?"

"No. Haven't had the pleasure. Or displeasure—I hear she's a bit of a nag."

"You might be, too, if you were running a house and three children."

"Must be a tight squeeze on the money Fairbairn makes. I think I'll remain a bachelor." Shaw had recovered and was ready to leave. "Will it be necessary to tell him about the talk we've had?"

"Won't mention your name to him."

"Thanks, Pete. I really wouldn't want to feel—"

"See you around." And you'd better stick around, Bristow thought as the door closed at last. He waited a few seconds, checked to see if Shaw was hovering in the corridor within listening distance, saw him enter the elevator. A young man in a very great hurry. Skillful, too, at dropping vague but poisonous hints: blackmail or need for money . . .

Bristow picked up the phone, called Doyle. "Extra care with Fairbairn. Could be in danger."

"Where did he go last night?"

"No farther than his backyard. Sat in a chair, looked at the stars. Does that often."

"Anyone else who knows about this?"

"Anyone who has been making a close study of Fairbairn and asks questions."

"Habits can be the death of us." Doyle was thoughtful.

"What news from Hansen or Taylor?"

"Taylor reports everything peaceful. How about you?"

"Ready to start typing. And sticking my neck out."

"I'll back you up. All the way."

"You're pretty sure now?"

"I know sewage when I smell it. Don't have to swim in it. Carl's one word on that recorded message was in the identical voice pattern as Shaw's."

"What about his check-out record on Saturday—time of exit?"

"I'll have that info later. Call you as soon as I hear."

Bristow locked his door, began typing out the basic points in Menlo's notes, adding his own contribution as an appendix. The final decisions were not his to make—that was something for the upper level to work out. He'd give the facts that had been uncovered and render his own opinion on a separate sheet. If his judgment erred, then his head would be cut off at his shoulders.

He wasn't an expert typist, usually too quick, with mistakes that had to be crossed out. Today, he typed carefully. Even so, the pages didn't look too good. But they were readable, and no outside eye had seen their contents. Anyway, he was protecting both Fairbairn and Shaw from office gossip: rumor could devastate the innocent man.

He typed a separate page: "Investigation not fully completed, but Shaw's statement seemed calculated to direct attention to Fairbairn. On the other hand, Fairbairn made no attempt to implicate Shaw, although he is developing— at this late date—some suspicions. It would seem that Fairbairn has been skillfully set up by Shaw and by Coul-on. These two definitely are linked. Coulton has also been connected with Waterman. All three should be closely investigated. Coulton may be the control."

He read over his statement and signed it with his identification number. Not the best piece of prose that he had ever written, but he had made his findings clear. Either I'll swim or I'll sink on this one, he thought as he slipped all the pages into an envelope and sealed it tightly. Yet, with Menlo gone, someone had to take a stand and point further investigation in the right direction. Right? He hoped to God it was.

He walked over to visit Miriam Blau, the envelope burning a hole inside his jacket pocket. "Keep it safe," he told her. "I'll collect it tomorrow."

"You're just like poor Frank," she told him. "Don't trust your own lockup. How is he? He must have had a premonition of his accident—the way he authorized you to receive his envelope." Her grave eyes in her thin, hawklike face lightened with amusement as she added, 'A young man—from Disinformation, he said—was here a few hours ago. Told me you needed the envelope that Mr. Menlo had deposited, but were too busy to come yourself."

"And?" Bristow asked quickly.

"I said, 'What envelope are you talking about? There's none here.' That seemed to set him back a little. Made some excuse that you must have been mistaken and rushed off. Didn't even stay to give me his name."

"What does he look like?"

"Medium height, thick brown hair—couldn't see his eyes—he wore blue-tinted glasses. About thirty years old, I'd guess." Miriam pushed a wisp of gray hair back into place in the tight coil around her head. "His identification tag wasn't visible, either. Seemed natural enough—his hand covered it, gripped the lapel of his jacket as if he were delivering a sermon."

"What color of jacket?"

"He was wearing a fawn gabardine suit—very nice too."

"Miriam, I've always loved you." Bristow gave her quick kiss on her pale cheek and left her startled for onc in her life.

A fawn gabardine suit, brown hair. A hundred me around this vast complex of buildings might fit th: description. But not one in that hundred knew about Men lo's notes. Bristow reached his office in a slight state o euphoria. Too bad that Shaw hadn't had time to find seersucker jacket—or a blond wig. A young man in . hurry, Bristow thought again. If he felt I didn't believ him, he will move fast, get rid of any possible evidenc: before he can be summoned upstairs to repeat his story We'll have to move just as fast. Bristow glanced at hi watch. There were still twelve minutes before the six-ter call from Vasek.

He phoned Doyle. "Any word about the check-ou times on Saturday night?"

"Got them half an hour ago—I've been trying to reacl you. Here they are: Shaw checked out at ten-twelve. Coulton and Fairbairn at ten-twenty."

"He left *before* them?" Bristow's heart sank.

"So the computer said. But I wondered. I talked, per sonally, with the guard who was on duty at the front desl that night. When prodded, he remembered that Shaw sud denly changed his mind about leaving—just after he hac been checked out and his identification deposited—anc dashed back to the elevator. Had left his desk drawer unlocked, he said."

"When did the guard see him again?"

"At ten twenty-six. They talked. Shaw joked about hi: forgetfulness. The guard left the original check-out time on record. Mr. Shaw was leaving, wasn't he? And as Mr. Shaw said, there was no point in messing around with computers. Temperamental, he called them. The guard agreed."

"Did Shaw join Coulton at the front door?" The guard

had a good view of that entrance, if he were paying attention.

"They went down the steps together."

"No car visible?"

"No car. They left in the right direction for the parking lot."

"I suppose you have the guard's testimony on tape."

"And he'll verify it in any court. Satisfied?"

"You bet! Sorry to press you about this, but—"

"I know, I know. We didn't find any stocking to match the mask. Not yet. But we came up with something else." Doyle's voice quickened. "Shaw has been discarding a lot of old cassettes—filled a plastic garbage bag with them. Some had been unscrewed, had come apart and the tapes were removed. We found a couple of cassette top sections—looked like all the others, except for two miniature scratches in their corners. I saw Menlo place them there himself."

"We've got him!"

"For the cassettes, yes. But not for—" Doyle broke off. Menlo had been his friend.

"You've had quite a day," Bristow said to encourage him.

"Not over yet. We're watching Fairbairn's place on Cherry Lane. Take care, yourself."

"I'll be home by seven-thirty. No late work." Tomorrow would be time enough to add two clinchers to his report, may it rest in peace in Miriam's keeping. In rising spirits, Bristow said, "Get a good night's sleep. Both of us." He was hungry, too. A long day since three eggs sunny-side up. "What's Taylor's last report?"

"Good," Doyle said, and ended the call. He could wish Bristow would pay as much attention to his own safety as he did to that girl's. A woman, actually; but they all seemed so damned young nowadays.

Bristow, reassured, settled down for a quiet two minutes before Vasek's call. He tried to clear his mind of all other thoughts. Be casual, he warned himself, don't let that buzzard think he has you jumping to his command. Let this nitwit American play it as cool as he does. The phone rang exactly on time, and he braced himself.

24

BUT WHEN VASEK'S VOICE CAME ONTO THE LINE, IT WASN'T so cool. "There are difficulties. We shall talk tomorrow. At four o'clock. And we will arrange our meeting. For Wednesday."

"Will your difficulties be over by then?" He is under surveillance, he has been traced. Bristow's calm vanished. "Anything we can do?"

"I will manage."

"Let us know if we—"

"Of course," Vasek said and left Bristow listening to dead air.

Joe's voice was saying, "Mr. Bristow—Mr. Bristow—are you still there?"

"Yes. What's wrong?" Joe's voice had sounded anxious, urgent.

"The tape you were going to collect—yesterday's phone calls—it's gone. I've been searching for the last half hour. I had it ready for you to pick up this evening. Thought Ken—my brother—had moved it. He was on duty this

287

afternoon when I was over at the hospital. But he didn't touch it."

"Who visited your office this afternoon?" Office? Joe's small living room.

"Three clients. They were collecting tapes of their messages—just as you do, Mr. Bristow."

"Take it easy, Joe. I'm not blaming you or your brother. Did Ken know these clients?"

"Two of them. The third said he was a new customer. Winston was his name. Ken couldn't find him on our register."

"And while Ken searched, Winston was looking through the bookcase where you stack the tapes." Labeled and dated, naturally enough. Joe was methodical.

"Didn't have far to look for yours—if he was the one who took it. But where else could it have gone? I'm sorry, can't tell you how sorry, never happened before—"

"Joe, ease up. No damage done." And Bristow hoped he sounded as if that were actually true. "But one thing is important, Joe. You were a good radioman. You can recognize a phone tap when you see it."

"A bug on my phone?"

"Have a look." It had to be Joe's phone. Doyle had made sure that his office was clean. "Were there any repairmen at your place recently?"

"Yesterday morning—just testing. There was a broken line." And then Joe swore steadily for the next few seconds, taking Bristow back all the way to Vietnam.

Bristow said again, "Have a look, Joe. And you might as well remove it. They've been listening to us for the last five minutes."

There was a long silence, ending with Joe on the phone once more. "I found it. Removed it, put it out of commission."

"What type?"

"Sophisticated. Probably could send and be heard for half a mile. Goddammit, Mr. Bristow—"

"Not to worry. I'll collect today's tape this evening."

And let Karen hear it, short and sweet as it was. "By the way, what excuse did Winston give Ken as he left?"

"He didn't. Just said he would see me tomorrow, straighten out everything."

"What did he look like?"

"Tall, thin. A rugged face. Brown eyes—they looked directly at you. Very pleasant in manner. Seemed a regular guy."

"European voice or American?"

"Real American. But we've got his voice on tape. I've a receiver-transmitter in the office, with its recorder in my bedroom. It's sound-activated. Turned on through the day, tape changed every two hours. So he's on the four-to-six recording. The police advised me to set it up—helps identify any burglars. I've a lot of equipment here, you know."

"Could I borrow that piece of tape?"

Joe considered for a second. "Sure, I'll have it ready for you."

"I'll see you within the hour."

"I'm real sorry—"

"That," Bristow said with a laugh, "is the last time I want to hear that word." But he was tight-lipped as he ended the call. Tall, thin, rugged face—it sounded like the Waterman he had first seen in Schleeman's club and then in Armando's. Easy manner, a regular guy. And so were all successful confidence men.

And how had Waterman—or whoever—got the idea, a good one, right on target, to bug my answering service? Coulton was the direct answer to that. He had attended the VIP meeting on the fabricated letters. He had listened to the Prague tapes and heard Karen report Vasek's exact words: Vasek would deal with Bristow and no one else in his department. Which proved that Waterman, if he was the one who pulled a fast trick on Joe's young brother, was linked with Coulton. Menlo's query on these two had become an exclamation mark.

Then Bristow wondered as he locked his desk and

prepared to leave, how would the Waterman-Coulton axis now be able to listen to Vasek's phone call tomorrow? That was a comic thought and kept him amused all the way to his car. One of the guards who patrolled the area was paying extra attention to the cars parked in this section, Bristow noted. Doyle's idea, probably. Bristow asked as he got into the Camaro, "No one put a stick of dynamite under the hood?" The guard didn't find that so funny, just nodded good day and paced on.

Suddenly, another question about Waterman came into Bristow's mind, and this one wasn't as comic. Why had yesterday's tape of recorded messages been stolen? For what purpose? Joe's telephone, tapped by one of Waterman's people, had given them Vasek's call word by word. So why steal the tape? It could teach them nothing new.

The question was repeated when he stood in the front room of Joe's small ground-floor apartment. Joe was still smarting, less from the blow on the back of his head than from the fact that a girl had done it. "Came in here looking sweet and cute, wanted to inquire about services and prices. Just when I was reaching for my list, she pulled a .22 on me, held it to the back of my neck, got today's tape—the one you were coming to collect, Mr. Bristow. Then she bashed me."

Ken, who was holding a towel wrapped around ice cubes to his brother's head, completed the story. "I came in—had been out at the supermarket—found him cussing and swearing. Wasn't knocked out—just a bit dazed. You know—I saw that girl getting into the car parked next to mine. A gray two-door Chevy—brand-new. But it was gone before I chased out after them."

"Them?" asked Bristow.

"The girl and the driver."

"Winston?"

"No. Not him. Light hair, big round jaw. That's all I noticed as I got out of my car with the groceries. Red in the face—the guy must have been hot in the jacket he was wearing. Shirt and tie, too." Ken, in short sleeves and wash pants, could only shake his head over the stranger's clothes. "Doesn't know Washington, that's for sure."

"How was the sweet cutie dressed?"

"The little bitch—" Joe said. "White pants—"

"Jeans, tight jeans," Ken added to that. "And a big loose shirt—made the pants all the—" He broke off as Joe glared up at him.

Joe took command. "Fair hair, long and straight. Face, tanned. Small and slight. Her voice—well, I've got her on tape." He looked at Bristow. "You want that sound-activated recording, too?"

Bristow nodded.

"What's going on?" Joe demanded. "I feel as if I'm in a forward combat area. Will they try more tricks for that phone call you're getting at four tomorrow? Well, I'll have my shotgun ready, stay here with Ken. I'll miss my basketball over at the gym but—" He shrugged his shoulders. "Boy, if I had my legs, she couldn't have pulled that stunt on me."

Would they try a third time to get hold of Vasek's tapes? Yet they had to learn what meeting he was setting up. "Why don't you make this police business? You have friends on the force. Get extra protection for four o'clock tomorrow, just in case—" Bristow paused. "May not be necessary, Joe. But it's better to take precautions. My fault that you're back in the front lines. But it won't last long. Next week, you'll have a good story to tell your buddies over at the Amvets' gym." He hoped he sounded as confident of that as his words. He added, with a smile, "You won't stop being my answering service, I hope."

"You kidding?" Joe's grin was back. He shoved aside the ice pack and smoothed his thin red hair in place. "Takes more than a bash on the head to do that. Frigging tramp—I'll be ready for her next time. I'll get you the recording—but keep it safe. I'd like to hear what a .22 sounds like when it's whacked on my skull." He swung his chair around, sent its wheels whirring toward his bedroom.

25

*B*RISTOW FOUND A PARKING SPACE AROUND THE NEAREST corner to his apartment. He locked his car, began the short walk home, with the recordings of Winston's and Cutie-Pie's voices—two miniature cassettes, wonders of the microchip age—safe inside his jacket pocket. Thanks to the delay at Joe's answering service, it was now well after eight o'clock. The streetlights were on, the houses brightly lit, too. Fragments of music from wide-open windows drifted into Muir, a pleasant accompaniment to his stroll. He was taking his time, observing the people on the sidewalks. Few in number, and all engrossed in their innocent business. Four late departures from a cocktail party, calling good-byes as they split into couples and reached their cars just ahead of him. Three people in full regalia leaving for some dinner party. Two women walking their straining Doberman. A late jogger on a slow run. Two men, at a leisurely pace, arguing about astrophysics. Everything seemed normal.

Just ahead now was the bookstore—closed. Above it,

Mrs. Abel's sitting room was lit. His own apartment, its windows dark, gave no signs of life. It seemed as deserted as he had hoped it would look.

Reassured, he crossed the street, approached his street entrance. In front of him, a car door swung open and a woman stepped out as she closed it behind her. Old, shapeless figure, he noted. A canvas shopping bag on one arm, a clutch of books in the other. They slipped, and she bent down to pick them up, shielded from the street-light by the shadow of the tree where she had parked her car. Too nimble for an old lady, he thought, suddenly alert. "Bristow!" The voice was held low. "Don't stop. Don't look. Go in! And wait!"

Nine more steps and Bristow unlocked his door, entered quickly, left it barely open. He drew back against one wall as his hand reached for his Beretta. He released its safety catch, waited.

The woman, bent with age, slipped inside and closed the door. He switched on the hall light. She turned the door's lock to secure it, then faced him, straightening her back, looked at him through heavily rimmed eyeglasses. Bristow's own inventory was quick but complete: a sallow face, wrinkled and furrowed; bobbed gray hair; a cotton dress, a drooping cardigan, sagging stockings, flat sandals.

"Not necessary," she said, pointing to the gun. Her voice had deepened. A man's voice, kept almost to a whisper.

"No?" Bristow's hand held steady.

"We talk in your apartment." The stranger almost smiled. "I did not expect such a warm welcome for a defector." His voice was still low, but now recognizable. He noticed Bristow's eyes. "We spoke at ten past six today. Tomorrow, we talk at four." The smile became real. "If you please, lead the way."

Bristow motioned with his pistol. "You first. And quietly." Then he followed Josef Vasek up the stairs.

On the first landing, Vasek paused to point at a door.

Bristow signaled no, up, silence. They reached the top of the narrow staircase, and Bristow halted by his apartment's entrance as Vasek, his attention focused on the exit at the end of the landing, went to investigate. "Back stairs. Outside," Bristow said softly and watched Vasek test the lock and chain. Vasek approved, now turned to the kitchen door that lay adjacent.

He was about to reach for its handle, but a sudden "No!" from Bristow stopped him. Bristow pointed to a small button-sized light glowing red on the wall above, and then to the mat lying in front of the kitchen's threshold. He didn't need to say, "The alarm is set." Vasek's foot was arrested inches from the mat, and he stepped back in time. He gave his second abrupt nod of approval and returned along the small corridor to stand beside Bristow at the apartment's front door and watch him unlock it.

The Beretta gestured to Vasek, and he entered first. He saw a dimly lit hall stretching before him, two men facing him with drawn revolvers. He swore and wheeled around, hurling his books at Bristow as he lunged toward the landing. Taylor's pistol butt hit him neatly on the back of his head.

Bristow picked up the books. His left arm had shielded his face automatically from Vasek's wild throw. Only one book had reached him, glanced off his shoulder. No damage done. "Pull him into the kitchen. Prop him on a chair. He'll be out cold for the next ten minutes. Search him."

"Handcuffs," Taylor told Hansen.

"No need," Bristow said, pocketing his Beretta. "He's a guest. Overnight." Tomorrow, we get him out of here, he decided, and rubbed his shoulder.

"He?" Taylor asked, already opening the canvas shopping bag.

"Definitely. And Hansen—leave the wig in place. The eyeglasses, too. He'd prefer to take them off himself." And why spoil all his fun? Bristow put his arms around Karen and kissed her. "All right, honey?"

"Now I am." She was still slightly dazed by the speed with which Taylor and Hansen had drawn their revolvers and moved to the door. "We heard a floor creak and some-one say 'No!' And then the knock—I knew it was yours, but the door opened and *that* came in." She looked at the sagging figure with its shoulders held by Hansen to keep it erect on a kitchen chair. The head, with a straggle of gray bobbed hair falling over a low forehead, dropped forward. Heavy glasses had slipped down to the end of a thick snub nose, rested on its upturn. "Is it really a man?"

"A friend of yours."

"Clothes and wallet," Taylor reported from his search of Vasek's shopping bag. "Canadian passport. Blank note-book; pen and two pencils."

"Try his shirt pocket." Vasek's hand had slipped inside it just after it was freed of his books. A touch-and-go moment, Bristow thought. Might have had to shoot his wrist, and that could have brought Mrs. Abel running upstairs—she was in her living room, not yet in bed with her hearing aid removed for sleep. He noticed now that Hansen and Taylor had silenced their footsteps with sneakers. Their two loose summer shirts were also some-thing new, and there was the good smell of stew from one of the pots on the stove over which a large hooded flash-light was perched. Another of these lights was on the kitchen table, new candles—thick and heavy—in the din-ing area. With shades and curtains drawn and one meager bulb replacing its usual bright lighting, this kitchen would seem dark enough from the yard and from the back of the houses on the next street. "You've been shopping, I see," he said to Hansen.

"Just picked up what we needed." Three visits to stores far from Muir Street, and one to Langley for equipment: not a bad afternoon's work, Hansen considered.

Taylor, without comment, had extracted a Smith & Wesson .38 from Vasek's pocket and laid it on the kitchen table. A silencer from the other pocket was placed beside the revolver. Then he lifted the wide skirt, removed a knife from a sheath attached to a garter. It, too, was dropped on the table. His hands searched the rest of Vasek's body, found a small transceiver tucked into a well-padded brassiere. He held it out to Bristow with one eyebrow raised. Bristow frowned, said softly, "Make it a natural accident." Taylor opened the back of the transceiver, examined its frequency circuit under the flashlight's beam, carefully eased a wire and pulled it hard, leaving it free enough to loosen any connection without being a noticeable break. He closed the transceiver and again raised a questioning eyebrow. "Back in place," Bristow said, and Taylor returned it to its padded nest. It could no longer receive or send any messages: switched on, there would be only a good imitation of the sound of frying. Why the hell did Vasek need it anyway? He was the lone wolf, entirely on his own. "Anything in the lining of his bag?" Bristow asked in a whisper.

"Nothing hard to the touch," Taylor said, but he knelt on the floor to search the bag again. "Zippered lining," he reported. "Concealed." He drew out a transparent plastic bag with three small tablets, white and round. "Looks like aspirin," he said as Bristow studied them under the light.

Aspirin, they were certainly not. "Get three plain aspirins from the bathroom cabinet," Bristow said. "Quick!" And Taylor was quick. He returned as Bristow finished the delicate job of opening the plastic container. Three bogus aspirin were replaced by the real thing. Taylor was back at the shopping bag, zipped up its lining as Vasek's head raised, his eyelids flickering. In front of him, he saw Bristow with his arm around a woman's shoulder. He looked at her twice, made sure. Behind him, Taylor left the shopping bag, now in good order, and moved quietly aside.

"It was no trap," Bristow said. "You are safe. Welcome to our foxhole."

Vasek's eyes left Karen, glanced at his weapons on the

table. "Can't be too careful when you are traveling," he said. His hand touched his breast for a brief moment; then, reassured, it dropped to his side.

"No need for them here. We have our own little arsenal."

Vasek shrugged his shoulders free from Hansen's support and rose. Again he looked around the kitchen, noting Taylor's revolver out of its holster. Next, his attention switched to Karen. He swept off the gray wig and bowed. "My thanks, Miss Cornell. I am in your debt. Perhaps you will identify me as being completely authentic and relieve these gentlemen's suspicions." He pulled off his glasses and some of the putty that had transformed his nose. "I took the advice you gave me in Rome. Contact lenses. But if I could get rid of them, wash and change— you might find me more recognizable." He picked up his bag. "Would you show me where?" he asked Hansen.

"It's—" Karen began in amazement.

"Yes," Bristow said, "that's who it is." He nodded to Hansen, who urged Vasek ahead of him toward the bathroom.

As Vasek was about to enter the hall, he paused to say, "Thank you, Bristow—I prefer to be nameless. Meanwhile." He looked at Hansen, at Taylor. "Your people?"

"Security."

"Is this house in danger?" He was suddenly alarmed.

"No," Bristow said. "Just Miss Cornell." There was a bitter edge to his voice that startled Vasek.

"I am sorry," he said stiffly. And entered the hall.

Karen's lips were tight. "He told me two weeks. He said in Rome he needed two weeks—and he was here in four days." Vasek's subterfuge seemed to upset her more than any mention of danger. She listened to the closing of the bathroom door. "Do you trust him, Peter?"

"As much as I trust any liar," Bristow said and hugged her. "How was your day at the office?" he asked to get her mind away from Vasek. Taylor, he noted, was removing the weapons from the kitchen table, finding a place for them behind some dishes that were packed into a small cupboard.

"Finished my rough draft." And it was good, she felt. Her account of the bombing on Via Borgognona was as objective as if she had been a disinterested observer with her own emotions ignored. And somehow, her description of the scene had seemed all the more immediate and hideous. "Schleeman will approve. I think. Did you call him?"

"Damn!"

"So it was that kind of day at *your* office?" she asked jokingly. But her eyes were anxious.

"Doyle must have phoned him about Menlo. They were all pretty close in their OSS days. He probably told him you had arrived and were resting up." Doyle could handle a good excuse, and Schleeman was experienced enough to accept a hint.

Taylor, until now seemingly oblivious, said, "Mr. Doyle contacted us at seven-thirty, asked if you had got home. I'll let him know. Do I report on Mr. Nameless?"

"I'll do that later. All I want to do now is wash and eat. Can you contact Doyle from here?"

"Can do. Hansen brought in a transceiver strong enough to reach him."

"Reach him anywhere?"

"Within a ten-mile radius. We also got a sound-activated recorder." Taylor pointed at the hall, high up on the wall, close to the molding.

"All set?" Bristow could see nothing—he'd have to climb up on a ladder for a close look.

Taylor actually smiled. "Only have to turn it on—once we're asleep."

"Do it now. Can it reach the dining area?"

"Sure can. Kitchen, front door, and that part of the hall. Not the rooms. Hansen and I will be taking shifts on a chair between your bedroom door and the living room."

"Just as well." Bristow glanced over at Karen, who was now setting two places at the dining table. "Our guest could be in danger, too. How far, by the way, could his little transceiver reach?"

"Not very far. A house on this street, perhaps. Three hundred yards at most, I'd guess." Taylor was about to leave.

Bristow stopped him, hesitated, then said, "Tell Doyle we'll need an ambulance here—five-thirty tomorrow morning. I'll explain to him later. Just get it laid on. And Taylor—there's a car about twenty feet north of our street entrance. Neutral color, couldn't see it clearly in the shadows. Dark gray or brown, perhaps. Two-door, certainly. Worth investigating. Could be someone inside." With a transceiver, thought Bristow. "Yes, tell Doyle it definitely needs investigating."

Taylor nodded and was on his way. An early removal, he thought as he entered the hall, and good riddance. If Mr. Nameless insists on taking his weapons with him, I'll ask if he's got a permit to carry them. And that thought brought a second smile of the day to Taylor's lips. A defector? One more bleeding headache.

Karen was saying, "I'll heat the stew. We ate at half past six. The men were hungry—and I really thought you wouldn't be here until midnight. Anyway, you probably want to talk alone with Vasek."

"It's my one chance. He will be in other hands soon."

"Thank heaven for that! Did you know he was coming here?"

"No. He isn't the confiding type."

"Except when it suits him." She was still angered by his lie which she had passed on in good faith. "In Rome, I had a nightmare after I met him in the church. He was a death's-head—a skeleton in his priest's cassock."

Bristow took her in his arms, held her close. "By tomorrow, you and I will never see him again. Don't worry about—"

"I'm not worried. I'm flaming mad. Wish I had never met the man. Won't even get that story he promised to give me whenever it could be told. Not that it matters," she said, and tried to laugh. All that mattered was Peter safe. "I've changed," she added in surprise. Changed so much. Where were all her ambitions now?

We both have, he thought, and kissed her.

They heard Vasek's voice, booming in good will as he at last left the bathroom. Bristow said, "I'll wash, won't be a second. Keep him smiling till I get back."

"Where will he sleep?"

"The living room. There's a couch or two armchairs or the floor." With a quick kiss on her nose, he hurried into the hall. "Be with you soon," he told Vasek, who was now dressed in a blue suit, slightly creased but presentable. He was thinner, too, and handsome: dark hair graying at the temples, clear-cut features, not a wrinkle showing on his smooth skin.

Vasek halted at the kitchen door, looking at Karen almost uncertainly.

"So nice to meet you again without skeletons dangling around," said Karen. "Do come in. I'm sorry about the subdued lighting effect. And we have the air conditioning turned low—it makes too much noise at full strength. How was your trip? Not too difficult, I hope." Chatter away, she told herself, like a babbling brook. Don't even be tempted to remind him that Aliotto died and he was responsible. As he was. Who would have thought that just talking to a man could get you killed?

Vasek seemed reassured and became a most charming though restless companion for the five minutes it took Bristow to return.

Karen lit the candles, saying, "It's dark enough to imagine you're in the most expensive New York restaurant. Stew is on the menu, but you can always call it *boeuf bourguignon*." What, she wondered, had he been looking for in those five minutes? He had wandered around, touching this, rearranging that, as he talked to distract her attention.

"Aren't you having dinner with us, Miss Cornell?" Vasek asked. He was now seated at the table, fingering the underedge of the plate set before him, lifting the wine bottle by its bottom to check the vintage. He relaxed: no small listening device anywhere; his wristwatch had registered not one bug.

"I've eaten. I didn't expect any guest, or I'd have waited. Tomorrow, perhaps?"

"Tomorrow." Vasek raised his glass of wine to her and watched her leave. "Was it wise—if she is in any danger—to bring her here? To your apartment?" He put down his glass without drinking.

Bristow settled in his chair, lifted fork and knife. "Why not? Karen is here for the same reason you came to this address. No professional in his right mind would believe I'd risk lodging either of you in my own home."

"True," said Vasek, and burst into laughter.

"Hey—keep it down!" Bristow warned him. "Sounds carry."

"A most careful man," Vasek observed with approval.

"A hungry one."

"You've had a busy day—no time for lunch?"

"Like you, I'm sure."

"Yes. A difficult day. A difficult week. You will want to hear the details—"

"Of course."

"And you'll have many questions to ask."

"And you'll have many answers to give. But," Bristow said, "why don't we leave that until later? First we'll eat and then we'll talk."

"For a little. I need sleep as well as food."

"Don't we all?" It was nine o'clock now. By ten, Bristow thought, I can stretch out on a real bed and relax. Vasek was making only a skillful pretense of eating and drinking until Bristow had finished half a plateful of stew and a glass of wine. At last, he set to, ate with zest. Supper was over in thirty minutes.

"Coffee keeps me awake," Vasek objected as Bristow poured two cups.

That's the idea, Bristow thought. He drank and again

noticed that Vasek waited, then forgot his objection as Bristow reached for the coffeepot and a second cup. A Byzantine world this man lived in. Real? Or his own creation? Did he really think I might drug *both* of us to catch him? If I had eaten little, would he have eaten at all? Bristow concealed his amusement, said gravely, "How do you get rid of the car?"

Vasek stared. "Car?"

"The one you left on the street."

"That is not my car. I used it. Temporarily. It was parked—no one there."

"Neat. But you took a chance."

"I take chances."

"True," Bristow said with a brief smile. "How did you recognize me?"

Vasek lit a cigarette, sipped his coffee. "Simple. I had a description and a photograph—as well as your address and phone number—from one of your colleagues. I also know you drive a Camaro."

"Which was parked out of sight from your car."

"But I saw you enter it this morning. It wasn't far from your door."

"You're an early bird." Bristow's light reply seemed to baffle Vasek. He said nothing. "In fact," Bristow went on, "you're early in everything, including your arrival in Washington. Brilliant. How did you manage it? Friday, late afternoon, you were a priest in Rome. Then—?"

"Then," said Vasek, "straight to a bus station. A change of clothes, hair, passport, and I was on my way to Zurich on a tour. Another change in identity, and I was in Paris. From there, a new passport and alteration in appearance brought me to New York."

At the latest, his arrival was on Sunday. And if he skipped Paris, took the Swissair flight from Zurich on Saturday morning, he could have been in New York early that afternoon. Bristow said, "Fabulous. Did you run into any trouble—any precarious moments?"

"In Zurich, yes. But only a brief alarm. I left the man—

a Czech agent who could recognize me—in the airport washroom."

"Permanently, I suppose."

"Most permanently."

"What name are you using now?"

"Vasek. Josef Vasek."

"The same as you used when you met Miss Cornell in Prague?" And let's hope that Taylor's sound-recorder is working loud and clear.

"Why not? It is my oldest name. I have a liking for it. I began my career in Prague, you know."

"Before you started using all those other amazing pseudonyms that we've gathered in your file?"

"The Farrago file." Vasek's amusement grew. "Quite extensive, I've heard—again by courtesy of your colleague."

And that's the second mention of our mole. Am I supposed to be breathless, ask in wonder who it can be? Bristow said casually, "Did you train him?"

"No need. He was well trained by the CIA."

"So you turned him. When?"

"Not difficult. He was at a period of his life when he was bitter—disillusioned—the Vietnam fiasco—"

"When?" Bristow insisted.

"After his wife died. A long illness that wiped out his savings. The kind of moment that makes a numbered bank account in Zurich sound attractive."

Bristow was suddenly wary. Shaw a widower? He had never been married, or else he had concealed it damn well. "We know his identity," Bristow said quietly.

"You know who he is?" Vasek was astounded. "You actually found Menlo?"

Bristow's spine stiffened. He stared at Vasek, couldn't speak.

Vasek pressed his advantage. "Or perhaps you uncovered the man Menlo had recruited to assist him? Also one of your colleagues, also in need of ready cash. Money is the root of all our success, wouldn't you say?"

"When was he recruited?"

"By Menlo? Two years ago, I believe. Wallace Fairbairn's young daughter had a bad accident on her bicycle—a lot of expensive treatment needed to get her walking again. But you remember, of course."

Bristow nodded. Fairbairn had borrowed money to meet some of the bills, but it had been paid back. Every dollar of it. That, Bristow knew. The two thousand he had lent Fairbairn had been returned within a year—a quiet transaction (Bristow's stipulation), about which not even Emma Fairbairn had known.

Vasek took Bristow's silence as a concession of complete failure. "Is it possible that you named the wrong man as your mole? One that Menlo had chosen for—what do you call it?—for a stooge. Shaw, I hear, is well suited for the part. An amiable idiot. But such men are always around."

"You're saying that Shaw was selected by Menlo to take the fall—if Menlo or Fairbairn was about to be discovered?"

"Yes. But you shouldn't be surprised. There are many such cases." Vasek was expansive in victory. "I remember in Moscow—" and he plunged into a long reminiscence about a similar dupe in his own department.

Bristow's attention was far away. His first impulse had been to take that soft white face and smash it down into a coffee cup. But he had mastered his boiling emotion, now sat motionless and let his cold thoughts race. Vasek had made one mistake: he had underestimated the speed of Menlo's intense investigation, the careful gathering of facts and circumstantial evidence that had let Bristow finish the job. Vasek didn't even know that the report was completed, probably thought that Menlo's death—he must have learned about the death somehow, otherwise he wouldn't have lied so boldly—would even halt the investigation or at least cripple it while Bristow started the belated task of gathering evidence all over again. Nor had Vasek learned that Bristow was in possession of Menlo's notes—a second mistake. Bristow was the man who had been out of touch, ignorant of what had happened during his absence in Rome. Let's stay ignorant, Bristow decided as he began to listen to Vasek's detailed anecdote. And stay alive.

"A very clever stratagem of the CIA," Vasek concluded at the end of his story.

"Sometimes we aren't entirely stupid."

"But it failed," Vasek reminded him.

"Well, we do. Now and again."

"You are still thinking about Menlo." Vasek was watching Bristow.

"Yes." Bristow shook his head. "It's hard to believe. You'll have to furnish proof, of course."

"Of course. Did you ever wonder why he kept himself so much apart? He resisted all friendship. Even his holidays in Nova Scotia—by himself—in lonely places—" Vasek seemed to hesitate. "We met there. Twice. A most suitable rendezvous. No one to see us but the salmon and a few speechless peasants."

Bristow felt sickened. Abruptly, he changed the subject. "Now about you. You must leave here tomorrow—for your own security. We'll take you to a safe house, see that it is well guarded."

"Where will that be?" The question was quiet but quick.

"I've no idea. Nor do I know who will be debriefing you. Many people, I think, from other sections. You are a very important man, Vasek." Bristow paused, said as a seeming afterthought, "Perhaps even more important than our political refugee who came asking for asylum four months ago."

"The one who calls himself Gregor?" Vasek was casual. "He's a friendly type—always says what he thinks will please you. But I hope your people will be on guard against that." Vasek frowned. "Menlo wasn't present at Gregor's questioning, was he?"

"Well—he could have been. Gregor asked for asylum through him."

"So Menlo vouched for him. Very clever. And Menlo no doubt persuaded his colleagues that Gregor's statements are trustworthy." Vasek shook his head in admiration of Menlo. "Where is Gregor now? Still being questioned? I did not think even his imagination could invent so much misinformation."

"I've heard he doesn't stay long in one place." Not with two attempts made to kill him. "A matter of security."

"I am relieved to hear your people take our safety so seriously. Mine will be a problem, too."

"We've had other defectors besides you and Gregor. None have been terminated or abducted as far as I know. But then, I don't deal with defectors. Only with words." With lying words, Bristow thought. "Disinformation is my field," he reminded Vasek with a smile. And I bet, he told the pale-gray eyes that were studying him, you have more fields of interest than that.

"How will you handle the problem of Menlo?"

"Not mine to handle. He's had a bad accident."

"Serious?"

"Could be fatal."

There was no surprise on Vasek's face, just mild amusement. "Perhaps," he suggested, "your colleagues from another section have already handled the problem for you."

Again Bristow restrained himself, said nothing.

"No more questions?" Vasek asked, preparing to rise.

"Not from me."

"When do I leave here?"

"Well—I'll have to make arrangements. No one expected you so soon. But give us a little time. We won't delay. For safety, it would be best to leave when the light is poor."

"It will be interesting to see how your people deal with my departure."

"Yes, you can compare our arrangements with KGB methods. By the way," Bristow said as he pushed back his chair and got to his feet, "did you write the three letters yourself? The letters you gave Miss Cornell to deliver to me?"

"Why do you ask?"

"They were masterly. One supposedly from the Secretary of State, another pretending to be from the Secretary of Defense, and a third—equally deceiving—from the President himself. A brilliant tour de force. They had your touch, I thought."

"In that case, I won't disappoint you. I composed them." Vasek paused, added quickly, "Of course, I had no idea of how they were to be used."

"You mean, with two assassinations planned to precede their publication?"

"That would only lead to worldwide disruption, to riots—anarchy. And war. Who could win a nuclear war?"

"Behold a pale horse," Bristow quoted, then paraphrased, "and its rider's name was Death, and Hell followed with him." It was the first time that Bristow had seen Vasek perplexed, but the Book of Revelations wasn't exactly approved reading in the Soviet Union.

In silence, they began to walk slowly into the hall. Before they would leave the area that Taylor's recorder covered, Bristow halted to say, "There is a joint agreement—between Moscow and Washington—that the letters will never be published by either side. Can we trust that agreement, or is it just another scrap of paper?"

"Now you are being too suspicious."

"If you had been caught or killed on your way through Europe, would it have been a broken agreement?"

"Possibly. But I am here. And I intend to stay alive."

And not make an escape and call it an abduction? Return secretly to Moscow, have the letters published and catch us out? "We'll make sure of that," Bristow said and led the way down the hall. "Sorry we've no extra bed. But the sofa in the living room isn't too bad. Undress in the bathroom, where there is plenty of electric light and no window to give it away. Don't open your curtains or the shade. And leave your door ajar to let some light into your room so that you can see your way around. Don't want you breaking an arm with a fall over the coffee table."

"CIA brutality?" Vasek asked with a laugh. He clapped Bristow on the shoulder and went into the bathroom, closing its door firmly.

Now he may try using his transceiver to reach the man who is waiting for instructions, Bristow thought. There will be no privacy in his room for any talk with a door ajar and Hansen sitting barely ten feet away from it.

On impulse, Bristow moved back into the kitchen and removed the large flashlight over the stove, then the second light from the table. In the dining area, the candles were out, but he dampened their wicks with the last drops of coffee. He switched off the kitchen's meager bulb, checked to see if the small red button was glowing over the back door, and returned to the dimly lit hall. Halfway along it, he handed one of the powerful flashlights to a surprised Hansen and bent close to him. "Take the flash to Taylor. Tell him I want to reach Doyle at eleven o'clock."

Hansen rose from his chair, padded silently to the guest room, while Bristow waited, his eyes on the bathroom door. Hansen was back almost immediately, but Taylor was with him, too. Taylor was whispering, "Mr. Doyle will be out of reach until eleven-thirty. Something is going down."

Can't have it all my own way, Bristow thought. "What is?"

"Didn't say. But we got a patrol car to investigate your street—the dark-brown two-door near this apartment."

There was the sound of movement from the bathroom. Quickly, Bristow pulled Taylor into the kitchen. They listened to Vasek's voice bidding Hansen good night, and as silence returned to the hall, Bristow asked, "Anyone inside that car?"

"One man. Chauffeur's cap and blue suit, waiting for a party to end, he said. Then as the cops began to search him, he changed his tune: he gave his name—Russian—and claimed diplomatic immunity."

"What?" Bristow recovered. "Did the cops have time to find anything on him?"

"No weapons—just a transceiver. They've moved the car and the Russian, taken them to the station to clear up this immunity business."

"He went quietly?"

"Better that than being arrested for loitering with intent."

"Okay, okay." As they reentered the hall, Bristow lowered his voice still more. "Any tricks, and use this." He tapped Taylor's holstered revolver. "Wound. Don't kill. Pass the word."

Taylor looked at him, nodded, moved silently down the hall, stopping to bend over Hansen's chair and whisper.

He got the message, Bristow thought, and entered his bedroom: emergency situation; be ready for anything.

Karen had been trying to read by flashlight, but she had fallen asleep, half-propped up on the pillow, her book lying spread-eagled on the floor. He placed the larger flash he had brought from the kitchen on his bed table, turning its powerful beam away from the window. Gently, he eased her head into a more comfortable position, then slipped off his shoes, dropped quietly beside her, lay staring up at the darkened ceiling. A few slow deep breaths, a loosening of his spine and shoulders, and he felt his body gradually ease. Lightly, he placed his hand over Karen's, let it rest there. His mind began to come out of shock.

Menlo... Menlo... No, don't think of Menlo and the venomous lies that were being woven around him: deal with that later. Now, think only of Vasek. Vasek and his connection with his embassy—was that why he had wanted to know the address of the safe house, so that it could be reported to the "chauffeur" in the car? So that his people would know where to find him and "abduct" him when he gave them the signal? Yet they had waited until the final stages of his plan. And he had been hunted by other members of the KGB. Their search had been intense, his danger as a "defector" had been real enough. Witness his alarm tonight when he found that Hansen and Taylor were Security and realized he had entered an apartment that needed to be guarded; or his panic and reaction when he entered and thought he was trapped, betrayed by me. It wasn't the first time that an intelligence officer had let a difficult and unwelcome guest be given that raw deal as the simplest solution.

Vasek—the man who took chances—his defection planned weeks ago as one sure way to get at Gregor, render Gregor's information suspect. Gregor was the target; everything else—Menlo and his section, our mole—was peripheral. And to be accepted as an honest defector, Vasek took his biggest chance: perhaps half a dozen, at a very high level, even fewer, knew of his plan. The rest of the KGB were told he was defecting, and their search for him only made his myth seem true and acceptable. But would they have killed him when he was found? I doubt that, thought Bristow. Their orders were probably to seize him and return him alive to Moscow. Even a man who is proud of the chances he takes might not want the risk of being shot by one of his own. Although tonight he seemed to have no qualms about killing a KGB officer in Zurich, some poor bloody fool who got in the way of his master plan.

And if I'm right, Bristow concluded, his pulse racing, his smile broadening, then he had no connection with the Sam Waterman cell—with Coulton or Shaw or any others who have been brought in to prevent their disclosure. They are peripheral, too. Only the Russian who claimed diplomatic immunity tonight is one of the few who knows Vasek is not a defector. He has used us all—the KGB and the CIA, Karen and me, everyone—but he didn't foresee one thing: we've got him. Yes, we've got him.

Bristow laughed softly. Karen, who had been watching

him for the last five minutes, raised herself on an elbow and touched his cheek. "Do I share the joke?"

He turned, drew her close to him, put a finger on her lips to warn her to speak low, pointed to the wall behind which Vasek lay.

"Later?" she asked. Always later—security, safety, security.

"Perhaps not so much later."

"When?"

"With luck, by tomorrow."

"And I'll hear the joke?"

"You'll hear everything." Sure, it broke the rules, but she had been in this case from the beginning. Karen knew more about it than most.

"I'll hold you to that promise," she warned him, her arms around him, her kisses on his lips. Then she laughed. "Are you going to sleep with your clothes on, darling?"

"I'm staying awake. A report I have to give—" he looked at his watch—"in thirty-five minutes." He would tell Doyle the essential facts: Vasek a fake but must be treated as genuine; one suspicion, and he will cut his losses and escape; special care, tightest security requested; full details will be given tomorrow morning—8:00 A.M.

"You do need sleep."

"Forgotten about it." He wouldn't be the only one who'd be forgetting sleep once Doyle passed on his warning. There would be several lights burning late tonight, and several tempers, too. "What about you?"

"Wide awake."

"Would you listen to this, honey?"

What now? she wondered, as he freed her from his arms and slipped out of bed. He opened the drawer of his night table, found the two mini-cassettes he had placed there along with the three white tablets before he had joined Vasek at dinner. Then he lifted the large flashlight and handed it to Karen as he got back into bed. "Hold that, darling. Give me some light on these things." He examined the miniature cases of the tapes. "I brought

them from Joe's—my answering service. He had two
intruders but recorded their voices. Just want you to listen, say nothing. Raise your hand if you recognize either
of them." He found the small switch that would start the
tape. "Okay," he said encouragingly and took the heavy
light away from her. "I'll play it at lowest volume, so keep
the machine close to your ear. This is a recording made
between four and six o'clock this afternoon." Waterman's
voice should be on the earlier half of it—Joe had returned
to his office by five. Bristow turned on the replay mech-
anism, held the mini-cassette to Karen's cheek.

She listened to various sounds; an unknown voice;
more noises of movements. And then, her eyes dilated in
astonishment. She raised her hand.

Bristow stopped the replay. "Well?"

"Sam Waterman."

"Definitely?" He ran back the tape just enough to play
the Waterman voice once more.

"Definitely," Karen said. "He may call himself Winston, but he *is* Waterman. What on earth was he doing in
Joe's office?"

"Snitching tapes of phone calls to me. Now, try this
recording, honey. It may be difficult." Perhaps impossible, Bristow thought. It had been twelve days since Karen
had heard Rita's voice in a Vienna café.

He played the second tape. First came Joe's phone
call, telling Bristow about Winston's visit. Next, sounds
of a wheelchair moving around; Joe's voice angry; Ken's
voice defensive as he left to buy some groceries. Movements again. Then a woman speaking American but with
a slight foreign accent picked up and emphasized by the
microphone.

Karen was suddenly alert. Puzzled, too. She signed
for the tape to be stopped, said, "Replay it, Peter. I have
to be sure." Again she listened intently. She looked at
him. "It can't be—"

Bristow switched off the recorder. "Can't be—?"

"The girl who came into the café with Waterman and Andreas Kellner. Rita."

"Are you sure that's her voice?"

"Rita said 'interesting' to rhyme with 'arresting'—said it often. One of her favorite words. And the woman on the tape—the same light voice, the suspicion of an accent, and 'interesting' used three times just the way Rita drooled it out. But—she isn't in Washington, is she?"

"I think you've just proved it." He replaced the mini-cassettes in the nightstand's drawer.

"And after she was so sweet and charming, she held Joe up—threatened to blow his head off if he didn't give her your recorded phone calls? That was Rita?"

"You heard her."

"What was the noise at the end? A blow?"

"With her revolver butt on the back of Joe's head. Nothing too serious. He sensed it coming, dodged a little. Could have been worse."

"The running footsteps were Rita's?"

"Yes. To meet her friend in the car that was waiting for her. A broad-faced man, light hair, looking hot and uncomfortable in a suit never meant for late summer in Washington."

"Andreas Kellner—"

"We don't know."

"It could be. With a tightly knotted tie?"

"He was pretty red in the face, I heard."

"It was Kellner," Karen said. "They go together—a team, I have thought. But why in Washington? Why your telephone messages?" I don't like this, she told herself. I don't like this one bit.

"Because," Bristow said, taking her hands in his, calming her sudden fear, "they are after Vasek. And Vasek made two calls to me, both of which they have stolen."

"Why? Did he arrange a meeting on either of them?"

"No. He promised another call tomorrow—at four o'clock—to set up time and place."

"Four o'clock—another lie," she said scornfully.

"He's the expert." Bristow looked at his watch again. "I'd better get moving. Lock the door. Open it only when I give that special knock." He hesitated, then moved quickly to a closet, found his Beretta in his jacket pocket. "Do you know how to use this?"

"No."

"Simple. Release this safety catch. You point, arm at full length, and squeeze the trigger gently. Got that?"

"I—honestly, Peter, I—"

"Take it, darling."

"What about you—if you think there's danger here?"

"Taylor will have a spare I can borrow."

"Danger from what—from him?" She nodded toward the living room.

"No more, I think. Not directly from him." The danger could now come from his KGB comrades who had been searching for him. Or from his co-conspirator, the friend with diplomatic immunity, who might be deciding that it was already the time to stage an abduction: better to have their plan aborted, and Vasek would agree, than be a prisoner of the Americans. "I'll get him away as soon as possible." I'll move up his timetable, Bristow decided. Ambulance at three, even two o'clock or earlier if Doyle can arrange that. He laid the Beretta on the table beside Karen, who was lost in her own thoughts.

"Peter—if they stole the tapes with Vasek's phone calls—" She hesitated, then plunged. "Perhaps they want to blot out any evidence that he had been in contact with you. Someone doesn't want him to *look* like a defector. But that's ridiculous, isn't it? Unless he isn't really a defector." The implications of that hit her. "Oh, no! It couldn't be all lies—a fake—and I was the innocent stupid little dupe—oh, no!"

He could only shake his head. "You're far from stupid, my love."

"Everything a deception—a pretense? Oh, God, no!"

"The three letters are no pretense—they are intended for use—a time bomb. But we'll defuse it." And as she looked at him, crushed and woebegone, he added, "Without you, darling, we'd never have got him here. We have him. He's caught."

Yes, she thought, caught with his own lies. And I aided them. "I'll recover," she said, trying to sound normal. "Just suffering from a wounded ego."

"If you'll cure mine, I'll cure yours. Miss Cornell, I love you. I love you very much."

"And I love you, Mr. Bristow."

"Show me—in half an hour," he said and entered the hall with a smile on his face that astonished Hansen.

26

By ten o'clock that Tuesday evening, Cherry Lane was at rest. Most automobiles were either garaged or parked in the short driveways of the neat well-spaced houses that lined this sleeping street—only a few were scattered along the curb where dinner guests had left them. Lighting was sparse, chiefly supplied from windows and front porches, and dappled by the shadows of the trees. Peaceful, thought Doyle's man as he finished a liverwurst sandwich and the last of the coffee from his Thermos. He pulled out his transceiver, spoke to the three men who were waiting around the Fairbairn house. From his car he had a clear view of its front entrance. "Jim here. All quiet," he reported. "How's it with you?"

"Quiet. The family is inside. We've scouted around the property line at the back of the house. Nothing."

"Nothing in Sussex either?" Sussex was the street that paralleled Cherry Lane, lay beyond it. It was new, some houses now occupied, two still in construction.

"Nothing."

"A false alarm?"

"Could be."

It will be a long dreary night, thought Jim, and signed off. He prepared for it by slumping down on his seat and lighting a cigarette. Two minutes later, he slid farther out of sight, dropped his cigarette in the ashtray. A car was traveling slowly along Cherry Lane, its headlights looming up behind him. He didn't risk raising his head until it had passed. Dark blue, he judged by the street lamp near Fairbairn's driveway; definitely a Maryland plate. Impossible to see if there was one man or two sitting in front of those damned headrests. No one in the rear seats, that was certain. He might have considered it was only a car in search of a friend's home—and in this district people could easily be wandering—but it was the second time in the last fifteen minutes that the dark-blue automobile had been driven steadily along this street. Completely lost or surveying the area?

Jim switched on the transceiver. "Walt? Dark-blue two-door, Maryland plate, proceeding for second time along Cherry. Now making a left into Devon." From Devon Road, it could swing left again into Sussex. He waited, transceiver in hand, until Walt reported back that no car had entered Sussex Street.

"Must have stayed on Devon," Jim said. "I'll alert the van. But keep watching."

"You, too."

Again, silence and boredom descended on Cherry Lane.

The man known as Barney had been an impatient passenger. "Look, Connie," he told the driver of the dark-blue Plymouth, "we've mucked around that road enough. You've told me the setup. I covered the whole area in daylight. I *know* it, I tell you. Let's get on with it."

"Nervous?" asked Shaw as he brought the Plymouth to a halt in Devon Road and switched off its lights. Sussex Street lay at the corner just ahead of them.

"I don't like waiting. I don't like two nights in a row. You should have let a few days go by—"

"We can't and we won't."

"How long do we sit here?"

"While I make sure you know exactly—"

"White house, black shutters, two stories, steep roof, two chimneys. Kitchen at one side, terrace at back with garden and chairs, low hedges separating neighbors' houses, trees all around."

"And a house almost completed to the rear—beyond his property line. That will give you a mark on his place."

"It would also be the quickest way in."

"Too direct. Therefore dangerous. Approach his back-yard from its side."

His . . . he . . . his. "What's this guy's name?"

"All you need to know is his height—five feet ten, if he's on his feet. And the color of his hair—fair—if he's sitting."

"*If* he's there," Barney added to that.

"He will be. Night is clear, stars are out—"

"You know one hell of a lot about him. But he might change his routine and stay indoors. What then?"

"We try again tomorrow."

"I won't be here tomorrow night. I'm flying out in the morning."

"You'll be here if you're needed."

Barney pulled on a pair of light surgical gloves. "Where's his pistol?"

Shaw drew it out of his jacket pocket, handling it carefully with a handkerchief. "Here! Remember, we need to keep his prints on it."

"I'll have to get pretty close to him if you want a suicide. That's taking a chance."

"Call it a challenge." Shaw took something small and folded from his other pocket and handed it over. "Stocking," he said curtly.

"I wear no damn mask."

"Don't wear it. Drop it. Behind the garbage cans at the kitchen door."

Barney stared at him. "You really know the layout."

"That," Shaw said, "is the only reason I'm here."

Barney looked at the stocking. His lips tightened. "Like hell I will. No time. Once you hear the shot, move up that street." He pointed to Sussex on their left. "I'll come straight out the direct way. Pick me up there. No delay. Got that?"

"Before you fire, you could drop—"

"You do it!" Barney tossed the stocking back. "I have my own orders." He stepped out, swearing under his breath. "Didn't have to give me such a walk."

"Not far. There's enough light." The stars were bright, the waning moon still full enough.

Barney left, slipping into the shadows, merging with the night's darkened colors in his black shirt and black trousers. He began following the line of sparse hedges and young trees at the back of the newly built houses.

No dogs at this end of Sussex Street, thought Shaw. Barney had it easy. I did all the scouting for him on Sunday evening—a good time to call on Fairbairn and commiserate with each other on Menlo's interviews that morning. No wife or kids to bother us, either—still visiting dear old Grandmamma. Yes, Barney had it easy: if I had brought him here blindly, parked at the other end of Sussex, he'd have two large shepherds to worry about. They were penned, of course, but they had powerful barks, could waken the whole neighborhood.

Shaw picked up the stocking, folded it neatly to replace in his pocket. He wiped the steering wheel clean and drew on his own pair of transparent gloves. He disliked driving with them, but he'd ditch the car, and Barney, once this job was over—Coulton would meet him near Friendship Heights. He settled to wait, wondering how he had ever been drawn into this circle of violence. All he had done was to follow the normal course of duty: report a large envelope, stamped by a Czech censor, delivered secretly

t a gas station by Bristow to Fairbairn. And Coulton had
»assed on the report as usual. Since then, deeper and
leeper into something they didn't understand. At least he
lidn't. Coulton? Never could tell about Coulton. He
eemed to take orders, but he certainly avoided situations
ike this one, didn't have to sweat it out while an imported
hug—A pistol shot cut through the night's silence.

Shaw switched on engine and headlights, made a quick
eft turn into Sussex. Three houses to pass before he'd
each the one under construction behind Fairbairn's place.
ts garden lights were suddenly ablaze, dogs had begun
»arking. A second shot rang out.

Shaw, nerves tightening, increased speed, reached the
ualf-built house as a man stumbled through Fairbairn's
ine of bushes. A black figure—could be Barney. A sec-
»nd figure, a third. Shaw jabbed the accelerator to the
loor, drove past Barney, who was halfway to the street,
aced its length, speeded around its curve that would bring
aim to the highway and safety.

But beyond that curve, at the first sound of firing, a
ight van had been drawn athwart the road. Shaw swerved
ind crashed over the sidewalk into a tree.

They pulled him out of the mangled car, stretched his
»ody on the grass. One of the men pointed to the surgical
gloves and shook his head. The other quickly searched
Shaw's pockets. "No weapon." Then he directed his flash-
ight onto a small folded piece of nylon. "Well, what do
you know!" he said in amazement as a dark-gray stocking
inrolled and dangled from his hand. "I'll call in our report."
He rose, gloves and stocking safely in his pocket, and left
or the van.

His partner waited for the irate householder to arrive
on the scene. She was an elderly lady who had delayed
n order to take the curlers out of her hair and pull on
some clothes less revealing than a nightgown and robe.
She was more scared than angry. "I was asleep—Oh, the
poor young man. Is he dead?"

"Looks like it. Head went through the windshield. Just

call the police, ma'am. Tell them a driver took the curv
too fast and went off the road."

"Oh, dear! He looks dreadful." She shuddered in syr
pathy.

"Please—just call the police. Stay inside. They'll har
dle everything." As she hurried indoors, he made for th
van. Quietly, it turned and headed toward Cherry Lan
"Jesus, he almost hit us. Must have been traveling at sixt
the damned fool." He turned to the man at the radic
"What's the news?"

"The police shot an intruder, caught him as he tried t
reach the car. He had dropped the revolver, but he wa
wearing gloves."

"So his fingerprints aren't on the gun. Hell, there goe
direct evidence."

"Except for the police bullet. He's got their slug in hi
shoulder."

"Saying anything?"

"Cursed everything and everyone in sight. Then h
clammed up."

"That figures."

"Calm the children," Fairbairn told his wife. "And kee
upstairs, all of you." And Emma—who had been con
plaining all evening about the invasion of their house an
garden by strangely dressed men, and what silly nonsens
was this, danger of what?—was now subdued enough b
the sound of two shots that she only nodded agreemer
as she hugged him in relief. He really had been in dange
she thought as she coaxed the children back into bed. /
burglar, she was explaining, but he had been chased away

Fairbairn stepped onto the terrace, watched a strange
clothed in black being taken around the side of the hous
toward Cherry Lane.

"Do you know him?" Jim asked.

"I've never seen him in my life."

"This way." Jim led him to his favorite chair. The seate

figure, wearing one of his old blazers, had the remains of its head mixed with shreds of its blond wig.

Fairbairn flinched. It could have been me, he thought. He said awkwardly, "Sorry about the argument I gave you when you first arrived."

"Well—it was all arranged at short notice. Didn't give us much time to brief you at length." Jim signed to one of the undercover policemen, who had charge of the revolver. "Don't touch it, just have a close look," he advised Fairbairn as he beamed a flashlight on a neat .22. "The assailant fired from about three feet away, reached for the dummy's hand, then saw the head was in smithereens. He dropped the pistol and bolted. But not before this detective caught him one on the shoulder. Neat job—we wanted him alive," he told that young man as he moved off to join his team. "Did you recognize the revolver?" he asked Fairbairn, who seemed frozen to the ground.

"It looked similar—to one I have—" Fairbairn broke off, staring at the smashed head of the wax figure.

"We'll never be able to use him again," Jim said lightly. "Poor old dummy."

"Symbolic." Fairbairn's voice was bitter. He came to life, moved quickly back toward the house.

Jim followed, found him unlocking a drawer in the study's desk. "I was out of this room for only five—six—minutes on Sunday—getting us some ice for our drinks." Fairbairn pulled the drawer open. He stared unbelievingly. "Yes," he said at last, "that was my revolver."

27

ALL WAS QUIET IN THE APARTMENT. BRISTOW REACHED his study, nodded to Taylor, who stood at the door. Doyle was now available and waiting at the other end of the two-way radio. Okay, Bristow signed, and Taylor left. He adjusted the headphones, kept his own voice low even if Vasek's room was halfway down the hall, and made his report on tonight's developments. Doyle listened intently, accepted all of Bristow's suggestions and requests. And then, once that business was completed, burst out with his own news: an attack on Fairbairn had failed; Shaw dead.

The stocking had been found on Shaw's body, an exact match, one of a pair. Fingerprints of the man arrested for attempted murder were the same as those found in Menlo's house. The label of a Zurich department store, concealed within the broad fold of the tie dropped on Menlo's floor, was identical with the one attached to the inside seam of the man's shirt sleeve. "Careless bastard," Doyle said jubilantly. "Too many successes in the past. That goes to a man's head. A failure or two keeps him cautious. He isn't talking, of course. And I'll bet he isn't Swiss. But we'll keep digging—Interpol or Interintell may supply a useful tip."

"Fairbairn?"

"He's safe. Reported to be a touch depressed. But he'll recover."

Fairbairn would. He was the type who always recovered. Next month, thought Bristow, he'll make a comic anecdote out of the whole incident.

"One last thing," Doyle said. "You'd better stop using your own car until this emergency is over. You can borrow one from us."

A neat reminder, thought Bristow, that a feeling of success could make a man careless. "I'll pick it up tomorrow. Meanwhile, you pass on my report. You know whom to contact."

"The sooner, the better. Take care."

Another neat reminder: to be the sole possessor of vital information was not exactly an enviable position. "I'll do that," Bristow promised. He left the study and found Taylor standing guard outside the door. "Ambulance comes at one-thirty. We wake him at one-fifteen. Okay?" Judging from Taylor's face, it was very much okay.

With extreme care, Bristow eased past Vasek's room, halted by Hansen's chair to whisper the same instructions, and at last could knock gently on his own door.

"A horrible way to live," he said as he dropped on the bed beside Karen. "A darkened house, tiptoeing around, whispering."

"I don't object to this part of it," she said as they lay with their cheeks touching and his arms around her.

"I'm getting rid of him tonight."

"How?" she asked in alarm. "Violence?"

"I hope not. With a little diplomacy, perhaps. Don't let me fall asleep. I'll have to rouse him at one-fifteen."

"Will he leave peacefully?"

"I think he will. He's probably calculating now that his chances are better elsewhere."

"Are they?"

"No." He kissed her. "Question time over. Tomorrow, ask all you want." In a house far removed from this apartment . . . He must make arrangements in the morning for that, before he picked up his report from the vault, added two more pieces of evidence to bolster his findings, and presented the whole package to the Director's office.

"You're worrying again," she told him gently.

He reached out to the flashlight and turned it off. "So let's do a little unworrying." He tightened his arms around her and smothered her laughter with kisses.

At one-fifteen, there was a soft tapping on the bedroom door. Good God, I'm late, thought Bristow as he swung his legs onto the floor, turned on the flashlight, drew on shirt and trousers, slipped his feet into his loafers. "Just stay there," he told Karen. "And once he has left, start packing." Then he was out in the hall to join Taylor and Hansen.

Packing? Am I being moved out, too? Not without you, Peter Bristow, she told him silently. But she stretched, prepared to rise and find her suitcase. She listened. No loud voices. No anger. No refusal from Vasek. Peter's diplomacy must be working well. Reassured, she got out of bed and began gathering dresses from the closet with the help of the flashlight.

But diplomacy had its limits. Vasek, dozing in the armchair, awakened the moment that Bristow entered the living room. At once, he was alert. And suspicious, although he made no comment as he picked up his shopping bag and followed Bristow into the kitchen with Taylor close to his heels.

Bristow turned on the meager light. "I thought it would be more comfortable to wait here."

"For what?"

"An ambulance."

"A car would be sufficient."

"But less safe."

"I do not wish to be strapped into any stretcher."

"Then you can walk and be an open target."

"You think this house is being watched? By whom?"

Not by your buddy from the embassy, buster. Bristow dropped the soft approach, decided on some plain talk. "By the people who removed two tapes from my answering service yesterday afternoon—tapes that contained your telephone calls to me."

There was only silence. Then Vasek said with some contempt, "So you had me recorded."

He knows damn well that all answering-service calls are taped, thought Bristow. "Standard procedure."

"Who were the thieves? Anonymous, I presume."

"No. Actually, they were two of your comrades, imported from Central Europe to help hunt you down. You know Kellner and Rita, don't you? And they know you. Don't forget Waterman, either. He's leading the chase, and you trained him pretty well. He first surfaced in Vienna on the day after you spoke with Miss Cornell in Prague. Quick, wasn't he? He now apparently believes you are in Washington. He's zeroing in on you, Josef."

Vasek's face was unreadable. He changed the subject, looking over at Taylor. "Where is the other guard?"

"Downstairs, waiting to unlock the door as soon as the ambulance arrives. He will let no one enter unless he can identify them."

"How many men will come with it? For my safety, of course," Vasek said with a heavy touch of sarcasm.

"Not counting the driver with his assistant—they'll stay with the ambulance and watch the street—there are four. Necessary for a patient who has just had a severe heart attack."

"I'll walk—I won't be carried!"

"All right, all right. The choice is yours." What was Vasek hoping for? To be seen by his embassy friend and be tailed to his new address? "We've tried to secure the street as much as possible. Cars parked within thirty yards of my front door have been moved away." That had an instant effect: Vasek stared. "For your safety, of course," Bristow added.

Vasek's calculations were over. He even smiled. "I thank you for all the measures. I hope my presence here has not put Miss Cornell in danger."

"In more danger," Bristow corrected him.

"At least," Vasek said, "you can thank me for bringing you and Miss Cornell together."

Vasek playing cupid? The vision was so preposterous that Bristow almost burst into a laugh.

The hall door opened, and Hansen appeared with two white-coated men following him.

"How does the street look?" Bristow asked.

"Quiet, sir. The stretcher is downstairs. I've checked all the men—know them well."

"Our guest may prefer to walk."

"That could be dangerous. The ambulance isn't parked directly in front of the house," Hansen said.

"Too obvious," Bristow agreed. He looked at Vasek, who had listened intently and was now picking up his bag. "Do you need that?"

"Just evidence of how I arrived—a demonstration to convince your colleagues that my disguises were credible enough to make my escape through Europe possible."

"A practical demonstration?" Bristow wondered how valuable the three white tablets must be to produce such an excuse. "Better get downstairs. The ambulance can't wait too long."

"My books—" Vasek said. "I'll have time to read, won't I?"

"Books? Oh, yes, the ones you threw at me. Have you seen them?" he asked Taylor and Hansen. "No?"

Taylor took his cue and looked blank. Hansen said, "Miss Cornell tidied up—"

"Then she'll find them for us," Bristow said quickly.

"Don't worry," he told Vasek. "We'll have them sent on to you. I won't forget. I promise you. Come on, we're wasting time."

The door was open. Vasek was being ushered out. No one had laid a hand on him. "We will meet again," he told Bristow. "Once everything is cleared—"

"Yes," Bristow said, "I'd like to hear the details of your journey. Must have been fantastic." He was the naïve and admiring American. Vasek accepted that and followed the two attendants and Hansen downstairs. Bristow watched them go.

At the foot of the staircase, Vasek gave a murmured command. Then he lay down on the stretcher and was covered by a blanket. The front door opened; and shut.

Bristow drew a long breath and stepped back into the hall, closed its door. Taylor, with a look of approval still on his face, reached a storage closet and extracted the three books he had stashed away last night. Bristow took them. Old editions with worn bindings: *Vanity Fair*, *Moby Dick*, *Great Expectations*. "Polishing his English, I see," Bristow said dryly and riffled through the volumes one by one.

Something at the back of *Great Expectations* caught his eye. The marbled paper that covered the inside of the binding seemed to have loosened with age and been pasted back. At least, its edges had been pasted—the center felt spongy, as if the gum or paste or glue didn't cover completely. A lower corner was peeling slightly, hadn't quite caught hold. He felt its tip—just the normal touch of paper, as if, like the center, it had been missed by the paste brush. "How do we get this paper removed—without damaging it? We'll have to replace it exactly."

"Steam," Taylor suggested and began filling the kettle.

Bristow was still looking at the lower corner; he tested it gently. Where would Vasek get any steam? "Just a moment," he told Taylor. "Let's see—" He lifted the corner with care, eased it up. Suddenly, the whole lower edge of the marbled end paper, and its outer side, too, came loose. Inside, flat against the binding, was a piece of flimsy paper. Slowly, he pulled it out. He unfolded the delicate sheet, smoothed it on the kitchen table. "Get that strong light," he told Taylor, "and we need a camera. I've one in the study."

"I've got a mini-job. Good for close-ups." Taylor glanced at the sheet of paper. "A map. Only a map of Washington," he said, partly astonished, mostly disappointed. Then he caught Bristow's impatient eye on him and hurried away.

Yes, only a map, but one made in great detail and in miniature scale; every street was lettered or numbered, and the surrounding portions of Maryland and Virginia marked with main highways. Bristow studied a red dot. Perhaps it indicated the embassy's safe house where Vasek could find refuge until he was smuggled out of the country. He had escape on his mind, that was certain. A map, the cash in his wallet—what had Vasek said? Money is the source of all our successes. But any unbribable guards wouldn't be drugged or poisoned by three aspirin tablets. How long would he stay as a defector? Two weeks, three? A couple of months? Long enough to establish his credibility with a few pieces of useful and true information, and then put an end to our faith in Gregor's reliability. Which only proved that Gregor was a most valuable source of real information, so accurate and trustworthy that Gregor must be neutralized if not destroyed.

Taylor was back. Six photographs were taken. "Just to make sure," Bristow said. The map, refolded and smoothed, was placed back in its central position under the marbled end paper. The self-sealing edges were pressed down and the lower corner left slightly unfurled.

Hansen returned as they were studying their handicraft with approval and relief. "Safe away," he announced. "Saw him into the ambulance. No one tailing. No one on the street, either. And I checked the parked cars—all empty."

"He changed his mind about the stretcher, I noticed."

"Pretty damn quick. Guess you put the fear of God into him."

"He has no God," Bristow reminded Hansen. "Now, here's our schedule. We pack. And leave before the light strengthens. At four-thirty."

"Pack all equipment?" Taylor asked.

"Everything. And don't forget your sound-recorder. In fact, I'll take its tape right now." *Just let Vasek try to deny he had ever written the letters, and our dinner conversation will leave him stuttering.* "I'll have that piece of film, too." Bristow looked at his watch. "A little over two hours before we start leaving. In your car. Okay?"

"Piece of cake," Hansen predicted.

28

THE GRAY CHEVROLET TURNED INTO MUIR STREET, LESS-
ened its speed as it traveled toward the bookstore. "Stop
here!" Waterman said. "Cut your lights!" Andreas Kellner, with a small smile playing around his lips, obeyed.
The American and his orders were amusing.

Rita, alone in the back seat, leaned forward to ask,
"Why here? This is too far away. Have we to *walk*?" She
didn't like the idea: not safe, even if this street was asleep
at three-fifteen in the morning. Besides, how could they
carry Vasek for fifty meters? Madness.

"There are no cars parked near Bristow's address."
Waterman's usual easygoing manner was fraying. "Do you
want ours to be the only one?" In Vienna, he had been
told this little sexpot was only a courier, a go-between
messenger. He was begining to wonder about that.

"There's nobody around to notice."

"That's why we delayed our visit." One reason why.
The other was Barney. No word from him. No report
from Shaw to Coulton, either.

"Delayed too much." Rita's idea had been to enter the apartment as soon as midnight was reached.

Waterman looked at her eager face. Was this urgency a sign of repressed fear? Since she and Kellner had arrived two days ago, she had talked incessantly about action: get the job done, get out. Or perhaps she enjoyed this kind of work.

Kellner was watching the dark street. "How are you sure we'll find Vasek here?" His English, unlike that spoken in Vienna, was fluent. He even had a London accent to match his tailored suit.

"Bristow is his definite contact." Coulton had vouched for it. "Bristow was named as that, by Vasek himself."

"Vasek told him on the phone that they'd meet tomorrow—"

"I know his methods. That phone call could have been for our benefit. He knew we were closing in. Why else did he abandon his motel room early this evening?" A set of sports clothes and a blond wig were all that Barney and Kellner had found.

"How did he know we were about to raid his room? I don't like this. Not at all," Kellner said. "Someone talked."

"No one talked. He sensed it. Sensed it was time to reach Bristow, and no more delay." There was a skeptical silence from Kellner. "Only five people knew we had traced him: Barney, both of you, myself and the man who passes on instructions to us."

"Your mysterious Fred," said Rita. "Does he exist?"

Coulton existed, all right, thought Waterman grimly. He should never have dropped the name Fred—a moment's lapse in caution.

"What about your contact at the embassy—didn't he talk with you today?" Kellner asked.

"He's been replaced. I met with his substitute. Gave me five minutes." That still rankled. "He arrived in Washington yesterday. From Moscow. He was more interested in the two tapes of Vasek's phone calls than in anything else. Said he could give us reinforcements tomorrow, but not before. I didn't actually name the motel. He was pressed for time."

"Idiot!" said Rita. "So he sent us chasing after some stupid tapes. We could have got them tonight."

"He's no idiot. The tapes must be significant." And who's to argue with a colonel in the KGB even if he was dressed as a chauffeur?

"We left Prague to find Vasek, not tapes." Rita's impatience was growing. "So let's find him." Damn these two-door cars. If she weren't blocked by Sam's seat, she'd be out on the sidewalk right now. "Come on!" she told him. "It's almost three-thirty by my watch. What's the delay?"

Kellner said quietly, "Barney. We need him. Isn't that right, Sam?"

"Could be on his way here. He knows the address." Waterman seemed unconcerned.

"Why hasn't he used his transceiver, got in touch with you?"

That had been Waterman's own question, but he hid his worry. "Not near enough, possibly. Its range is limited."

"Where is he?" Kellner demanded.

"On another assignment."

"Are you responsible for that? Or was it your Fred's idea?" Kellner's quiet voice ended. In sudden anger, he said, "You two have something more in mind than Vasek's capture. Nothing comes before that! Nothing!"

"I know," Waterman said. "We want him as much as you do. He will name names. His words. I have reliable information on that. If he does, Fred and I—and our group in Washington—will be uncovered."

"What other assignment was so important?"

"A complication. Also involving our security. So we are dealing with it." At least, Fred Coulton is dealing with it. I just take his orders.

"And risk losing Vasek?"

"No, we won't."

Rita said, "Then move now! We can do without Barney. You come in his place."

"That's not my function."

Kellner said smoothly, "In Vienna, you came with us to introduce an American journalist. Tonight, you came to direct us around Washington streets and make sure we lost any tail. But at this moment, you are here and Barney is not. We go into the apartment together. Or we don't go. My report to Prague will cover these facts."

"I am—"

"I know. You are an outlet for disinformation, a valued one, I've heard. But you've been trained in other skills, too. We need them now!"

"I am unarmed. I brought no—"

"Not any more." Kellner reached across to the glove compartment and found his spare revolver. "Take it. You know how to use it."

"We'll rouse the whole neighborhood if we have to—"

"With silencers?" Kellner asked.

"I'm ready," Rita said. She checked her own revolver and slipped a heavy ring onto her left hand. "One little jab from this," she told Waterman, who had turned to stare at her, "and Vasek will be flat on his back in two seconds." She laughed as she waved the ring on her finger right under his chin and watched him draw back. "Surely you didn't expect Andreas to carry Vasek downstairs all by himself, did you? We really do need you," she added sweetly.

"What about Bristow?"

"You deal with him." She tapped the pistol in Waterman's hand. "Might help to solve that complication you talked about."

"We'll drive nearer the doorway," Kellner said. "There's been no movement in this street. They're all asleep." He started the engine, edged the car along the curb to the bookstore. "No talking. Silence once we enter."

"The door will be heavily locked," Waterman warned him.

"And I know how to unlock it." Kellner drew the car to a gentle halt, stared up at the apartments above the bookstore. "Which floor? Did your Fred help us with that much information?"

"I scouted the bookstore myself. The woman who owns it lives above her shop."

"So the top floor is our target," Kellner said and switched off the engine. "Move!" he told Waterman. "Rita—leave that handbag; bring the electric torch." They stepped out of the car. With a last glance up and down the street, Kellner joined them and set to work on the lock. "Keep watch!" he told Waterman in an angry whisper.

Rita had eased her revolver into the belt of her well-fitted pants and now held the flashlight over the keyhole with one hand while she twisted the loose ring on her other hand so that it faced inward. With sudden pressure on its central stone, it could release the prongs that appeared to hold the fake gem. It worked well. She had used it before. But at those times, the prongs—stabbed against a wrist or the side of a neck—had ejected cyanide. Lucky Vasek, he was only going to sleep for an hour. Perhaps not so lucky. A traitor would not find Prague so enjoyable. Promotion for us, she thought; we managed it where others failed. But if Vasek wasn't found here—She looked at Waterman, and her lips no longer smiled.

He noticed that swerve of her head, sensed a threat. Then he averted his eyes, kept them scanning the silent house, the empty sidewalks. He could still hear Kellner's angry whisper and wondered on the reversal of their roles. He was now taking orders instead of giving them. A protest was useless. Kellner had become a different man from the amiable figure he had met in Vienna. Kellner—and Rita, too—were much more than they had seemed. Much more, he thought, his tension mounting with his sense of helplessness.

At last, the lock was turned. Ready to open the door, Kellner whispered his last words. "They want him alive. Wound, if need be. Don't kill. These are our orders." He took the flashlight from Rita and led the way inside. The entrance hall was lit, the first landing, too. Above that, the staircase headed into darkness.

Softly, slowly, they reached Bristow's door.

It was almost half past two, Bristow had noted when he returned to their bedroom. "Sorry about the delay." His voice was normal, no longer a need for murmuring and whispering.

"Trouble with Vasek?" Karen asked quickly.

"No, no. He's gone. I just had to examine the books he brought with him—after he left."

"Vasek really has left?" It had all been so quiet, she thought.

"He has. And we're leaving, too, packing up, all of us." In haste, Bristow began filling his bag with the help of a flashlight. "By tomorrow, we'll even be using electricity again. This has been a pretty miserable time for you, honey." And she had taken it like a trooper. There she was, sitting cross-legged on the bed at half past two o'clock in the morning, watching him with a smile, letting his excitement run on. He finished packing, placed his bag beside her suitcase, typewriter, bag, and briefcase. "Not my usual way of life," he assured her.

"What? You don't play host to a defector every week?"

"Back to analysis and evaluation for me. I'll keep clear of defectors, leave them to counterintelligence." He was now setting the alarm clock, placing it on the bed table within his reach. "It will ring at three-fifteen. Gives me forty minutes before I rise and get dressed. We leave at half past four." He fell into bed, too tired even to pull off his clothes. He reached for her hand, closed his eyes. "Bliss," he said.

"Where do we go when we leave here?"

"You'll stay at Doyle's house through the day. All

arranged. And I'll be at the agency. A lot of—" His voice was drifting off. "I'll collect you in the evening, and we'll—" There was silence.

"Go where?" she asked. But there was no answer. He was deep into sleep. He needs it, she told herself: last night he hadn't had anything like three hours of sleep; twice she had opened her eyes briefly, found him wide awake. As she was now. Except she wasn't as troubled as he had been. Worries are over for all of us, she thought as she looked at his face: all cares banished. Her spirits soared. Then she lay back, wondering once more how she could ever have fallen in love so completely and so quickly. Perhaps you didn't judge love by the length of time you had known each other—it was the depths of time that mattered.

She began rearranging her own life. The New York house would be sold. They'd live in Washington—no more commuting for her; she had hated it, she might as well admit, a drag on energy, a waste of leisure—but not in this apartment. Surely Peter would agree. Each time she entered the kitchen, she would think of Vasek and his arrival, and that was one memory she didn't need. Memories ... Schleeman had been right. They could tie you to the past, could make you captive. Silken chains.

The alarm sounded. Bristow's arm went out, his hand silenced it, then slipped from the clock, brushed against the revolver that lay on his table, fell back on the sheet, and was motionless.

Karen was smiling as she rose and crossed around the bed to his side. She lifted the clock and held it near the flashlight to reset it for three-forty-five. That would give him ample time to get ready. He needed all the extra few minutes of sleep he could get. In the meantime, she herself would shower and prepare to face another day. As she replaced the clock on the table, she glanced at the revolver he had borrowed from Taylor—a nasty, mean-looking object with a silencer attached. Surely, there was no longer any reason to have it at hand? As for the Beretta, she had forgotten about it. But she certainly didn't need it to brush her teeth, she thought as she gathered her clothes and her handbag with its cosmetic pouch inside—comb, powder, lipstick. It felt heavier than usual. A small suspicion struck her, so she opened the bag and found the Beretta. Peter, Peter, she told him silently, aren't you just a bit too careful? She repressed a laugh and went into the hall, closing the door quietly behind her.

"Hi!" said Hansen. He was up on a stepladder in the hall, near the bedroom door, disengaging some wires that had been hidden by the molding at the edge of the ceiling.

She took a few steps to reach the ladder, pointed up at the wall—Peter was asleep on the other side of it—and kept her voice low. "What on earth is that hole?"

Hansen came down a few steps, dropped his voice, too. "Just needs a little plaster—Taylor had to dig into it a bit." Briefly, he showed her a small gadget, replaced it in his pocket. "All the better to hear with," he said. "We had a warning signal in our room connected with it, too."

"And I never noticed it!"

"No one did." He looked at the wires still to be dealt with. "Won't take long. Another ten minutes and I'll be in the shower."

"Where's Taylor? Asleep?"

"He's on his two-way radio. That's his post."

So we are keeping in touch. Cautious people, these. "I'll have the bathroom free for your shower in ten minutes. Fifteen?" she corrected herself.

"Fifteen," Hansen said cheerfully and climbed toward the ceiling, opening his knife to gouge out a well-hidden wire.

She hurried past the bedroom and living-room doors, reached the bathroom on the opposite side of the hall, switched on its light. Fifteen minutes, she warned herself as she slipped off dressing gown and nightdress, washed her face, brushed her teeth, ran the shower, and stepped into its cool steam. That was another thing about this apartment, she thought: not enough hot water. But the bathroom light was strong, and once she was dressed, she could apply make-up accurately. She reached the last stage of combing her hair four minutes ahead of her allotted time. Just then, she heard a sound, a thud on the hall floor. Had Hansen slipped, fallen from the ladder? She turned from the mirror, comb in hand, to unlock the bathroom door. She had it only half-open when she stopped. A woman's low voice was asking, "Bristow?" A man's voice answered, "No." A third voice hushed them both.

For a moment, Karen stood paralyzed. Then she reached into her handbag lying open on the ledge of the washbasin at arm's length, grasped the Beretta, dropped the comb, flicked off the light, pulled the door wide. She drew to one side as she looked down the hall. Hansen on the floor, motionless. Three people moving away from him toward her, one man almost at the bedroom door and a woman following. He waved his pistol, pointing it toward the living-room door. The woman passed him as he waited for her to reach it. Karen raised the Beretta and fired. Nothing happened. Safety catch, safety catch—she released it, no time to aim, fired a warning shot.

Bristow heard it. He was already on his feet. The thud in the hall had wakened him. Only a second of disorientation and his hand had gone out to warn Karen, found her gone. He swung his legs out of bed, grabbed the revolver on his table, switched off the flashlight. Silently, he reached the door, felt for its handle, yanked it open. On the threshold, only one step away, a man was aiming at the bathroom. Bristow whipped the butt of his revolver down on the man's head, moved clear of the falling body. At the living-room door, a woman had turned to shoot at the bathroom, too, then swerved around to fire her second bullet at him. Bristow dropped low. The bullet passed over his head. Taylor stepped from the study and shot her in the right shoulder.

Her revolver clattered to the floor. She grabbed hold of her wounded arm as if to stifle its pain. A fleeting look of astonishment, of anger; a faltering step, a low moan;

and her knees buckled. She fell, clutching her shoulder, lay still.

Swiftly, Bristow reached the bathroom. Karen was unhurt. She had drawn close against the wall at one side of its entrance, was standing there transfixed with horror, her eyes seeing only the hole that gaped in the tiles on the opposite wall. "Karen—"

"Look out!" yelled Taylor, taking aim at a man who had just emerged from the kitchen. Bristow wheeled around, his revolver pointing.

"All right, all right!" Waterman said quickly, threw aside his weapon, held up empty hands. He calmed his voice, hid his frustration: no quiet escape by the back door— locked, chained, an alarm's red signal showing it was set—they would have stopped him on the stairs. At least, he had avoided the shooting gallery. "I fired at no one. I'm not responsible for that," he protested as he looked at Hansen's body. "She is!" Waterman nodded toward the girl and started slowly toward them.

"Stay where you are!" Bristow kept his eyes on Waterman, his pistol aimed while he sensed Karen coming to stand by his side. He slipped his free hand around her waist, gripped it tightly. She was still shaken.

Waterman stared in complete amazement, looked from Karen to the Beretta she held, then back to Karen. He recovered, said with amusement, "So it was you who fired that shot." The only one without a silencer. "I ought to have guessed. The smart reporter always on the scene. Or is this a new line of work, Miss Karen?"

She ignored him, watched Taylor's brisk movements as he gathered up the weapons on the floor and hurried to dump the load with a clatter somewhere in the kitchen. Almost at once, he was back in sight, stood looking down at Hansen. One shot in the back. Taylor took off his jacket and covered the body. With set face, he picked up Hansen's knife. It had fallen as he tried to leap down from the ladder, too engrossed in his job to hear the front door's lock being quietly turned. Taylor tore down a long strip of dangling wire, slashed it free, cutting it into three pieces as he came along the hall. He caught Waterman's arms from behind, pinned them back, wrapped a piece of wire around his wrists, and tied the ends. "Shut your mouth!" he told Waterman, who had begun to protest.

Next was Kellner. Taylor bound his hands, noticed no bullet wound. "He's alive. Out cold. You hit him?"

"Hard," said Bristow.

"Not hard enough." Taylor moved on to Rita. "Don't understand this one. I didn't fire to kill—just caught her right shoulder." He touched her neck. "Not dead. Fainted?" But she wasn't the fainting type. He turned her on her face, pulling her left hand free from its clutch on her wounded shoulder, and gathered her wrists to tie them together at her back. "What the hell's this?" He looked down at the heavy ring on her left hand, its face turned inward. He stared at the prongs that had pretended to hold its stone in place. "Came loose with her grip?"

"Careful with that!" Bristow warned as Taylor removed the ring and held it out for them to see.

"What the hell is it?"

Bristow thought of Vasek. "Perhaps some kind of injection needle."

Waterman laughed. "Dear little Rita put herself to sleep. Oh, it's harmless now—shot its bolt. Lucky it wasn't carrying her usual cyanide. She threatened me with it, you know. I was forced to—"

Bristow cut him off, saying to Taylor, "Get help. Three extra cars."

"They're on their way. I was talking with Doyle when the shot was fired. I said, 'Mayday,' stepped out, left our connection open. Sorry I was late."

"Two seconds only. No damage."

"One second is enough," Taylor said grimly, looked along the hall at Hansen. "They shot him in the back." He left abruptly. At the study, he paused to say, "I'll fill Doyle in," and closed its door.

Waterman had noted the look on Taylor's face as he

left. "I did *not* shoot your agent. I'm not a killer. I am
political—" He saw only anger in Bristow's eyes. "Karen,
you know I'm not a criminal. You've worked with me,
you know I'm no murderer."

"Then why did you come here? To congratulate me
that I escaped alive from a bombing in Rome?" Her voice
was cold, contemptuous. She has recovered, thought
Bristow with relief. She is out of shock and as angry as
I am. Her eyes traveled past Waterman, rested on Hansen's body. "As a man, he was worth a hundred of you,
Waterman." She turned to Bristow, "Couldn't we carry
Hansen into the bedroom?" Her voice had softened; she
was close to tears. "Peter—did they have to kill—"

"Better leave him until the others get here," he said.

Waterman sensed Karen's sudden emotion. "I've told
you the truth. Please believe me, Karen. I did not kill
him. I could have shot your Peter when he came out of
that door." He nodded toward the bedroom. "I didn't."

"True," said Bristow. "But you thought Rita would take
care of me. Didn't you? The way that your man took care
of Menlo? The way he tried to take care of Fairbairn?"

Tried? Barney had failed. Waterman stared at Bristow,
began to calculate his remaining chances. Slim, now. If
Barney had been taken alive, very slim indeed. Escape
was the only way out—not a plea of innocence, not a
protestation of ignorance. If he could move closer to
Karen—if he could loosen the grip of the wire around his
wrists still more, slip his hands free, be ready to grab her
and her little pistol—yes, he might make that front door
with her as a shield. Keep talking, he told himself. The
knot on the wire could slip. Not easily, but with enough
time it would give. And he had another half hour before
Bristow's people could possibly arrive. "You know," he
said with a smile, "if you are looking for the man who
ordered Menlo's death, and Fairbairn's, and his assault—
you've got the wrong guy. I'm not important, Bristow. A
cog in the machine, as you are."

"So you're pinning all blame on Coulton?" It was a shot in the dark, but it seemed to have hit its mark.

"Coulton? Who's he?" The words were casual, the eyes tense.

"The man you were meeting last Friday evening at a very quiet club in Washington. Before you left for Rome. Remember?"

"You're crazy." Waterman took a few steps toward Karen. "What's he talking about?"

"Back!" Bristow said sharply. "Back where you were!"

Waterman retreated a pace. He leaned a shoulder against the wall, made a show of boredom. "Do we all have to stand here while we wait for your cleanup squad?"

"Keep standing, and turn around."

"Just thought Karen would be more comfortable sitting down in your living room."

"Turn around!"

Slowly, Waterman obeyed. Another half hour and he might manage it; but now the knot still held, even if it was eased slightly, and he could feel Bristow's eyes on his back. There must be some way, something that he could do. He tightened the muscles of his wrists, slackened them, tightened, slackened. Little by little, painful as it was. Then he heard the other man coming along the hall, saying, "Ten minutes and they'll be here. Driving at ninety—no traffic problems this time in the morning." Ten minutes. Waterman's hope began to fade.

Bristow said, "Handcuffs, Taylor. This one"—he indicated Waterman—"thinks he's Houdini. And that one on the floor has stirred twice, probably faking a concussion."

"Won't be a minute." Taylor was as good as his word. He was back with two sets of handcuffs, his own and Hansen's. He snapped them in place—Waterman first, Kellner next. Waterman felt the cold bite of the metal added to the pain encircling his wrists, and his vague hope turned to despair. Coulton got me into this, he thought, Coulton will get me out. Or is Coulton trapped, too? His depression plunged into the depths of failure complete.

Taylor had examined Rita's wrists and tightened the wire around them. She was still totally unconscious—a powerful drug, whatever she had used. Lying there, with a face so sweet and innocent, she was unrecognizable from the girl with the grimacing mouth and wide eyes who had fired to kill. That magnum she had chosen to use, far too heavy for her; her aim would have been surer with a lighter pistol. She couldn't always depend on a man's broad back as her target from ten feet away. Hansen, blasted open—Taylor was gripped by a rush of deep anger. She's the new breed of women, is she? Terrorist-trained, no doubt about that. Something rotten had been added to this world of ours. Next time I come up against one of them, I'll not aim for a shoulder. That, I promise.

Taylor moved toward the study, controlled his emotion enough to be able to speak. "I'd better keep in contact. As soon as they enter this street, I'll get downstairs and let them in."

"Okay," said Bristow. Waterman has given up, he thought, noting the slackened hands, the drooping head. Unless he decides he'd rather be dead than face his future. One lunge toward us, and I'd have to shoot him. I'll be damned if I'll help him commit suicide.

"It sounds," said Karen, watching Taylor enter the study, "as if the emergency is over. Really over."

"Yes." But I'll believe it, thought Bristow, when I see Doyle and his men come through that front door.

"Then I don't need this," she said with relief and handed the Beretta over to him. He took it, slipped it into his belt, kept his eyes on Waterman and the revolver ready. "My aim," she admitted, "was awful."

"Where did the bullet go?" He dropped a kiss on her head as he pulled her close to his side.

"Into the ceiling, I'm afraid. A panic shot. I forgot the safety catch." She shuddered. She would remember that moment forever. Even now, it reached out and laid an icy finger on her heart. "I was almost too late."

"But you weren't." His eyes left Waterman to linger

on her face. "You weren't, my love." Without that warning, we would all be scattered on the floor, shot in cold blood as Hansen had been.

Suddenly, she threw her arms around him, kissed him fiercely. "You could have been killed. You might have been dead. I thought—I thought I had lost you and—" She broke off, kissed him again and again.

Taylor ran past them, tapping Bristow on the shoulder. "They're here!" he said, left the door open as he reached the landing and raced down the stairs.

Waterman came to life. "Time for my exit, I see." He started walking to the door.

"Waterman—stop!"

Waterman laughed, increased his pace. "Shoot a handcuffed man in the back? Let Karen do that job—she's always been good at it!"

Karen flinched, then shook her head.

Bristow's jaw was set, his eyes hard. "He won't get far, and he knows it. A cheap shot, Karen. His specialty." He's lucky I wasn't facing him with his hands uncuffed, but he knows that, too.

Waterman reached the door as a group of men entered. He kicked the first man hard in the groin, shouldered Doyle heavily aside. The third man wasn't caught by surprise; he was Taylor. He drew and fired as Waterman lunged at him. He didn't aim at the shoulder, either. He aimed for the hipbone and gave Waterman something to curse for the rest of his life.

29

AFTER WEDNESDAY'S PREDAWN ASSAULT, THE PEACE AND quiet of morning in the Doyle house seemed incredible to Karen. And miraculous. And normal, she kept reminding herself—a word rarely appreciated until you found yourself facing hideous danger. But it was over; and she completed her readjustment from last night's fears by setting to work. It was always the great pacifier.

By midafternoon, her article on the terrorists—their background and history, the bombing and Martita's planned escape, the cost in human lives, the scenes of destruction both inside the hall and outside in the street—was completed and corrected, typed into presentable copy, ready for mailing to the *Spectator* by an obliging Mrs. Doyle when that unflappable lady went marketing. Not even a six o'clock breakfast in her kitchen for four strangers, with herself presiding in blue dressing gown and pink curlers, had dented Mrs. Doyle's equanimity. It was the antidote they all had needed, including a grim-faced Doyle: something simple and true, honest and kindly—the reverse of what they had seen and sensed since Vasek appeared at Peter Bristow's door. Tonight, thought Karen, we'll all sleep.

With thanks in her heart, she spent the next half hour daydreaming on the chaise in Mrs. Doyle's guest room, which had been her working space today. From downstairs came the distant sounds of voices and a drift of music, even once a burst of laughter—not from Taylor; it must have come from Hansen's replacement, as young and cheerful as he had been. That thought put her on her feet, made her start rearranging the clothes in a suitcase that had been packed for her Rome visit. So many new memories gathered in the last six days, putting the old ones to rest in the past. Where they belonged. Carefully, she refolded *la Contessa*'s elegant sweater. I *will* invite her to dinner, Karen decided; and Giovanni, too. I'll send him a copy of my article on terrorism and write "Thank you" across its by-line. Schleeman will be astonished by it—not quite what he intended when he sent me to Italy. Schleeman . . . I should call him. But from here? Will that endanger the Doyle house?

She almost laughed. A week ago, she would have gone downstairs, picked up the telephone on the hall table, and without hesitation made several calls. But if last night's terror had taught her anything, it was caution. Imminent danger seemed to be over, but Doyle had left two of his men stationed here when he went off with Peter this early morning—Doyle to visit Hansen's wife and two children before he filed his report to—to whom? To the Powers That Be, she called them. Peter was with them, too—had been since eight o'clock—would he be free by six, as he had hoped, to collect her and take her—where? She had learned more than caution in this last week. She had learned trust. Trust and reliance on someone else, a strange right-about-face for an independent woman who had taken pride in being self-sufficient. Now she was entrusting her whole future to someone she had known for only twelve days.

But Peter had not only saved her life; he had given it new meaning, new hope.

She heard a telephone ring, then footsteps running upstairs. Taylor's voice came with his knock on her door. "A call for you, Miss Cornell." And when she opened the door, startled, half-afraid, he reassured her by adding, "The alert must be over. Mr. Doyle told him he could call you here."

"Mr. Bristow?"

"No. He has gone back to the apartment to collect his car. The call's from a Mr. Schleeman. His secretary is on the line. Do you want to talk?"

"He's my boss. I'd better, don't you think?" She hurried toward the stairs. The emergency must really be over. "So they arrested Coulton?" His name had been mentioned in a cryptic exchange between Peter and Doyle at breakfast. Coulton, whoever he was, seemed to be the last loose string that needed to be snipped off.

Taylor—and it was a mark on his new acceptance of her—replied frankly, "As far as I could make out from the reports coming in, he didn't stay around to be arrested."

Karen halted at the foot of the staircase. "You lost him?"

"Not us," Taylor said quickly. "He skipped before State's Security called on him this morning. Well, I'll be pushing off now. We are packing up our gear. So goodbye, Miss Cornell. Good luck to you."

They shook hands solemnly. "And to you," Karen said. She picked up the receiver. Schleeman's secretary was efficient as ever, but even more long-suffering. "At last," she commented before she brought Schleeman on the line.

"Ah," he said, "the elusive Miss Cornell. And where the dickens have you been?"

"Lying low in Washington. Didn't Mr. Doyle tell you?"

"Apart from the fact that you were well and safe, as little as possible. What's been going on, Karen?"

"Too much to tell you now."

"Yes, that's what Bristow said."

"He called you?"

"At lunchtime. Seemed busy."

"He was."

"And you?"

"I finished an article for you. About Rome. It's in the mail."

"The mail? Why don't you hand it in to me? I'd like to hear—"

"I'm taking ten days off, Hubert. I do need some rest and recreation, you know."

There was a brief silence. "I guess you do. Sorry about Rome. My fault. I admit. Shouldn't have sent you—"

"It worked out well. In a way, I have to thank you for that." She couldn't resist dropping her small bombshell. "I'm getting married."

"Well, now—" Schleeman was startled. "My guess is Bristow. Right?"

"Right."

Then Schleeman sounded worried. "Are you sure, Karen? Really sure?"

"Yes. I'm not backing out this time."

Again a small silence.

"I mean it, Hubert. Stop worrying about Peter. I'd never do anything to hurt him." She had been on target about Schleeman's reaction: he was definitely relieved as he now gave his warm congratulations. You men, she thought—but with affection—and listened to his next query. "We'll live in Washington," she answered. "I'm selling the New York house—"

"Thank heaven." A memory trap, he thought. Best that she was free of it. "Commuting's no way to live—a few days here, a few days there."

"I've found that out."

"You'll be staying in Georgetown?"

"I don't know. . . . Not in Peter's apartment, I think." She remembered the expression on his face this morning when he had taken one last look at the hall just as they were leaving. There had been no need for words.

"You can't live on cloud nine," Schleeman reminded her.

"Well, we can always buy a tent and camp out in Langley Forest." She had him laughing, a good moment to say, "I'll keep in touch. Story worrying about either of us, Hubert. My love." And she ended the call before he could start asking questions about the defector.

As for Schleeman, the defector was much on his mind. Arrived and in good hands, was all that Bristow had said; and then had added an apparent afterthought which was probably the main purpose of his phone call. "You can pass the word—discreetly. You're the first to hear of it, Hubert." So, thought Schleeman as he prepared to leave for a dinner with friends of the press, I've been authorized to spread an unauthorized leak. And I'll do it. Just following a hunch that it is somehow important that a message should reach those who are interested in this defector.

Schleeman left his office in high good humor, astonishing those he greeted, his irritability and short temper of the past few days completely banished. The office relaxed, made its own speculation about this change, and all of them wrong.

By half past four that afternoon, Bristow was free to leave. Doyle himself elected to give him a lift to Muir Street to pick up his car. It was a good opportunity, the last they would have, to compare notes on the day's meetings.

"Thanks for backing me up," Bristow said as they cleared the gates of Langley.

"You didn't need much corroboration."

"Didn't I?" Bristow shook his head. "I overstepped a few boundary lines. Beyond my authority. You heard that remark, didn't you?"

"What time did you have to alert other sections? Don't expect a medal. All you'll ever get is your name carved in a plaque on the wall with dates of birth and death—if killed in action. You nearly made it, too."

"I made one thing definitely." Bristow was suddenly

angry. "A mistake. A big one. I didn't examine that damned fountain pen."

"Taylor said it looked normal—not the usual thick, heavy article. But he should have checked it. He'll get a reprimand for that."

"Keep him out of it. I didn't mention his name."

"Then I'll reprimand him."

"Why? He was working at high speed—no time at all— Vasek was about to wake up and take notice. Anyway, what could Taylor have done? Remove that cyanide pen? Warn Vasek that we were onto his game? And what kind of performance would he have put on then at his inter- rogation? Taylor isn't to blame. I'm taking responsibility."

"You did that," Doyle said dryly. "And without any explanations, either."

"They always sound too damn much like excuses."

"And that would never do, would it now?"

"I was there. I should have tried to disarm it and replace it. Then—"

"Disarm it? How? You're no expert in that. And that little pen is the latest model, trust Vasek to have one. All you'd have had was an ejection of cyanide gas right in your face. You'd have got your name on the Honor Roll; that's for sure."

"Death from heart failure doesn't count."

They both smiled at that. The tension eased. Doyle said, "When Vasek was asleep, they found the pen in his bag. They had time to disarm and replace it. He'll never know until he tries to use it. Anyway, the big consolation for you is that your report was accepted and action is being taken. That's something. Everything's under con- trol."

"Except for Coulton."

Doyle tapped his two-way radio. "I keep hoping. Strange. We went after a mole and unearthed another one—the big one, too."

"But he got away."

"We'll see."

"How the hell did he get a Top Security rating? A week ago last Monday he attended a special session along with people from the White House, State, Defense, National Security. Was even asked for his expert opinion on forged signatures. State must be—"

"Not their fault. His security clearance was already established before he ever joined the Bureau of Public Affairs—was passed on to them by the Treasury. Before his time there, he had been issued Top Security clearance by the Oval Office. Fifteen years ago."

"What?"

"We had a President who was suspicious about forged checks. Coulton was brought in to solve the problem. And that made him."

"It was roses, roses all the way," Bristow said.

Doyle looked at him sharply.

"But who," Bristow went on, still thinking of Browning's verse, "cast the myrtle in Coulton's path right into the White House?"

What the hell had myrtle or roses to do with anything? Doyle concentrated on entering Georgetown. Cross Key Bridge, short distance on M, a left into 33 and up O Street. Then right into Dumbarton and another left. "Look," he said at last, "if you're worrying who made things easy for Coulton, drop it. Not your business or mine. That's for State's Security office and the FBI to uncover. They'll be concentrating on his track record right now; you can bet your last dollar on that."

"Okay, okay. I heard you." As they turned another corner, Bristow said, "My car's along here. I parked last night a little distance away—"

"I know." Roses and myrtle were still rankling. "I had it checked over this morning after you left the apartment."

"Keys?" Bristow asked with a smile.

"Who needs them nowadays? There isn't a car that's lockproof." The radio signaled, and Doyle slowed up to answer. He drew to the side of the pavement on the quiet little street. The report was on Coulton. His Mercedes had been found near the docks in Baltimore. "Got that?" he asked Bristow as he switched off the radio.

"Coulton is home free."

"Could be. One thing about the KGB—they take care of their own."

"Hey—what's going on?" Bristow was looking straight ahead. Last night, there had been a line of parked cars fore and aft of his. Now, the cars were gone, leaving the Camaro in lonely state. And three tall youths, hands in the pockets of their tight jeans, sneakers on their feet, were circling it closely, peering through its closed windows, then straightening up to glance along the street. One drew his hands out of his pockets, his head swiveling as he made a last quick check on the nearest pedestrian and found none close enough to stop him. His thin arm reached for the car door.

Bristow was out and running as the Camaro's door was opened. It had been left unlocked. No key had been used. He yelled a warning. "Beat it."

The youth froze, with one long leg already stepping inside. He pulled it out, slammed the door, and bolted. His two friends raced ahead of him.

Nothing happened.

Bristow halted, felt foolish, returned to Doyle. "Damn me for an idiot. Thought it might be booby-trapped. The door was un—"

At that moment, the bomb exploded. A small one, neat, nicely aimed at the driver. No pillar of fire, no spreading flames. Merely a black and twisted wreck of the Camaro's front seat and windshield.

Bristow stared at it bleakly. At least, there had been no people passing close, not much damage to the wall beside which he had parked—no houses there, just a garden. One small tree seemed to be the only casualty.

"Get in!" Doyle ordered. "Do you want to spend the evening making statements at some police station?"

Bristow recovered, stepped into the car.

"I'll take you back to Langley. You can use one of our

cars meanwhile. You know, those kids would have been DOA without benefit of heroin—if we had arrived five minutes later."

"And five minutes earlier?" Bristow gave one last glance at his Camaro as they passed it. Hell, he thought, I liked that car. "Guess I wouldn't have been keeping my six o'clock date." Then his control broke, and he said savagely, "Coulton's last word?"

"He didn't have much time to plan anything. Let's see—" Doyle calculated. "Your Camaro was checked and found clean around five o'clock this morning. Coulton left his house in a taxi at six, evaded surveillance when he reached the airport, disappeared. Someone had his Mercedes waiting for him. That's certain, at least." Doyle pursed his lips. "Not much time," he repeated. "Of course there are KGB operatives in Washington. Could have used one of them."

"Could use them again." Bristow was thoroughly depressed. "How long will this go on?" He was thinking of Karen. He couldn't, and wouldn't, drag her into any more danger. So what did he do—tell her they had to separate? "For how many weeks? Even months?"

"Not long," Doyle said encouragingly. "Just until Coulton's safe in Moscow. Then their interest in you could be over. They might have been worried about what you would do to upset his plans. Take that as a compliment."

Bristow said nothing.

"I was dropping the guards watching over you and Miss Cornell. I think I'll countermand that order. For a couple of days?"

Bristow was grim-faced. "Or a couple of weeks."

"My guess is that he's halfway to Cuba by this time."

Bristow was silent.

Doyle pulled the only rank he could. "I've been around longer than you have—been on the job for near thirty years. So believe what I'm telling you."

There was still no comment from Bristow. His silence lasted across the Potomac into Arlington. Then, as he became aware of green meadows and trees, he roused himself from a strange mixture of thoughts: ideas, doubts, and plain anxiety. He glanced at his watch.

"You'll make your six o'clock date," Doyle told him.

"I've a couple of phone calls to make."

"Want me to let Miss Cornell know you'll be late?"

"But don't mention the bomb. Just tell her—tell her I've a load of work ahead of me. Will you?"

Doyle didn't like it, but he nodded.

"Thanks. Thanks for all you've done. I've given you a lot of trouble in these last two days."

"That's my business," Doyle said and then reached to turn on his radio as it signaled. It gave the final report on Coulton. He had boarded a Mexican freighter at nine that morning. Identified from his photograph by three dock-workers. Sailed at ten o'clock. First stop, Havana.

"What did I tell you?" Doyle was elated. His guesses, he could now admit, were sometimes wrong. This time, on target. "You're off that hook, Bristow! When he reaches Cuba, he'll fly off to Moscow. First plane available, I'd say. A slick escape—he had help, of course; must be valuable to them. But he won't be operating around here any more. He'll probably be given some desk job in Moscow for the rest of his life. It's the pattern." He looked at Bristow, saw no answering smile. "So what? We didn't catch him, but we spiked his guns. He's a marked man outside of the Iron Curtain. No more infiltration into high places for him. No more bomb threats, either."

"It wasn't Coulton who ordered my death."

Doyle's flood of words ended. He could only stare at Bristow.

"If you had about two hours' notice to clean out your desk, destroy anything incriminating, reach Baltimore, would you worry about anything else?"

He had a point there, thought Doyle. "Then who—"

"Vasek. Prearranged. Once he made contact with me and was accepted as a bona-fide defector, he didn't need me any more. In fact, he'd see me as an obstacle to any new scenario he was planning to create. So eliminate me; silence any testimony I could give that would contradict his story."

"He'd never get away with that."

"He'd make a damned good try. Such as—he came to America as a defector, telephoned me, suggested a quiet place where we could meet along with one or two of my colleagues. But I refused, insisted he must come to my apartment. I was alone, no other representatives from Central Intelligence—only a couple of guards who didn't know who he was and a girl who'd say anything I told her to say. We were lovers, weren't we? So I trapped him, invented lies to end his credibility, and made him a prisoner. Why? For my own benefit—Bristow's ambition wanted full credit for the capture of a KGB agent: promotion, more power." Bristow's laugh was short and bitter. "I know this technique, Doyle. I've studied it for years."

"I believe you," Doyle said. "I heard what he had to tell about Menlo in that talk you had over dinner." The sound-recorder's tape had been played at the final meeting that afternoon. "So did your friend Holvec." He would be heading the team of Vasek's interrogators—had known Menlo, worked with him at times, respected him. "Did you notice Holvec's face? Hear his four-letter descriptions of Vasek?" Then Doyle's amusement at that recollection faded. "When d'you think the bastard will go into his new act?"

"As soon as he senses he's a prisoner. He'll try to prove he's an honest-to-goodness defector. And if I'm not around—" Bristow shrugged.

"It's still hard to believe. I mean, character assassination is his line."

"And twisting facts and manipulating history."

"But—having someone terminated?"

"All for the good of his cause, Doyle. And if I'm right, that answers another question: why he had the tapes of his phone calls to me removed from my answering service. They'll be obliterated by this time."

"Waterman did that!" Doyle reminded him sharply. "Waterman was no ally of Vasek, either."

"Who ordered Waterman to do it? He didn't need the tapes. He already knew what they contained. He had the telephone in my answering service bugged."

"Someone—not Vasek but a friend of Vasek—ordered him to get these tapes? Someone with clout—" Doyle was now thinking aloud. "Had to be. Waterman wouldn't have obeyed him otherwise—taken the risk of stealing something he didn't need."

"What about clout at the embassy level—someone who knew Vasek's real mission?"

"By God—the man who waited outside your apartment, claimed he was a chauffeur and then switched to diplomatic immunity at the police station! Although, mark you, his car hadn't any diplomatic plates. But if he arranged for the bombing, how the hell did he know you drove a Camaro? He's new here, arrived on Saturday, a press attaché, so-called."

"Vasek knew my car by sight—let that slip—a small remark to make me rattled."

Doyle shook his head. "You don't rattle so easily."

"I am now. If I wasn't eliminated in the first attempt, what follows? A second try?"

Doyle took a full minute to answer. "I think I'd call Holvec."

"I'm doing that." Chris Holvec had asked to be updated on any further developments. An attempt on Bristow's life certainly qualified. "I'm also calling Maynard Drayton. He's with the State Department."

"Using diplomatic channels? Might be your best bet, if Drayton comes through. Do you know him well?"

"We're old friends." And Drayton's anger over Coulton must have lit Drayton's slow-burning but powerful fuse. Not only over Coulton's infiltration and escape—his very presence at an upper-level meeting to discuss the problem of three letters of disinformation would be a rank offense that smelled to heaven.

Well now, thought Doyle as they were passed through the gates at Langley, if Drayton had enough guts to summon that Soviet so-called press aide, tell him he was in danger of being booted out of the country for conduct unbecoming a diplomat and gentleman, that could crimp the little bastard's style. Vasek's friend would get the message: no more car bombings, no apparent accidents to anyone who had talked with Vasek on his arrival. Anyone... "Did Miss Cornell hear any part of Vasek's conversation with you?" Doyle asked suddenly.

"No."

"Then she's not in danger, thank God."

No longer in danger from the Vienna cassettes and their revelation of Waterman, Kellner, and Rita. No danger from Coulton, either: his ring was smashed. Bristow drew a keep breath. "Only," he said, "when she's with me."

Doyle glanced at him quickly as he drew to a sudden halt in front of Bristow's office building. Bristow was out at once, hurrying toward the steps. Doyle raised his voice. "I'll have a car waiting for you here."

Bristow waved back, entered the doorway.

Good luck with your telephone calls, thought Doyle as he reversed, turned, and headed for home. Arrange Bristow's transport, give Karen the message, supper, and twelve hours of blessed sleep.

There was one benefit in talking things out with Doyle. Bristow had the basic points in order and could telephone an adequate but short report to Chris Holvec. Holvec, interrupted in the replaying of Vasek's sound-recorded conversation, was relieved the call wasn't a talkative rehash of today's meetings—he had a lot of work ahead of him. He had managed to procure the Prague cassettes and intended to study them thoroughly. "Just wanted to learn about our boy from the moment he contacted Miss Cornell," he explained. "Now, about your problem, Pete.

You'll have to stay alert for the next two or three weeks. Sorry about that, but we need the time. As long as he thinks he's establishing his credibility with us, he may feed us an item or two of real information. We can't let that slip. You agree?"

Unwillingly, Bristow agreed. Three weeks were more likely than two, could even stretch to four if Vasek furnished any interesting leads.

"What we could attempt—and this is stealing your credit, Pete—we could drop a hint now and again, convince him you had little to do with his case. Your only job was to alert us and steer him into our safekeeping. We investigated, we uncovered. The credit goes to us. Not you. Sorry. But it could end any future interest in you. You agree?"

"Yes. It's a safeguard." Vasek would be given a long stretch in prison—illegal entry, false passport, concealed weapons, conspiracy—but he could be released in less than a year; it had happened before, an exchange for some hapless American arrested in Moscow.

"Our boy has too much pride in his talents. He wouldn't feel so hurt if he thought it took ten men to unearth him. But one man alone—I ask you, Pete!"

"Okay. He's all yours, Chris. From the beginning." The phone call ended, and not one mention of Vasek's name. Bristow's amusement over that was brief. Three or four weeks . . . How did he break the news to Karen? We were talking about a wedding in ten days. Thoroughly discouraged, he dialed Maynard Drayton's number.

But this call, lasting much longer, was something of a surprise. Drayton was overflowing with unusual excitement. He had a story to tell and plunged into it without waiting to hear why Bristow had called him. It was a word-by-word account of an FBI report made today, after two agents had visited the garage that had sheltered Coulton's Mercedes for the past five days. The owner needed some prodding, but eventually admitted the Mercedes had been there last night.

When had it left?—This morning.

When?—Pretty early.

How early?—Around six maybe.

Who had driven it away?—No idea.

A man or a woman?—A man.

How had he arrived at the garage?—In his car.

Where was it now?—Not here. The man had returned
for it.

How did he get back to the garage?—By taxi.

When?—Just before eight.

What kind of car?—Dark-brown, two-door Fiat.

Its number?—Didn't notice.

"But," said Drayton, "a young mechanic did notice.
And it's the same car the police picked up last night outside your apartment. The driver's name is Dmitri Suslov—*no* relation to the Suslov we all knew once—he
owns the car, actually. He claims diplomatic immunity,
of course."

"So I heard."

"How?"

"We're interested in Suslov, too. A recent arrival in
Washington, I understand. Just in time for our defector's
appearance here."

"Defector? Oh?—yes. Prague—"

"He surfaced yesterday."

"Good!" But Drayton was more engrossed by the connection between Coulton and Suslov. "We obtained a photograph of Suslov, sent it to the garage immediately. Two
mechanics identified it—the owner was absent. And it
was Suslov who left the brown two-door Fiat for a couple
of hours this morning while he drove the Mercedes away.
Next time it was identified, it was near the docks in Baltimore. So now we have enough cause to take the necessary steps. We are requesting Suslov's immediate
departure from Washington."

"How soon?" asked Bristow quickly.

"By the end of this week."

"Friday? Saturday?"

Drayton was mystified. "Does one day matter, Peter?"

"Yes. We think Suslov arranged for a car bombing today. He could be planning another unpleasant surprise."

"Whose car?"

"Mine."

"Badly damaged?"

"Front seat was totally wrecked."

"My God!" A brief silence. "A lucky escape."

"There might not be a second one."

"I see." Another pause. "I'll press for Friday at latest."

"My thanks for that, Maynard."

"Not at all. Don't want to lose a good tennis partner. When do we have our next game?"

"When you finish all that paperwork on Suslov."

Drayton laughed. "It's been quite a day."

"That it has," Bristow said. Thoughtfully, he replaced the receiver. Two days—with Suslov now conscious of watchful eyes even from his own embassy: it wouldn't like us to go public with the proof that has turned up. Two days were a damned sight easier to excuse to Karen than three or four weeks. Easier for me to handle, too, he thought as he left for Doyle's promised car. Perhaps I'm chicken, but I don't enjoy living with a perpetual glance over my shoulder.

30

THE EVENING LIGHT STILL HELD, CASTING A GOLDEN GLOW over the fall and rise of meadow and woodland. "I think I know where we're going," Karen said, breaking the awkward silence. Or do I? She wondered. She glanced at Peter, who seemed to be intent on driving. Not that the traffic was as heavy now as it had been on that Saturday when they had first met. Nor were they being followed, except by two security agents who were keeping a tactful but definite eye on Peter's car. A borrowed car. Had he been so pressed for time that he hadn't picked up his Camaro? And wasn't the emergency over? So why were Doyle's watchdogs back on duty? No explanations offered by Peter, either. He seemed to have retreated into another world. No easy talk, no banter, no teasing, no smiles, no laughter... Something has happened, she thought, something has gone wrong. Between us?

She had a sudden fear, tried to find an answer that would divert it. "Did they accept your report—all the evidence?"

"They listened. And Doyle's own report was pretty conclusive."

So it wasn't today's business that had gone wrong. They were leaving the highway now, entering a lane darkened by the trees that lined its ditches. "I do know this road," she said and felt cold with its deep shadows. She made an effort, said lightly, "What's its name?"

"Cedarhill."

"Where are the cedars?"

"They died off one summer. Had to be replaced by maple trees."

"Must have been years ago." The maples were full-grown. "How large is the house, actually?"

"Not as large as it looks. Can't be more than eight or nine rooms. But there will be enough space for the security men over the garage. They won't be in your way."

My way? What about our way? "Are we expected there? I thought you could use it only on weekends."

"I phoned Madrid this morning. Everything's all right."

But this stilted kind of talk isn't. "Who is the owner, anyway?"

"John Fitch—we're old friends. School and college."

"An enormous upkeep—gardeners and housekeeper even when he isn't here."

Bristow gave his first smile since he had collected Karen at the Doyle house. "Fishing trip?" he teased her. "No, he doesn't make any more money than I do. He inherited this place from his uncle, who was also his guardian, along with a trust that pays for the upkeep. He can't use it much—that's the big snag. Foreign Service."

"I thought he planned to come for Labor Day. That's this weekend." Which didn't give them much time here. Another move? She was tired of living out of a suitcase.

"Well, the best-laid plans can go haywire." Then he said almost to himself, "They certainly do."

A change in plans? Ours? she wondered and felt a sudden depression grip her.

"He's being transferred to Morocco. May be home for

a week at Christmas." Bristow became aware of her silence. "He's glad to have you around. Lights, people moving about."

"A glorified house sitter?" Her voice had sharpened.

Bristow looked at her in surprise. "As his guest, Karen. And the house doesn't need anyone to discourage burglars—just needs some life in it. It's well protected with every alarm system available. Uncle Fitch saw to that. I'd never have brought you here unless I felt it was safe."

As if to support that truth, they arrived at gates that were firmly closed. "That's the way they'll be until you leave," Bristow said and stepped out of the car to use the intercom that connected with the house. He waited there until the car that had followed them from Doyle's house appeared. He spoke into the phone, the gates swung open, and both cars could enter before the gates closed again. "There's a high wall of steel mesh all around the place," he said as he drove up the short curve of driveway.

"I never noticed it before." And the gates hadn't been closed, either. Why now? The emergency was over.

"Trees and bushes are a nice disguise. But I wouldn't try to scale its top. Uncle Fitch valued privacy if not his possessions."

"Electric shock? Isn't that illegal?"

"Noise isn't. There are enough alarms to bring out the local police, if not the fire brigade and the Boy Scouts, too. We used to test it every Fourth of July."

The driveway straightened, ended in a circle before the redbrick house. Set on a gentle rise of ground, it dominated the long stretch of grass that Karen well remembered—a green slope ending in a boundary of trees; and beyond, a small pond where two people had sat, relaxed, talking easily. Why so easily then? Why so self-consciously now? They had been circling around everything important, talking about anything and anyone except themselves. Something is wrong, she thought again and looked blankly at the two-storied house with white pillared doorway and window frames contrasting with black shutters.

She scarcely noticed the rose-colored welcome it gave her as it lay bathed in the warm rays of sunset.

Their car stopped before the shallow steps of the entrance. Bristow reached into the back seat for her suitcase, bag, typewriter, and briefcase, carried them in two loads up to the front door. The car behind them had turned into the garage adjoining the house, where a gardener waited to direct the two security guards to their quarters. All well arranged, everyone knows what to do except me, Karen thought as a middle-aged couple—no doubt bequeathed with the house—took her luggage into the hall. She made no move.

Bristow returned, opened the car door for her.

"What about your bag, Peter?" It still lay on the back seat.

"Come on, honey." Slowly she got out of the car. "I'll see you into the house—"

"Peter! Am I staying here alone?"

"For a few days. It's better that—"

"Why?"

"I've a lot of work to finish. I left some papers at the apartment, and I'd better look over them. Thought I'd stay there tonight—I'll be at my desk until twelve or later."

This can't be happening: the same kind of excuses she once had made when she was backing away from someone she had imagined she loved and found she didn't. But it could be happening: too short a time, too quick a decision, too rushed. They had been thrown together by a crisis, shared all its tensions and emotions. Now the danger was over, and they had come to their senses. Oh, no! she thought, and she stopped and faced him.

"Karen," he said, taking her arm to accompany her up the steps.

"Oh, no!" she said aloud and drew free. "Why bring me here—*here*—to tell me—" She felt hot tears stinging her eyes. She turned blindly and ran over the grass, away from the lighted doorway. She stumbled on the uneven ground. He caught her before she fell, held her.

"Karen!"

"Why didn't you tell me, straight out? I can face truth, even when it hurts. but not evasions, not—"

He kissed her, violently, a long searing kiss, his arms tightening around her. Then he looked at her, brushed the tears from her cheeks, pulled her close to him. "I love you, Karen. I love you. And you know it." He felt her relax against him. Gently he asked, "What was that all about?"

She shook her head. "Something—something from the past. It seems I never forgot it." Or forgave myself.

"Forget it now. This is the present. This is me—no one else." He kissed her eyes, her cheeks, her lips.

"But why were you going to leave me?" Her voice was small, the words almost inaudible.

"For your safety," he was forced to admit.

"Waterman is caught—there's no danger now."

"A bomb went off. In my car. This afternoon." She stared at him, couldn't speak. "It was timed to explode two or three minutes after the driver closed his door. And all I could see as I looked at the front seat—a black, twisted wreck—was you sitting beside me, both of us buckling up, preparing to drive off." He paused. "As we might have done. I nearly phoned you to ask you to meet me at Muir Street, drive here with me."

Her eyes still looked at him with horror.

"Not to worry," he told her, easing his voice. "No one was hurt. The bomb was triggered by a boy who was about to steal the car. He saw me, swung the door shut, and ran."

"But if you had arrived before the boy—" She couldn't finish. "Oh, Peter! Who set the bomb?"

"We'll probably never know. But we think we do know who arranged it."

"Who?"

"His name—at present—is Suslov. In a couple of days, he'll be gone. Booted out of the country."

"Not arrested?" Her indignation and anger had overcome fear.

Bristow was smiling as he slipped his arm around her waist and began leading her to the house. "Diplomatic immunity."

"You take it so lightly."

"Do I? When I was willing to ruin our arrival here?" Might have ruined more than that, he thought. I handled this badly. "Just bear with me, Karen. Stay here for two or three days. That's all I was asking."

"If you are going back to your apartment, I'm coming with you."

"No!"

"But yes!" She looked at him, touched his cheek. "When I was in danger, what did you do? You flew to Rome, stayed beside me. So either I'm coming with you or you remain here. Why not, darling?"

"If a second attempt is made—"

"This place is safe, or you wouldn't leave me here. And we are safe—no Suslov followed us. Your work is over, the job's done. You're still on leave anyway, aren't you?"

"I am not dragging you into any more danger, Karen."

"So you think that if you are a marked man for the next two or three days, you ought to keep far away from me? That's crazy, completely mad."

"Crazy?" He was angry.

"You alone in the apartment, ready to face Suslov and let your Beretta shorten two days to two minutes—was that the idea, Peter? But how can anyone face a bomb hurled through a window?"

That stopped further argument cold. "Pretty far out," he said. "Where did you pick up such wild notions?"

"In Rome." She shivered. Dusk had fallen, and with it the dew. "Let's go in. At least, have dinner with me. If you must leave, then I leave, too." She looked up at him. He had taken off his jacket, draped it around her bare shoulders. "I mean that."

Yes, she meant it. He gave up. Not entirely against his own judgment, either. For the first time this evening, he was admitting he was exhausted, in no shape to travel or stay alert. It might not be a bomb hurled through his window—that was unlikely. But it could be a fire started in a ground-floor bookstore, and Mrs. Abel above it, deeply asleep. "You're a powerful arguer," he said as they reached the car. He hesitated, still debating with himself.

"Only when I'm desperate." She looked back at the deep shadows spreading over the stretch of grass, at the blackened outlines of trees that sheltered the pond. It all began there, she thought. "I really believed Vasek's story." She could smile at herself now. "The eager little reporter, so earnest about it all."

Bristow's eyes had followed her glance. "And beautiful," he said. "I didn't know whether to look at you or listen. But I did both."

"And started all your troubles. Including me."

"That's one I want to keep with me for the rest of my life." He lifted his bag out of the back seat.

She laughed and held out her hand. He grasped it firmly. Together, they mounted the steps and entered the house.

About the Author

HELEN MacINNES was born in Scotland, grew up there, was graduated from the University of Glasgow, and later studied at University College in London. After her marriage to the late Gilbert Highet, they lived in Oxford, where he was a don at St. John's College. In 1937 Mr. Highet was invited to lecture at Columbia University and, except during his distinguished war service as a high-level member of British Intelligence, the Highets made their home in New York. They became United States citizens in 1951.

Miss MacInnes started to write for publication in 1939. Her first novel, *Above Suspicion*, was an immediate success and launched her on a spectacular writing career that has made her an international favorite. Her previous nineteen novels have sold well over twenty million copies in America alone and have been translated into twenty-two languages. Each of her novels has been a best seller and a book-club selection. Several have been adapted as films.

Miss MacInnes is recognized as the creator of remarkably acute and supremely exciting novels set against a background of meaningful present-day events. In the genre of highly literate suspense, she is unrivaled.